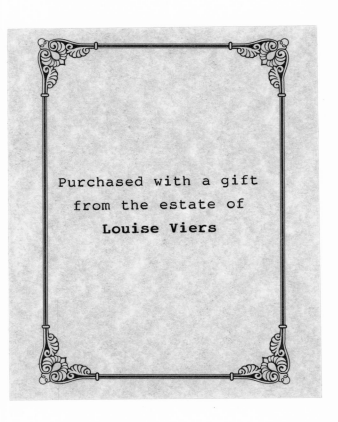

TARNISHED
IMAGE

Also by Alton L. Gansky
in Large Print:

A Ship Possessed
A Small Dose of Murder
By My Hands
Distant Memory
Jack on the Tracks
Marked for Mercy
Stardust
Terminal Justice
Through My Eyes
Vanished

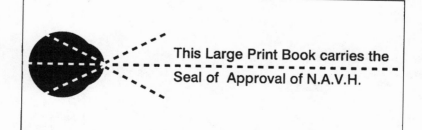

This Large Print Book carries the
Seal of Approval of N.A.V.H.

TARNISHED

IMAGE

Alton L. Gansky

Thorndike Press • Waterville, Maine

Published in 2003 by arrangement with WaterBrook Press, a division of Random House, Inc.

Thorndike Press Large Print Christian Mystery Series.

The tree indicium is a trademark of Thorndike Press.

The text of this Large Print edition is unabridged. Other aspects of the book may vary from the original edition.

Set in 16 pt. Plantin by Warren S. Doersam.

Printed in the United States on permanent paper.

ISBN 0-7862-4821-1 (lg. print : hc : alk. paper)

*To my brother, Richard.
This one is for you, Bubba.*

Acknowledgments

Every novelist owes a debt to the people who help make a project like this possible. The lucky author will have an assertive and knowledgeable agent, a publisher who is willing to make the work a success, an experienced editor to acquire and oversee the myriad details that surround every book, a line editor who keeps the author from revealing his ignorance about the English language, and a family to provide support.

In my case, I'm fortunate to have all this and more. I wish to express my gratitude to my agent, Claudia Cross, for returning my phone calls (and for allowing me to borrow her name, which I use liberally throughout the manuscript); to Daniel P. Rich, the president and publisher of WaterBrook Press, for giving me the opportunity to share my stories; to my editor, Lisa Bergren, for her guidance and for finding something of value in what I do; to Lila Empson for her keen eye as she reviewed the manuscript; and to my family who continue to show their support in new ways.

I would also like to express my thanks to the many experts who gave of their time and knowledge to keep me on track with the technical and specialized matters that appear in this book. Any such matters correctly conveyed are in large part due to them. Any errors are exclusively mine.

Prologue

Sierra de Agua, Belize, Central America
1990

Perspiration dotted his forehead and streaked his cheeks. Raising a tremulous hand, the young man wiped his face. He grimaced. Pain pierced every joint; every muscle protested the movement with scorching agony. His skin felt aflame, and his head throbbed percussively. A small and pathetic groan issued from his parched throat, passed split and swollen lips, and joined the guttural emanations of the other fifteen patients.

He closed his eyes for a moment and then reopened them, focusing on a large blue-green fly that rested on the white mosquito netting that surrounded his bed. The fly was motionless except for its front legs, which it furiously rubbed together like a famished man rubbing his hands

9

before a banquet table. Unfortunately the netting that kept him safe from insects also kept out the light, sweet breeze that wafted in through the open windows spaced throughout the ward. The breeze played a lullaby on the supple leaves of nearby trees, but the young man could not sleep; he could only wait and hope the disease that incapacitated him would leave as quickly as it had come. He doubted that it would.

He was fourteen and until a week ago was strong and full of energy. He had run where others walked, and he had loved nothing more than playing soccer after school with friends. Four of those friends were on the ward with him now, and two others had already died. Soccer no longer occupied his mind, only survival.

A movement outside the netting caught his eye. A woman in a white smock stood next to his bed.

"How are you feeling?" she asked. Her American accent was sweet to his ears.

"Bad, doctor. Really bad." His voice was weak. "Are my parents here?"

"They were, but I sent them home," she answered without emotion. "It's best that they not see you right now. You don't want them to get sick too, do you?"

He shook his head slowly. Bolts of pain ripped down his back.

"You're a good son," the doctor said. The young man watched as she raised a large hypodermic and removed the plastic cover that protected the big-bore needle. "I need to take another blood sample."

He didn't want to give blood. He was tired of giving blood. He wanted to go home and to sleep in his own bed. Still, he offered no objection.

The doctor pulled back the white netting and leaned over him. The blue-green fly took flight. Deftly she plunged the needle into a vein just below the crook of his elbow. When she was done she raised up the hypodermic and studied the red fluid contents. She grinned and closed the netting. "Try to get some sleep. Maybe your parents can see you tomorrow."

The young man smiled weakly and watched as the woman with dark hair walked away.

Closing the door behind her, the woman in the white smock secured the lock. It was the only room in the small outlying clinic capable of being locked, and she was the only one with a key. Turning, she faced a ten-by-fifteen room filled with laboratory

11

equipment and a computer terminal. A broad table, upon which rested a large, rectangular glass box that looked like an aquarium without water, dominated the room. A small white piece of paper had been taped to the glass container. It read: *Aedes aegypti.* Carefully carrying the syringe of blood she had drawn from the teenager on the ward, she made her way to the table and gently set it down.

She felt a moment of sadness for the boy. He would be dead in two or three days. This fact bothered her some, but not unduly; she had, after all, been responsible for his disease.

She leaned forward and placed her face near the glass surface and closely studied the container's inhabitants. A smirk spread across her face. She raised a hand and drummed her fingers on the glass. A thousand mosquitoes swarmed into frenetic flight. Her smirk erupted into laughter.

Glancing at the blood-filled syringe she said aloud, "Is anyone hungry?"

1

La Jolla Shores, California
1999

The August sun hung high in a deep turquoise sky and poured its effulgence down on the beach. David O'Neal took in a long, deep breath through his nose. The air was perfumed with the smells of salt water, warm sand, and suntan lotion. The day was hot, and he could almost imagine a sizzling sound coming from the well-oiled bodies of sunbathers who joyfully roasted themselves in the sun's intense light. Not David. He preferred to lie on his reclining lawn chair in the full shade of the beach umbrella he had rented from a local vendor.

The cry of gulls and terns overhead blended with the gentle sounds of rolling surf to compose a relaxing symphony that lulled him to the edge of gentle slumber — something to which he would happily surrender. This was the first real day off he had taken in sixteen months of steady, grinding, mind-shredding work. Yet despite the unrelenting pressure, high learning curve, and foreign nature of his job, he would not trade one moment of it.

Being the director of Barringston Relief, the largest relief organization in the world, was as fulfilling as it was demanding. Since assuming the position after the death of his friend and employer A. J. Barringston, David had traveled to twenty-four countries, getting acquainted with the heroes who labored in the worst possible conditions. He had made a return trip to Africa, where he spent time in Rwanda, Republic of Congo, Burundi, and Sudan. He also toured the relief work his organization had recently established on the island nation of Madagascar. His travels took him to famine-stricken North Korea, where farmland had failed to recover from devastating floods. Several weeks were spent in South and Central America. He walked along the Appalachian Mountains and the inner-city streets of Los Angeles, Dallas, Miami, and New York. Everywhere he went, he saw the worst possible conditions; he also saw the brave men and women who faced those elements with passion and aplomb.

David O'Neal worked with the same tireless passion of his predecessor. The broad expanse of the world and the unrelenting need of the suffering now defined his life, which had once been expressed in church work. The enterprise of relief was now the power that energized his soul. It was his work, his dream, his service, and his worship. He thanked God for it every day.

Today, however, he was not Dr. David O'Neal, head of Barringston Relief. No, this day he was just plain old David, citizen of the beach on a searing hot August afternoon.

Through drowsy eyes, he scanned the beach. Children scampered joyfully along the shore while others built sandcastles with their parents. Fifty yards out in the water, bodysurfers struggled to find a wave with sufficient energy to carry them in its foamy grasp. It was a futile effort, for the rollers were nearly as still as the air was calm. Only gentle waves made their way to the sand to flop lazily on the shore, spreading diaphanous froth on the sand. That was fine with David. It meant that he could relax more and worry less about Timmy.

Like the other children along the strand,

Timmy was enjoying the water. David spied him as he raced forward into the ocean, leaping wildly over the two-foot waves as if they were moving hurdles. Once the water was waist high, Timmy would leap boldly into an oncoming wave only to surface rubbing his eyes and coughing. He was having a great time.

Unlike the other children, Timmy stood just over six feet tall and was nearly twenty-four years old. Despite his adult height and age, he was still a child within. His intellectual and emotional development had been tested and compared to that of an eight-year-old. While many who met the boy-man were bathed in pity, David often found himself admiring him. The young man was resilient, strong, and chronically cheerful. Every day brought him new joy and a renewed zest for life. Living was an unending adventure. Not a bad way to live, David had thought many times.

Timmy had known a hard life, living on the streets where other homeless people frequently beat him. A.J. had rescued him from just such a beating years ago. A.J. was the closest thing the boy had ever had to a father. Now that he was gone, David filled that role.

Assured that Timmy was well, David

once again closed his eyes and waited for the simple sleep of relaxation to envelop him.

A muted sound jarred him from his trance: a ringing, electronic and annoying. Glowering, he reached for the cell phone that had been tucked away in a tote bag he used to carry towels and sunblock. He had to search for a moment before finding it.

"David O'Neal," he said, after snapping open the small folding phone.

"Dr. O'Neal," a tinny and distant voice said through a haze of static, "this is Osborn Scott. Sorry to bother you on your day off."

"No problem, Oz," David said. Osborn Scott was a new addition to Barringston Relief. A quiet, capable man and driven scientist, Oz — as he insisted on being called — normally stayed to himself, preferring his work to social contact.

"How was your trip to Belize?" Osborn asked. Even over the phone, he seemed distracted.

"Fine, but puzzling. I'm afraid I came home with more questions than answers."

"Are people still getting sick down there?"

"Yes. It's not an epidemic yet, but it's worrisome. All our research doctors know is that it's viral. But I don't think you called me to talk about Belize. What's up?"

"I need to show you something," Osborn said.

"Can it wait until tomorrow?"

"I think you might want to see this sooner than that." Osborn's voice was tense.

"Is there a problem?" David asked. He could feel his stomach tighten. If Osborn was concerned, then David's life was about to become far more complicated.

"I'd rather not talk about it over the phone."

David sighed. "OK, I'll be there in about half an hour. That's the best I can do."

"That'll be fine." Osborn hung up.

A puissant feeling of disquiet replaced the sense of peace that had permeated David only moments ago, and for good reason: Osborn Scott was the head of CMD, the catastrophe monitoring department. If he was as concerned as he seemed, then something frightening was in the works.

Seated on the three-foot-high concrete wall that separated the sand from the cement walkway that paralleled the shore, a thickly built man with a marine-style haircut carefully aimed a small camera in the direction of the person he had been assigned to follow. He depressed the shutter button. *Click.* The picture was recorded, not on an emulsion of film, but on an electronic chip inside the body of the camera. The image, and the scores like it he had been taking since David O'Neal arrived at the beach, would not need processing. Instead, the camera would simply be downloaded onto the hard drive of a computer. From there the pictures would be used any way his boss decided. He had no idea what that would be, and he didn't care.

The camera he held was an amazing and expensive item. He had been reminded of that fact many times by Jack and that pencil-necked geek with whom he was to leave the camera. "Ten thousand dollars," they had said several times as if he were some dumb high school kid who was borrowing the family car for the first time.

Click. Another shot. *Click.*

The assignment was boring. Sitting in the hot sun, dressed in a pair of brown walking shorts and a white T-shirt, the man waited patiently for his target to position himself so he could snap a usable picture. Unfortunately, that meant prolonged periods of inactivity as David lay quietly in the shade of an umbrella. The retarded boy had been much easier to photograph. He had not stopped moving since arriving at the shore and stood in the sun most of the time. His pictures would be the best. The man wished he could say the same for the ones of David O'Neal. He would just have to wait and see.

The thick man watched as David gathered his things together, returned the rental umbrella, and walked to the car with the young man close behind. The man took another ten pictures then opened a palm-size cell phone. He dialed a number. An answer came on the first ring.

"Jack, here."

"He's moving," the thick man said evenly.

"Got it." A moment later the connection was broken. Jack was never one for long conversations. No matter. At least now he could get out of the sun. There was no need to follow David O'Neal. They knew where he was going, and people would be waiting — people with cameras like his as well as high-end video equipment. The phone call O'Neal had received that prompted his departure had been monitored and recorded. The truth was, everything there was to know about David O'Neal was known, and every place he went someone would be nearby, watching, recording, and waiting.

Standing, the thick man stretched, yawned, and placed the cell phone back in his pocket. He strolled to his own car.

The fifty-three-story Barringston Tower cast a lengthening shadow on the four-lane downtown street that passed in front of it. David never ceased to be amazed at its beautifully designed exterior. Instead of sterile glass and cold concrete that had become the redundant theme of many mid- and high-rise buildings in the heart of San Diego, the Barringston Tower was adorned with earth-tone pebbled panels. Along each floor were planters brimming with hearty plants. Each time David saw the structure he was reminded of artist renderings of the Hanging Gardens of Babylon.

Turning the wheel of his Ford Taurus, David steered the car through the drive that led to the first of two subterranean parking garages. Near the central bank of elevators was a parking place marked with a sign: DR. DAVID O'NEAL, CEO, BARRINGSTON RELIEF.

One minute later he and Timmy, still dressed for the beach, were standing at the basement elevators. Timmy shivered despite the heat of the day. His swim trunks and white T-shirt were still wet; sand clung tenaciously to his bare feet.

"Thanks for the hamburger, David," Timmy said as he hugged himself in an effort to ward off his chill.

"It was the least I could do after making us leave the beach early. I appreciate your being a good sport about this."

"You're welcome." Timmy shivered again. "I still feel cold, David."

"I think you may have a little sunburn. That's why you feel cold."

"A burn can make you feel cold?" Timmy asked, puzzled.

"Sometimes, Timmy, I know it doesn't make sense, but it works that way."

"Oh," he replied innocently. "Will it hurt?"

"The sunburn? A little, but I have some stuff to make it feel better."

A soft chime announced the arrival of the elevator cab. The two stepped inside, and David removed a small plastic card from his wallet and inserted it in a slot next to the control panel. Immediately the doors closed and the elevator began its rapid rise to the fifty-third floor.

"When we get to our floor, Timmy," David began, "I need you to take our stuff to the apartment and put it away. You can take a shower and watch television. I have to meet with someone for a few minutes, and then I'll be up. Can you do that?"

"Sure," Timmy said. "Can I have a soda?"

"Absolutely," David replied with a big grin. "Just be sure to put your wet clothes in the bathroom. I'll deal with them later."

"OK."

The elevator arrived at the top floor and opened its doors. Timmy, arms filled with towels and the tote bag, stepped out and walked toward the penthouse apartment he shared with David. When the mantle of leadership passed from the murdered A. J. Barringston to David, the board of directors insisted that he move into the large flat. He resisted, feeling that it was an unneeded extravagance. Worse, it would remind him of his friend lost to a violence David had yet to overcome. Nonetheless, he acquiesced.

It wasn't long before David realized the importance of living in the suite. Directing Barringston Relief's worldwide efforts was not a nine-to-five job. Since becoming

CEO he had averaged fourteen hours a day working when he was in the country and more when abroad.

The luxurious suite presented some problems, as did the entire Barringston Tower. Visitors often assumed that monies that could be used in hunger relief and other efforts were being spent on the magnificent high-tech building. More times than he could count, David had explained that the building and everything in it, as well as the staff of nearly five hundred, were largely subsidized by Barringston Industries. Barringston Relief paid no rent or utilities for the use of the top ten floors. Barringston Industries occupied the thirteen floors below that, and the remaining thirty floors were leased to various businesses. The lease money from those organizations paid for the building and the cost of its operation.

The enigmatic Archibald Barringston, founder of the global construction company that built high-rise structures in scores of foreign countries, led Barringston Industries. Twenty years prior, he had given a ten-million-dollar jump-start to his son Archibald Jr., known as A.J. to everyone. A.J. had guided the relief agency from its inception. Today it was the largest nongovernmental organization in the world.

Monies for the actual relief work came from several sources. First, people from around the world made donations. Since almost all of the relief organization's overhead and operational expenses were covered by other sources, more than 90 percent of contributions received by individuals and businesses went directly to relief work — a higher percentage than any other relief organization. Substantial funds were gained from patents on research done by Barringston scientists and engineers. Barringston Relief did more than take meals to the hungry; it was the leader in the development of the biotechnology necessary to end famine and related diseases. Side benefits from this research improved crop production in the United States and other countries. Profits from these products were poured back into the relief work.

The elevator descended one floor, and David exited into a lobby. The lobby was empty except for a few chairs and potted trees situated around the perimeter. Three departments — communications, political analysis, and catastrophe monitoring — shared the floor. A large pair of oak double doors led to each office complex. The

CMD was behind the doors to his left. David entered.

Casually he strolled through the half-dozen cubicles that delineated individual work areas and tried not to look conspicuous. Although there was no formal dress code for employees and attire ran the spectrum from jeans and polo shirts to three-piece suits, David's swim trunks, sandals, and San Diego Padres T-shirt was stretching it. When he had left the beach, he had planned to head straight to his apartment, change clothes, and quickly make his way to the CMD offices. That plan had changed when Timmy made his disappointment about leaving the beach early known by lowering his head and extruding his lower lip. David knew he was being manipulated, but he couldn't help feeling guilty for making Timmy leave the beach so early. He made things right by promising to stop for a hamburger and shake on the way home. That had added an additional twenty minutes to the trip. David had promised to meet Osborn in half an hour; he was now late.

Osborn's office, a twenty-by-twenty room with a teak desk and credenza and floor-to-ceiling windows on two walls was in the corner of the tower and overlooked the dense cluster of buildings of urban San Diego. From fifty-two floors up it was a captivating view. Osborn, a stately, middle-aged, African American, was not looking at the view. Instead, his eyes were fixed on his computer screen, peering through small, wire-rimmed glasses.

"I'm sorry to have taken so long, Oz," David began, "but I had to work a little diplomacy with Timmy."

"No problem," Osborn answered without looking up from his screen. "Let me show you something."

David walked over and stood behind him. On the large color monitor was a photo of the Gulf of Mexico and the Caribbean Sea. The picture was detailed, showing mountains, valleys, rivers, and overhead clouds.

"What am I looking for?" David asked.

Osborn picked up a pencil and pointed at the monitor. The sharpened end touched the glass screen with a discernable tap. "Here, fifteen degrees north by about seventy degrees west."

David leaned forward and squinted. "That clump of clouds?"

"Yeah." Osborn leaned back and scratched his chin thoughtfully. "Except it's more than a clump of clouds. It's a tropical storm, a big one, and I'm sure it's on its way to being a hurricane."

"Hurricanes happen every year," David replied. "I don't think you called me here to show me a new one."

"We've already had two this year," Osborn said as he leaned forward and tapped a key on the keyboard. Instantly, the map zoomed out to reveal more of the area. Osborn clicked the key once more and the map shrank. David could now see the entire eastern seaboard. "The first two started well out in the Atlantic and moved toward the coast, but each turned north and never made landfall." As he spoke, Osborn traced the paths of the previous storms. "No harm, no foul. This one, how-ever, is sure to hit something."

"Like what?"

"Too early to tell. It's not even a proper hurricane yet, but it will be. And I think it's going to be a monster."

"How can you tell?"

"Gut feeling, right now, but this is what I do. This is why you hired me last January. I study catastrophes; it's my science, my pas-sion."

That was true enough. Barringston Relief had been heavily involved in fighting world hunger. Its considerable resources were aimed at meeting immediate and long-term needs. David had added another dimension to the work: emergency aid to victims of cataclysm. Each year millions of people were killed, injured, or left homeless by natural disaster. It was David's dream to abate that pain. That's when he hired Dr. Osborn Scott, one of the highest acclaimed students of catastrophe. His reputation was global.

"So you think it's going to be a problem?"

"It's going to be a problem all right. I just don't know how big a problem." They studied the map for a few moments. "I'm sure the news media will be broadcasting word about the storm, but until more data is in, they will be guessing where it will make landfall. We know a storm is out there and that it's going to be a problem for somebody. That's about all we know right now. I'll give you my best guess though."

"OK."

"If I were a betting man," Osborn began, "I'd wager that this fellow will reach hurricane status tonight or early tomorrow and that it will take a northwesterly track." Once again he pointed at the screen. "Worst-case scenario: It grows to a four or five, plows across Cuba, picks up steam in the Gulf of Mexico, and makes landfall again somewhere around here." He pointed to New Orleans.

"That would be bad," David said seriously.

"That would be *very* bad," Osborn corrected. "In the next three days, David, people will die and homes will be destroyed. You can bet the farm on it."

David reached for the telephone on Osborn's desk and quickly punched in the number of his personal assistant on the keypad. A second later, he spoke. "Ava, I need you to set up a meeting with the RRT. Make it for —" he looked at his watch, "four-thirty. That'll give everybody a couple of hours to rearrange their schedules."

David listened for a moment then said, "No, better put us in the big conference room. I'm not sure how long we'll be meeting, so you'd better arrange for some coffee, water, that sort of thing. Thanks, Ava." He hung up.

"I think convening the rapid response team is wise," Osborn said.

"It can't hurt. Besides, I'd rather be ahead of the game than behind. I'm going to clean up while you prepare to make a presentation. Bring whatever information you can and be ready to answer questions. You're the authority on this, and the team will need all the info you can give them."

"I'll be ready," Osborn said resolutely.

"Don't take this the wrong way, Oz," David said, "but I hope you're wrong."

"Me too," Osborn answered. He paused then continued, "But I'm not.

Indian Ocean
Depth: 21,645 feet

Slowly . . . steadily . . . unfailingly . . . the jigsaw pieces of the Earth's crust moved, not by feet, but by meager inches each year. The plates expanded as the fluid rock beneath the pieces purposefully produced new crust while other plates patiently gobbled down the existing shell, melting and blending it with the mantle beneath. Not a day passed, not a minute ticked by without the ancient ballet continuing.

Overhead rested a four-mile-thick blanket of salt water and fluid, always in motion. It was a concert conducted since creation, a dance of endless movement.

With almost intelligent tenacity, the Indo-Australian plate slowly twisted clockwise, creating pressures, magnifying stress, subducting with a plate eight hundred miles east and diverging with its sister plate fifteen hundred miles west. In its center a portion of crust sixty miles thick fractured, elevating a slab of rock the size of California in a titanic eruption of power. With it rose six hundred twenty-five thousand cubic miles of ocean.

Two minutes after it began, the eons of stress relieved, the ocean floor resumed its sluggish dance only slightly altered, gliding in restful moderation.

Not so the ocean.

The conference room was a large trapezoid, wider near the double entry doors and narrower by ten feet at its head. David stood with his hands clasped behind him and faced the gathered executives of Barringston Relief. Ten pairs of eyes returned his gaze. Behind him was a large and technically sophisticated projection screen. To his right was a computer terminal.

The room itself had no windows, the result of purposeful design meant to decrease distractions. The walnut-paneled walls were adorned with pictures taken of Barringston Relief work around the world.

A large walnut table dominated the

center of the room. Seated around the table was the rapid response team — the RRT — comprising the ten department leaders, each an expert in his or her field.

"First, let me thank each of you for re-arranging your schedules to be here," David said. "I believe this is the first time we've met like this since the inception of the team six months ago. Two hours ago, Dr. Osborn Scott brought a serious matter to my attention. I've asked him to bring us up to date. Oz, if you would, please." David stepped back and took a seat.

Osborn stood and took his place at the head of the table. He carried no notes. Before he began, he paused at the computer terminal next to him and tapped in a command. On the floor-to-ceiling screen behind him a satellite photo appeared in bright colors. He stepped to the side to avoid impairing anyone's view.

"This is the latest satellite photo from the NOAA. As you can see, it is of the Gulf of Mexico and the Caribbean." Facing the image, he pulled a penlike device from his pocket and clicked on a small switch. A low-power laser emitted a thin beam that appeared as a small red dot on the satellite image. Aiming the pointing device at a smear of clouds, he continued. "This accumulation of clouds is a massive tropical storm that is quickly growing in power and size. The National Hurricane Center has named the storm Claudia. While it's too early to say with certainty, I estimate that there is a better than 90 percent chance that this storm will grow to hurricane status and do so quickly, perhaps as early as tomorrow morning. When it does, it is sure to cause severe damage.

"It's impossible to predict the track a hurricane will take," Osborn continued. "But because of its present position with Venezuela to the south, several Central American countries to the west, Cuba and the Caribbean Islands to the north, we can safely say that some country, most likely several countries, will be adversely impacted by this storm. Someone is going to take a beating."

"How strong a storm do you anticipate?" Kristen LaCroix asked. Kristen was the director of public relations. She was a bright woman with deep red, shoulder-length hair. She was also David's closest friend.

"Prognostication is a tricky business," Osborn answered, "but I think it's going to be a four, possibly a five."

"You had better explain that, Oz," David

said, wanting to be sure that everyone understood.

Osborn nodded. "Hurricanes are rated on a scale of one to five, with category five being the most severe. Wind speed and barometric pressure determine a hurricane's category. For example, Hurricane Andrew devastated Florida, annihilating several towns and cutting a swath of destruction thirty-five miles wide and creating severe damage over a much wider area than that. It had sustained winds of one hundred forty-five miles per hour with gusts up to one hundred seventy-five. Before it was done, it left forty dead and caused twenty-five billion dollars in damage."

"That was a category five?" Kristen asked.

"No," Osborn replied. "That was a category four. A five is described as catastrophic and maintains winds of one hundred fifty-six miles per hour or greater with gusts that top two hundred miles an hour. In addition, it brings a storm surge of eighteen feet or more."

"Storm surge?" asked Tom Templeton, director of inter-agency relations. His department maintained communications with other relief organizations worldwide as well as with governmental agencies.

"Yes," Osborn answered. "Most people think that a hurricane's winds are the most dangerous part of the storm, but the wind is just one segment of the problem. The storm brings a water surge with it. This surge is like a mound of water that is pushed along by the winds. When the hurricane strikes the shore, this mound of water, which may rise twenty feet above its normal level, instantly floods the surrounding land, taking everything — cars, houses, and people — with it."

"I take it that category-five hurricanes are unusual," Kristen said.

"The U.S. has only endured two in its history. A four is bad enough."

"How bad is bad?" Bob Connick, Barringston Relief's chief financial officer asked.

"Factors vary," Osborn answered. "Much depends on where the hurricane strikes. Developed countries, where sophisticated warning systems exist, fare far better than undeveloped countries. Those systems, however, are wonderful when it comes to saving lives, but they can do nothing to diminish property damage. To give you an idea of what a hurricane can do, I'll share a few examples.

"On October 7, 1737," Osborn continued, "a typhoon — which is the same thing as a hurricane but occurs in the western Pacific or Indian Ocean — struck near Calcutta and sank twenty thousand ships and killed three hundred thousand people. On October 1, 1893, a hurricane similar to this one originated in the Gulf of Mexico," he motioned to the satellite image, "and moved ashore near Port Eads and the Mississippi coastal region. It took eighteen hundred lives. In 1900 a hurricane came ashore at Galveston, Texas, and killed six thousand people. The city was largely destroyed and was later rebuilt — seventeen feet higher than the high tide level."

"But those all occurred a century or more ago," Bob Connick protested.

"True. Today we can evacuate many of the people, but there is still a horrible price to pay. In September 1989, not all that long ago, Hurricane Hugo blasted through the Caribbean islands from Guadeloupe to Puerto Rico before ripping through North and South Carolina. Hugo killed five hundred people and left several billion dollars worth of damage. And as I said earlier, Hurricane Andrew did over twenty-five billion dollars worth of damage in Florida in 1992 but took only forty lives, thanks to technology.

"But don't let the low death toll confuse you," Osborn said. He was now pacing in front of the looming image of the tropical storm. "These storms are still dangerous, far more so than most realize. November 1995 saw Typhoon Angela strike the northern Philippines with winds in excess of one hundred forty miles per hour. The devastation was unbelievable: more than six hundred dead and two hundred eighty thousand homeless."

"Do we need to tell anyone about this?" David asked.

Osborn shook his head. "No, the experts already know, including the NCEP and other agencies. My concern is Mexico and Cuba."

"NCEP?" Kristen inquired.

"National Centers for Environmental Prediction in Miami, Florida," Osborn answered. "The National Hurricane Center is associated with them. They already have a plan of action for such storms, and they will be monitoring it as well. I have a friend there who will share information with us. As I said, the real problem is Cuba and possibly Mexico."

"How so?" David asked.

"Many parts of Mexico are populated by small, impoverished towns. There's a good chance that thousands will not get advance warning, and even if they do, they will not be able to move out of harm's way fast enough. That will only be a problem if the hurricane doesn't veer north, as I expect it to do. Cuba is the concern. While Cubans are familiar with hurricanes because they deal with them every year, a hurricane of this size may be too much. Unlike Americans in the U.S. with large landmass, freeways, and surface streets, the people of Cuba have no place to go. Getting on a boat sure isn't going to help. Those with access to hurricane shelters will be safe, but the others . . ." Osborn shrugged.

David stared at the image of the storm for a moment, then swung his chair around to face the others. Before him were the department heads of communications, medical relief, political analysis, volunteer facilitation, public relations, resource distribution, and transportation coordination, as well as the chief financial officer and the inter-agency liaison — all capable people, trained and dedicated to global relief. They were all experienced with long-term projects in famine and plague. Meeting catastrophe-related needs, however, was something new for them. For nearly six months, they had been working as a team to provide quick response to stricken areas while working in concert with other agencies and governments. This would be their first real test.

Turning back to Osborn, David said, "All right, Oz, break it down for us."

"The following scenario is subject to change," Oz prefaced. "Tomorrow morning, tropical storm Claudia will be upgraded to a hurricane. It will continue to gather strength over the warm waters north of Venezuela and move in a northwesterly direction. I believe it will veer north in time to hit Cuba and hit it hard. The storm will slow over land but will regain its power and intensity once north of Cuba. It will then continue on until it makes landfall on the southern coast of the U.S. The eye-wall will most likely hit Louisiana and Mississippi."

"You sound very confident about your prediction," Bob Connick said.

"Call it scientific intuition," Oz responded. A moment later he said, "It's not confidence you hear — it's fear."

David stood. "OK, folks that's it. I would like to see brief summaries about your department's readiness in two hours.

Let's get to work." Turning to Osborn, David said, "Thanks, Oz, you made everything clear."

"I hope so, David. I have a bad feeling about this. A really bad feeling."

Cox's Bazar, Bangladesh
7:47 A.M. local time

Akram Kazi felt the loose sand under his feet give way with each step. Grains slipped between his bare feet and the sandals he wore. Pressing his chin down on the tall stack of newly washed white towels he carried, he struggled to make certain he didn't spill his load. It was his job to carry towels from the resort's laundry to the small white shack in the middle of the beach where tourists and traveling business executives freely retrieved them after a swim in the ocean. It was just one of the many services that Holiday Resort offered its guests.

Akram hustled along the sandy beach that ran in front of the hotel. The August heat would soon have the guests lining the shore, sitting under umbrellas to protect them from the fierce sun. Akram hurried. He had many things to do, including wiping off the tables of the outdoor café.

Already, guests were being seated and eating breakfast. Akram was running late.

Thirty hastily taken steps later Akram was at the three-meter-by-five-meter shed. *"Assalaa-mualaikum,"* he said, wishing peace to his coworker.

"Wallaikum assalaam." Zahid Hussein, the employee who tended the shed, returned the traditional greeting, but it was clear that he was upset. "It is about time, Akram. I have no towels to give, and already people are asking for them."

"It is not my fault," Akram protested. "The laundry was not done with them. I could not bring you wet towels, could I?"

"No excuses. You have made me look bad before our guests. I will not tolerate that."

"The towels were not ready —"

"Enough," Zahid interrupted. "Do you see that man over there? The one with the big belly?"

"Yes." The man, portly with fish-white skin, reclined on a lounge chair.

"He wants a towel. Take him one and apologize for your actions."

"But I have tables to —"

"Take him a towel and do it quickly."

Akram acquiesced. Zahid was older and

had seniority. Everyone had seniority over him. But that didn't matter. In just two months he would move to Dhaka, the nation's capital, to attend college. It was a fortunate opportunity from Allah, who had already blessed him many times. He could read, unlike 65 percent of other Bangladeshis, and he had a hunger for knowledge. So he worked, saving every taka and paisa, and looked forward to that day when he would study at the University of Dhaka. He longed to be a teacher, like his father before him. Education was the only way his tiny country could climb out of the pit of constant despair and depredation.

Approaching the white man with the big belly, Akram held out a clean white towel in his right hand. Since personal hygiene was done with the left hand, it would have been an insult to use it for something so personal as a towel.

"Thank you, young man," the middle-aged guest said.

"I offer my apologies for not having your towel ready when you requested it." Akram raised his right hand to his forehead, palm slightly cupped, offering a traditional salute.

"No problem, buddy," the man said.

American, Akram thought. *His accent is American.*

"It's just a towel. Everything is OK."

The man touched his index finger to his thumb to form a circle. Instinctively, Akram looked away. It was an obscene gesture, highly offensive. Of course, the American didn't know that. The gesture, Akram had learned, was common in the Western world and simply meant that things were all right. Still, the sign shocked him. Akram had learned many things about foreigners since coming to work at the Holiday Resort two years ago. They were always doing something offensive: pointing with their index fingers, showing the bottoms of their feet, passing food with their left hands. It was simple ignorance on their part, and Akram had learned to endure it.

"Thank you for your kindness," Akram said, his eyes diverted to show humility. "Is there anything else I can get for you?"

"Nope. Nothing at . . ." The American's voice trailed off. "What . . . what's going on?"

"Sir?"

"Out there, boy, look!" The man pointed to the ocean. The offensive gesture was lost on Akram when he turned to see the ocean rapidly retreating from shore.

44

"Don't tell me that's normal." The man lumbered to his feet.

"I have never seen such a thing," Akram said, his eyes wide. "The ocean is leaving."

Slowly he and the American began to walk toward the tide line. Looking up and down the beach, Akram could see that other guests and employees, compelled by curiosity, were doing the same. The beach itself was unique, being the longest unbroken strand on the planet, but this was something before unseen.

"Look at this, will ya," the guest offered. "Fish and crab for the taking."

Akram had noticed it too. The now exposed ocean bottom was littered with crabs and other crustaceans. Fish flopped on the wet sand, slowly suffocating in a blanket of air.

"What do you suppose did this?" asked the pudgy man.

Akram shook his head. "I don't know. Maybe I should tell my manager —"

"Wait! Do you hear something?"

Tilting his head slightly as if to line up his ears for better reception, Akram closed his eyes and listened. "Yes — a roar, a rumble." He opened his eyes and looked at the guest. The man's face was drained of all color, his mouth slack, and his eyes wide. Again he pointed out to sea, and then he crossed himself.

"Hail, Mary, full of grace . . ." the man began. He crossed himself again.

Akram turned to see what had so terrified the man. "Allah, have mercy," was all he could say.

80 kilometers SE of Bhubaneswar, India
Altitude: 2,200 meters

The Cessna Skylane RG airplane bounced slightly as it passed through a thermal. The pilot, an East Indian named Rajiv Kapur, paid no notice to the bump — his mind was elsewhere. Below him the deep blue of the Bay of Bengal was turning a shade lighter as the plane flew over the shallower waters of the continental shelf. Above him the sky was a crystalline blue. It was a beautiful day for flying and even a more beautiful day to be home celebrating the birthday of his five-year-old daughter, Jaya. Normally, Rajiv would be happy to chart a leisurely course back to Bhubaneswar and then to his home in the town of Puri outside the city, but not today. He wanted nothing more than to be with his wife and child.

He checked his airspeed again: 156

knots — 75 percent power, just what it should be. The craft was capable of over 160 knots, but that was pushing the engine harder than necessary, especially on a substantially long flight like the one he was taking from the Andaman Islands 735 miles behind him.

A devout family man, Rajiv was proud of the daughter his wife had given him. Jaya had stolen his heart, as had countless daughters across the world done to their fathers. He soon learned that his little girl knew the secret passages to her father's soul. Jaya knew those avenues well and could melt her normally stern father with a simple glance and a flash from her obsidian eyes. She could manipulate him like no other, and Rajiv loved it. As he flew, his mind filled with the image of his little girl: smooth, brown skin, coal-black hair, shiny eyes, and a bright smile that beamed. She could laugh in such a contagious way that a roomful of adults would find themselves giggling like children.

Rajiv arched his back to stretch out the kinks of three and a half hours at the plane's controls. He shifted in his seat and checked his navigation indicators. Not that he needed to. He had been making flights like this one for over ten years. He often bragged that he could fly to the Andaman Islands blindfolded as well as to any airport on the eastern coast of India. Still, he was a cautious pilot. Caution mixed with courtesy had made him one of the busiest charter pilots in the area. Next year he hoped to add another plane to his "fleet" of one.

"What's that?"

The voice dragged Rajiv from his revelry. He turned to his passenger, Mr. Julius Higgins of London, a jovial man with shiny white hair and a broad mouth. He and his wife, a woman with hair as dark as her husband's was white, were recently retired and were sightseeing in India. "I'm sorry, Mr. Higgins. What did you say?"

"That," Higgins replied nodding out his window. "Looks quite odd, don't you think?"

Rajiv peered across the small cabin and out Higgins's window, but couldn't see anything. Instinctively he looked out his own side window. What he saw made his heart stutter. Even from an altitude of over two thousand meters he could see the ocean being drawn back like a blanket off a bed, leaving long streaks in the mud and sand of the ocean floor.

"Have you ever seen anything like that

before?" Higgins asked. "I mean, does that happen all the time?"

Rajiv could not speak; he just shook his head.

Higgins turned to his wife who was in the seat behind him in the four-passenger plane. "Wake up, dear. You don't want to miss this. Something unusual is happening."

Groggily, Mrs. Higgins opened her eyes. "What? What's wrong?"

"Look out your window," Higgins replied.

"Amazing," she exclaimed, then she smacked her husband on the back of the head. "Why aren't you taping this, Julius? That's why you have the video camera in your hand."

"Oh, right," Higgins said. A moment later he was pointing the video camera out the window. "Try to hold the plane steady, chum."

Rajiv just stared out the window and tried to make sense of what he was seeing. In a few more minutes they would be over land with the ocean behind them and unable to see the drama below. Slowly, Rajiv turned the Cessna and took a course parallel with the shore. To his left was the heavily populated coast; to his right, open ocean.

A gasp came from the back. Rajiv turned to see Mrs. Higgins with a hand to her mouth, her eyes wide in fright. Another gasp, this time from Mr. Higgins.

"What? What is it?" Rajiv blurted.

No one answered. His clients sat stone-like in their seats, gazing watchfully out their windows. The terror in the cabin was palpable. Julius Higgins rigidly held the video camera to his eye. Instinctively, Rajiv leaned to the side to see the monster that had horrified his passengers. The sight struck him hard, like a vicious punch to the stomach. His heart beat rapidly, pounding so hard that Rajiv thought it might burst from his chest.

A ribbon of white, sinuous as a snake, raced toward the coast. So long was the ribbon that Rajiv could not see its ends. The line of water tumbled and churned and grew. Without thought, Rajiv banked the plane hard and pushed on the yoke. The craft responded without hesitation, and the invisible hand of acceleration pressed everyone back into their seats.

"What are you doing?" Higgins cried out.

"I must see," Rajiv said.

Higgins glanced at the altimeter in the

instrument panel. The white indicator arm spun as the Cessna plummeted. "Are you trying to kill us?" he shouted above the now roaring engine. Rajiv did not respond.

Rajiv kept his eyes fixed on the surface of the glistening earth below and then, after an eternity of moments, pulled back on the yoke. Slowly the plane leveled in its flight. The craft cruised at 175 knots, one hundred meters above the newly barren ocean floor. Rajiv, consumed by the image before him, was only barely aware that Julius Higgins had resumed taping. He blinked, then blinked again, but it was still there and it appeared to be growing.

A wave. Rising. Building. Charging with locomotive speed. A wall of water. A cliff of ocean.

"Dear Lord," Higgins said. "It's a tidal wave."

"It's huge," his wife added.

"I'll say. That thing has got to be around twenty-five meters."

Twenty-five meters, Rajiv thought. *Twenty-five meters or better, and it's growing.*

Again, Rajiv banked the plane and raced for shore. This time he maintained his altitude. Urgently he snatched the microphone from his radio set and raised it to his mouth. He keyed the device and began to speak rapidly in Hindi. "Mayday, Mayday, N20355W with emergency traffic."

"This is Bhubaneswar tower, 355W. State your emergency."

"Wave. Tsunami headed your way." Rajiv's voice was breathy as he struggled to keep his emotions controlled.

"What?" came the surprised response of the air traffic controller.

"I'm forty kilometers southeast of Puri. I see a large wave —" Just then the watery monster raced beneath them. Rajiv checked his airspeed.

"How fast are we going?" Higgins asked.

"We're going 165 knots," Rajiv replied, "about three hundred kilometers per hour."

Higgins shook his head. "Three hundred kilometers per hour and that thing is pulling away. It'll hit the shore in less than five minutes."

"Say again, 355W, please." The air traffic controller's voice was tense.

Five minutes, Rajiv thought. *Five minutes wasn't enough time to do anything. Not enough time to get into a car and drive to safety. Not enough time to seek shelter. Barely enough time to pray.*

"Please repeat, 355W."

Rajiv did not respond. What could the controller do? Instead he watched as the wave raced away from them, outdistancing them with each passing second. The wall of water was rising and racing toward the coast, toward Puri, toward his home. And there was nothing he could do about it.

But he would try.

Pushing the throttle to the stops, Rajiv made a vain attempt to catch the fluid behemoth. The engine roared, then screamed in protest. Rajiv did everything to speed the Cessna along — trimmed the propeller, eased all — but it did no good. Only a jet could catch the wave of destruction ahead of him. At the moment, the wave was the fastest thing on or above the ocean. Rajiv would arrive moments after the wave struck shore.

Squeezing the yoke until his knuckles turned white, Rajiv attempted to will the plane to fly faster. He even pointed the nose down to make full use of gravity. His airspeed rose to nearly 200 knots, but it was not enough. He could not descend forever. Soon he would have to level off or die. Maybe dying would not be so bad.

If only he could be there with his family, with his wife and his beautiful Jaya, then maybe he could help or at least hug them one last time. It was a foolish thought, but men are allowed foolish thoughts when their loved ones are in danger.

As the wave approached the shore, Rajiv saw it crest. A second later a spray of white rose high in the air and then quickly rained down. The plane flew over the shoreline a minute or two after the wave broke. Rubble bobbed around on the churning cauldron of cold seawater. What had once been houses were now little more than fragments, kindling. As quickly as the wave had arrived, its destructive tide receded, taking with it the debris of buildings, cars, boats, and bodies.

Rajiv was now flying a mere thirty meters above his hometown of Puri — close enough to see detail that would forever be branded in his mind. Next to him Higgins continued to tape. Rajiv felt an overwhelming sense of anger at the man for being so unmoved by what had just happened, but that dissolved when he saw a single tear stream down the Englishman's cheek.

Below was utter carnage. The streets were littered with debris as though an atom bomb had been unleashed. The wave had not cared if it destroyed the wood huts of the poor or the fine homes of the rich.

Little was left. Bodies of men, women, and children were strewn about; some of them lay naked, the wave having viciously ripped the clothing from their bodies.

Two minutes later, Rajiv circled a decimated stretch of ground. A missile attack would have left more structures intact. Homes, offices, schools, and people had been turned into the flotsam of fate.

"Why are we circling?" Higgins asked softly.

Rajiv did not answer. He stared out the side window.

Higgins sighed. "Is that where you lived?" he asked kindly.

Rajiv nodded slowly and continued to gaze at the wreckage of what had been his middle-class home. Gone were the white stucco house, the small courtyard, and his family. This was where he had lived. Now gone. All gone.

Below he could see a small yellow tricycle implanted next to a fractured stone wall — the birthday gift he had purchased for Jaya.

Tears came unhindered.

2

San Diego, California

The cafeteria on the forty-seventh floor of Barringston Tower bustled with activity and was filled with sensuous aromas of finely prepared food. The cavernous room was much like any other cafeteria, except the quality of the fare was equal to that of the best restaurants. Here executives from Barringston Industries shared tables with workers from Barringston Relief.

David, Timmy, and Kristen LaCroix sat at a table next to a picture window that overlooked the bay. The San Diego skyline twinkled in the darkness. The moon, full and rich, hung above the water and cast soft, ivory light on the city below.

Kristen stared at the moon. David stared at Kristen. Timmy made gurgling noises with his straw as he attempted to free the last drops of a chocolate shake from the bottom of a large glass tumbler.

"Timmy," David said, "that's a little noisy, don't you think?"

"I guess so," Timmy replied. "I like it."

"Go easy on him, David," Kristen said. "It *is* chocolate, after all."

"Yeah," Timmy echoed. "It *is* chocolate, after all." The three laughed, then Timmy asked, "Can I go back to the room? I wanna watch TV."

"Sure," David said.

"I'll get your dishes," Kristen said. "You run along."

"Thanks," Timmy replied. A moment later he was gone.

"You're doing a fine job with him," Kristen said. "Not everyone would be able to handle that kind of responsibility."

"He's a good kid. He's really not that much trouble."

"Is he still having nightmares about the attack?"

"Sometimes." David shrugged. "Aren't we all?"

"I suppose. It's not easy seeing someone gunned down like that. I wish Timmy hadn't seen A.J. die. He loved him so much."

David nodded. He wanted to avoid the subject. Watching his mentor and friend killed had cut him deeply. Sixteen months had not brought a full healing, and the wound still bled. David wondered if sixteen years could.

Kristen reached across the table and gave his hand a gentle squeeze. The simple gesture carried a message of strength, support, and love. David returned the tender squeeze and smiled.

"It's a beautiful moon," Kristen said. "It reminds me of something."

"Would that be a warm night in Ethiopia as the two of us sat on a bench in front of a hotel in Addis Ababa gazing at the same moon? Would it remind you of our first kiss?"

Kristen smiled warmly and said, "Actually, it reminds me of a pancake."

"What?" David laughed. "Oh, you do wax poetic, Miss LaCroix."

"Just trying to lighten the moment."

"I appreciate that."

"Did the others get their readiness summaries to you as you asked?"

David nodded. "Every report on time. It looks good. All we need to do now is wait until we know where the hurricane will hit."

"Osborn seemed pretty serious in the RRT meeting," Kristen observed.

"He's an earnest man and takes his work seriously. He thinks that this may be one of the larger hurricanes to hit the area."

"But he doesn't know?"

"He doesn't know yet. He will. He's the best there is at this sort of thing."

"I don't really know him," Kristen admitted. "What can you tell me about him?"

"He's one of the few intellectual giants in the world. I read an article he wrote for *Scientific American* about weather-related cataclysms and the efforts to monitor them. I picked up the issue because it contained an article about new drought conditions in Africa. It also started me thinking about how ill prepared we were for a sudden catastrophe.

"I had always assumed that the Red Cross and the Red Crescent could handle anything that came their way, but I found out how untrue that assumption is. Generally speaking, the Red Cross, the International Red Cross, and the Muslim-led Red Crescent are remarkably efficient, but like all organizations they are limited in what they can do. I wondered if Barringston Relief could supplement their efforts. I also wondered if we could predict some of these disasters.

"That's where Osborn Scott came in. I did a little research on him and discovered that he's considered tops in his field. He's earned two doctoral degrees, one in meteorology and one in geography. I approached him about leading a department that would monitor and catalog catastrophes so that we might be better able to respond. At the time he was with the California Institute of Technology and reluctant to leave. I told him about our research arm and gave him a tour of the labs on the forty-ninth floor. He was dutifully impressed, as was I when I first came here. Once I assured him that he could continue his research and pick his own team, he agreed. And that, dear Kristen, is how Dr. Scott became one of our own."

"What do you know about him personally?"

"Personally? Not much. He's single and devoted to his work. He passed the security check, if that's what you mean."

"No, that's not what I mean. What do you know about him as a person?"

David sat quietly. Finally he admitted, "Not much, I guess."

"Men," Kristen exclaimed. "I think he's more than concerned about this hurricane, David. I think there's some history there, probably painful history."

"You picked this up from the RRT meeting?"

"I learned from the best." She winked.

David was an authority on public and interpersonal communication. Before going to seminary in the San Francisco area, he had earned a master's degree from the University of Arkansas. He was especially adept at reading body language. It was his skill as a speechwriter that had prompted A. J. Barringston to hire David in the first place. And David had needed the job.

Only a few people knew of David's painful past, that while he was the pastor of a growing church, his wife had left him for someone in the congregation. An unwanted yet uncontested divorce followed, along with depression and loss of confidence. He had regained his confidence and shed his depression during a heartrending, eye-opening trip through Ethiopia last year. Today he was a new man who, through adversity and sorrow, had regained his faith. Still, he kept his emotions to himself and was slow to form relationships. Only Timmy and Kristen had broken through. He loved them.

Because of his recent pain, he never pried into the lives of others.

"All right," David conceded. "What should I have noticed?"

"His agonizing concern," Kristen replied. "I know he didn't say anything about it, but you could see it in his eyes. This thing has him scared. Now before you interrupt me, let me say this: We are all concerned about the hurricane and the lives it will affect. That's why we work here. But his concern was different. There was fear in his eyes and his mannerisms. Surely you noticed."

"Actually, I hadn't. I was trying to take in all he was saying and formulate some plan of action. I was preoccupied."

"That's understandable. All the decisions fall on your shoulders now. I have less pressure and, therefore, more freedom to notice these things."

"So you think something has him scared?"

Kristen nodded. "I suspect something has happened to him, something he doesn't talk about."

"Do you think I should be concerned that he may crumble under the stress?"

"No, but he might need a friend. Just like you needed A.J. when you came here."

David looked out over the moonlit water. A small boat cruised slowly through the harbor. "I'll be sensitive to the situation," he promised. "Thanks for the advice."

"The pleasure is all mine. Just one of my many skills."

"Yeah, but can you fill a coffee cup?"

"What? You want me to refill our cups? I'm the one with a bum leg." Kristen had been born with her right leg shorter than her left, requiring that she wear a custom thick-soled shoe. She walked with a slight limp.

"Bum leg, huh. You forget. I watched you traipse all over Ethiopia a year ago. I couldn't keep up with you."

"You still have to get the coffee."

David sighed and then smiled. "I think I'm being taken advantage of."

"You love it," Kristen countered.

He did.

"Nice acceptance speech," Jack LaBohm said as he turned to face his boss. The light of a dozen chandeliers that hung from the ceiling of the reception room in the five-star Walston Higgins Hotel in New York City reflected off her long, thick mahogany hair. Her brown eyes sparkled attractively. Her lips, brightened by a barely red lipstick, parted to reveal immaculate teeth. He had never seen her so beautiful. She was dressed in a long, clinging, yellow evening dress that rippled in effortless, fluid motion when she walked.

Jack had watched as she mingled among a roomful of reporters and scientists. She beamed a smile at each person who caught her eye, politely shook any hand offered, listened to idle chat, and received buckets of praise. She was the consummate guest. Few would guess that she possessed a fierce determination and explosive temper that had left many who angered her quaking like a leaf in a tornado.

"It served its purpose," Dr. Elaine Aberdene replied, flashing the well-rehearsed, disingenuous smile. "It seemed to go over as planned."

"Better than planned, I would say. You had them eating out of your hand. May I get you some more champagne?"

"No. I just want to get out of here."

"I would think you would want to eat up all this praise. Being named Scientist of the Year by *Science Review* magazine is pretty heady stuff. Great food, other scientists, an awards presentation, not to mention the big write-up in next month's issue. Enjoy it. You deserve it all."

"I've won honors and awards before," Aberdene answered coolly, her voice low so as not to be overheard. "This is just another one. An important one to the company, granted, but it's just another award. How do you think it will impact the market?"

Jack shrugged, then said, "Hard to predict. It will be good, no doubt about that. We should pick up half a point on Wall Street, maybe more, depending on how the news media handle it."

"They should be favorable."

"I think so. Finding an effective treatment for dengue fever is the kind of stuff that makes news."

"But not front-page news," Aberdene said quickly.

"True. Dengue isn't much of a problem in this country, so the true impact of the work will be wasted on many. Pity."

"It is a pity," she agreed.

"Shame we can't do something about that."

Aberdene made direct eye contact with her aide but said nothing. An unspoken message was conveyed in the simple glance. He was tall, with dark hair, hazel eyes, and a perpetual five-o'clock shadow. He was her facilitator. When something needed to be done in this country or on foreign soil, Jack LaBohm got it done. He was the man with contacts, the mover and shaker. He never questioned an order, never backed down from a confrontation, and never betrayed a loyalty — especially when it came to Dr. Elaine Aberdene and Aberdene Pharmaceuticals.

"Are things going according to design?" she asked.

"Everything and everyone is in place. It's just a matter of time." He raised the champagne glass to his lips and took a sip. "Actually, it's been easier than hoped. All we need is a little more time, and our problem should be resolved."

"Hopefully, not too long. If we're not careful, everything could go up in smoke. I haven't worked this hard to let that happen now."

"There's nothing to worry about," Jack said soothingly. "I have done everything you've asked. All you need to do tonight is look glamorous and be charming."

"It's hard to be charming in these shoes," Aberdene complained, shifting her weight. "Why do they let men design women's shoes? Has there been any more mention of Belize?"

"Not much. He mentioned it in a phone call but didn't say anything other than a short reference to the new outbreak. He doesn't suspect anything."

"He will, though. He will."

"How can you be sure?"

"I've encountered the Barringston people before. They do more than provide Band-Aid relief. They try to change things. They also have one of the finest medical research teams in the world. They can afford to hire the leaders in any biological field. I'll bet you that they have folks working on this thing right now. We should be doing our own work instead of sipping champagne in a ballroom. When do we leave?"

"I still think you should stay in New York for a day or two. Catch a Broadway show, eat at fancy restaurants —"

"I don't want to stay," she snapped bitterly. "I want to get back to my work. When do we leave for San Diego?"

"The limo is waiting; the jet is fueled and ready. All you have to do is give the word and we're gone."

"Consider it given."

David found Osborn seated at his desk, holding a small stack of papers and staring at his computer screen. David stood silently in the doorway and watched the man who had yet to notice him. Osborn's brow was furrowed, his lips pulled tight. Every few moments he would type something with his free hand and then frown.

Kristen's words came back to David. Was something else bothering Osborn Scott? Or was he just an intense man intent on doing his job the best he could?

"Can't get the station you want, Oz?" David said.

Osborn jumped, startled by David's words. "You frightened me. I was lost in my thoughts."

"So I see." David smiled. "It happens to me all the time. Sorry to sneak up on you."

"No apology is necessary. We did have a meeting." David had set the evening meeting after receiving the readiness reports. "Have you had dinner yet?"

"No, I'm not hungry."

"Well, be sure you eat when you are. We need you on top of your game. You're the brains behind this situation."

"I don't know about that, but I'll do what I can."

"Anything new?" David walked to Osborn's desk and peered at his computer screen. A spreadsheet filled with numbers and formulas filled the monitor.

"Not really. I've been on the phone to several hurricane monitoring groups gathering all the information I can. I have also been asking their opinions."

"And . . . ?" David prompted.

"They're concerned. It's not unusual to have tropical storms and hurricanes in the area, but this is shaping up to be a monster. It will be a full-fledged hurricane by sunup on the East Coast. I've been running some calculations on potential track and force. It's difficult without hard data, but using what I have, I've verified my best-guess scenario."

"Will there be more hard data coming?"

"Yes. A satellite is watching this thing right now. In addition, weather monitoring stations will give us key factors like barometric pressure, size, and direction. The Fifty-third Weather Reconnaissance Squadron of the U.S. Air Force Reserve flew one of their WC-130 planes through it late today. The information is relayed to the National Hurricane Center for evaluation. I hope to have that information soon. Tomorrow, members of the NOAA's aircraft operations center will send out one of their P-3 Orion aircraft. They carry a little more instrumentation. After that we will have a good picture of Claudia."

"They actually fly into these things? Isn't that rather hazardous duty?"

"Absolutely. I got to do it once. That was enough for me. The information is, however, invaluable to prediction and research."

"So you'll be able to update us frequently?"

"Yes, my whole team is on it right now."

"That's good," David said. He paused, then asked, "Are you OK with all of this?"

"What do you mean?"

"It seems to weigh pretty heavy on you. Kristen thought that maybe there was something about this storm that's bothering you."

"I'm OK, David. Really. I just take all this very seriously."

"We all do," David added.

"Perhaps, but I know what one of these things can do. I've studied them up close several times. Hurricanes, tropical storms, all of it. I've lived through dozens of them gathering information, making observations." Osborn softened his voice. "They're beautiful, David, filled with might and energy. I used to love them as an artist loves a painting, or as a director loves films. I thought they were to be admired, appreciated."

"But now you feel differently?" David prompted gently.

Osborn nodded. "Somewhat. I still think they are things of wonder. But what they leave behind is ugly."

David studied Osborn for a moment. He

could see a memory, a recollection of pain, in the scientist's distant gaze. "Do you feel like talking about it?"

Osborn shook his head. "Nothing to talk about, and nothing would change if I did."

"Excuse me, Dr. Scott," a voice said behind David. David turned to see a young woman, maybe twenty-five years of age, with long, straight blond hair. She was one of the five people Osborn had brought with him to form his team. "I'm sorry to interrupt, but we just received the data from the Fifty-third's reconnaissance of Claudia." She stepped in and handed a single piece of paper to Osborn. David could see that her face was drawn.

"Thank you," Osborn said. He glanced at the paper. Seconds later he looked up at her and asked, "You wrote these down correctly? You're sure these are the numbers?"

"Yes." There was no hesitation.

Osborn returned his attention to the paper and shook his head. "It looks like science wins and the Gulf of Mexico loses. Thank you, Betty." The young woman nodded and left.

"What do you mean?" David asked.

"Claudia is going to be a great storm to study. It's also going to be one of the worst to strike the area." He began to read numbers off the page: "Eight hundred eighty millibars, closed cyclonic system, surface winds thirty meters per second and climbing . . ."

"Meaning?" David asked.

"It's bad, David. The atmospheric pressure is very low at 880 millibars. Standard pressure at sea level is 1,016 millibars. The lower the pressure the worse the storm. Back in 1988, Hurricane Gilbert was measured at 888 millibars and Typhoon Tip in the Pacific came in at 870 millibars — the lowest ever."

"You said it was a closed system."

"Yes, convection and the earth's rotation have caused the storm to spin and to feed on itself. This baby is already a hurricane, and as the convection continues over the warm waters it will increase the wind speed. The storm will pull tighter and become more powerful."

"So your gut feeling was right," David said.

"Yeah, I guess so. Somehow, I don't feel very good about that."

A ringing filled the room. Osborn turned and answered the phone then handed it to David. "It's Gail in communications for you."

David took the phone. "Yes, Gail." He

listened, and closed his eyes. He lowered his head. "When?" Listening. "What about our people?" More listening. "Stay with it, Gail. I want to know where every worker is." He hung up.

"That wasn't good, was it?"

"No," David said softly. "A tsunami hit the coastline in the Bay of Bengal. We don't have details, but our workers in India and Bangladesh have reported it."

Osborn spun in his chair and began typing. Seconds later text appeared on the screen. "This computer is constantly online with the Internet. I use a service that screens certain news for me. Associated Press usually has the first word on such things. That's what this is." He pointed at the screen. "Not much information, but it confirms what you just said. Let me get my team on it right now."

"I'm going up to communications. I want to know what's going on. Let me know when you have something."

Without waiting for a reply, David exited the office, taking the sickness of fear with him.

The room was dark, which was just the way Archer Matthews preferred it. Expensive miniblinds were drawn closed, blocking out the light of day. The gentle glow of a large computer monitor struggled to push back the mantle of darkness that cloaked the room; the pale light shone on the drawn face of Archer as he meticulously and adroitly manipulated the pencil-like pointing device that he held in his right hand. As he moved the device along its vinyl pad, the action was repeated electronically on the screen. Drag, click, click, drag. He had performed the act countless times that day, the day before, and weeks before that.

Setting the device down, Archer leaned back in his chair and rubbed his bleary blue eyes. He had the look of a weary traveler — pale skin, thin frame, and blond-brown hair that hung in his eyes. He also had a brooding, volatile countenance that others tolerated only because of his skill at the computer.

The dull pain of a headache began to tighten on his temples, and his back was strained from sitting in his high-back leather chair for hours. He was weary, not just because of the work, but because of the Problem. The Problem. His Secret. The ever-present It. Only a few were privy to the concealment. He refused to talk about It and only barely acknowledged Its existence. Yet despite his efforts to ignore

It, It refused to ignore him.

A new weariness embraced him, not one that came from long hours at tedious, sedentary, mind-numbing work, but one that came from a body at war with itself. How long had it been? More important, how long would it be? Still there was hope, and that hope lived and breathed because of the work he was now doing.

The phone rang, jarring Archer's mind and dragging him from his introspection. The sudden sound frightened him at first, then the fright gave way to heated annoyance.

"What?" he said, snapping up the receiver. He listened intently for a moment. "First set went out this morning. I still have work to do on this piece, not that we need it. I don't understand —" Again he listened, his mouth drawn tight in frustration at being cut short by the caller. "Understood. I'll be done by morning."

Angrily he hung up the phone, sighed heavily, rubbed the back of his tense neck, and resumed his work.

His head still hurt.

His back still ached.

And, worse, his conscience still haunted him.

3

The tension in the conference room was tangible, palpable, as though it had a life of its own. David sat stone-still as he listened to Osborn Scott, who once again stood before the assembled RRT. The large screen behind him was blank.

"Here's what we have so far," Osborn was saying. "A little less than four hours ago a substantial earthquake took place on the floor of the Indian Ocean. Early readings from the various seismic stations in the area indicate a quake in the neighborhood of a magnitude 8.8. That will likely change a little after more detailed analysis, but not significantly. There is some confusion and much speculation since the quake occurred in a normally stable area of the Indo-Australian plate. These things normally occur along subduction boundaries in the Pacific Ocean where there is greater seismic and volcanic activity."

"What is subduction?" Kristen asked.

"The earth is covered with a semirigid crust called the lithosphere. This crust floats on a molten mantle of liquid rock and is broken up into a number of geologic plates. These plates are constantly moving, albeit slowly. Where these tectonic plates meet, one of several things can happen. First, they can push together to form an undersea ridge — a mountain range. Or, second, they might move away from each other, allowing the mantle below to rise and create new crust. Third, they can slip by each other in a lateral movement, or, fourth, one plate may subduct, that is, have its leading edge pushed down and under an adjoining plate. Sometimes this happens slowly, others times quickly. Anytime there is a sudden movement there is an earthquake."

"But this didn't happen at a plate boundary?" David asked.

"No. It was fairly close to the center of the plate. There have been a few earthquakes in the center, but not many. This is surprising. If I were a betting man, I would have wagered against such a thing happening at that location. Nevertheless, it did. That's one thing about science: You can be surprised at any time."

"So this earthquake caused the tidal

wave?" Kristen inquired.

"Tidal wave is the wrong word. The wave that struck the coastal regions of the Bay of Bengal had nothing to do with the tides. It was the result of a sudden seismic occurrence. The accurate term is *tsunami*. It's a Japanese word that means 'harbor wave.' But to answer your question, yes, the earthquake caused the tsunami."

Osborn paused for a second. "Let me explain. Imagine an area of ocean floor. Above it is several miles of heavy seawater. Think of it as a column of water over the seabed. Have you all got the picture in your mind?" Ten heads in the room nodded. "OK, here's what probably happened in the Indian Ocean. Centuries of stress fractures a piece of the crust, hundreds of miles long, and thrusts it upward twenty or thirty feet. Now what happens to that column of water above it?"

"It has to move too," Kristen offered.

"Exactly, but here's the kicker. Water can't be compressed. So when this massive sliver of crust is pushed up, it pushes up all that water above it. In this case, over twenty-one thousand feet of water was suddenly pushed upward. Immediately after that, the ocean surface seeks its own level. Gravity insists on that. That sudden rise and fall of the ocean over the earth-quake causes a wave, and that wave moves out away from its point of origin in a circle, like what you'd see if you threw a pebble into a pond."

"How big is this wave?" Bob Connick, the CFO, asked.

"At sea, about three feet high."

The room filled with incredulous mur-muring. "Three feet?" Connick objected. "That's not big enough to capsize a row-boat."

Osborn shook his head. "We need to forget images from movies like *The Poseidon Adventure*. Don't let that fool you. It's true that if we were on a cruise in the Indian Ocean and a tsunami came by we wouldn't notice it. It wouldn't even spill the drink in your glass. Ships at sea seldom notice a tsunami. That's because the ocean is so deep that the wave travels below the surface with only a slight bulge above. The danger occurs when the massive wave hits shallow water." He held up his forearm to simulate a wave and slowly moved it in front of his body. "The wave continues on, sometimes altered by undersea geography, until it reaches shallow water. In the deep ocean the wave can move at jetliner speeds — upward of five hundred miles an hour."

"Five hundred miles an hour?" Kristen said with disbelief.

"Yes, and unlike waves you see at the beach, a tsunami can cross an ocean in a few hours, hit a continental shelf, and bounce back across the ocean. In 1960, for example, a tsunami created by an earthquake off Chile reverberated through the Pacific for over a week."

"So what happens when it hits shore?" David asked.

Again, Osborn raised his forearm vertical. "The bottom of the wave strikes the shallow seafloor. This does two things. First, it slows the bottom of the wave." He tilted his arm so that his palm moved forward while his elbow remained fixed. "This slows the wave considerably. Instead of racing through the ocean at several hundred miles an hour, it slows to freeway speeds. Second, the wave, which has been hidden below the surface, now begins to rise. By the time it hits land it can be between fifteen feet and two hundred feet in height."

There was silence. David tried to imagine a wall of water two hundred feet tall. His mind flashed back to yesterday's beach trip with Timmy. He could see Timmy frolicking in the surf. In his mind one of those waves rose high above the beach before crashing down like the collapsing wall of a brick building. The vision made David shudder.

The phone next to David rang. It was his administrative aide, Ava. "Yes. Thanks, Ava." David hung up the phone and picked up a remote that was near the head of the table. He pointed it at the large screen and pressed a button. The blank screen was replaced with the live image of a middle-aged man in a suit seated behind a news desk. They were seeing a CNN newscast. David turned up the volume.

". . . undetermined number of dead and leaving tens of thousands homeless. This highly populated coast was devastated by the first tsunami and suffered even more damage with the second . . ."

David shot a puzzled look at Osborn. "Two waves?"

"I'll explain in a minute."

The anchorman continued, ". . . reports are being received from the East Coast of India to the West Coast of Burma. Hardest hit was the low-lying region of Bangladesh. Scientists are stating that this may be one of the largest tsunamis on record. The video footage you are about to see was taken by a tourist flying over the wave just before it struck shore. The tourist, Julius Higgins, and his wife were vacationing in India and had been on a return flight from the Andaman Islands aboard a small charter plane."

The image of the anchorman was replaced by the uneven video picture of open ocean. The muted voices of the travelers could be heard. The picture was startling: A white band of churning water was moving quickly across the blue ocean surface.

"Amazing," David said.

The conference room was plunged into silence as the dramatic image unfolded. Even from the air, the growing size of the wave could be appreciated. The band of white became a swollen, green wall of water. The camera had stayed fixed on the enigma as it crashed on shore. Ocean spray shot skyward, and buildings twisted unnaturally until they fell in chunks into the boiling flood. Cars tumbled, and debris, propelled by the immeasurable force of the wave, shot through the air like shrapnel from a bomb. Minutes later the inundation began to withdraw to the sea in deadly swirls and eddies of flotsam and bodies. The flooded streets emptied as if a giant plug had been pulled somewhere offshore.

So rapid was the watery withdrawal that floating debris whipped around like the blades of a blender. The retraction of the surge was as hideous as its advance.

The anchorman reappeared on the screen. He looked shell-shocked. "As you can see, great destruction was left in the wake of the wave. Early reports state that Cox's Bazar, a resort community in Bangladesh, was destroyed utterly. We will have more on this as new information is made available."

David clicked off the screen and, like the others, sat in stunned silence. Osborn was the first to speak.

"I have made the study of catastrophe my life's work, but I have never seen anything like that."

"How extensive is the damage?" David asked.

"Too early to tell," Osborn answered. "It will be a few more hours before we know with any certainty."

"What's this about a second wave?" David felt sick.

"Remember when I said that the wave goes out from the seismic event like ripples from a stone tossed into a pond? Well, the pebble causes more than one ripple. Tsunamis work the same way. The wavelength

— the distance between the waves — can be about six hundred miles. That means that the second wave would strike a little over an hour later. That wave is less intense, as are subsequent waves after that. The initial tsunami does most of the damage, but the second wave is a killer too. The locals see that the water has receded and return to the shore area to retrieve their belongings and look for lost loved ones. By the time they realize that a second wave is on the way, it's too late."

David rubbed the back of his neck and sighed. Turning his chair he faced the RRT members. "It's time to get to work," he said. Of Gail Chen, the quiet, intense department head of communications, he asked, "Any word of our workers?"

"We had two works going on in the affected area," she replied, brushing away her straight black hair from her brown skin, "one in Vishakhapatnam, India, and another in an orphanage outside Cox's Bazar. We have been unable to connect with either one. We have some people in Calcutta who are trying to make physical contact, but that is going to be difficult because of the destruction and chaos."

Gail Chen didn't say it, but everyone understood her intent: There was a good chance that Barringston Relief staff had died in the catastrophe.

David already knew the answer, but he asked the question for those who didn't. "How many of our people were . . . are in the damaged area?"

"Five in Bangladesh, six in India."

"Stay with it, Gail. I want our best people on the communication boards. We have the finest equipment available; let's make sure we get everything we can out of it. In the meantime, I'll personally contact their family members and let them know we're doing everything we can. Let's not give up hope."

"Yes, sir."

"Albert, how are we fixed on resources?"

"Resources, medical, food, and temporary shelters are in good supply, but none are in the area. I'll need to draw from our reserves in Tanzania, but it can be done."

David nodded. He went around the table formulating a plan of action. Food and tents would be sent, and so would medication. Barringston Relief wasn't big enough to handle this alone. It would work closely with other organizations. Tom Templeton would handle those contacts.

The discussion went on for twenty minutes, each person clearly defining a next step. The discussion was fast paced and intense. So much so that it took Osborn several attempts to get their attention.

"Yes, Oz, what is it?" David asked.

"I think we may be overlooking something here."

"Like what?" Kristen asked.

"Hurricane Claudia. I know that what has happened in the Bay of Bengal is disastrous, but let's not forget that another tragedy is just a day away."

The reminder sobered David. Osborn was right. They were facing catastrophes on both sides of the world. David shook his head, "Two major natural disasters occurring within days of each other. What are the odds of that?"

"Better than most realize," Osborn answered. "In fact, it's not unusual at all. Multiple natural disasters are common, but they are not always this intense."

"Common?" David said.

"Sure. August 1992 saw a volcano eruption in Alaska as well as an earthquake. Shortly after that, Hurricane Andrew struck the Bahamas and tore through the southeastern states of Florida and Louisiana. A week later Tropical Storm Polly inundated eastern China and took 150 lives. Typhoon Omar impacted Guam and the Philippines. In Afghanistan, flash floods swept through the valleys of Hindu Kush, killing hundreds. Most people aren't aware of these events because many of them take place on foreign soil. You're not aware of it because Barringston Relief has been primarily concerned with hunger issues."

"You're not saying that another catastrophe is on its way, are you?" Kristen asked.

"You must understand," Osborn said firmly. "Catastrophes are not unusual, they are the norm. They happen every year. Some years are worse than others, but every year has its share of disasters. I can't tell you if there will be another one soon or not, but there will be others."

"But how can we deal with multiple disasters like this?" David asked. "We have many resources, more than some countries, but the well is not bottomless. How do we help everyone?"

"You don't," Osborn said. "You have to make choices. Some you will save; others you will be forced to lose."

The comment shocked David. "That's not what I want to hear, Osborn."

"Nor is it what I want to say. It is, however, a fact of life. Choices must be made, and as far as Barringston Relief is concerned, you will have to make them."

Cueva del Toro, Cuba

Seven-year-old Angelina Costa Ruiz strolled along the white sands of the Peninsula de Guanahalabibes near the town of Cueva del Toro. The warm sand stuck to her bare feet, and a stiff breeze ruffled her dark brown hair. She loved the shore, with the cry of gulls, the smell of salt, and the rolling waves. Twice a year her father would take a weekend off from the Center for Agricultural Engineering in Havana, where he worked as a senior research scientist, and drive to his sister's house. They would make more such trips, but gas for the family's old Ford was difficult to come by.

Papa worked hard and spent many hours at things that Angelina did not understand, but she did understand that a weekend at the beach with her cousins was more fun than school. Turning, she looked back at her father who lay upon a towel in the sand, a straw hat covering his face, his dark skin glistening in the sun. He looked so alone, and Angelina wished for him a new wife and for herself a new mother.

It had been six months since Mama died. Cancer, Papa explained. But it had been so sudden, so fast. Now it was just she, Papa, and her older sister, Juanita. Juanita was engaged to be married in October, and soon the house would grow by one when Juanita's new husband moved into their home on the outskirts of the city. Roberto, Juanita's fiancé, was a kind man and always had a joke for Angelina. He was tall and skinny with big eyes that flashed when he laughed. He was also a teacher like her mother had been and helped Angelina with her homework when Papa was working late — something he did almost every night.

"The future of Cuba is in biotechnology," Papa always said. He was proud of the work he did, and Angelina was proud to have such a smart and respected father.

The shrill sound of children at play caused Angelina to redirect her attention to her cousins as they frolicked in the ocean, splashing each other and diving under the small rollers that lumbered toward shore. Five cousins. Angelina's family was small compared to her aunt's. It was fun being around so many children, like being at recess in school. Still, Angelina preferred her own company. Papa said that her mother had been the same way: quiet and thoughtful.

She missed her mother so much. Tiny tears began to float on her eyes. Papa did the best he could. When he was home, he even tried to braid her hair like Mama had done. Papa was a smart man, a good scientist, but he knew nothing about braiding hair. More than once, Juanita had had to undo what Papa had done. They often laughed about it together, but neither would say anything to Papa. He was the best father any child could have, even if he was gone a lot and couldn't braid hair.

Yet as good a father as Papa was, a little girl needed a mother. Someone to tuck her in at night and tell her stories and teach her about cooking and about growing into a woman. Perhaps she should pray for a new mother. Papa didn't believe in God, but Mama had. She had said, "When you're sad or frightened, pray. There's power in the prayer." Twice a month, Mama would go to a little church that was a twenty-minute walk away. The people met in a small, old building with walls covered in peeling white paint. They prayed there too. When Mama had first become ill, Angelina prayed. She prayed hard. She prayed often. But even so, Mama died.

Angelina hadn't prayed since.

At first she had been angry with God. How could He take her mother? He was God, what did He need with her? Angelina needed her Mama more than God did. Now that months had passed, she no longer felt that way. She still missed Mama, but she was no longer angry with God. She didn't know when that change had happened, but it had. Now she was beginning to pray again. Would it be right to pray for a new mother for herself and a new wife for Papa? Perhaps God would understand.

A gust of warm wind startled Angelina. Sand blew past her feet and stung her bare legs. Quickly she shut her eyes and raised her arms to cover her face. It was blowing harder now, swirling, twisting. She could hear a faint moan as the wind blew past her ears. Was this God talking?

Seconds later the wind was gone. Angelina looked at the other children as they stood in the surf. They too had covered their eyes against the sudden breeze. Now that the breeze was gone, they looked at each other and resumed their play.

Odd, Angelina thought. *I don't think I like that.* She looked in the direction from which the wind had come, but could see only boats on the ocean and large billowy clouds in the sky.

Juanita had said that Mama lived with the angels above the clouds. The thought made Angelina happy. A new warmth filled her. Except Mama wouldn't live above those clouds. Mama liked pretty things, and the distant clouds were dark and puffy and looked like old bruises.

No, Mama wouldn't live above those clouds.

David pushed the play button on the remote for the fourth time in the last twenty minutes. He was seated behind the custom teak desk that stood near the large picture windows that made two of the four walls of his office. Across from the desk and on the opposite wall was an entertainment center that housed a large-screen television. The television was a tool, not a luxury. Barringston Relief was a global operation, and the monitoring of international news necessary. In addition to that, many reports from relief workers abroad came via video. This allowed the staff not only to read or to hear a report, but to see events with their own eyes. Consequently, every executive office was equipped with a television and VCR.

No sound came from the television; David had muted it, preferring instead to take in the images without the voice of the aircraft's passengers. He was watching the same video that had been played in the conference room. The communications department routinely recorded such special broadcasts and distributed them to those departments that might be affected by the news.

David was in awe of what he was seeing. Despite the visual proof before his eyes, he was having trouble believing that such a monster could rear its head so quickly and cause so much damage. It was, after all, just water. He knew the illogic of that thought. Osborn Scott had made it very clear that water was dangerous in many situations. David had seen news coverage of floods in the Midwest that had literally carried two-story houses for miles before depositing them, broken and twisted, along a muddy bank. In essence, this tsunami was a gigantic flood that had traveled through the ocean at five hundred miles per hour and impacted the shore at over seventy miles an hour. At that speed, water was not the soft, giving liquid that people used every day — it was a wall nearly as solid as brick.

A knock on the door jarred David from his thoughts. "Come in," he shouted as he pressed the pause button on the remote. Timmy peeked around the corner. "Hey, come on in, buddy."

"Hi, David," Timmy said as he entered. He walked straight in, then stopped abruptly, turned, and went back to shut the door that he had left open.

"What are you up to?" David asked with a big smile.

"Nothin'," Timmy replied. "Mrs. Winters just left."

"Did you learn anything new today, buddy?" Mrs. Winters was the tutor that David had hired to work with Timmy. Although Timmy's mind would never develop beyond that of an eight-year-old, eight-year-olds were capable of doing many things, including reading. There were many good books on the market for minds as young as Timmy's. David was committed to helping him grow to his full mental and emotional potential.

"Yeah, we read a Dr. Seuss book. It was neat."

"I like Dr. Seuss. He uses a lot of rhyming words."

"Yeah." Timmy noticed that the television was on. "Are you watching a movie? I wanna see a movie."

"It's not a movie, Timmy. It's from a newscast."

"Oh," Timmy said with disappointment. "Is that the ocean?"

"It's called the Bay of Bengal, and the shore you see is India. Someone took this video while they were flying in an airplane."

"Neat!"

"Well, not really Timmy. Unlike a movie, real people got hurt, not actors."

"Oh," Timmy replied. David had explained to Timmy the work of Barringston Relief. "Are you going to help those people?"

"We're working on that right now, Timmy."

"Can I see?" he asked, nodding at the television.

David hesitated, wondering how Timmy would respond to such devastation. "I don't know, Timmy. It's not pleasant."

"I don't care. It's important, and you're always saying that I should know important things."

David studied Timmy for a moment, attempting to discern his motivation. Timmy was a sensitive person who often felt the pain and sadness of others. Seeing the tape could prove traumatic. On the other hand, it might help him understand better the work of Barringston Relief and why David had to travel so much.

"OK, Timmy, but if it frightens you, or if you have questions, then you must tell me. OK?"

"OK, but movies don't scare me."

That wasn't true. More than once David had had to leave a theater with Timmy because a movie monster was too frightening for him to handle.

"If it does, though, you promise to tell me?"

"Sure."

"OK, then." David rewound the tape to the beginning. "This happened in India and other countries near India. It was morning there." David pressed the play button.

"What's that?" asked Timmy, pointing at the screen.

"It's a giant wave."

"Like what we saw at the beach?"

"No, Timmy, those were small waves. This wave is much bigger and much stronger."

"How big?"

"We don't know yet, but Dr. Scott thinks that it may be between 150 feet and 200 feet tall."

"Wow." He paused and wrinkled his brow. "How tall is that?"

David paused the tape. "Come over here." David walked to the window behind his desk. "You see that building across the street? The white one?"

"Yeah, it's smaller than our building."

"That's true. Our building is fifty-three floors high. That one over there is only fifteen stories. The wave on the video would be about that tall, maybe even a little taller."

Timmy's eyes widened in disbelief. "Wow! That's lots bigger than the ones at the beach."

"Much bigger," David corrected.

"Yeah, much bigger."

Turning back to the television, David began the tape again. Timmy was wonderstruck. David watched him as the boy watched the video. Timmy took it all in, the sudden explosion of the wave's power, the wreckage left behind, the torn buildings, and the lifeless bodies.

When the tape was over, Timmy turned to David and asked, "Why?"

"Why what?"

"Why did that happen?"

"There was an earthquake under the sea. It caused the wave."

"No, I mean, why did God let that happen?"

David was nonplussed. It was not the question he had expected. Since David had taken on the responsibility for Timmy, he had been taking the boy to church. A year and a half ago, when his wife had deserted him, David had quit praying. It was during his first trip abroad to Ethiopia with A.J., Kristen, and others to Ethiopia that David had regained his spiritual balance. Since then he had been faithful to attend and support a local downtown church whenever he could. He took Timmy and Kristen with him. Timmy was now showing new spiritual roots.

Timmy's spiritual sensitivity proved remarkable. He had developed a real hunger for matters of faith, often quizzing David to distraction. One of David's great joys was watching Timmy study the illustrations in a children's picture Bible that he had purchased for him.

"What do you mean, Timmy?"

"Why did God let the wave happen?"

The question was a deep one with which theologians had struggled for centuries: Why did God allow pain and suffering?

"There's no easy answer for that, Timmy."

Timmy looked at the now blank television screen. Clearly the answer had not satisfied him. "Oh."

David felt his stomach turn. This was an important question for Timmy, and David was uncertain how to answer. After four years of college, three years of seminary, and an additional two years to earn his doctorate, as well as over a decade of pastoral ministry, he felt that he should have all the answers to questions like this, but he did not. He did not have a response for Timmy, and he did not have an answer for himself. He knew the various philosophical arguments — pain is needed so that joy can be appreciated and similar platitudes — but he found those wanting.

Many times David had held dying children in his arms, children too weak to receive the nourishment that Barringston Relief had brought too late. He had helped dig mass graves and hand-feed people too frail to pick up a spoonful of rice. He carried medical supplies to outlying areas of Africa and told stories to children in Brazilian orphanages. Each effort was rewarded with more peace than anything he had ever done, but in the still, quiet nights, the same question would come to mind. He was determined not to demean the suffering or insult God with simple one-line answers to such a profound question.

Timmy was staring at David, waiting for an answer. "Timmy, I don't know."

"Were those bad people?"

"No, they weren't bad."

Timmy pushed out his lower lip, something he did when pondering some difficult concept. "Did they do something wrong?"

"No."

"Did they make God mad?"

"Not that I know of, Timmy. The world is filled with sadness and pain. It always has been that way, and it always will be."

"Are there children in India?" Timmy asked.

David nodded. "There are children everywhere, Timmy."

"Did they die too?"

A sigh escaped David's lips, and he hung his head. "Yes, Timmy. Many children died because of the wave."

"I don't get it."

"Sometimes bad things happen. We live in a world that is dangerous. Sometimes something happens like a tsunami — that's what the wave is called — and many people are affected. It's part of living on our planet. That doesn't mean that God made the big wave, Timmy. The big wave is an act of nature."

"Nature made a wave that God couldn't stop?"

"No, that's not what I mean —"

"Could God have stopped the wave?"

"Well, yes, I suppose He could, if He wanted to."

"He didn't want to?"

This wasn't working. David was struggling to help Timmy make sense of a tragedy and was failing miserably. "I wouldn't say it like that. You're asking a very difficult question, Timmy. I'm not sure there is a good answer for why tragedies like this happen."

"If we was in India —"

"*Were* in India," David corrected.

"If we *were* in India, on the beach and everything, would we be dead?"

Closing his eyes, David thought for a moment. How should he answer that question? David decided that the truth would still be the best approach. "Yes."

"I don't get it."

A sadness seeped into David, like water into a sponge. David wished for a clear and concise answer, but he knew one wasn't available. He could try to explain some of the things he had been taught, arguments like "Death isn't always a bad thing," "Everyone dies sooner or later," and "Bad things happen to good people." But none of the things he had studied could adequately answer such a difficult question. Timmy's mind was limited in development, but he was amazingly sharp with those things he could understand.

There were some people who would offer simplistic answers, but those answers came when people failed to question deeply and honestly. They took platitudes like pills. There were many spiritual questions that humans couldn't answer — not in this life anyway.

"You know, Timmy," David finally said, "at the moment, I don't get it either."

4

Osborn Scott pressed his fingers to his temples and rubbed. He closed his eyes and took in slow, deep breaths. Weariness ached within him; fear percolated in his mind; his stomach felt like a vat of heated acid. Opening his eyes again he looked at the data sheet in front of him. It contained information from NOAA's Aircraft Operations Center. Earlier that day, their P-3 Orion aircraft had flown through Claudia, which had been fully upgraded to hurricane status with good reason. NOAA verified information of the earlier fly-through by the Fifty-third Weather Reconnaissance Squadron. The barometric pressure at the storm's center was abysmally low at 875 millibars, and wind speeds had already surpassed one hundred forty miles per hour. Tomorrow it would be worse.

Part of Osborn felt excited. This was a once-in-a-lifetime — no, a once-in-a-century storm. Scientists waited all their lives for the opportunity to study such an event. The excitement waned. This was more than a storm, it was death packaged in wind and rain. Most would see a monstrous cyclone, but Osborn recognized it for what it truly was: a six-mile-high, fast-moving, ravenous, unrelenting demon — a demon that would not be satisfied without a sacrificial oblation of life and property.

And there was nothing Osborn Scott, Barringston Relief, or anyone else could do about it except watch impotently.

The news media were already carrying the story. Every broadcast and cable network told of the impending meteorological invasion. Maps appeared on television screens, and impeccably dressed weathermen and women pointed to the circling white clouds. Each quoted the National Hurricane Center and made prognostications. That was a good thing, Osborn knew. The sooner people knew, the sooner they could protect themselves. Except no one yet knew where Hurricane Claudia would hit.

Tomorrow they would have a better idea, and they hoped that would be soon enough.

Osborn pulled open the right-hand desk drawer, removed a five-by-seven color photo in a battered metal frame, and studied it. Slowly he passed his finger over the young faces of the group in the photo. All so young. He paused as his fingers reached one face, that of a youthful woman with a brilliant smile and straight, shiny blond hair.

The image blurred as Osborn's eyes filled with tears. In his mind, the hair was no longer the beautiful locks portrayed in the photo; instead the hair was wet, tangled, and matted with blood.

Slamming his eyes shut, Osborn fought the images that played in his mind like a movie on a screen. He took a deep breath and willed himself to think of something else, anything else. He would not, could not, endure the memory again. It brought too much pain, too much mental agony.

Blond hair. Wind. Blood. Water. Blood.

Quickly he put the photo away and slammed the drawer, but it did no good. Osborn Scott was doomed to live the event over one more time — one more agonizing, soul-shredding time. And he was powerless to stop it.

Words ricocheted in David's mind as he gazed out the window of his office. Fragments of sentences and pieces of paragraphs bounced about with no loss of energy, never settling. Osborn's answer to David's question would not go away. How do you help everyone? "You don't," he had replied. "You have to make choices. Some you will save; others you will be forced to lose."

David shook his head. Those were unsettling words he did not want to hear. He knew that no matter how large Barringston Relief became, there would be people out of reach of its help. The pending hurricane was bearing down on Cuba and other areas like a medieval dragon swooping down from the sky on an English village, and the monster wave churning hundreds of miles of coastland into a mass of twisted debris only made matters worse.

Many would send help. Countries would mobilize food and medical aid, but no matter how fast things happened, people would die or be left homeless.

Pictures as clear as any taken by a camera flashed in his mind. David could see the carnage, sense the pain. He was thankful to be a part of an organization dedicated to helping others, but he knew that it wouldn't be enough. Still, they would do their best. Lives would be saved, and families sheltered and fed. He wished he could do more, and he prayed that nothing else would go wrong.

"Nice office," a male voice said behind him.

David turned and saw two men in suits standing in the doorway to his office. One was an African American who stood about David's height but was more stoutly built. He wore a dark blue suit with an equally blue paisley tie. His face was pleasant and adorned with a slight smile that elevated a thick mustache.

Standing next to him was a man in a light gray suit. His face reflected no emotion at all.

"Thank you," David said with uncertainty.

"Did you have this designed for you?"

David glanced around the room. It was a good-sized office, simply adorned and furnished with a glass-topped desk, matching conference table, and walnut credenza. Several leather chairs were opposite the desk.

"No," David replied. "I inherited it when I became head of Barringston Relief. May I ask who you are?"

"The head of Barringston Relief?" the man said with a tone that showed he was dutifully impressed. "Then you are, indeed, Dr. David O'Neal?"

"I am," David answered. "What can I do for you?"

The man reached into the inside pocket of his coat and pulled out a small leather wallet, opened it, and showed his identification to David. The man in the gray suit mirrored the act.

"I'm Agent Bennett Hall of the FBI, and this is Detective Wilson of the San Diego Police Department. The first thing you can do for us is to step away from the window and stand in front of the desk."

"I don't understand." David was perplexed.

"I'll be happy to explain things in a moment, sir, but first do as I say, and step away from the window and stand in front of the desk."

"But," David began, "I don't —"

"I understand that," Hall said firmly. "Just do as I ask."

David complied and stepped to the center of the room.

"Please turn around and place your hands on the top of your head."

"What?" David responded loudly. "You're not serious."

"I am serious, sir. Turn around and put your hands on your head and interlace your fingers."

Again David complied. His heart raced and he felt his face flush. "There must be some mistake." David felt a hand seize his own. A second later, David felt something cold, smooth, and metallic touch his right wrist. He heard a small click and a muted ratcheting sound. He was being hand-cuffed.

"What is going on?" David demanded in a voice louder than he intended. As he spoke, the FBI agent turned the cuff so that it dug into David's wrist and smoothly guided David's hand behind his back. Before David could speak again, his left hand was dragged behind him and shackled with the other cuff.

"I asked a question," David fumed over his shoulder.

Agent Hall ignored David and asked a question of his own. "Do you have any-thing in your pockets that might stick me? Needles? Knife? Anything sharp?"

"Of course not."

"It's a routine question, Dr. O'Neal," Hall said evenly as he patted David's pockets. After the cursory pat down, Hall reached in David's pockets to pull out whatever he found: keys, wallet, and an ATM receipt.

"Tell me this is a joke." David was simultaneously filled with fear and anger.

"I'm afraid not, Dr. O'Neal," Hall said. "You are being arrested. We have a warrant."

"For what?"

"That will all be explained later."

"You'll explain it right now," David demanded.

Hall turned David so that he could face him. The small smile he had brought into David's office was gone, replaced by a firm, professional stare. "No, I won't. And making demands of me will only make things worse."

"What could be worse?" David asked.

"Oh, there are many things worse. Much worse. And you don't want to know what they are. Isn't that right, Detective Wilson?"

"Absolutely."

"But this is impossible. Don't you know who I am?" David was flustered and felt stupid over the last remark.

"I know who you are, Dr. O'Neal," Hall replied evenly. "Until recently, I admired you and this company. But I guess I'll have to rethink all that now, won't I?"

"I don't know what you're talking about."

"They never do," Hall said to Wilson, who chuckled.

"David, I forgot —"

David turned to see Timmy standing in the doorway, his mouth open, his eyes wide with disbelief.

"Timmy —"

"What are they doing to you?" Timmy asked loudly. Turning to Hall he shouted, "You leave him alone. You leave him alone!" Timmy charged forward, his hand raised in a fist.

David knew that Timmy had the mind of a child but the body of a grown man. In anger, Timmy could hit hard enough to injure. Out the corner of his eye he saw Hall tense and start for Timmy. David reacted.

"Timmy, no!" he shouted and stepped in front of the young man, interposing his body between Timmy and Hall. "Everyone stop!" David commanded.

Timmy halted in his steps just inches away from David.

"Listen to me, Timmy," David said firmly, fixing his eyes on Timmy's. "Are you listening to me?" Timmy was staring at Hall. "Look at me, Timmy. Look at me now."

Slowly Timmy diverted his angry gaze

from Hall and stared at David. His eyes began to fill with tears. David felt tears flood his own eyes. Timmy was just trying to protect him, to come to his aid. Seeing David with his hands behind his back and two strangers standing menacingly nearby had frightened him.

"Timmy," David said softly but firmly, "these are policemen, and they're here doing their job."

"Where are their uniforms and badges and —"

"One is a detective, and the other is with the FBI."

"Like on television?" Timmy asked.

"Yes, like on television."

"But what are they doing to you?" Timmy demanded. "Why are they here?"

For a moment David was tempted to make up a story, but chose the truth instead. "They think I've done something wrong."

"That's crazy," Timmy shouted. "He didn't do nothin'. He's my friend. You leave him alone."

"Timmy, that's enough." David's voice was stern, like that of a father speaking to an errant son.

"But you ain't done nothin' wrong," Timmy protested.

"I know, but I need to go with them so I can straighten all this out. OK?"

Timmy didn't answer.

"I need you to be strong. You must settle down. OK?"

"OK," Timmy conceded. "I guess."

"Good," David said, easing the edge in his voice. "Thank you. Now I want you to do something for me, OK?"

Timmy nodded.

"Go next door to Ava's office and ask her to come in here. Can you do that for me?"

"Yeah," Timmy answered with a pout. "I guess.

"OK. Go do that right now."

Timmy looked at the two men once more, then quickly walked from the office. Seconds later he reappeared with David's administrative assistant, Ava.

"What . . . What's going on?" she stammered.

"I'm being arrested, Ava," David said with an outward calmness that belied his inner turmoil. "I need you to do a couple of things. First, call Bob Connick and let him know what's happening. See if he can get someone from legal to help me out. Also, let Kristen know what's going on."

Kristen was not only David's closest friend

but also director of public relations. She might be required to answer questions of the media; he didn't want her caught off guard.

"OK," Ava said. "But I don't understand. Arrested? For what?"

"That's a good question," David said turning to face Hall.

"Well, for starters, fraud," Hall said.

"Fraud?"

"It will be explained to you during your interview at FBI headquarters. Now it's time we left."

"No!" Timmy shouted.

"Timmy," David said firmly. "Go with Ava."

"But —"

"Do as I say," David demanded firmly.

Tears began to streak down Timmy's cheek. He wiped at them with the back of his hand.

"It's going to be all right, Timmy," David consoled. "Trust me. I'm going to be fine. You'll see." David could see that Timmy didn't believe him. "Trust me, Timmy. Please."

Timmy lowered his head and walked from the office with Ava, who had gently taken his hand.

Agent Hall took David's elbow and

motioned toward the door. "It's time to go, but before we do there's one more small bit of business." Hall pulled a small white card from his coat pocket and read from it. "You have the right to remain silent . . ."

After acknowledging his Miranda rights, David walked from his office, his hands cuffed behind his back.

They exited through the lobby. Agent Hall was on one side, his hand firmly holding David's arm. As they approached the glass doors at the front entrance, David could see a throng of people, some with cameras. The press. David felt his heart sink. Two uniformed security guards who worked for Barringston Industries struggled to keep the reporters back.

"Could we go out another way?" David asked quickly. The last thing he needed was this to become a public event.

"No," Hall answered succinctly. "Our car is at the curb."

"Couldn't the detective here drive it into our underground garage?"

"No," Hall answered. "We've wasted enough time."

The lobby doors opened into a rising swell of cameras, microphones, and people.

The reporters jostled each other for position and shouted out questions: "Is it true, Dr. O'Neal?" "Can we have a statement?" "What is your response to the allegations?"

David lowered his head, making no eye contact. He said nothing. He had seen news footage of people who had been arrested being led through crowds like this. The suspects would bow their heads, turn from the cameras, or even, when possible, cover their heads with coats or their shirts. David now understood why.

Hall and Wilson pushed through the crowd without comment until they reached the curb where a dark sedan was parked. Seconds later, David O'Neal, his hands still cuffed behind his back, was driven away. As the car left the curb, David turned to see the crowd and wondered how they had known he was being arrested.

Across the street from the Barringston Tower, a thick man with a military haircut watched with satisfaction as David was led through the crowd of reporters. As the dark sedan in which David was seated pulled from the curb, the man removed a small cell phone from his brown sports jacket and dialed a number. When the ring was replaced by a voice, he said, "It's done." He hung up.

"Can I help, Papa?" Angelina shouted against the wind. Powerful gusts of air pressed against her small body. Her hair flew about her face in tangled strands and whipped at her skin. The unrelenting wind stung her eyes. Rain swept across the yard and peppered the house like grains of sand.

"Get inside, Puppet," her father ordered. "It's not safe out here."

"But what about you? It's not safe for you either."

"I'll be there in a moment," he shouted. "As soon as I'm done here."

Angelina stared at the large flat plywood sheet her father struggled to hold against the window. Her uncle was hammering nails through the plywood and into the house.

"Get inside, Angelina! Now!"

Still dressed in her bathing suit, Angelina turned and trotted for the doorway. The drops of rain propelled by the wind stung her flesh like a thousand ant bites. There were new tears in her eyes now — tears of fear.

Inside the small house was the entire Marquez clan: five children huddled near their mother, Maria, Angelina's aunt. The youngest ones were in tears; the older ones sat wide-eyed. Angelina stood in the middle of the living room, uncertain of what to do or say next.

"Are they finished?" Maria asked firmly. Angelina knew that she was trying to be brave for the children and for her, but her aunt's fear was as real as the loud hammering from the nails being driven into the walls.

"Almost." Each window in the house had been covered with a sheet of plywood, leaving the house dark and confining, lit only by a ceiling lamp. Silently Angelina turned and watched the front door, waiting as each eternally long second ticked by. A new fear welled up inside her, the kind of fear that only a child who has lost a parent can feel. What would she do if she lost her father too? *No!* Angelina told herself. *That would not happen. She would not let it happen.*

Angelina began to pray again.

It had all happened so quickly. Two hours ago they were on the beach enjoying the sun and ocean. The children played under the watchful eye of Maria, and the

118

men dozed. Angelina had become bored with her little stroll along the shore and had returned to keep her father company. Sitting by his outstretched body, she had listened to him snore and had giggled. He sounded like an old car. A small portable radio was on the towel next to him. Angelina, wanting something more melodious than her father's snorts and wheezes, turned it on. The sudden sound startled her father.

"What are you doing, Puppet?" he asked as he rubbed his eyes. "I was having a wonderful dream."

"About a woman?" she teased.

"No, about food."

Angelina grunted and reached for the dial on the radio. A man was speaking, and she wanted music. Just before her hand touched the radio her father grabbed her arm and held it.

"Papa! What are you doing?"

He shushed her. "Listen." A moment later he was on his feet and gazing at the horizon. Angelina had joined him, squinting into the ever-increasing wind. She had heard the word that had frightened him: *hurricane.*

The door opened with a resounding slam that reverberated throughout the room. The wind outside moaned and howled. Angelina watched as her father and uncle staggered into the room, drenched by the pounding rain. With quick motions, her father closed the door, using his weight to offset the invisible hand of wind that resisted him.

Once the door was shut he spoke. "Wind is picking up fast. The storm is on its way."

"Will we be OK?" Maria asked.

"The windows are boarded, the doors shut. As long as we stay inside we should be fine."

Angelina crossed the floor, reached up, and wrapped her arms around her father's waist. Outside, the wind howled, moaned, and whistled around the corners of the house as if uttering an ominous threat.

5

The interview room was a ten-by-twelve concrete-block chamber with a small, heavily scarred wood conference table. David sat at one end of that table and waited. He had been sitting alone in the room for nearly an hour, and his frustration was quickly compounding. That frustration was added to the fear, confusion, and anxiety that churned and bubbled in his stomach like an evil alchemist's brew. He looked at the mirror — a two-way mirror he surmised — and wondered if he was being watched.

The trip from his office to the FBI building in Kearny Mesa took just over twenty minutes. Once inside he was patted down again and his handcuffs were removed. He was allowed to make a phone call, which he used to tell Ava where they had taken him, and shown into the interview room. There he had been read his Miranda rights again. The next hour passed with excruciating torpidity. No one waited with him. No one talked to him. He sat alone, his mind flooded with confused thoughts.

On the trip over, David had questioned Agent Hall repeatedly, but Hall was uncommunicative. David stood and began to pace the room. He knew that such behavior would signal his anxiety to anyone who might be observing him through the two-way mirror, but he did not care. He had a right to be anxious. He had been arrested in his own office, in front of Timmy, and dragged through a horde of reporters. He was innocent of any wrongdoing, he knew that. Still he felt dirty, tarnished.

David rubbed his wrists where the handcuffs had been. He could still feel their cold, metallic grip. His mind whirled with images: pictures of Timmy's tears, the faces of the reporters, the expression on Ava's face. His frustration was quickly ripening into anger. He wanted to throw something, but there was nothing in the room except the table and the four chairs around its perimeter. And while throwing a chair might have some momentary gratification, it would not help his cause.

Focus, David, he told himself. *Set the emo-*

tions aside and focus your thoughts. Use your brain. Clearly, there has been a mistake, and all this will be taken care of shortly.

His conversation with himself only mildly calmed him. No matter how many times he reassured himself that his arrest was little more than a police faux pas, he failed to be convincing enough.

The door, a gray metal slab, swung open, creaking as it rotated on its hinges. Agent Hall entered, followed by a man David didn't recognize.

"Are you comfortable enough, Dr. O'Neal?" Hall asked.

"Not very," David answered.

"I understand," Hall said without sympathy. "You were kept waiting, but Mr. Overstreet insisted on being here during our interview."

David turned to the man Hall had just mentioned. He was tall, with a solid build and black hair speckled gray. His eyes were a piercing green and reflected a keen intelligence. "May I ask who you are?" David inquired evenly.

"Certainly," the man said extending his hand. "I'm Calvin Overstreet, your attorney."

Reluctantly David took the man's hand. It felt enormous and powerful. Everything about the man gave an impression of strength. "My attorney? I'm afraid we've never met."

"We haven't," Calvin said, motioning to the chairs. The three men took seats, David at one end of the table, Hall at the other. Calvin sat at the side between them. He turned and faced David as if Hall weren't even in the room. "Mr. Barringston called and asked me to represent you. I've had the privilege of providing legal counsel to him over the years."

David cringed inwardly at the revelation that the elderly Archibald Barringston knew of the arrest. "I thought someone from our legal department might represent me."

"Good people, one and all," Calvin said with a broad smile. "But they are not criminal attorneys, and it appears you need someone experienced in criminal matters."

"A good one," Hall interjected.

Calvin turned and cast an unfaltering gaze at the FBI man. He then turned back to David. "Have you been asked any questions by Agent Hall or anyone else?"

"No. I told them in the car that I wanted an attorney present during any questioning."

"Very prudent," Calvin said with a nod.

"Now, before we go another step, I need to know if you want me to represent you. That part needs to be official."

"You say Mr. Barringston sent you?"

"Yes. Your aide, Ava, called him, and he immediately phoned me."

David hesitated. He didn't know this man, but he did know Archibald Barringston and trusted him completely.

"Let me tell you two more things, Dr. O'Neal," Calvin said. "First, Mr. Barringston is paying all legal fees. You need to have no concern about that. Second, you need me. This is no small matter."

The last phrase sounded ominous to David, and it hit him hard like an unexpected punch to the stomach. Could he be in that much trouble? David nodded silently, then uttered just one word, "Yes."

"Very good," Calvin said. "As your attorney, I now advise you to offer no information without my consent. You are to talk to no one about these matters. Not to friends, family, or coworkers. Any remarks you make, whether in a room like this or in casual conversation, can be used against you. Do you understand?"

"Yes," David answered, feeling comforted that Calvin, who was showing himself to be aggressive, was there to help.

"Fine," Calvin said. "Agent Hall wants to ask you some questions. I will let you know whether or not to answer them. Refusing to answer a question is not an admission of guilt; it is an exercise of your rights. Understood?"

"Yes," David answered. "But I don't even know what the charges are. They mentioned some nonsense about fraud, but that's all."

"Nonsense, huh?" Hall interjected. He leaned back in his chair and crossed his arms. "You've become a very popular man over the last few days, Dr. O'Neal. A great many people want to talk to you. In fact, there was quite a debate as to who would have the honor of arresting you."

"What do you mean?" David said. A serious, determined expression crossed his face. He was quickly moving from confusion and concern to irritation. "Could you be less cryptic?"

"Was I being cryptic?" Hall asked innocently. "All right then, let's get to it. We have sufficient evidence to believe that you have been involved in mail fraud in which money raised by Barringston Relief has been skimmed off and placed into an offshore bank account —"

126

"That's ridiculous," David objected loudly. "I'm paid a straight salary, and I don't handle the books. I get a weekly report and that's it. Not to mention I have only one bank account and one savings account, and they're in this country."

"We know about those accounts," Hall responded, leaning forward over the table. "And so does the IRS and the inspectors at the postal service. We also know about the three accounts in an offshore bank in the Cayman Islands."

"I have no accounts in the Cayman Islands," David asserted.

"That's not what the president of the Americas Bank says," Hall responded. "According to our investigation thus far we have determined that you have sequestered close to thirty million dollars in those three accounts. That's an awful lot of money, don't you think?"

"Your investigation is flawed," David retorted firmly. "I have no accounts outside this country."

Hall held up a hand. "Wait, there's more. The INS is interested in you too."

"The Immigration and Naturalization Service has interest in my client?" Calvin asked calmly.

"Very much so," Hall said with a grin

that caused his mustache to bunch up under his nose. Turning to David, Hall said, "Have you ever heard of Cross-World Shipping?"

David looked at Calvin, who nodded. "Yes. They're a South American shipping line that we contract to carry food and medication for us. Barringston Relief has worked with them for several years. What about them?"

"On a tip," Hall answered, "the Coast Guard boarded one of their ships two miles out of San Diego Bay. A search revealed nearly five hundred illegal immigrants in the hold of the ship. And not in very good condition, I might add. They were dehydrated, ill, and had been abused. The skipper of the ship had never been in trouble before and was most cooperative. He didn't want to lose his master's license, so he gushed forth with information. In that information your name came to the forefront. He gave a written statement in which he said you hired him to smuggle aliens into the U.S."

"Absurd!" David shouted.

"Is it?" Hall asked. "We have the captain's statement and statements from five hundred illegal immigrants from Guatemala, Honduras, and Belize. They each stated that they paid ten thousand dollars for passage to this country. They also said that the arrangements were made through a Barringston Relief outlet. In Honduras it was an orphanage; in Belize, a medical center."

"I don't believe it," David said. Unconsciously he rubbed his temples. His head was beginning to hurt.

"We believe it, Dr. O'Neal," Hall said. "The INS believes it, and the Coast Guard believes it too."

"It's not possible," David said. "I've done nothing wrong."

"Do you know how many times I've heard that?" Hall asked bitterly. "Don't you think it would be better if you cooperated with us?"

David looked up and made eye contact with Hall. "Yes," he said softly. "Yes, I do."

Hall leaned back in his chair and smiled.

"I assume what you want is the truth," David said.

Calvin started to speak, but David cut him off.

"All right, here's the truth. Everything, and I mean everything, you've just told me is a lie, I have no accounts in an offshore bank. I have skimmed no money from contributions. I know nothing about the smuggling of illegal aliens into this country. That's the truth, Agent Hall. It is the pure, unadulterated truth. I know it's not what you want to hear, but that's too bad. As God is my witness, I'm innocent of all those charges."

The room filled with silence. David stared at Hall, waiting for a response. Calvin studied David. Hall, his jaw tight, his lips pursed, sat motionless. At first no one moved, no one spoke. The silence grew heavy.

Finally, Calvin cleared his throat and said, "If this concludes the questioning, I will be taking my client home."

"No one is going anywhere," Hall snapped. He stood, walked to the door, opened it, and said to someone in the hall, "OK, bring it in."

Hall stepped back and held the door open as a man in a suit, another agent David assumed, pushed a metal cart into the room. The cart carried a television and a VCR. The man plugged the two electronic devices into a wall socket and left.

"What's this?" Calvin asked.

Hall didn't answer. Instead he picked up a black case, removed the videocassette it held, and plugged it into the player. After switching on the television, he pushed the play button and stepped to the side wall. He didn't bother to watch the tape; instead, he stared unblinkingly at David.

He wants a reaction, David thought and then determined to give him none.

The television screen came to life, first with a blizzard of white and black dots that was quickly replaced by a pure, unbroken blue. A second later an image appeared of three men sitting around a conference table in a room David did not recognize. The darkness outside the windows indicated that the event had occurred long after sunset.

The two men were strangers to David, yet he knew the third one very well. David was watching himself meet with two people he had never before seen. Blinking several times, David instinctively leaned forward to get a closer look at the impossible scene before him.

"Is there audio with this?" Calvin asked.

"No," Hall admitted. "Just the pictures, but that doesn't matter right now."

"What's the significance of this tape?" Calvin inquired.

"Do you see the man on the left of your client?" Hall asked. "That's Luis Torres, captain of the *Emerald Green*, the cargo ship boarded by the Coast Guard. The man on Dr. O'Neal's right is Arturo Lozano. INS tells me he heads an alien smuggling syndicate out of Mexico. But it gets better. Watch."

The image played out on the screen. The unheard conversation at times seemed tense. Three minutes into the tape the David O'Neal on the video motioned to someone off screen. A second later a tall woman with flowing red hair entered the frame carrying a brown briefcase. She was super-model beautiful and dressed in a clingy, shimmering blue evening gown. Setting the briefcase on the conference table she leaned over and gave David a long and passionate kiss. When she finally ended the embrace, she gently caressed David's cheek and whispered something in his ear. On the screen, David laughed and said something. The other two men joined in the laughter. Even without sound it was easy to tell the bawdy nature of the comment.

David watched himself open the briefcase and turn it first toward the man on the right, then toward the man on the left. The briefcase was filled with money. David closed the case, secured its latches and pushed it over to the man Hall had identified as Arturo Lozano. Lozano quickly opened the case again, pulled out several bills, and handed them to the woman. She smiled graciously and seductively. The three men laughed again.

Abruptly the tape ended.

"Pretty convincing, don't you think, Dr. O'Neal?" Hall asked.

David was devastated. His head reeled; he felt nauseous. "It's not real," he said weakly. "That's not me. It didn't happen. I've never met those people before. I've certainly never met that woman before."

"Not real?" Hall snapped. "Is that not your face we see on the tape? Of course it's real, and you know it."

"No, I don't!" he shouted and stood to his feet.

Calvin was on his feet too, his hand firmly placed on David's shoulder. "Sit down, David. Sit down now."

Reluctantly David complied.

"That's not all," Hall said. "I don't want to give away all my secrets, but I can tell you that we have copies of bank statements from the Cayman bank. We have bank documents with your signature."

"There can't be bank documents," David protested. "I've never been to Grand Cayman."

"Is that a fact," Hall said. "It so happens

that I have photos of you entering and leaving the bank."

"That's impossible," David shouted.

"Not only is it possible," Hall shouted back, "but it's a fact. The only thing that is impossible is you getting away with this."

"I have done nothing wrong."

"Do you expect us not to believe our own eyes?" Hall countered. "Come on, Dr. O'Neal. Let's put this charade to rest and save the hardworking taxpayers some money on this investigation. Confess and we can all get on with our lives."

"I have done nothing wrong," David repeated.

"Enough," Calvin interjected forcefully. "David, you will say nothing more. Nothing. And you, Agent Hall, will stop browbeating my client."

"Don't push your luck with me, Overstreet," Hall said. "Your past will not help you in this case."

"Either charge my client or I'm taking him home," Calvin said.

"He's going to be charged all right, and when this is all said and done, Dr. O'Neal will spend the next decade or two of his life behind bars. And not even you can stop that."

"We'll see about that," Calvin said.

"You know what the saddest part of all this is?" Hall said, turning his attention back to David. "My wife and I have been regular contributors to Barringston Relief. We thought we were doing a good thing. Well, no longer, Dr. O'Neal, no longer. I've got a feeling that many of your other contributors are going to feel the same."

David sat in silence and shook his head. "I'm telling you the truth. Why won't you believe me?"

"Because the evidence says you're lying, that's why." Hall took a deep breath. "By the way," he continued, "the Justice Department is freezing all of Barringston Relief's assets."

"You can't do that," David objected. "People depend on us for food and medication. If we fall behind in delivery, many could die."

"You should have thought of that sooner, Dr. O'Neal." Hall stepped to the door and opened it. He turned back to David. "If people die, it will be your fault."

David felt like he had been kicked. Nothing made sense. Nothing was real. It was as if he had been caught up in a suspense movie.

Hall turned to Calvin. "Give him good counsel, Overstreet. He's going to need it."

Hall left the room.

"This is beyond all comprehension," David said morosely. He was looking down at the table in the interview room, his hands clasped in front of him, fingers tightly intertwined. "I don't understand how any of this can be."

"David," Calvin said quietly. "We need to talk."

"I know what you're thinking, Mr. Overstreet," David said. "If I were in your shoes and I had just seen that tape, I'd be looking for a way out of here — a way to get as far from me as possible."

"I doubt that," Calvin said. "You're not the type to quit on people in need."

"What now?" David asked.

"We talk for a few minutes, and then I get to work."

"I don't know what I can say to convince you that I did not do any of the things with which I am charged."

"I believe you."

"How can you believe me?" David asked with incredulity. "Even I can see that the evidence is overwhelming."

"That's why I believe you," Calvin said with a smile. "This is too perfect. There is too much evidence, and it's too neatly wrapped. Plus, there's something wrong with that video."

"Like what?"

"I don't know, but I'll figure it out. Something about it doesn't seem right — doesn't fit."

"It's not me," David said with conviction. "I can assure you of that. I've never seen those people, I've never met with them, and I've never kissed that woman. I think I would have remembered that."

"No doubt there," Calvin agreed.

"What happens next?"

"You'll be transported to the county jail where bail will be set. I'll post the bail, and we'll be on our way."

"Isn't there a court hearing or something first?" David asked.

"Usually the bail is set according to a schedule. I think you'll be home tonight. Maybe tomorrow, depending how far along the paperwork is."

"That's a relief. Is it true what Hall said about freezing Barringston Relief's assets?"

"I'm afraid so, David. They don't want you transferring money out of the country . . ." David looked up sharply and Calvin read the unvoiced statement. "I know you haven't transferred any funds, but the

Department of Justice thinks you did."

"This is a nightmare."

"No, it's not," Calvin corrected. "It's as real as it gets, and we're going to respond accordingly. It's time to get to work."

David looked up at Calvin and studied him. "Mr. Overstreet, I appreciate your help, but I've given my life over to aiding the starving and ailing of the world. This could ruin it all. It's not just my life we're talking about here, it's the lives of countless thousands of unnamed people. Children who struggle daily to hang on to life. Add to that the number of workers that Barringston Relief has around the world as well as in our various offices, and the number of affected people becomes enormous. So you'll understand my intent when I ask, Are you good at what you do?"

Calvin Overstreet leaned forward and spoke in a measured tone. "David, I'm the best man you can have on your side. That's not arrogance; it's a simple statement of fact."

"What did Hall mean when he said your past won't help you?"

"Hall and I go way back," Calvin said. "We worked together, right here in this office."

"Worked together?"

"Yes," Calvin said with a nod. "I'm a fifteen-year veteran of the FBI."

"Now you practice criminal law?"

"And tax law. It's an odd mix, I admit, but I don't take every criminal case that comes my way. Only those in which I believe the accused is innocent."

"Why do you believe I'm innocent?"

"Mr. Barringston said you were, and that's good enough for me. Besides, I'm a pretty good judge of character."

David was starting to feel relieved that Calvin was on his side. "May I ask why you left the FBI?"

"Sure," Calvin answered. "I sent an innocent person to jail. I believed at the time that she was guilty, but ten years later I found out I was wrong. When she went to jail, she had an eight-year-old daughter; by the time she got out, her daughter was eighteen. That's a lot of years to miss. My mistake cost her a big hunk of her life and the opportunity to watch her child grow up. Not to put too fine a point on it, David, I destroyed her life and that of her family. I can't forget that. Unfortunately, I can't undo it either, but I can do my best to make sure it doesn't happen to someone else."

David sat in silence and looked at the

man who had so easily opened himself. "I don't know whether to be reassured by your commitment or concerned about your past mistake."

"Be reassured, David," Calvin said with a short laugh. "Now let me ask you something. How good is your memory?"

"Pretty good. Why?"

"Because it's time to dig up the past, David. It's time to dig up the past."

6

Aldo Goldoni turned the rearview mirror of the delivery van toward himself and studied his reflection through ice-blue eyes. He wore a brown cap that sported the initials WPS — World Parcel Service. The same initials were painted in gold on each side of the van. The bill of the cap rested just above his eyebrows, which were the same coal-black color as his hair. Aldo bent the bill of the cap, giving it a smooth curve. The cap gave him the finished look he was searching for. He smiled at himself and picked up the two packages that rested on the seat next to him. One was small, only five-by-eight inches; the other was roughly the size of a briefcase.

Before exiting the car, Aldo scanned the front of the Barringston building. The media people who teemed there earlier were now gone, each no doubt trying to make a deadline or wanting to be the first to report the story about the head of a local charity being arrested by the FBI. Also gone were the beleaguered security guards who valiantly and successfully had kept the reporters at a distance. There was no doubt that at least one guard would remain in the lobby, maybe several. That didn't matter to Aldo; he had the uniform and the identification to pass through those doors. He also knew that WPS made deliveries to this building several times a day. Today would be no different.

With packages in hand, Aldo stepped from the van and briskly jogged up the six wide concrete steps, through the large glass doors, and into the ornate lobby. As he had expected, he was greeted by a middle-aged man in a gray security uniform seated behind a semicircular counter.

"Hi," Aldo said, flashing a smile.

"Hi," the guard answered warily. "Where's Richard?"

"Got sick," Aldo answered easily. "Flu or something. They called me in to finish his shift. Normally, I work in north county." He shook his head in mock disgust. "This was supposed to be my day off."

"That flu can be bad," the guard said. "Had a touch of it myself just last week."

"It looks like you survived it all right."

"Knocked me off my feet for a few days,

but I'm doing OK."

"Glad to hear it," Aldo said. "Do I need to sign in or something?"

"Nah," the guard grunted. "Which floor you headed to?"

"Um," Aldo turned the package and pretended to read the label. "I need to find a Kristen LaCroix in public relations. What floor is that on?"

"She's with Barringston Relief," the guard answered after consulting the computer that sat on a desk behind the counter. "You want the fifty-second floor, east wing. It's not too hard to find."

Aldo started for the bank of elevators that were situated in a wall behind the guard.

"You gotta take one of the ones on the right," the man said. "Those are the public elevators. Just punch fifty-two, and the girl in the lobby there will help you."

"Thanks," Aldo said, beaming another smile. "You've been a big help."

"I can sign for those," the woman behind the receptionist desk said firmly. She was short with straight black hair and narrow eyes.

"Normally that would be great," Aldo said sweetly, "but I'm afraid I have to deliver these personally."

"Personally?" The woman raised her eyebrows. "My signature has always been good enough in the past."

"It has nothing to do with you," he replied with a little laugh. "It's something new at WPS. We now offer direct-to-person delivery on certain items. Some people send confidential stuff with us, and they get annoyed if the wrong person signs. We hope this new service will make them happy."

"It's a nice idea, but you're going to have problems with it. Many office buildings are like ours with certain secured areas. If that package had to go over to communications or the research lab, then you'd never be able to deliver it. Areas like that are restricted."

"That's a good point," Aldo conceded. "Is public relations one of those areas?"

"No. I guess you lucked out." The woman pointed down a hall. "The last office on the right is a corner office. That's where you'll find Kristen LaCroix."

"Thanks," Aldo said and started down the hall.

A dozen steps later he was standing at the open door of Kristen's office. He watched her in silence for a moment. She was lost in thought, her head down as she read the pages on her desk. Her hair was a stunning red, and she wore it to her shoulders. Aldo knocked on the jamb. Immediately Kristen looked up. Her deep blue eyes were captivating despite the weariness they reflected.

"Yes?" Kristen asked.

"Kristen LaCroix?" Aldo asked. "I have a delivery for you." He watched as she blinked a few times, signaling her confusion at seeing a deliveryman at her door. "The sender wanted to be sure it went right to you."

"What is it?" Kristen asked.

"I'm just the deliveryman," Aldo said with a grin.

"I guess you wouldn't know, would you?" Kristen said. "Is that other package for me?"

"No, ma'am," he replied as he tucked the other parcel under his arm and held out a clipboard with paper on it that contained several signatures. "If you would just sign here."

Kristen took the clipboard, looked at it for a moment, shrugged, and signed her name. "There you go," she said, handing the clipboard back and taking the small package from Aldo's outstretched hand.

"Just one more thing," he said sheepishly. "Is there a rest room on this floor?"

"Yes," Kristen replied. "Just go back down the hall. It will be on the right, near the elevators."

"Thanks," he said and quickly left the office with the other package still under his arm. A short time later, Aldo Goldoni exited the rest room empty-handed.

Kristen leaned forward over her desk, resting her elbows on the smooth wood surface, and rubbed the back of her neck with her hands. The muscles in her neck and back were hard and tight from tension. She took in a long, measured breath, held it, and slowly released it in a whisper of exhalation. She tried to make sense of everything.

David's arrest had changed her orderly, systematic world into immediate chaos. Her desk was cluttered with messages and requests from news media, department heads, and others who wanted to know more. The problem was that she knew nothing more than some stranger in a coffee shop down the street.

It was Timmy who had alerted her to David's arrest. He had burst into her office in tears, his eyes and face red from fear and frustration. "They're taking him away!" he had shouted.

"Who?"

"The men. The policemen."

"What?"

"They're taking him away," Timmy had cried again.

By the time Kristen had made her way to David's office, he was gone. Only Ava remained, standing in shocked stillness at what she had witnessed. In telling the story to Kristen, Ava broke into tears. Timmy joined in the weeping. Only Kristen remained dry-eyed, not for lack of concern, but because her mind was racing to understand all that had happened and to discern what needed to be done. Still, the news made her feel weak, and her stomach hurt as if she had been seized by some vicious flu.

Now she was dealing with the early fallout. As the public relations director, it was her job to field all calls from the press. There had been scores of them. She gave them each the same answer: "We at Barringston Relief have no comment at this time."

It was a bad situation made all the worse by the familial nature of Barringston Relief. Unlike the corporate world that was divided into owners, managers, and workers, Barringston Relief was more like a family. While there were too many people for anyone to know everyone, there was still a closeness knit from the nature of the work. Any Barringston employee arrested would adversely affect all the others. In David's case, that truth was even more potent, especially for Kristen.

She had fallen in love with David nearly two years ago when they had traveled to Africa to tour the famine areas. It had been a slow and halting relationship. David was fresh from his unwanted, unsolicited divorce. David had been crushed. By his own admission he had lost all motivation and direction, causing him to resign the church where he had been pastor for fifteen years. Even after coming to Barringston Relief as a speechwriter for A.J., he had been slow in coming out of his shell.

It was in Ethiopia that he had found his catharsis. Daily faced with death and seeing the heroic struggle of the famine stricken and the unrelenting drive of the relief workers, David had regained perspective. He had found himself and his God again. He was a changed person.

Kristen had fallen in love with that new man.

The relationship had moved forward slowly, which was fine with Kristen. She was in no hurry to force it to a new level. She knew that such things did best when they were left to grow like a flower — provide the water and food it needs, and the flower will blossom. So would their relationship.

It was their emotional connection that made all this so hard. Not only was David the new head of Barringston Relief, but he was the one she loved. Detachment was impossible. She wanted to scream at the media, letting them know that this was all a huge mistake, a monumental blunder. David could not be found culpable for any crime. Yet she had to remain professional in tone and in action. So she responded to the questions evenly, professionally, and without visible emotion. Inside, however, her heart twisted and burned like lava in the crater of a volcano.

Leaning back in her chair, Kristen rubbed her weary eyes. She had wanted to run to David's side, to hop in her car, and to race to the jail, but she knew it would be futile. They would never let her see him. Not now, not yet. To confirm this she had called the firm's legal department. They told her what she already knew. There was nothing for her to do but wait and carry out her duties.

Opening her eyes, she looked at her cluttered desk. Normally she was tidy to a fault. David had jokingly accused her of being able to organize an anthill. Spread across the top of her desk were message slips, a pad of paper, and several files. There was also the package the delivery man had brought.

He had struck her as odd, although she couldn't put her finger on it. He was pleasant enough and reasonably attractive, but not very tall. In fact, she doubted that he was much taller than she. Normally, the delivery men just left the packages in the lobby. It was unusual for one to come right to her office.

What was that package anyway?

She picked up the parcel and studied it. It had no return address, just her name and the Barringston Tower address. The package itself was light and had a familiar feel to it, an everyday weight and shape. Peeling back the brown paper, she discovered a videotape. There was no label. The cassette was plain, black plastic, just like hundreds she had seen before.

Curious, she stood and walked to the

TV/VCR monitor across from her desk and inserted the tape. After turning on the TV, she activated the play button. The tape began to run.

Walking back to her chair, Kristen watched as the snow on the screen became a cobalt blue and was replaced by an image of three men seated around a table. Using the remote she had brought back to the desk with her, she turned up the volume. There was no sound. The tape had no audio. Still, the drama was clear enough. She watched with sickening fascination as the man she loved plotted with the other two men and then allowed himself to be kissed passionately by a beautiful woman.

Mesmerized by the scene that played out before her, Kristen failed at first to notice the tears streaming from her eyes.

The setting sun glistened off the distant ocean draping pearls of reflection along its undulating surface. The sky was changing from blue to gray as the marine layer of clouds slowly rolled in. Elaine Aberdene turned from the window of the twenty-second floor of the Aberdene Pharmaceuticals building, leaving behind the beautiful seascape of La Jolla. She faced the two men with her in the plush office. A television played silently from its perch in a black enamel entertainment center. A news anchorman was speaking, but no words were heard. The sound had been muted after the lead story had aired. At the moment she cared about nothing else.

"So it's all working?" she asked. She carried a clear, round glass sphere the size of a baseball in her hand. The paperweight had been a gift of a one-time suitor. Embedded in the glass was a single, delicate mosquito.

"Perfectly," Jack LaBohm said, rubbing his chin. "Just as planned."

"The media seem to have taken to it," Aberdene said. "At least they believe it."

"The media will believe anything," Archer Matthews croaked with disgust.

"And you're convinced that they'll discover nothing?" Aberdene asked firmly, ignoring for the moment Archer's impertinence.

"There's nothing *to* find," Archer boasted. "There are no tracks to follow, no clues to pick up. I delivered perfection, just as you ordered."

"And am I not making it worthwhile for you?" Aberdene demanded.

Archer nodded solemnly. "Yeah, you are."

Turning to Jack she pressed for more information. "What about that little Italian man . . ."

"Aldo Goldoni," Jack offered.

"Goldoni," Aberdene said softly as if she were rolling the name around on her tongue. "He's in place? He's working out?"

"He comes highly recommended," Jack said with a broad grin. "Very professional."

"I don't think I want to know who or what recommended him, do I, Jack?" Aberdene asked.

"Probably not."

"Can I go now?" Archer asked with a whine, "I've been working twenty hours a day for weeks. I'm beat."

"In a few minutes," Aberdene said, brushing aside a wisp of mahogany hair from her forehead. "How are you coming on the other project?"

"You don't need it," Archer answered. "This one's good enough. It's fool-proof."

Aberdene narrowed her eyes and stared at the anemic-looking man who sat on her leather couch. "I didn't ask for your opinion," she said strongly. "I want to know the progress of the other project."

Archer crossed his arms and sat in silence.

"Maybe you should ask the question, Jack."

Jack smiled and took two steps toward the seated man.

"OK, OK." Archer threw his arms in the air. "It's going great. I'm right on schedule. Two, three days tops, and then I'll be done."

"You told me you'd be done tonight," Jack shot back.

"You think this is easy? You think anyone can do this? If you want fast, you'll get mistakes. You choose."

"Two days," Aberdene commanded. "That's all you get. I don't want anything to mess this up. There's too much at stake here."

"If anything gets messed up, it won't be from me," Archer proclaimed. "Just give me time to do my job and get a little sleep, and you'll have more than you wanted."

"Just remember the schedule," Aberdene said. "You need me. Remember that too. You need me."

"And you need me," Archer countered. "That's the deal, isn't it? I do what you want, and you give me what I need. It's a business deal. Just stop treating me like a slave. I'm a professional. I'm the best there is at what I do."

"That's why you're here, little man," Jack chimed in.

"And why are you here — *big* man?"

Jack started toward Archer again but was cut off by Aberdene.

"That's enough, boys. I'm not impressed with all this macho stuff." Walking over to her gray-and-white desk, Aberdene set the glass paperweight down. "You can go now, Archer. Get a good night's sleep, but be on the job early tomorrow. Got it?"

"Yeah, yeah," he said, standing to his feet and walking to the office door. "I got it all right." He closed the door behind him.

"Are you sure he's trustworthy?" Jack asked, his eyes still fixed on the door.

"He's safe. I have what he needs. I have his life in my hands, and he knows it. He'll do what I tell him to do or he will pay the consequences."

"He's awful full of himself, isn't he?"

"Creative people usually are, Jack. Now leave him alone."

Jack frowned. "So what now?"

"Watch and wait for the moment. We've evaluated all the possible scenarios. We're ready to respond to their next step."

"Plan the work and work the plan. Is that it?"

155

"That's it. Soon all that will be left of Barringston Relief will be a vague memory."

"Perhaps we should pop some champagne."

"Not until it's over — completely over."

"When will that be?"

"When I say it's over and not before." Aberdene returned to the desk, picked up the paperweight, raised it to her eyes, and studied the winged insect entombed in the glass. A grin, dark and amoral, spread across her face. "And it will be over soon."

David lay motionless on his back and stared at the white ceiling of his cell. The mattress upon which he lay was thin and secreted a vague odor of disinfectant. Small pellets of perspiration dotted his brow. The central air conditioning of the jailhouse weakly moved the tepid, cigarette-laced air around and carried with it the haunting moan of air forced passed the metal register. Unconsciously, he rubbed his index finger and thumb together, mildly aware of the oily film that remained in his pores from the fingerprinting ink and the soapy, premoistened towelette he had been given to clean his hands.

His mind raced; his emotions churned and bubbled like water set to boil. One moment he felt fierce anger at the injustice he was forced to endure; the next moment he wanted to cower in fear. The desire to strike out would exchange turns with the nearly overwhelming need to weep. Like a child caught on a runaway roller coaster, David's feelings were bouncing back and forth with soul-jarring jerks.

He sat up and looked around the cell. There were two beds, each a thin, heavily used mattress resting on a flat metal surface cantilevered from the wall. The floor was bare concrete. On one wall was a metal toilet and sink that some institutional designer had melded into a single, ugly, utilitarian unit. The only window in the room looked out over the receiving area of the jail. There was no view to the outside.

The muffled voices of guards and detainees echoed down the halls. Occasionally a uniformed officer peered in through the window and watched David. He was on suicide watch, not because he had given the impression that he was suicidal, but because his attorney, Calvin Overstreet, had arranged it. By calling in favors with his former FBI colleagues, he had been able to keep David from being confined with the other prisoners — some-

157

thing Calvin said could be unpleasant. By having him placed on suicide watch, David could have the equivalent of a private room. This was even more important since word of his arrest had been broadcast on television. Many of the detainees awaiting trial had access to the television room, and it was likely that they would have seen the report. No one could guess what their response might be.

David buried his face in his hands. None of this seemed real. Even as a minister he had never been inside a jail. Not even to visit someone. Now he was an inmate, at least for a short time.

Fear-propelled questions began to buzz through his mind. How would he explain this? What would he say to the people at Barringston Relief?

The images of two faces floated to the forefront of his mind: Timmy and Kristen. David could still see the frightened, confused expression on Timmy's face as the police had led David from his office. David loved Timmy and knew that that love was returned in like kind. Seeing the young man tortured by an event he couldn't understand stoked the fires of David's emotions. Timmy was now his charge. David should be there to take care of him, but he wasn't. He was locked in a small room and under the strict surveillance of his jail keepers.

Then there was Kristen. By now she had heard of the arrest and would be concerned. How was she dealing with all this? Judging by the number of media people who had been waiting out front when the FBI escorted David from the building, she would be overwhelmed with calls.

As he thought of Kristen, David's heart sank. He loved her dearly. She had been a rock of strength for him when he first came to Barringston Relief. She had spoken plainly, but never unkindly. They were kindred spirits, and David thanked God every day for bringing her into his life. He wanted to see her now more than ever. He wanted to talk to her and gaze into the deep blue of her eyes. His fingers hungered to stroke her thick red hair. He wondered if things would be different now.

Standing to his feet, David began to walk around the room, something he was prone to do when deep in thought. Back and forth across the tiny cell he paced, forcing his rampaging emotions to order and then pressing them to the back of his mind. Control was the key here, he told himself. Much of that had been taken away from

159

him, but he could still control his response to the situation. David knew that if he did not discipline his emotions, his emotions would manipulate him. So he paced, denying the emotion, encouraging the intellect.

Timmy would be all right. There were many people in Barringston Relief to look after him. Most likely, that job would be seized by Kristen. Since Timmy lived in the building in David's suite, he would be fine. Kristen was a sharp and purposed woman, not subject to overreaction. She too would be fine. The real question was what to do next. Confined as he was, there was little that he could do physically, but he could apply his intellect to the problem.

Comforting himself with Calvin's promise of a quick bail release, David undertook the difficult task of putting the arrest behind him and solving the problem at hand. The arrest, questioning, and booking had made him feel dirty, soiled. He didn't belong in this place. He was an innocent man. What he had to do was keep his wits about him and fight to reestablish his integrity.

The images from the video rushed to the forefront of his thoughts. He had never seen the other two men in that video, and he had certainly never been kissed by that woman. *You may be middle-aged,* he said to himself, *but you're not so old as to forget something like that.* One thing was certain: That event never happened. And if the event was unreal, then it must be fabricated. But why? By whom? Such a fabrication was an elaborate affair and must have been difficult to arrange. Why go through so much trouble? Who hated David that much?

And there were other matters with which to deal. He knew he was innocent, but how could he prove it? The tape was a convincing piece of evidence. If roles were reversed and he were an observer instead of the accused, he would have trouble disbelieving his own eyes.

This brought Calvin Overstreet to mind. David had been impressed with the attorney and was glad that Mr. Barringston had retained him on David's behalf. Calvin had professed his belief in David's innocence, but David wondered if that wasn't little more than a lawyer's attempt to comfort his client. Still, the man had seemed sincere, and he certainly seemed to know his way around the situation.

During their meeting in the interview room, Calvin had coached David about many things. "Remember," he had said, "don't talk to anyone about this. If the FBI or anyone else wants to question you, insist — demand, if you have to — that I be present. That is your right. Don't talk to anyone in the jail, not the guards, other prisoners, or the janitor. Say nothing to them. Don't even talk out loud to yourself. Anything heard can be used against you. If you are put in a cell with another prisoner, don't talk about your arrest or anything else. The prisoner could be an undercover agent put there to hear anything that may help their case."

"Would they really do that?" David had asked in shock.

"It's been known to happen," Calvin answered. "I also want you to begin a mental rehearsal. Imagine any question that may come your way and formulate an answer. I want you mentally prepared for the next interview. Also know this: When they question you, they will attempt to fool you into making statements that they can use."

"What do you mean?"

"For example, they won't ask you if you've ever met Arturo Lozano. Instead, they'll say something like this, 'Is this the first time you've met with Arturo Lozano, or have there been other times?' Now if

162

you answer with a simple no, then it implies that you've met with him before. So be sure to take as much time to answer a question as needed. Say, 'I have never met with Arturo Lozano.' You can and must give more than yes or no answers, unless I tell you otherwise.

"Also," Calvin had continued, "they will mix difficult questions with easy ones. This confuses many people. They'll say something like, 'How long have you been transferring money out of the country, Dr. O'Neal?' You, of course, deny doing any such thing. Then they'll ask a no-brainer, 'You actually live in the Barringston Tower?' You answer yes, and then they hit you with an incriminating question for which they also want a yes answer, such as, 'Did you have help transferring the money?' Do you see what I mean? It's an attempt to play with your head. You must keep your wits about you at all times. You must work from here," Calvin said tapping his forehead, "and not from here." He tapped his chest. "Brains and not emotion will get us out of all this."

"And faith," David had added.

Calvin had studied David for a moment and then nodded. "You'll need a lot of that, Dr. O'Neal."

David had taken Calvin's instructions seriously. He had spoken to no one and had felt a strong sense of relief when he was put in the cell. At least he had time to think without the interruption of other prisoners. David trusted Calvin. He had to. He was well over his head in trouble.

7

Kristen wanted to go to bed. The day had worn on with a horrible, grinding slowness. now it was over, at least for a little while. Since arriving for work at eight, she had put in twelve straight hours. Her eyes burned, her back hurt, and her heart ached. The latter she attributed to the video of David. It was as she was gathering her things to leave that she thought of Timmy. She had not seen him since David's arrest. Normally he busied himself with light janitorial work in the building, but he had not been by to collect the trash as he usually did.

With David gone, Timmy would be alone. Kristen picked up the phone and punched in the number that would ring David's top-floor suite. There had been no answer; just the electronic message manager. Next she placed a call to maintenance and asked the building engineer if he had seen Timmy.

"Nope," he answered. "I haven't seen him

all day. Is he OK? He never misses work."

"I'm sure he is, but I'll check on him." Kristen hung up the phone.

A feeling of concern encircled her. Leaving her office, she made her way to the cafeteria. Timmy had a notorious appetite for snacks, especially at night. Perhaps he was feeding one of his many cravings for sweets.

The cafeteria was nearly deserted. A few employees were scattered about the room, seated at tables and eating meals. Kristen spotted Timmy sitting alone at a table in the middle of the large room. As she approached him, she saw that he was staring down at what must have been at one time a piece of pumpkin pie. Timmy was smashing the dark orange-brown pie on his plate. The small dish was covered center to rim with mashed pie.

"Hi, Timmy," Kristen said.

"Hi," he replied without looking up.

Kristen took a seat. "Doesn't the pie taste good?"

Timmy just shrugged and continued to flatten the pulpy mass.

Reaching across the table, Kristen laid her hand on Timmy's wrist. "Put the fork down, Timmy."

"Why?"

"Because I want to talk to you. OK?"

Timmy dropped the fork and placed his hands in his lap. He didn't look up at Kristen.

"Are you all right, Timmy?" she asked.

He shrugged. "Yeah, I guess so. I don't know."

"You're worried about David, aren't you?"

Again he shrugged. "He said it would be all right, but I've been waiting for him and he's not back, and it's dark and I don't know where he is. I've been waiting and waiting and waiting." Tears dripped from his red eyes.

Kristen was heartbroken watching the boy-man in tears. His anxiety was palpable. "Sometimes things happen in life that are hard, Timmy, and we must learn to be strong."

"But he didn't do nothin'," Timmy protested. "David wouldn't do nothin' wrong."

The images of the video she had seen crashed forward in her mind. Like Timmy, she had always believed that David was as good a person as anyone could be. But there was the tape . . .

"It's like those wave people," Timmy said, wiping at his eyes again.

"Wave people?"

"Yeah, David showed me the movie of the big wave over in the Indians."

"Indians?" Kristen was baffled, then it hit her. "The tsunami in India? David showed you that news report?"

"Yeah, India. The big wave. Killed all them people. David said they weren't bad people, but the wave killed 'em anyway."

"And you think something bad is going to happen to David?"

"It could! It could!" Timmy was weeping loudly. "They're going to take David away from me, just like that bad man took A.J."

Timmy had never recovered from the horrible sight of his friend and guardian A. J. Barringston being shot by the Somali warlord Mahli. The trauma no longer affected Timmy's daily life, but it could still rear up in times of stress or anxiety. For Timmy there was no greater fear than seeing someone he loved taken away. He had lost his parents and been abandoned on the streets of San Diego. He had seen his best friend killed, and now he had witnessed David's arrest.

"You come home with me tonight, Timmy. That way we can keep each other company."

"But what if David comes home? I'll be gone."

"He'll know to call over to my house."

"What's going to happen to David?" Timmy asked a little more calmly. "Bad things like the wave people?"

"No, Timmy," Kristen said with a gentle smile. "Nothing like that. We'll have to wait and see. A lot of smart people are helping him."

"Real smart people? Smart people like you?"

"Very smart people," Kristen said. "Come on. Let's go home. We'll come back in the morning. OK?"

Timmy paused in thought as if weighing the options. "OK," he finally said. "I ain't been to your house before."

"It's not fancy, but it's comfortable."

"Do you have cable TV?"

"Yes, Timmy," Kristen said with a grin. "I have cable TV and a VCR. Maybe we can watch a movie."

"OK." Timmy paused in thought again. He asked, "Is David really going to be OK?"

"Yes, Timmy, he's going to be fine." Kristen's words carried more conviction than she felt.

Osborn Scott sipped at his cold coffee, studied the latest satellite photo of Hurricane Claudia, and shook his head. Things were moving from bad to worse. The storm had picked up in intensity and speed. He had been holding out for a miracle, a sudden drop of energy, but no such miracle was forthcoming. Claudia would impact Cuba tomorrow and would do so as a category five. The damage would be horrendous, and no power on earth could stop it.

Like an ancient prophet, Osborn could see the destruction in his mind as clearly as if it were on television. Small houses and huts would be demolished by two-hundred-mile-per-hour winds; the faces of buildings would be stripped away. A storm surge better than twenty feet high would lay waste to anything in its way, as would wind-driven waves thirty feet high. And there was no place where the people of Cuba could run except to shelters. Most would survive; many would not.

His mind raced back to 1997 when Hurricane Pauline, a Pacific storm, ravaged Acapulco and surrounding regions, leaving over four hundred dead and thousands homeless. By all standards Pauline had been a moderate hurricane; Claudia would be stronger by tenfold.

Archibald Barringston stood behind

his expensive, high-backed chair and drummed his ancient fingers on the black leather. His mouth was drawn tight, and he cast an angry, unwavering gaze through gray eyes at the man who sat opposite his desk. Behind him, the darkness of night oozed in through the large window that overlooked the bay.

Nearly eighty-nine years old, Barringston had seen it all. He stood tall and straight and exuded a power that belied his advanced years. All his friends were either retired or dead. Barringston, however, still ran a multibillion-dollar construction company. No one had the courage to suggest he step down. He had often said the only thing that would take him away from his teak desk was a hearse.

Age had etched deep creases in his forehead and cheeks, added dark spots to his skin, and thinned his blood, but it had left his mind untouched. A battle of wits with Archibald Barringston was a battle soon to be lost, as many had discovered.

"Surely you see my point," Bob Connick said. He was a heavily jowled man, with pale eyes and a nose a half size too large for his face. His cheeks, normally a healthy pink, were drained of color, betraying the anxiety he felt.

"I understand, all right," Barringston said firmly. "It's your motive I question."

"I assure you that my only motive is doing what's best for Barringston Relief."

"Cutting David off at the knees will be good for Barringston Relief?"

"This whole situation is bad, Mr. Barringston. The Justice Department has already seized our assets. They even took some of our computers. We can't move money, and if we can't move money, we can't move food to stricken areas. We have workers in scores of countries that are dependent on us for their personal and relief-oriented supplies."

"How does relieving David of his duties help that?" Barringston asked strongly.

"By assigning the control of monetary decisions to someone else, we may be able to get our assets free sooner."

"And just who should receive that responsibility? You?"

"I *am* the chief financial officer, Mr. Barringston. There's nothing untoward about my assuming those extra responsibilities. I'm the one most familiar with the overall operation and the day-to-day money transfers."

Barringston stepped from behind the chair, turned it, and sat down. He said nothing. He sat in cold silence and studied Connick, as if his ancient eyes could pierce his persona and read the truth in every line of the man's life.

Connick cleared his throat. "I will be sending a memo to the other board members informing them of the emergency meeting tomorrow. Because you are the senior member of the board of directors and because of your involvement in your son's start-up of Barringston Relief, I thought I should inform you personally."

"A nice gesture, Connick," Barringston said. "It's good to see that you have my interest at heart."

"I do, and that of Barringston Relief."

Barringston didn't acknowledge the comment; he was too angry. There had been a time in his life when he would have erupted at such arrogance and insincerity. Now, tempered by age and maturity, he responded differently. He let the force of his person and reputation do the work for him. Many had been cowered by his quiet resolve.

"Mr. Connick, I'm just shy of my eighty-ninth birthday. That makes me an old man. Because of my age, some dismiss me as a crank or a mentally enfeebled old codger."

"I would never think such a thing."

"It would be a mistake if you did," Barringston snapped. "As an old man, I've reached the point where I care very little of what people think of me. There's a freedom in that, Connick. I no longer feel the need to be polite or to cater to the sensitivities of others. I'm a simple man with simple tastes and a huge hunger for success. That's why I am where I am."

"You have achieved a great many things, Mr. Barringston. I'm proud to know you."

"Well, let's see if I can change that," Barringston said pointedly. "I have built Barringston Industries on three principles: hard work, honored promises, and loyalty. I taught those things to my son, A.J., and he put them to work in Barringston Relief. I did more than provide the initial start-up capital for the company you work for, and I do more than provide rent-free offices in this building. I concern myself with all that goes on. That's why I sit on the board of directors, Mr. Connick.

"After my son was killed," Barringston continued, "I led the board in its decision to appoint David O'Neal as my son's successor. I did so, not because he was the most qualified or had the most experience, but because my son saw something great in him. A.J. was right. David O'Neal has led Barringston Relief to new heights. He may eclipse all that my son achieved."

"There is no doubt that David has done some wonderful things, but —"

"Don't interrupt," Barringston said sharply. "I'm not finished."

"Sorry."

"I am an astute judge of character, Mr. Connick, and I can tell you that David is innocent of these bogus, trumped-up charges."

"Sir, I don't mean to be rude, but I have seen the video the police have. In fact, a copy was delivered to all the department heads. I'm afraid it's quite convincing."

"I got a copy too, Connick, and I'm telling you it doesn't mean a thing."

"But —"

"Are you listening to me?"

"Yes, but —"

"I can't explain the video yet, but I know David."

Connick shook his head. "I'm sorry, but I can't agree. The evidence is over-whelming. Our assets are frozen, and our work will begin suffering in the next day or two. A hurricane is bearing down on Cuba and will strike within hours, and a tsunami has struck the coastal regions of the Bay of

Bengal. We have personnel missing on that one. Barringston doesn't need to have its leader in jail on felony charges. Too much is at stake here."

"I know what's at stake, Connick," Barringston snapped loudly. "I know it very well. But we do not shoot our wounded. Over the last sixteen months, David has worked himself to exhaustion to save as many lives worldwide as possible. Does that sound like the actions of an embezzler and an alien smuggler?"

"I don't know what could motivate David to undertake such crimes —"

"I do," Barringston interjected. "Nothing. Certainly not money."

"But the video —"

"The video is a lie."

"You can't be sure of that."

"I can be sure of one thing, Connick. If the situation were reversed, David wouldn't be so quick to convict you."

Connick sat dumbfounded.

"I'll tell you something else. I will fight you on this every step of the way. You will not find a friend in me on this issue. And I am not a man to be trifled with."

"With all due respect, Mr. Barringston, we must set our emotions aside for the greater good of Barringston Relief. Too many lives depend on us."

Archibald Barringston rose to his feet and leaned over the broad desk. He pointed a crooked finger at Connick. "You send out your memos, Connick. You send them out to every person on the board. You send me one too — and attach your resignation to it."

What little color remained in Connick's face drained. "I'm . . . I'm . . . sorry Mr. Barringston, but I don't work for you. I work for Barringston Relief, not Barringston Industries. You're not in a position to fire me."

"Not at this moment, but you might be surprised at what can happen in a board meeting. Now get out. I've had all of you I can stomach tonight."

Slowly, Connick rose to his feet and stared at Barringston. His gaze was quickly broken by the unflinching, penetrating gaze of the old man. A second later, Connick left.

As the office door closed behind Connick, Barringston turned and gazed out the window into the dark San Diego night and wished that he truly felt the conviction of his own words.

This was the worst part of it, Aldo Goldoni

thought as he slowly lowered himself to the floor, his nose a mere inch from the tightly woven carpet of his hotel room. With a powerful thrust of his arms, he pressed himself into full push-up position. He paused for ten seconds, then lowered himself, inch by inch until his nose once again hovered just above the floor. He had no idea how many push-ups he had done, nor did he care. *Waiting. I hate the waiting.*

Everything was in place. The plan was fully formulated and memorized. The targets were identified. All he needed was the go-ahead, the word that would free him from the mundane task of killing time.

Another push-up. His muscles burned with the effort; ripples of pain raced through his nerves. He was enjoying every second of it. For him the pain was a sign of success and his endurance of it a testimony to his strength of mind and emotional resolve. It had always been that way. Even as a child, when his father, nearly insane from the massive quantities of drugs he put into himself, would punish Aldo with beatings or burn him with cigarettes, Aldo would endure the pain stoically. It was proof of his power, his determination, his nearly omnipotent will.

Aldo had learned to endure everything.

As a child he learned to tolerate the hatred of others, to withstand the cruelty of children, to hold up under frequent beatings by neighborhood gangs, to be nonchalant about his fractured family — a drug-addicted father and a streetwalking mother. No pain was greater than what he endured as a child, and he had survived that. There was no pain with which he could not deal. Loneliness, fear, and anxiety meant nothing to him. He had trained himself to be the perfect machine: functional, emotionless, dependable.

But he still hated waiting.

He had carried out each duty to which he had been assigned. The tapes were delivered, the Barringston Tower security system analyzed, the meager security guard force and the targets monitored and their habits logged. Nothing was missing, nothing lacking, nothing to do but wait for the word.

Aldo Goldoni did another push-up. He was not a big man, standing just over five foot seven and weighing precisely one hundred fifty-two pounds, yet he was fit; his body was a mass of tightly strung, well-exercised muscles. He made it his goal to be thin. Bulky muscles would make him stand out, and in his line of work he needed to blend in, just as he did when dressed as the WPS delivery man. No one questioned him, and most took no notice of him. That's the way it was supposed to be.

He lowered himself to the floor again, but this time he remained there, halfway through the exercise. His back was straight, his arms bent at his side, his bare chest lightly touching the carpet. He remained motionless, suspending his weight by his hands and feet. Seconds turned into minutes. Each of those seconds brought more tension in his muscles, more pain to his body. It was exactly what he wanted. The pain was proof of his existence; his endurance was proof of his mastery.

He was invincible. No one, no thing, could ever stop Aldo Goldoni. He had seen to that.

Aldo forced his mind away from the intense protestations of his body and made it focus on the job he had been assigned. He had done this work before. Terrorism, crime, and violence were his stock in trade, and it paid him well. The poverty of his youth was gone. Now he drove whatever car he wished and stayed in the best hotels. The room he was in now cost three hundred dollars a night, and he considered it middle grade. That was just one of the perks of his work. He was always in demand, and he always delivered. He would do no less on this assignment. The fact that people were harmed and often died because of him mattered not at all. Such was the nature of his work.

David O'Neal and Kristen LaCroix, Aldo knew, would soon learn that.

"Mind if I sit here?" Long, slender, tan legs worked their way down the steps, making soft splashing sounds as they pushed aside the pool water.

Calvin Overstreet looked up at the woman from his seated position on the pool steps. She was tall, with short black hair, and vivid blue eyes. Those who saw the two at parties and social functions often classified her as the perfect trophy wife. What they could not know was that Calvin deeply loved the woman he had married twenty-five years ago.

"Actually," Calvin said with a smile, "I'm waiting for a beautiful brunette to join me."

"I am a beautiful brunette."

"Well, this one happens to be my wife."

"I am your wife," she said playfully.

"In that case, you are more than welcome to share my seat. It happens to have
a beautiful view of the water."

Jenni laughed. "It happens to be *in* the
water."

"That explains why my feet feel so
damp," Calvin joked.

Jenni sat on the step next to her husband. "What's bothering you?"

"What do you mean?"

"You've been sitting on this step in the
shallow end of the pool for the better part
of forty-five minutes. You're starting to
look like a prune."

"It's not the water, it's my advancing
years."

"You're not that old," Jenni said.
"What's on your mind?"

A warm breeze blew along the surface of
the pool, causing little ripples. Calvin
gazed down into the water. "I've taken on
the David O'Neal case."

"The man from Barringston Relief? I
saw the news report. Is it going to be
tough?"

Calvin nodded. "Yes. Maybe impossible.
Archibald Barringston sent a copy of the
tape to me by courier. I've watched it a
dozen times. The videotape is extremely
incriminating, and such evidence has done

well in court. The DA is going to have fun with this one."

"Why did you take the case?"

"Old man Barringston asked me to, and O'Neal was a friend of A.J.'s. I felt an obligation. Besides, something isn't right."

"Not right?"

Calvin turned and faced his wife. The back porch light combined with the pool lights to reflect off her tanned face. She was an insightful woman and keenly intelligent. She had been a wonderful mother to their two children, who were now grown and gone. "I can't put my finger on it, but all my legal alarms are going off. Everything is just too perfect."

"You think he's innocent?"

"I told him I did, and at the time I meant it. Now I'm having second thoughts."

"Don't," Jenni said.

"Don't what?"

"Don't have second thoughts, Cal. You have the best instincts possible. Your first impressions are almost always right."

"Almost, but not always."

"Don't start that again," Jenni said firmly. "No one's perfect. You had every reason to believe that woman was guilty. Besides, all you did was arrest her; the courts put her in jail."

"On information I provided and on testimony I gave."

"You're not in the FBI anymore. You have a successful and respected legal practice. I think you ought to stop beating us up over a mistake you made years ago."

"Us?"

"Sure," Jenni said. "Our love has intertwined our souls. When you hurt, I hurt."

"I'm just tired, Jenni, that's all." He cupped some water in his hand and splashed it on his face. "And maybe a little afraid."

"Afraid?"

Calvin nodded. "I'm afraid that someday I may do just the opposite of my last mistake and help a guilty person go free."

"You think this O'Neal man is guilty?"

Calvin shook his head. "Not in my heart, but my head says to look at the evidence. I'm giving myself conflicting advice. At times I don't know which to listen to."

"When you proposed marriage to me, were you listening to your head or to your heart?"

Calvin chortled. "My heart, dear. I was listening to my heart all the way."

"Well, that turned out pretty good, didn't it?"

"More than pretty good," he said leaning

over and kissing her gently on the lips. "It was the best decision of my life."

"Then learn to trust your heart more," Jenni said, stroking Calvin's damp hair. "By the way, how did Mr. Barringston get a copy of the tape?"

"Someone had it delivered."

"Convenient."

Calvin nodded, now lost in thought again. "Yeah, too convenient."

"Do you want to take a few laps with me?" Jenni asked as she pushed away from the steps.

"Normally, I would jump at the opportunity," Calvin answered, "but I've got a bail hearing tomorrow. I want to make sure I've got all my ducks in a row. One night in jail is enough for someone like David O'Neal."

"Suit yourself," she said and then began to swim the length of the pool with long purposeful strokes. Calvin watched as the woman he loved moved fluidly through the water.

"Well," he said to himself, "maybe a couple of laps wouldn't hurt."

8

The wind no longer moaned — it screamed and squealed like a banshee. The walls of the small Cuban house shook with each new blast, as did the heart of Angelina.

Angelina was perched on her father's lap as he sat with the others waiting for the storm to pass. The electricity for the lights was already gone, and the storm, coupled with the plywood-covered windows, left the house dark and tomblike. The only light came from a single storm lantern in the middle of the room. It cast large and ominous shadows on the walls behind them. Ghosts. The ghosts Angelina was sure they would all become.

"I'm frightened, Papa," Angelina said for the fourth time.

"Me too," her father answered. "It's all right to be frightened as long as we remain calm."

Angelina nodded in silence. Some of the other children wept.

"This is a bad one," Maria said as she drew her youngest to her. "Maybe the worst."

No one answered; their silence was agreement enough. Heavy tropical storms and hurricanes were common in Cuba, but no one took them lightly.

The wind hammered the house, driving the drops of rain with such force that it sounded as if a thousand children were outside throwing handfuls of pebbles at the walls.

"Look, Papa," Angelina said, pointing to the front wall. Rivulets of water streamed down from the ceiling. "The house is leaking."

"The wind is doing that," her father answered. "It's pushing the water under the eaves and through the wall."

"I don't like it," she protested. Her father kissed the top of her head and held her even more tightly. Angelina knew that he didn't like it either.

Seconds that would normally pass unnoticed now oozed by with maddening slowness, and with each tick of the clock the wind screamed louder, the walls shook more, and the fear grew thicker.

There was a new sound, a pounding, like shutters slamming against the house. Except the house had no shutters. Banging, slapping. Angelina drew herself into a ball on her father's lap. "What's that?" she asked.

"It's the plywood," her father said. "The wind is pulling it away from the window."

"But you nailed it," Angelina protested. "I saw you."

"It wasn't enough. Maybe we had better —"

The plywood was gone. A gust of invisible power peeled it from the window. Angelina watched as it sailed away. A second later the glass in the window reverberated to the beat of the storm, rattling, shaking, bowing with the pressure. Her father had started to stand when the glass gave way in an explosion of shards that filled the room. Angelina felt herself being lifted from her father's lap and slammed to the sofa as he attempted to cover her with his own body. Maria and the children screamed.

Half a moment later her father was on his feet. "Everyone into the bathroom. Right now!" Before Angelina could speak, her father snatched her up from the couch and carried her in one arm. He then seized one of her cousins. Her uncle did the same with two of the smaller children. Rain was pelting them as they raced across the room and down the hall toward the only bathroom in the house. "Inside, everyone," he said as he set Angelina down.

"But, Papa, there's not room for everyone," Angelina said, stunned by the violence of the last few seconds.

"Get in," her father commanded. "Put the youngest children in the bathtub. The rest of you sit on the floor." Everyone complied. As soon as they were in, Angelina watched as her father and uncle stepped away from the door and disappeared into the house.

"Papa. Papa! Come back."

No answer.

"Papa!" Angelina started to rise, but Maria put a hand on her shoulder. Angelina stared at the open bathroom door, wishing with all her might that her father would reappear. "Pa-paaaa." Her scream was muted by the howling demonwind.

Glass breaking. Another window had been exposed and had exploded. Still, no Papa. "Papa, come back. I need you."

Nothing.

Tears raced down Angelina's face and mingled with the water from the storm. Her heart ached. Instinctively she knew that her father was gone, like her mother. She knew that she was alone — orphaned.

She was wrong. A shadowy figure appeared in the door, struggling with a large rectangular object. It was her father. "Put this mattress over the bathtub," he shouted against the invasive noise of the storm. "Cover the children." As soon as the mattress was moved into place with the help of Maria and two of the older children, he disappeared again, but this time for just a moment. They had another mattress. Angelina realized that he must have dragged them from the children's bedroom.

Struggling, they lifted the mattress up and passed it into the room. "Cover yourselves with this," he ordered, then stepped into the crowded bathroom and shut the door. Once seated upon the floor, he held up one end of the mattress. The other end was wedged on the tops of the sink and toilet. Children cried, and the wind screamed ferociously like some ancient beast.

It was dark in the room and the air was becoming stale, but Angelina didn't mind. Her father was seated next to her, and that was all that mattered.

The wind continued its attack, as if it had will and reason and had selected this house to be the object of all its fury. The walls vibrated like the skin on a bass drum. There were snapping and popping sounds.

"What's that, Papa?" Angelina asked in the darkness.

"The shingles on the roof are being torn away. We can expect to get wet soon."

"Get wet again," Angelina corrected.

"Yes, wet again. But we should be all right."

Minute after minute passed, and the storm grew worse. The sound of the wind was maddening. It was as if the storm sought voice to speak of the evil it intended to do and of the lives it hungered to take. Pounding, thumping, slamming, pushing, the storm continued on. Angelina wanted to rest, to close her weary eyes and sleep, but she could not. Every second brought a new and frightening sound. The storm could not only be heard, it could be felt as if it had a weight all its own. Water began to pour in through the ceiling in relentless streams.

As the storm's intensity grew, all conversation ceased. The noise of the wind was too loud to allow even the fearful cries of the younger children. But Angelina spoke anyway. Not to anyone in the room, but to God. She prayed and prayed hard. She prayed for her life and her father's and for the lives of her uncle, aunt, and her cousins. As the storm pounded the house, Angelina wondered if God was able to hear her petition over all the noise.

Minutes were hours, hours were days. Time seemed to cease its flow. Only the storm continued to move.

Then it stopped.

There was silence — beautiful, blessed silence.

Only the soft sound of water dripping could be heard.

"It's over," Angelina exclaimed. "It's all over."

"No, my little angel," her father corrected. "We're in the eye of the storm. When that passes, the winds will begin again, this time in the opposite direction. It's not over. We have to go through it again."

Angelina felt a sadness flood a heart already filled with fear. "Again? We have to go through it again? I don't want to go through all that again."

"I know, Angelina. I know. But we will."

Rajiv was little more than a zombie, a mindless, soulless being wandering among the broken vessels of humanity. Where once had been a thriving town, there remained nothing more than flotsam, splinters of existence scattered consistently and completely. No buildings stood; only the occasional block wall remained intact. The market area was gone, the houses were gone, and his home was gone. Automobiles were sprinkled everywhere like toy cars in a child's cluttered bedroom.

Standing amidst the rubble, Rajiv took in the surroundings around him and attempted to fix his bearing by some landmark. There was none. The best he could tell, he was standing where his kitchen used to be. Kicking aside boards swollen with water, he found the concrete foundation that had faithfully supported his home. It was all that remained. Even the debris that so thickly covered his property belonged to others, washed to their resting place by the powerful reverse surge of the retreating wave.

What had it been like? Rajiv wondered. *Did they know it was coming? Could they hear it?* In his imagination made vivid by sorrow, he could see the family already gathered for the birthday party. Each would be dressed nicely, each with a gift. They would have been waiting on him. Perhaps they felt something, perhaps his sweet Jaya had skipped to the window just in time to see the towering . . .

No! Rajiv commanded himself. *I will not think this. I will not see this.* But he did. The vision came to his mind uninvited and would not leave. It played brightly and loudly. It would not be ignored. It refused to be evicted. Quickly and as powerfully as the monster wave had crushed his town, the vision of his family's destruction pressed irresistible, pervasive tentacles into his thoughts — impossible to kill, impossible to sever.

Rajiv clenched his fists and beat them against his forehead to drive the image from his mind. He felt no pain in his hands as he clenched them so tightly that his fingernails scored his palms. He did not feel his hands pounding his head. Only the pain in his heart was noticeable, and that raged like a fire. And still the image of the devil-wave crashing down on his family with immeasurable force played in his thoughts. He was spared no detail.

Down the road, or at least where the road had been, Rajiv staggered and stumbled. He fell time and time again as he tripped over the wreckage — shattered boards, bits of home, and bodies. He looked, he studied, he examined everything for a sign of his family, simultaneously filled with hope and fear of success.

Around him others, neighbors who had been away at the moment the ocean turned evil, also wandered, also looked, also hoped. Aide workers scampered among the rubble, wanting desperately to help and finding the task beyond their worst nightmares.

Walking. Looking. Walking. Looking. Then . . .

On the ground, near an overturned car, Rajiv saw something that jarred him from his stupor — a flash of sun off a bit of glass. A picture frame, familiar in size and design. Bending down, Rajiv picked up the photo and saw his family. They were all smiles. They were happy. Now they were gone.

Rajiv could stand it no longer. His legs folded beneath him, and he crumpled to the ground. Tears fell from his eyes, his breathing came in ragged, raspy breaths. Bands of emotional steel tightened around his chest, and his stomach became a pot of churning, burning fire.

He howled in agony, not caring who heard or saw. He wept loudly and fell to his side on the sharp debris. Rolling on his back he turned wet eyes to the cobalt-blue sky above him and cursed whatever gods there were, hoping, pleading, that they would end his life too.

"Two million dollars!" David exclaimed as he walked down the wide, pea-soup-green corridor of the downtown San Diego County courthouse. "That's steep."

Calvin shook his head. "Not really. Even though you don't possess much personal wealth, you have had access to a large amount of capital. One of the charges against you deals with the illegal transfer of funds. There's the possibility — in the court's mind — that some of the money may be available to you and that you might skip the country. You have traveled world-wide, after all."

"I assume that's why they insisted on taking my passport?"

"You would do the same thing in their shoes. Actually, they could have withheld bail. I think we should count ourselves lucky. Especially since Mr. Barringston put up the money."

"How do you thank someone like that?" David wondered out loud.

"You don't. He's a good man to have as a friend."

"What now?" David asked.

"We get out of here. I've arranged for a

car and driver to meet us outside the main entrance. The media are there, and they want to ask you a lot of questions. Don't say anything to them. Is that clear? Say nothing."

"Won't that make it seem as if I'm hiding something?"

"That's why we're going out the front door. I don't want it to look like we're avoiding them. When we get there, let me do all the talking. I'll handle everything. You just look confident."

"I'll do my best."

"You'll do great. Just keep quiet. Let's go."

Calvin led David down the hall and through two large glass doors. A mass of reporters and photographers greeted them. Questions were fired in machine-gun fashion. Cameras snapped photos. Film crews aimed expensive video cameras at David.

Stopping at the top of the wide concrete stairs that defined the entrance, Calvin held up his hands and signaled for the crowd to be quiet. The roar turned to murmuring, the murmuring to silence.

Flashing a large smile, Calvin spoke. "I know you are eager to question my client, but I also know that you are professional enough to know that he will not — and this is at my insistence — answer any questions. I can tell you that my client is innocent of every charge brought against him and that I will conclusively prove that in court."

"What about the tape?" someone called out.

"I am not free to discuss any evidence that might be used in this case, but I can promise you that my client is innocent."

"How much was the bail?"

"Two million dollars," Calvin answered without flinching.

"What will happen to Barringston Relief?" a reporter asked.

"It will continue to save lives," Calvin snapped back. "That is its mission, and that mission has not changed."

"Is it true that Barringston Relief funds have been frozen by the Justice Department?" a reporter with a microphone inquired.

"I have been told that is the case, but as soon as the Justice Department realizes that such an action will result in the deaths of hundreds of humans across the globe, then I believe they will release the funds."

"Dr. O'Neal," a male reporter in an expensive suit called out. "Why did you steal the money? And how much were you paid for smuggling illegal immigrants into this country?"

Calvin snapped his head around and glared at the reporter. He pointed a finger at the man. "Sir, I have told you that my client is forbidden to answer questions. Clearly that comment was too complex for you. I was willing to stand here and answer any questions you fine people had, but I see that a commitment to a professional approach is absent. I will answer no more questions."

The crowd groaned, and a few turned toward the offending reporter with murder in their eyes.

"One more question —"

"No," Calvin said loudly, grabbing David by the arm and pulling him through the crowd. "I thought I was dealing with professionals. It appears I was wrong."

"But —"

"There will be no more questions and certainly no more answers," Calvin snapped. Forcing his way through the crowd, he led David to a large, dark Lincoln Continental. As they approached the vehicle, a heavily built, ominous-looking chauffeur opened the door to the backseat. Both men entered.

"I can't believe this is such a media

event," David complained sourly.

"Big-dollar corruption and the scandal of a beneficent organization and its leader breaking the law is an irresistible story."

"But none of it is true."

"When have you known that to make a difference?" Calvin said flatly. "Besides, you were arrested, and that in itself is news."

"That one reporter seemed convinced of my guilt," David said, peering out the darkly tinted window at the crowd.

"The one I accused of being unprofessional?"

"Yes, the guy in the expensive suit."

"He's not a reporter, he's an actor," Calvin explained casually. "I hired him to ask that question."

David stared at his attorney dumbfounded. "What?"

"Look, David. It's my job to protect you and to get the very best trial — the fairest trial possible. Assuming this goes to trial. I didn't want us standing out there saying no comment to every question that was asked of you. That would make you look guilty. I wanted just enough time to assert your innocence and then get out. If the news media are going to be angry over the skimpy information available to them, I want them angry with me, not you. I want you to look as harmless and innocent as the day is long. So I set up the situation. It worked rather well."

"But isn't that rather dishonest?"

"David, you're in a lot of trouble. This is no time to be naive. The media can be careless and dishonest. If I don't do everything in my power to control them and this situation, I'm going to have a difficult time finding jury members who haven't already formed an opinion.

"Modern legal logistics in high-profile cases have demonstrated that much of a case is tried in the media. If that happens with you, then I plan to win in the media."

David sat in silence as he took in all that he was hearing. He had no taste for and very little understanding of legal matters. Those were always things for someone else to handle. Now he had been dropped in a caldron of boiling legalities that he could not fathom.

"Let's go, driver," Calvin said. Then to David, "Trust me. You must put your full and unbridled trust in me."

David nodded. There was little else he could do.

In the dispersing crowd of media, one

man watched intently as the dark sedan carrying David O'Neal pulled away. Purposely, he lowered the small Super 8 camera he had been holding and scratched his temple. The wig of short brown hair he wore was making him perspire, and his scalp itched.

Aldo Goldoni had continued to tape as the car pulled away, being sure to zoom in on the license plate. Most people lived their lives without a thought regarding privacy. Aldo knew that gathering information on anyone was easy. All it took was a little knowledge, desire, and some experience. By just blending with the crowd, he had not only learned who David's attorney was — information he could have gleaned from a newspaper report — but also the measure of the man, the way he handled himself. He had also been able to observe David O'Neal's condition. O'Neal looked resolute and unflappable, but his eyes and slightly hunched stature betrayed a weariness and confusion. He had not enjoyed his night in jail. For Aldo, that was a good sign.

Nothing got by him. He had trained himself to be observant and skeptical of all that he saw. In his line of work it could spell the difference between success and failure, life and death. That's why he had picked up on the plant in the crowd. Overstreet must have hired someone to portray an unethical reporter so that he would have an excuse to leave. Aldo admired that and made a mental note to learn more about Calvin Overstreet, Esq. He was not a man to underestimate, but then neither was Aldo Goldoni.

The hot water of the shower cascaded on the back of David's neck, bringing only small relief to his tense muscles. His time in jail had made him feel dirty, as if simply being in the building had soiled him deep into his pores. He had shampooed his hair twice and scrubbed his body with soap like an obsessive-compulsive.

Calvin had delivered him to the Barringston Tower where he had quickly made his way up to his penthouse suite on the top floor. No sooner was he in his apartment than he stripped himself of the clothes he had been wearing for the last thirty-six hours, brushed his teeth, shaved, and began showering. He wanted to stay in the shower forever, listening to the mild roar of the water, feeling the cleansing steam, experiencing the penetrating warmth. The shower enclosure not only kept the water in, but at least in David's weary mind, kept the world out.

Since David's apartment was on the top floor of a commercial building, he had an inexhaustible source of hot water. He knew, however, that he could not stay in the shower forever, no matter how tempting the thought. He would have to face the world one day at a time, perhaps one hour at a time. His mind was clouded with questions that hung over him like a thunderstorm over the mountains. And like a thunderstorm, his thoughts would release lightning bolts of fear and uncertainty.

After a half-hour of wet seclusion, he turned off the water and stepped from the shower. He had made a decision. He would live each day as normally as possible, taking care of business, doing what must be done — and he would start immediately.

David entered his office and sat down behind his desk. He studied the files neatly arranged on its surface. It was a testimony of his assistant Ava, who, by the simple act of continuing the workday as if nothing had happened, was stating clearly her belief that all would return to normal.

On the desk were several folders,

each marked with a clearly printed label: MEMOS, TSUNAMI, HURRICANE CLAUDIA, RESOURCES, and half a dozen others. The desk also contained a neatly stacked pile of phone messages. David scanned those quickly. Most were routine; a few were from the news media. On the latter, a note, written in Ava's precise style, read: *Referred to Public Relations.*

David set aside the phone messages and picked up the folder marked HURRICANE CLAUDIA. It contained a bare-bones update of the storm:

Hurricane Claudia made landfall western extreme of Cuba at 11:45 P.M. EST. Category Five; sustained winds 190+ mph; gusts to 225 mph. Damage unknown. Damage in Jamaica and the Caymans currently being assessed. Early reports indicate massive destruction and great loss of life. Present course puts Claudia at New Orleans, tomorrow early. Advisories have been issued by all pertinent agencies. Osborn Scott.

David felt shell-shocked. He reached over to the phone and punched the intercom button. "Ava?"

"Yes," she answered cheerfully. "It's good to have you back. Are you all right?"

"I'm fine, thanks. Could you see if we have any news footage of Hurricane Claudia? Perhaps something from the Caymans or Jamaica."

"I'll get you everything I can."

"Great."

"Would you like some coffee or something?"

"Coffee sounds good. Oh, and Ava, thanks."

"I'm here if you need me."

David released the button. Next he opened the file marked TSUNAMI. The top page of the file was a brief from Osborn written in the same terse style:

Tsunami damage is still being assessed. Early estimates by Indian and Bangladeshi governments place the loss of life at nearly 15,000. International Red Cross and Red Crescent place the number higher. Figures are expected to rise sharply. Communication reports no contact from our field workers in Bangladesh.

An ache grew inside of David, a deep, penetrating sorrow. So many lives lost, and more would die in the hours ahead. He knew the problems were far from over. In the hurricane and tsunami areas, new dangers would soon arise. There would be a lack of food and fresh water. Disease would be rampant, taxing even the most prepared nation. Looting and crime would skyrocket. Then, for the survivors, the slow, agonizing rebuilding would begin. Many, perhaps most, would rebuild without the presence of loved ones.

It was time for Barringston Relief to . . . Realization took David's breath away with a sudden jolt. Quickly he grabbed the folder marked MEMOS and opened it. There were several, but the one he was looking for was on top:

To: All department heads and board
    members
From: Robert Connick, CFO
Re: Asset restriction

As most of you know, recent events have led the Justice Department to take action against Barringston Relief and its CEO. Part of that action included the freezing of all funds. We are unable to move monies as needed. I am, therefore, calling an emergency meeting of the Barringston Relief board of directors to discuss this extremely urgent problem. We will, of course, discuss the video you all received. The meeting shall be held at 4:00 P.M. in the large conference room. In addition to the members of the board, I am asking that each department head be present to answer questions. I know that each of you is extremely busy, but this matter must be addressed.

At first David felt a sense of indignation at Connick's impulsiveness, but then he chastised himself for the thought. Of course, Connick would call a board meeting. David had been in jail, no one knew if bail would be set, and Connick was the CFO. If funds were frozen, he'd be the first one affected. Had David not been in jail, he would have called the meeting himself and consulted with Connick immediately. Connick was doing the correct thing.

David read the memo again. What was this about the department heads receiving a video? The realization hit David hard. Quickly he glanced at the top of his desk again and saw what he had missed before

— a videotape. Seeing a black cassette on his desk was not at all unusual. Tapes from field workers to tapes of news reports were routinely sent to him. He snatched this one up. There was no label.

Stepping from his desk, he crossed the office to the entertainment console that held his television and VCR and inserted the tape. It was as he had feared. Someone had sent the tape to all the department leaders in Barringston Relief. That meant that not only did the entire firm know of his arrest, they had also witnessed the alleged crime. How many of them would be able to disbelieve their own eyes?

There was a knock at the door. David stopped the tape and turned, expecting to see Ava. Instead it was Kristen and Timmy.

"David!" Timmy said, bounding across the room and hugging David with such force that it nearly knocked him over. "You're back! You're back!"

"Easy, buddy," David said with a chuckle, returned the embrace. "Did you miss me?"

"Lots. I was afraid you weren't coming home ever again."

"What, and leave you alone? Never going to happen, buddy. You're stuck with me."

"I like being stuck with you."

"That's good, Timmy." David freed himself from the embrace. "You weren't in the apartment when I came home. Where were you?"

"I was doing my job, 'cuz I didn't do it last night." Timmy bounced on the balls of his feet with excitement. "I went to Kristen's house last night, but I didn't sleep real good."

David looked at Kristen, who had remained at the door. She was leaning against the jamb, her arms folded in front of her. To David she looked weary, stressed. Even the blue-and-white double-breasted cardigan jacket she wore seemed to hang loosely.

"Thank you for watching Timmy," David said to her.

"Timmy is always a pleasure," Kristen said slowly. After a pause she continued. "I thought you might call me when you got in."

"I just arrived in the office a few minutes ago."

"I see you got a tape too." She nodded toward the VCR. Her words were terse, but spoken softly. David could tell she was hurt.

"I'll tell you what, buddy," David said to

Timmy. "Are you done with your work?"

"Yeah."

"OK, why don't you run upstairs and watch some television."

"OK," Timmy said, then asked, "They're not going to take you away again, are they?"

David shook his head. "I'll be home later. I have a meeting at four, but I'll be up after that and then we'll have dinner together."

"Can we go out?" Timmy asked enthusiastically.

"Sure. I'll even let you pick the restaurant."

"Cool," Timmy exclaimed. David watched as the young man left the office.

In the corner of the room were a pair of matching sofas and two padded leather chairs. David motioned to the seating area. "You have something on your mind, Kristen. Come on in and tell me about it."

Kristen stood motionless for a moment, then crossed the office and took a seat in one of the chairs — removing the opportunity for David to sit next to her. David sat in the opposite chair.

"Let me guess," David said softly. "You saw the video and you're upset."

"I think I have a right to be upset,"

Kristen replied coolly. "I'm as under-standing as the next woman, but this is too much of a stretch."

"That's not me in the video," David said matter-of-factly.

"It certainly looks like you." Her words, laden with pain, had a bite to them.

"I'll grant you that, but I can tell you that it was not me. I can't tell you who that is, but it's not me."

Kristen crossed her arms again but said nothing.

"Have I ever lied to you, Kristen?"

"Not that I know of," she snapped harshly.

David sighed loudly and took a deep breath. He wondered how he would respond if the roles were reversed. "I don't blame you for being upset. The video is very convincing. It might even be con-vincing enough to land me in prison. But it is not real. I have never lied to you, and you know that. I'm not lying now. I can't prove my innocence. You will either have to trust me or not."

More silence.

"What do you want from me, Kristen?"

It was her turn to sigh. "I don't know, David," she said, shaking her head. "This is . . . beyond me. I want to believe you. I don't enjoy being angry. You know how much I love you."

"And I love you too. I would never, never do what that tape shows." David leaned forward. "I need you to believe me, Kristen. I can stand to lose many things, but I don't think I can stand to lose you or Barringston Relief. As it stands now, I may lose both."

A tear ran from Kristen's eye. David knew that she was not prone to such displays of emotion. He had seen her cry only once before, and that had been at A. J. Barringston's funeral. That lone tear was testimony to how much the video had hurt her.

"I plan to fight this, Kristen. I will not roll over and play dead. If I have to fight it alone, I will, but I'd rather face this with you by my side."

"Do you really think it's that easy?" Kristen said loudly. "Do you think that I can turn my emotions on and off like a faucet? I have seen the man I love, the man I've trusted with my love and my heart, kissing another woman. I have seen it with my own eyes."

"No, you didn't," David countered strongly. "You saw a tape of someone who looks like me. I've been set up, and you're falling for it."

"I am not a stupid woman, David. I know what I saw."

David tensed. "And I am not an immoral man. I am telling you, that was not me. I can't explain how that tape came to be, but I can tell you before God and everyone that was not me."

"I wish I could believe you," Kristen said.

"You can. It's your decision. I can't make you believe me, but I know you're capable of it. Like you said, you're not a stupid woman. Think, Kristen. Think. Have I ever done anything to make you believe that I could behave in such a fashion? Has there ever been anything in my words or actions to make you think that I am capable of such impropriety?"

She shook her head slowly. "Not known to me."

"Not known to you?" David was exasperated. He had spent his years building a life based on Christian values and mores. But all that was now crumbling like an ancient and decayed facade. It was inconceivable that a lifetime of righteous living could be destroyed in such short order. David was well aware of those spiritual and political leaders who had destroyed their images by misbehavior. Their downfalls were understandable and carried a sense of justice. Had David been guilty of the crimes, he would accept the fallout, but he was innocent. Apparently, he was one of the few who believed that.

"Kristen," David said softly, "I can stand the accusations of others. I can tolerate the media and the police. But I can't stand losing you. What good is it for me to convince the world that I'm innocent if I can't convince you? But I'm not going to give up. Stand with me or leave me, but I will prove my innocence or go to my grave trying."

Another tear. "You won't have to go it alone. I'll stand by you. My mind tells me that I shouldn't; my heart says that I must."

"Your heart is right." David rose to his feet, walked to Kristen, and held out his hand. She took it and stood. He drew her close. The perfume of her hair was inviting, comforting. He kissed her on top of the head and held her tight. "I will prove my innocence to you. Somehow, some way. I need more than your tolerance, I need your belief."

"I . . . I can't give that to you. Not after what I've seen. I'll stand with you, help you, continue to love you. But that's all I can do right now."

His heart fell and shattered like crystal on concrete. Of all the things that happened in the last twenty-four hours, this was the worst. A portion of David's soul began to die.

Allowing herself to be embraced, she buried her face in his chest and wept softly. An empty sadness filled David, but only for a moment. Soon the sadness was replaced by boiling anger. Her pain set off a complex set of emotions in him that included an enormous flood of fury and resolve.

I don't know who's doing this, David thought, *but they just crossed the wrong man.*

9

Punta Gorda, Belize, Central America

Beu Ribe pushed the dusty rag along the top of the battered wooden pew. Back and forth she dragged the cloth, rubbing the worn varnish as she had done every week for the last fifteen years. She looked at her hand. Its color was dark, a tribute to her mother's Mayan blood. The skin was rough, chapped, and wrinkled from her sixty-two years of hard and impoverished life. It trembled slightly.

She continued to work down the long pew. Already this afternoon she had cleaned twenty-two pews and had only four more to go. Then she would sweep the bare stone floor. It was her ministry, her way of contributing to her church. With no money to put in the offering box, she contented herself with a physical contribution. Besides, Father Donovan had more important things to do than clean the chapel. It was a work she enjoyed.

Today, however, she did not feel like sweeping the floor, or even finishing the dusting. She was sore. Her muscles ached, and her joints protested each movement, no matter how small.

Halfway along the pew, Beu stopped and sat down. Her chest heaved with each inhalation, and she felt hot. Looking at her hands, she saw that the tremors had intensified.

I must have the flu, she thought to herself. Slowly she leaned forward and rested her arms and head on the back of the wood bench in front of her. Her mouth was dry, and her eyes were beginning to ache.

"Are you all right?" a kind and soft voice asked.

Beu looked up and saw Father Donovan standing at the front of the church. "I may be ill, Father."

He walked over to her. "What is it? Are you sick to your stomach?"

"Somewhat," she answered weakly. "I'm tired, and my bones hurt."

"Is it your heart?" the worried priest asked.

Beu slowly shook her head. "My heart feels fine, Father. I'll be better in a minute, then I can finish."

"You are finished right now," he said firmly. "If I let anything happen to you, the congregation will hang me by my ears from the nearest palm tree."

A weak smile crossed Beu's face. She knew the priest was trying to cheer her. "Perhaps . . . perhaps I should go home."

Father Donovan touched the back of his hand to her forehead. "You're burning up."

"I feel cold."

"You have a fever. I'm taking you to the clinic."

"No," she protested weakly. "My grandchildren —"

"Are old enough to take care of themselves for a few hours. I'm taking you to the clinic."

"I have no money," she said.

The priest shook his head. "The clinic is operated by an American company. They do not charge their patients. Let me help you up."

With strength spawned from unshakable character more than physical capacity, Beu stood and, aided by Father Donovan, walked from the church, the dust rag still in her hand.

"What's wrong with her?" the priest

219

asked the young woman doctor. She was small with shiny ebony skin.

Before answering, she placed both hands into the side pockets of her white smock and gazed down at the nearly delirious Beu Ribe. She shook her head. "I will run some blood tests, but I'm afraid it may be serious. We've had five other cases like this over the last three days, and we think there may be more on the way. We also have a clinic in the north at Orange Walk, and they have been reporting the same thing. It seems to get worse each year."

"What, doctor?" the priest asked. "What gets worse?"

"Dengue hemorrhagic fever," she answered flatly. "There are always a number of cases of dengue fever, and those are seldom serious. When a patient is infected again, however, they sometimes develop the hemorrhagic form. It can be deadly."

The doctor turned away from the bed and walked the corridor formed by the rows of beds on opposite walls. Father Donovan followed. "The disease is caused by a virus that is carried by mosquitoes. The insect feeds on an infected person and then transmits the virus to others when it feeds again. The mosquito — *Aedes aegypti* it's called — is common in tropic lands like this one. It's a day-feeding insect and very prolific.

"The government," she went on, "has done its best to eradicate the mosquito, but it's nearly impossible. It can breed almost anywhere as long as there is standing water. Coffee cans, old discarded tires, it doesn't matter. If there is standing water, then the insect can breed."

"I'm familiar with the disease, but I thought it struck mostly children."

"That's true normally. It's also what concerns us most." The two walked from the ward into a small reception area and then outside. The setting sun hovered over the western jungle. "We know of four major strains of the disease, but this appears different. It may be a new strain. Every year there are tens of millions of cases worldwide, most of them involving children. More than one hundred tropical and subtropical countries have experienced a dengue outbreak. That's for a normal year. Statistically, over two-fifths of the world's population is at risk."

"This new virus is worse?" the priest inquired.

"Much worse," the doctor answered. "It has a short incubation time and advances to a dangerous level in the body quickly.

The mortality rate is very high."

The priest nodded solemnly. "Perhaps I should remind my congregation about this. They could check their property for standing water and maybe protect themselves."

"That is a good and wise idea," the doctor said.

"Is there anything else I can do?"

The doctor studied the priest for a moment. "I'm sure they would appreciate your prayers and visits."

"I will do that. Is there anything I can do for Beu Ribe?"

The doctor shook her head sadly. Father Donovan knew that the only thing he could offer the faithful Beu now was last rites.

David was the last one to walk into the large conference room. As he did, the idle chatter that had filled the cavernous space quickly died. Seated around the table were the six directors of the board and the heads of each department in Barringston Relief. All eyes turned to him. David, however, directed his gaze to the end of the table where he, as president and CEO of the organization, always sat. Seated in his spot was Bob Connick.

"I didn't expect you to be here,"

Connick said, standing to his feet.

"So I see," David answered flatly as he walked to his seat and waited for Connick to step aside. It was clear to David that Connick was disappointed with his presence. Gathering his notebook and papers, Connick yielded the spot and took a place at the other end of the table. David stood in front of his chair and took in the expressions of the others in the room. Some looked embarrassed, others concerned, many confused. To his right was seated Archibald Barringston, who offered the only smile. Halfway down and to his left sat Kristen, her face drawn and weary.

"I know," David began, "that my presence here is a surprise. Thanks to Mr. Barringston's kindness, I was released on bail earlier today. Since then, I've been doing my best to get back on track."

David set a leather notebook down on the table and opened it. "You are all here because of a memo sent by our CFO, Bob Connick. I believe he was right in calling the meeting. I am, however, not willing to relinquish my position. I wish to make something clear to each of you. I am not guilty of the charges brought against me. You have each received a video that ostensibly shows me dealing with known criminals and discussing certain illegal activities. That video also shows me" — he paused, looking for the right word — "cavorting with a young woman. The video is a lie. You are probably saying to yourselves, 'But I saw it with my own eyes.' What you saw was a contrivance. I'm not sure how, or what the purpose of the video is, but I will find out. I will prove my innocence to you and the world."

Bob Connick cleared his throat. "David, I'm sure that each of us feels —"

David quickly raised his hand, cutting off the CFO. "I'm not finished, Bob." Tension filled the room. "Some things must be made clear from the outset. I have no plans to step down from my position or to assign it to another. That would be an act of a guilty man. I hope you will support this. You, of course, have the power to remove me from my office. If that is your intent, then let's get to it. As moderator of this meeting, I ask if there is anyone here who wishes to make a motion that I be relieved of my duties?"

David stood silent and waited. Purposefully he made eye contact with each person in the room, giving each an opportunity to speak. Lastly, he looked directly at Bob

Connick and waited. The silence became heavier, thicker.

"All right, then," David finally said. "It appears that a motion is not forthcoming. That means we can get down to business." David took his seat. "Let me bring you up to speed. Mr. Barringston has posted a two-million-dollar bail for my release. I understand that money came from his personal funds. Is that correct Mr. Barringston?"

"It is," Barringston replied firmly. "No monies from Barringston Industries were used. And since I do not have the authority to use Barringston Relief monies, I invested my own."

Looking at the old man, David felt a strong sense of kinship. Barringston was going the extra mile for him. Even the word *invested* was his way of showing support for David.

"Thank you, Mr. Barringston. Your confidence in me means a great deal."

Barringston offered only a slight nod.

"In addition," David said to the group, "an attorney has been chosen and is now working on the matter. After a preliminary review, he has told me of his belief in my innocence. All I can ask of you is that you withhold judgment until the matter is settled."

Several in the group nodded.

"I have also instructed our legal department to begin the necessary work to release the freeze on our assets. This will take a court injunction and will most likely fail, but we're pursuing it anyway. The Justice Department has a job to do, but so do we. I intend for us to carry out our plans. Each of you will be kept informed. Nothing will be held back from you.

"Also," David continued, "I want you to feel free to come and talk to me at any time. Get me out of bed if you have to, but don't hesitate. You have questions. That's normal. I will be as open as anyone can."

David paused. He felt weary, worn. He struggled to sit straight, shoulders back, head held high. He wanted to project an image of confidence and control. The board and the department heads needed to see a man with his hands tightly on the reins of the organization. They didn't need to see the truth. Inside, David was awash with emotions as turbulent as the ocean in a storm, and he feared that his veneer might crack and reveal his inner turmoil.

"Seated around this table," he said, "are the best business people in the country. You are here because of a commitment to make a difference in the world. None of that has changed. Our task is the same. We will not surrender that because of this . . . event."

David paused, then asked, "Is there any comment?"

"Yes," Barringston said. All eyes turned to him. Age had diminished his physical stature, but his intellect, experience, and reputation made him a giant in the eyes of the others. "Unity is paramount here. The world must not see a divided organization. Such division would imply guilt and uncertainty. Either would undermine the work. Everything we say and do will be scrutinized by our employees and the media. I think we need to agree here and now that all media comments go through the public relations office and only that office. We also need to show unity in front of the other Barringston workers. If you can't do that, now is the time to speak up." Barringston turned to face Connick. The old man's gaze carried the unspoken message.

"Very well," David said after a moment. "Before we brainstorm about the asset freeze and receive an update on the tsunami and Hurricane Claudia, let's talk about another matter. I would like us to call a conference for tomorrow afternoon.

Is that possible, Kristen?"

"Yes," she answered. "Several reporters have asked if we'll be holding one soon."

"Good," David said. "Let's schedule it for about two o'clock. Does that work OK?"

Kristen nodded.

"Do you really think it's a good idea to speak directly to the press?" Connick asked.

"Yes," David answered quickly. "In a controlled situation. When I left the jail, my attorney forbade me from speaking. This will be different, more controlled. It will also be on our turf and in our timing. He will review my written statement before the conference. As a rule he doesn't want me talking to the press, but this allows us a forum to express my innocence. It's important that we appear up-front and forth-coming on all matters. Being innocent isn't enough. My innocence must be clearly shown. This is the best first step. Do we all agree on this?"

Several answered yes; others just nodded. Connick did neither.

"Second," David continued, "I've prepared an internal statement to be delivered to all employees here in the building and overseas. Communications will have to work out the logistics of getting it to all our field workers, but I'm sure they can do that. Is that true, Gail?"

"Absolutely," Gail Chen said. "I can have it to most of our workers within a couple of hours. A few will take longer, but everyone should have it within a day."

"Good," David said. "I knew your department was up to the task. Now, let's move on to other matters. I need to hear from you about the asset freeze. What can we do to ensure that the work goes on uninterrupted? Can we transfer overseas materials to the most needy areas? How long can we operate without the ability to transfer funds? There are many questions to answer, so let's get started."

First one person spoke, then another. Within a minute the formerly subdued meeting erupted in an exchange of ideas. David understood that it wasn't business as usual, but it was as close to being so as could be expected.

David dropped into his chair and released a heavy sigh. The evening darkness poured into the office through the windows. The meeting had lasted for three emotional hours and had left him drained and edgy. He wanted to go up to his apartment, lock the door, unplug the phones, and go to bed, but he had promised Timmy a dinner out. He didn't want to disappoint the boy.

Rubbing his eyes he glanced at his desktop. Ava had been in and tidied up the jumbled contents. The files were neatly stacked to his left, and message slips were placed in the center of the desk. The first note was from Calvin. It read, *Call at any time.*

Picking up the phone, David quickly entered the number. He didn't recognize it but assumed it was Calvin's home. A woman's pleasant voice answered.

"This is David O'Neal," he said wearily, "I'm returning Calvin's call."

"Oh, yes, Dr. O'Neal," the woman said. "He's out by the pool. Let me take the phone to him."

David pictured Calvin enjoying an August night by the pool as his wife brought him a remote phone.

"David," Calvin said a moment later. "How are you holding up?"

"Tired, Calvin. I feel like I could sleep for a week."

"Emotions will do that to you. Did the board meeting go OK?"

"How did you know about that?" David

inquired with surprise.

"Mr. Barringston called me. He said that your CFO might want to cause trouble, and he was looking for a legal opinion on the matter. Did he? Cause trouble I mean."

"Not really," David answered. "I don't think Bob Connick is motivated to do that. He's a very cautious man. I think he was merely being protective of the firm."

"Money men usually are cautious and protective."

"I'm still the CEO, and we're working on plans to keep things moving forward." David noticed a large envelope at the top of his desk. As he picked it up, he wondered why he hadn't noticed before.

"That's good to hear," Calvin said. "I think we need to meet on a couple of issues. When are you available?"

The envelope was addressed to him, but it had no return address.

"David? You there?"

"I'm here, Calvin. I'm sorry, I let myself get distracted. How about tomorrow morning, say, nine o'clock?" David turned the envelope over. There was nothing written on the back. Pulling a letter opener from his desk drawer, he cut open the mailer.

"Tomorrow at nine will be fine," Calvin replied. "It might be good to have Mr. Barringston there."

"OK," David said. "Do you want me to call him?"

"No, I'll do it. Have a good evening, David. And get some rest."

"I will. Thanks." David hung up the phone, reached in the package, and extracted two eight-by-ten photos.

David's heart seized in his chest and began to pound wildly. His stomach constricted, and he was nearly overwhelmed with nausea.

He dropped the photos to the desk, closed his eyes, and wished them away. They were still there. With tentative hands he picked up the photos and willed himself to study them.

One was a photo of Timmy at the beach. He was standing waist deep, looking back to the shore. Behind him a small wave had crested and was hitting him in the back. Timmy's eyes were wide with surprise, his arms thrust in the air as the cool water embraced him. It would have been a comical picture had not someone traced the image of crosshairs over the boy's head. At the center of the crosshairs a small red dot had been painted. Carefully lettered words were written in the upper left corner: *To die will be an awfully big adventure.*

The second photo was similar except it was a picture of Kristen as she left her home. She was looking forward as if she had just left the house and was walking to her car. The same crosshairs were drawn over her image with the painted red dot splashed between her eyes. Her photo also had neatly lettered words: *Let us go in; the fog is rising.*

The message was clear. Timmy and Kristen were in danger. David didn't understand the cryptic messages penned on the photos, but he did understand their intent.

Snatching up the phone, he punched the redial button. A moment later he had Calvin on the line.

"Can you come over?" David asked quickly.

"What? Now?"

"Yes, if possible. I wouldn't ask if it wasn't important."

"Can't you tell me what this is about?"

"Not over the phone. Just get over here." David hung up without waiting for a reply. He studied the photos. Someone was trying to intimidate him, and they were succeeding. But what did they want?

David dropped the pictures, picked up the envelope again, and looked inside. A small piece of paper was wedged at the bottom. He quickly extracted the note. Now he understood. The note read, *Be careful what you say. Confession is good for the soul.*

Again David snapped up the phone. This time he dialed Kristen's extension. There was no answer. He hung up the phone and attempted to quiet the acidic fear in his stomach. He picked up the phone again, this time placing a call to security. His anxiety rose when he learned that her car was gone from the parking lot. The next call he placed was to Kristen's home. Her answering machine picked up. David left a message requesting a call when she got in.

There was one other call to make. This one to his own apartment. No matter how much it upset Timmy, David could not take him out. The danger was just too great.

"OK, what's all this about," Calvin said as he strode into David's office.

"Thanks for coming," David said. Without additional words, he handed the photos to Calvin.

Calvin studied them for a moment before gently setting them on the desk. "Is there anything more?"

David handed him the note. This time Calvin took it between two fingers at the upper right corner. David watched the motion and realized his mistake: He had been handling the photos and notes like any other documents on his desk and had given no thought to fingerprints. David felt stupid and feared that he may have destroyed important information.

After reading the note, Calvin set it down next to the photos. "These are people who are close to you?" he asked pointedly.

"Yes," David answered. "The young man is Timmy, and I'm his guardian. I took over after A.J. was killed. He's learning disabled."

"And the woman?"

"Kristen LaCroix, head of public relations and my girlfriend."

Calvin nodded and took a seat opposite David's desk. "Where are they now?"

"Timmy's up in my apartment. Kristen left for home about forty minutes ago. I left a message for her to call me when she got in."

"Has she?"

"No, and I'm getting worried," David answered.

"Call her again. Right now. I want to know where she is."

David responded immediately, but there was no answer.

"Would she screen her calls?" Calvin asked.

"I doubt it. She's very good about returning messages. What's going on here?"

"First things first, David. You were right to call me about this. Someone is working you over big time. That someone may be dangerous. I want to make sure everyone is safe. Is there a place other than her home where she might stay? I don't think it's wise for her to be at home alone."

"We have employee apartments on the forty-seventh floor. Some of our people work long hours and often stay the night. We could put Kristen in one of those."

"OK, do that. It will be easier to protect her. Then —"

The phone rang. David snapped it up, listened for a moment, then mouthed the words, "It's her."

"Are you all right?" David asked.

"Sure, why wouldn't I be?"

David wasn't sure what to say. He didn't

want to frighten her, but he wanted her safe.

"You still there, David?"

"Could you come back to the office?" David began, but he was interrupted by Calvin.

"Let me have the phone," Calvin demanded. David handed him the receiver.

"Ms. LaCroix," Calvin began firmly. "My name is Calvin Overstreet, and I am David's attorney. We have just received some information that makes us believe that you could be in danger."

Calvin paused, listening.

"Ms. LaCroix," Calvin said, "I think it's best that we be cautious about this. Here's what I want you to do. As soon as we hang up, you double-check all your locks and windows. Don't open the door to anyone —" Again Calvin listened. "No, it's not silly, and this is not a game. Please do what I say. After you check the locks, I want you to find a place away from all windows. Sit in the bathroom if necessary, but stay away from the windows. Do you understand?"

There was another pause. David watched as his attorney nodded his head slightly. "Good. I'm going to pick you up and bring you back here. I want — Yes, Ms. LaCroix, I do believe that it is necessary. Don't worry about packing anything. We'll get whatever you need later. Understood? Good. David will give me the address. I should be there in . . ." Calvin looked questioningly at David.

"She lives in Chula Vista. It'll take you about half an hour."

"I'll be there in thirty minutes," Calvin continued. "I'm wearing a dark blue polo shirt and beige pants. I'll be driving a white BMW. I'll knock on your door three times, pause, and then three times again."

Calvin shook his head. "No, it's not cloak-and-dagger, Ms. LaCroix. We've never met. I don't want you opening the door to the wrong person. Now, here's David again."

David took the phone.

"Is this really necessary?" Kristen asked.

"Have you ever known me to play a joke like this?"

"No, but life is full of surprises lately," she said quickly.

The words stung David. "Kristen, just do what Calvin has asked you to do. OK?"

"Yeah, I guess so. But I don't like it."

"Thanks, Kristen, I'll see you soon." David hung up the phone. He turned to Calvin. "I'll write the address down."

"While you do that, I'm going to make a call."

"To whom?"

"The FBI," Calvin answered. "They might be able to tell us more about these photos. Besides, they need to know about all this."

"I shouldn't have touched the photos, should I?"

"You had no way of knowing. Most likely the perpetrator wore gloves anyway. This doesn't look like the work of an amateur."

"Do you understand the comments on the pictures?"

"I recognize the one on Timmy's photo, the one that says 'To die will be an awfully big adventure.' It's from J. M. Barrie's *Peter Pan*. It's something that Peter says in the play."

David cast a quizzical look at Calvin.

"My mother loved that play. We had to watch it every time it came on television. You know, the one with Mary Martin as Peter Pan. I've seen it so many times I can almost quote the entire play."

"What about the other?"

Calvin read the line aloud: "Let us go in; the fog is rising." He shook his head. "It doesn't ring any bells with me."

"I've never heard it either, but I feel like

it may be important."

"In situations like this, everything is important." Calvin picked up the phone and dialed. "Write down that address and any directions you can give me. I don't want to waste any time."

Archer Matthews threw the half-eaten slice of pizza back in its grease-stained box and dragged a paper towel across his face. He studied the image of David O'Neal that appeared on his computer screen.

"Can't we move a little faster?" Jack LaBohm asked irritably.

"Nope," Archer replied. "You want the best image possible, don't you?"

"Yes, but —"

"No buts, Jack. Perfection takes time and cooperation."

"You know I think you're an arrogant little —"

"I've reached the point in my life where the opinions of others don't interest me. That happens to people in my situation. We get rather apathetic about such mundane things as the hurt feelings of others."

"I didn't say my feelings were hurt. I just wanted you to know that I despise you immensely."

"See there. And you didn't think we had

anything in common. Now shut up and smile."

"Again?"

"What's the matter, Jack, does it hurt your precious little face to smile? Is the process too complicated for you?"

Jack pursed his lips and furrowed his brow. The image of David on the computer did the same.

"That's a lousy smile, but it's a good test just the same." Archer laughed at his little joke. "OK, you can relax for a minute."

Jack LaBohm leaned back in his chair and mindlessly picked at one of the many white dots on his face.

"Leave those alone," Archer ordered. Or we'll have to start over and that would make your boss very unhappy."

"Elaine Aberdene is your boss too."

"For the time being," Archer conceded.

"I'm sick of these dots," Jack complained.

"They're necessary. It's the only way I can transfer your facial expressions into the computer. Without them the digital camera array couldn't track the movement of facial muscles."

"So when I smile, O'Neal smiles too. Is that it?"

"Just like before, except I'm being a little

more cautious this time. Putting in more detail."

"Shouldn't you have done that on the first tape?"

"The first tape is fine. Unflawed. This one is the next step up. No one, and I mean no one, will be able to find fault in this tape. Not even David O'Neal's mother could tell the difference."

"Technology is amazing," Jack said as he looked at the picture-perfect image of David.

"Actually," Archer corrected. "I'm amazing. Now let's do it again. This time I want a real smile."

Jack leaned forward and placed his head in a semispherical device. He could see the tiny lenses of the twenty-four cameras that would track each movement of his face.

"OK," Archer ordered, "smile."

Jack complied, as did the computerized version of David's face.

"No wonder women can't resist you," Archer said sarcastically. "Tilt your head to the left. Good. Now the right. Good. Open your mouth. Hmm."

"Hmm, what?" As Jack spoke, the mouth of the computer David moved sympathetically.

"An open mouth is just a dark cavity on

the screen. I'll have to do a little touch up, but it won't be a problem. This is going to work perfectly."

"It had better," Jack threatened.

"It will. I promise you that. It will."

The white BMW pulled away from the curb. Aldo had watched as the dapper-looking man escorted Kristen from her home to the car. Before entering the car himself, the man had surveyed the surroundings. He was a cautious one, but that was to be expected. O'Neal wasn't likely to have some shyster representing him on such a serious matter. Nor would he send just anyone to pick up Kristen. Aldo had been told by his crew that monitored the phone tap on O'Neal's telephone that Calvin Overstreet would be stopping by for Kristen.

Aldo studied every gesture made by Overstreet. He moved with prudence and forethought. Most likely the man had some training, military or maybe police. Since O'Neal's phone was monitored constantly, Aldo had been warned of Overstreet's arrival. Not that it mattered, for he was tucked snuggly away in a van with tinted windows. He did have some concern, however. When the lawyer had looked in his direction, he had frowned at the sight of the van. Did he suspect the surveillance?

"What does it matter?" Aldo said to himself. The photos that had been left on O'Neal's desk was the tip-off that the LaCroix woman was being watched. What did matter was that she was out of the house. That was no surprise. It was an anticipated event in the plan. There was a better than 90 percent chance that such a thing would happen.

As far as Aldo was concerned, it was an advantage. Where else would they take her except back to Barringston Tower? That would put the woman and the retarded kid in the same area.

"Nothing like having all your ducks in a row," he said to himself. His job was so much easier when the marks did his work for him.

10

Angelina held tightly to her father's hand as they stood in the devastated living room. The second half of the storm had been as bad as the first, rattling and shaking the house as if a giant had ripped it from its foundation. The noise of the wind had been horrific and was punctuated with the sounds of exploding glass and cracking lumber. The family had remained crammed into the tiny bathroom for over four hours. The mattresses they had used to cover themselves had weighed heavy upon them as the roof, stripped of its shingles, let rainwater pour in like a waterfall.

Now the storm was gone, and so was much of her aunt's home. The roof sheeting had remained in place over the back of the house where they had huddled in a desperate attempt to hide from the storm. The same could not be said of the rest of the house. Angelina looked up through rafters into puffy, wounded gray skies. Around her were the fractured remains of a family's possessions. A bomb could not have done more damage.

"Is it really gone, Papa?" Angelina asked softly, squeezing his hand.

"Yes," he answered in a whisper. "The storm is gone, but not its effects."

A muffled sound caught Angelina's attention. She turned and saw Maria frozen in disbelief, her hand raised to her mouth, her eyes wide. Around her stood her children, like a brood of chicks. Her husband placed his arm around her shoulders in a vain attempt to console her. Angelina walked to her, being careful not to step on any sharp debris, and gave her a hug. "It will be all right, Aunt Maria. You'll see. Everything will be all right." Maria stroked the young girl's hair but said nothing.

Returning to her father, Angelina asked, "Where is the storm now, Papa?"

He looked at the clouds and said, "Havana."

The word sent a chill through Angelina. *Havana.* That's where her home was, where her sister, Juanita, was. Looking around the razed house, Angelina wondered if their own house would soon look the same.

Outside, the damage was even worse. Lumber, fractured and splintered, covered the ground, its sharp spearlike edges pointing in every direction. Dead birds were scattered in the rubble. A lone dog limped by in the distance.

"Look, Papa," Angelina said pointing down the street. A piece of plywood, just like the pieces that had been nailed to the window frame, was wedged through the windshield of a 1958 Chevrolet sedan and protruded rigidly from the vehicle. Across the street rested a large section of someone's roof.

The sudden absence of the wind and the crushed and stripped homes made Angelina feel as if she were on another planet.

The stillness was oppressive as the realization of the destruction set in. The fear was gone now, but it had been replaced by another consuming emotion — despair.

No one spoke. Even Maria had stopped her weeping. The shock of what they were seeing had leveled their emotions as surely as the hurricane had leveled the area. There was nothing to be said. No words could bring understanding or closure. The storm had come and done what it did. That could not be changed.

Sensing the depression that filled those around her, Angelina offered the only words she could think of. "We are all alive."

Her father looked down at her for a long moment, then surrendered a small, reluctant smile. "Yes, we are, Puppet. Yes, we are." He picked her up and hugged her deeply. She returned the hug, wrapping her small arms around his brown neck. "Yes, we are."

"I love you, Papa," she whispered softly, burying her face in the crook of his neck. "I was afraid for you."

"I love you too, Puppet," her father replied. "You were a very brave girl." He then kissed her on the cheek and wiped away a tear from his eye.

An aching sadness filled David as he watched the woman he loved study color copies of the pictures he had received the night before. She lingered over them, her eyes darting back and forth as if she was memorizing every detail in the photos. She paused over her picture. The crosshairs and symbolic dot of blood forced a noticeable shudder. Despite the personal nature of her photo, she seemed more moved by the one of Timmy. She was oblivious to the others in the room. Calvin and Barringston sat quietly, waiting for the appropriate time to move forward.

Outside, the sun continued to climb its steady path toward midday as it had done for countless years, untouched by the angst of the world below it.

David reached across the corner of Barringston's desk and took Kristen's hand. "Are you all right?" he asked softly. Kristen had been invited to the nine o'clock meeting after being told about the photos. She was now as involved in this as David and had as much at stake.

She nodded. "It's just so . . . so hard to believe. To think someone is out there right now, thinking about killing me and Timmy. It's mind shattering."

"You're showing a great deal of strength considering the situation," Calvin offered. "Many people would panic."

"I'm tempted," Kristen said with a forced and meager smile. "I see why you were so insistent last night, David. You were right to demand that I stay in Barringston Tower."

David gave her hand another squeeze.

"We can't be too careful," Calvin said. "These pictures aren't a prank."

"Is that why we're meeting in Mr.

Barringston's office instead of David's?" Kristen inquired.

"Yes," Calvin said flatly. "It's not beyond reason to think that David's office is bugged with listening devices. I've arranged to have the office swept while we meet."

"Swept?" Kristen said.

David answered. "Calvin has asked a private security firm he knows to do an electronic sweep of my office, your office, my apartment, and a few other areas to see if there are any electronic bugs."

"How do we know that Mr. Barringston's office doesn't have listening devices?" Kristen said.

"We don't," Calvin replied. "I'm playing the odds. He or she or they, whoever it is, can't bug the whole building. Of course there are other ways."

"Such as?" Barringston asked.

"In rooms like this with large windows nearby, an experienced operative can, using a special electronic device, listen to our conversation through the window. The glass vibrates with each word spoken. That vibration carries our words."

"That's why you insisted on having music playing?" Barringston said as he looked at the portable boom box near the floor-to-ceiling window in his office. The speakers of the radio were directed at the window. It was playing Beethoven's sixth symphony.

"Yes," Calvin answered. "Even the White House, in certain rooms, pipes music at the windows. The window then vibrates to the music and not to the voices inside."

"Well, there's one good thing about these pictures," Kristen said. "It sure proves David's innocence."

"Not in the eyes of the law," Calvin said. "We still have a long way to go on that. I took the actual photos to the FBI this morning and had a talk with Agent Hall. He wasn't impressed, but he agreed to send them to the lab. I even got him to put a rush on it. I've also notified the local police, but there's not much they can do at the moment."

"Does Agent Hall really think I manufactured the photos?" David was incredulous.

"He didn't say as much, but I suspect that's his thinking."

"Why would I do that?"

"To throw suspicion off yourself," Calvin answered flatly. "He doesn't like you. He's not all that crazy about me either. He thinks I sold out the bureau when I left to practice law."

"So what do we do now?" Barringston asked.

"Let's talk security," Calvin said, opening a brown file folder and setting it on the edge of Barringston's desk. "Kristen, I think it's best for you and Timmy to remain in this building as much as possible. Also, we need to bolster the security in the building, especially on Barringston Relief floors. Can you limit the people who go up to your floors?"

David nodded. "Our employees use a special set of elevators. Right now they operate like any other elevators. They are equipped to read magnetic cards. The cards carry a code that takes the employee to his floor, but they can be bypassed by pressing the floor button. That's so workers can go between floors and also so delivery people can have access to the offices."

"Delivery people like the person who delivered the tape to Kristen?" Calvin asked.

"Yes," David felt a wave of fear wash over him. The thought that someone could walk into Kristen's office at any time stunned him. "However, we can set the elevators so that only those with cards can use them."

"Do that," Calvin said. "Anyone else should be escorted by security. We should hire a security firm to augment the small force you have now. How much training does the building security have?"

"Not much," Barringston admitted. "Mostly they're retired men who keep an eye on things and report any trouble to the police."

"We need more than that," Calvin said. "I know a good local firm. They do a lot of work for the defense and aerospace industry. They can have a bonded and trained crew here within a day."

"Do you think it's really that bad?" Kristen asked.

"I doubt you're in any real danger at the moment, but harming you could be part of a backup plan. I just don't think we should be taking chances."

"Backup plan?" Kristen repeated.

"I think the goal is to discredit David, not to harm you or Timmy. Whoever is doing this wants to influence David. That's the meaning of the note's *Be careful what you say*. The photos and note arrived shortly after the decision to hold a news conference. That's the second part of the note, *Confession is good for the soul*. They want David to confess at the news conference."

"But why?" Barringston asked. "What's the point?"

"Well, that's the big question, isn't it?" Calvin responded. "David, right after your arrest I asked you to think about who might want to frame you. Have you done that?"

David shook his head, "I've tried, but I can't come up with anyone who would go to such lengths to hurt me. There are a few people in foreign countries that object to our work, but none are capable of doing this. At least, none that I can think of."

"Someone has motive and means." Calvin turned to his notes. "I've been reviewing the charges against you, David. They fall into two categories: embezzling and smuggling aliens into the country. The embezzling will fall by the wayside when the Justice Department does an audit of the books. I doubt that our mystery person could arrange for Barringston Relief monies to be transferred to an offshore bank. Not unless they had someone on the inside — something we can't discount — or electronic access to your accounts.

"The thing that bothers me is the alien connection. They're saying that you arranged for the smuggling of foreign nationals from . . ." Calvin looked at his notes. "From Honduras, Guatemala, and Belize."

"What bothers you?" David asked.

"Guatemala and Belize border Mexico. Wouldn't it have been easier to cross Mexico on land and cross the border into Texas, New Mexico, or Arizona? Why offload them in San Diego? The odds of being caught doing that are very high."

"People are smuggled in by ship all the time," David said. "Thousands of Chinese come to this country illegally each year."

"But that makes sense, doesn't it?" Calvin said. "How else would an Asian get to the United States except by ship or air. A ship from Central America could make much shorter trips to Texas, Florida, and other states. Why sail through the Panama Canal and up the Pacific to offload in a highly supervised port like San Diego?"

"Perhaps that was the ship's scheduled port of call," Barringston said. "Maybe it was expected to be there and the immigrants were just a side — I hate to say it this way — cargo."

"I suppose," Calvin agreed, "but why Belize? How many illegal immigrants come from Belize?"

"I don't know," David said. "But that may be the connection. I just returned from Belize a week ago."

"You did?" Calvin said with surprise.

"Yes. We have a couple of medical clinics in the country. Every month or so, I take a trip to see our field workers. There's a troublesome disease down there. Our doctors are not only providing medical help to those in the outlying areas, but are doing field research."

"What kind of disease?" Calvin asked as he took notes.

"Dengue hemorrhagic fever," David answered. "It's a nasty disease. DHF is not unusual there or in any tropical or subtropical area. But this version of the disease is resistant to treatment, incubates faster, and has a higher mortality rate."

"I wonder if that's the connection," Kristen asked.

"If so, I don't see it," David said. "The only connection is that I was in Belize and that some of the aliens on the ship are from there."

"What about the disease?" Calvin said. "Could the people framing you have something to do with that?"

"I don't see how," David responded. "How does anyone benefit from DHF? I think we're stretching here."

"Perhaps." Calvin rubbed his chin.

"Someone sees a connection," Barringston said. "Whatever it is, they take it seriously. The photos are proof of that. Whoever sent them is crazy."

"Crazy like a fox," Calvin rebutted. "I did some checking on those quotes. A reference book on quotations was all I needed. I was right about the one on Timmy's photo, the one that read 'To die will be an awfully big adventure.' It's from Barrie's *Peter Pan*. Act three, to be specific. The other quote — 'Let us go in; the fog is rising' — took me a little longer. Those are reputedly the last words of Emily Dickinson. The words she spoke before she died."

"I don't get it," Kristen admitted.

Calvin looked at her and then the others. "Whoever sent those pictures has a fixation with death. That should make us all very uncomfortable."

David's stomach tightened as the elevator began its descent from his fifty-third-floor office to the lobby. It wasn't the dropping motion that caused the discomfort but the thirty reporters who waited for him in the lobby.

The news conference had been called for two o'clock. It was now ten minutes past that time. David knew that his being late would not improve his image, but he had wanted to review his notes one more time.

The gathering was taking place in the lobby, which was spacious enough to accommodate up to one hundred people. The lobby was the choice of Calvin, who had been concerned about security. "Anyone can forge a press pass," he had said. Calvin had also insisted that Kristen, who was responsible for media relations, not go down to the lobby. She chose to go anyway, making it clear that a couple of photos were not going to intimidate her from doing her job.

The elevator doors parted. David took a deep breath. With posture erect, he strode into the lobby like a man without a single care to trouble him. A wood lectern had been placed in the corner of the lobby. It faced out to the fan-shaped seating area of folding chairs filled with reporters. As he walked toward the lectern, Kristen stepped behind the wood stand. David stopped and waited.

"Hey, mister," a young boy's voice said. David felt a tug at his suit coat. Looking down, he saw a boy about eight years old wearing a San Diego Padres baseball cap and a dirty shirt. "Hey, mister," the boy said again. He was holding a brown paper folder.

David smiled and said softly, "What is it, son? This is kind of a bad time for me."

"A man wanted me to give ya this," the boy said, lowering his voice and holding up the folder. "He gave me twenty bucks to give it to ya. He said he'd give me twenty more if you would open it right now. I need the money, mister. I got a sick mom. Will ya open it? Please? It means a lot to me. Please. I need the other twenty."

The boy's voice rose with each plea. Several of the reporters turned to face him.

"OK, son, OK. Just settle down." David took the folder.

"Go on, open it so I can get my money."

David glanced around the lobby. He saw only bewildered reporters and a concerned Kristen. He flashed them all a smile and raised his index finger to indicate that he needed a minute.

"All right, son," David said. "Let's see what you have here." The envelope was not sealed. No sooner had he reached in than he knew it was another photo. He could feel its smooth surface and the weight of the paper. His heart sank. Slowly he extracted the picture. Its image made his stomach flip, his heart pound like a kettle drum. David felt the color leave his face and his mouth go dry. Quickly, he slipped the photo back in the folder.

"What's your name —" David began, but the boy was gone. David turned to Kristen and nodded. He knew her well enough to know that she sensed his distress.

"Thank you for coming, ladies and gentlemen," Kristen began drawing the attention of the reporters back to herself. "We appreciate your interest. I know you are busy people, so allow me to introduce to you the head of Barringston Relief, Dr. David O'Neal."

Kristen stepped away as David took her spot behind the lectern. He set his notes down and took a moment to look at the gathering before him. Men and women sat in metal chairs, many with notepads, many more with small tape recorders held out at arm's length. At the back of the group were several men with video cameras mounted on tripods. As soon as David looked up, the lights from the video crew blazed on, bathing him in bright, stark white. David could hear the clicking and clacking of camera shutters as they added bursts of light from their strobes to the already overilluminated scene.

The new photo blazed in his mind, demanding attention.

David paused to allow photos to be taken and the video cameras to be adjusted. Then he spoke.

"I wish to add my thanks to that of our public relations officer, Ms. LaCroix. You folks have certainly kept her busy over the last couple of days. I may have to bill your organizations for her overtime." A light laughter emanated from the crowd.

David wondered what to do. The purpose of the photo was clear. There was no cryptic message this time. Just one line: *Confess or else.*

David looked up at the waiting crowd of reporters. Each had fixed his attention on him. He had to say something, but his next words could spell the difference between life and death. The future, his and that of others, was counterbalanced by his next comments.

He tried to weigh the pros and cons, analyze in seconds the potential effects of his next action. His senses became acute. He could hear every foot shuffle on the floor, every note page turned. His heart thundered with explosive beats. His throat seemed to be closing, constricting. He could feel the blood rush through his veins like water through a high-pressure hose.

He had to do something, say something.

They were still looking at him. Waiting. Watching. He wondered if the person responsible for the picture was seated among the reporters, watching and enjoying David twisting in the wind of fear, like a spider suspended from a lone strand of webbing.

Call off the news conference? Say nothing? Make no commitment one way or the other? Flee? Run from the room? Confess to something he didn't do? Take the burden upon himself? Pay the price of the guilty even though he was innocent?

The picture, the picture.

No. No. No. David straightened his spine and raised his head. He would not be intimidated. It was a picture and nothing more, and it was a lie, and somehow he could prove it, and it was wrong to give up, and surrender wouldn't guarantee the problem would go away, and there were thousands of people who would be affected, and . . . and . . . God would not abandon him. He knew that. He was doing everything right. He had help in the person of Archibald Barrington who believed in him, Kristen who loved him, Calvin Overstreet who guided him, and God who empowered him.

No, David resolved. *It will take more than a set of lies to cower me, to pound me into submission. Not now. Not ever. I will stay with the plan.*

"I wish to make a brief statement," he said with a calm that concealed the turmoil he felt. "Two days ago I was arrested on several felony charges. I have been released on bail and so am able to stand before you now. It is my understanding that your organizations received a videotape incriminating me for the crimes of which I am accused. In light of such a video, you must be wondering what I can possibly say to you short of a confession. Well, I shall speak the truth. I am innocent of all charges leveled against me. I cannot explain the video to you other than to say that the person who appears in it is not me."

The photo was a lie. It wasn't true. It could never be true.

"I wish I had more answers for you than I do. I can tell you that I was not then, nor have I ever been, in league with those who smuggle and abuse illegal aliens. Barringston Relief exists for the purpose of alleviating suffering, not adding to it. My life is wrapped up in that goal. I have not and

263

will not do anything that would damage the goals of Barringston Relief or its employees.

"As we stand here," David continued, "several hundred dedicated Barringston workers labor in the worst possible situations. Some have suffered illness, physical attack, and terrorism. Some have died on the field of service only to be replaced by other noble souls. I would never do anything that would sully their reputation or the dignity of their work. I would certainly not do so for material gain."

Push the image out of your mind. Push it back. Give it no room.

"Where does that leave us?" David asked. "With a great many questions. I can tell you that the matter is being looked into as we speak. It is my hope that the truth will be known shortly so that I and many others can get back to work.

"Before I take questions, I must ask your patience. As professionals who have covered many matters that deal with the courts, you know that there are some things I will not be able to comment on. Now, are there any questions?"

The picture, the picture.

David felt weak, sick. He wondered if he hadn't just triggered an avalanche that would not only bury him but crush the lives of those whom he loved.

"Who is your attorney?" a reporter on the first row asked.

"Calvin Overstreet," David answered.

"How much was the bail?" another reporter asked.

"Substantial," David replied. "And I must add that the bail money did not come from Barringston Relief." David looked down at the brown envelope. He could see the picture in his mind as if he had been endowed with X-ray vision. Pangs of anxiety pierced him.

"Are you saying that someone is trying to frame you?" asked a woman whom David had seen on television.

"Yes."

"Why would someone do that?" the woman reporter asked. "What do they stand to gain?"

"We don't know yet. Extortion, perhaps."

The questions came slowly at first, then more rapidly. David answered or refused to answer each question posed. Calvin had spent two hours briefing him on what he could and could not address. The time with Calvin had been more intense than what he was experiencing at the news conference. Thirty minutes later, David stepped from the lectern exhausted in mind and body. A run up the stairway from the lobby to the fifty-third floor would not have tired him as much. Kristen came to his side. They started toward the elevator.

"You did very well," she said kindly.

"Thanks, but I don't think they believe me."

"They will before it's all over. I didn't believe you at first either. When the facts are out, the world will know."

David replied with a weary nod.

"There's more, isn't there?" Kristen asked. "That boy gave you an envelope. When you opened it, you looked like someone had just slugged you in the belly."

Again David nodded. "Not here. I need to call Calvin and have him come over —"

"Dr. O'Neal?" The male voice came from behind him. David lowered his head. He did not want to give a one-on-one interview.

"I'm sorry," David began as he turned. "I can't grant any personal interviews." When David turned he saw not a reporter but a teenager. He was tall and thin, and his dark hair was shaved close to the scalp on the sides but long on top. He had an aquiline nose that seemed too large for his acne-laced face. "I'm sorry, I thought you were a reporter."

"I may be able to help you," the young man said.

"Oh?" David responded suspiciously. Was this another game perpetrated by his tormentors? He glanced at Kristen, who looked as leery as he felt. "How so?"

"It's about the video they showed on television the other night." His voice was deep and slightly raspy, typical of late developing teens. "There's something wrong with it."

"Wrong?" David raised an eyebrow.

"Yes," the boy looked nervous. "My name is Greg Cheney, and I'm a sophomore at San Diego State University. I'm majoring in television production, so I spend a lot of time looking at video. Actually I want to work in Hollywood someday doing computer animation, but that may take awhile. I have to finish my degree and then —"

"Greg," David interrupted. "You were saying something about the video being wrong."

"Oh, yeah. Sorry. I'm a little nervous. I think it's fake."

David smiled. "I know it's fake. I just

don't know how to prove it."

"I do," Greg said. "At least I think I do. But I can't tell you. I have to show you. Do you have a VCR?"

"Yes." David was becoming suspicious again. He had been warned by Calvin to be careful about strangers, yet this boy seemed genuinely nervous. Nothing in his body language showed deceit.

"OK," David said. "Let's take a look at what you've discovered."

Greg smiled broadly. "I didn't think you'd listen to me. I mean, I want to help."

"Greg, I can use all the help I can get."

11

"He got the package?" Aberdene asked. She was seated behind her desk. In her hands was a two-foot-long, six-inch-diameter, clear plastic tube. Inside the tube a hundred mosquitoes clung to its smooth surface.

"Absolutely," Jack said confidently, his eyes nervously fixed on the container. He and Archer were seated on a leather couch opposite the desk. "He got it all right. I thought he was going to lose his lunch when he opened it."

"You saw him open it, Jack?" Aberdene pressed.

"I wasn't actually there," Jack admitted, "but I saw the video Aldo shot."

"He was there? How wise is that?"

"He was lost in the crowd of reporters," Jack explained. "Since no one can identify him, he can disappear in a crowd quite easily."

"But O'Neal continued with the news conference anyway, and instead of confessing he maintained his innocence. The picture failed to elicit the proper response. Why is that, Jack?"

Jack turned to face Archer, who returned the glance with a broad grin. He was having fun watching Jack squirm.

"He was in a tough spot, Dr. Aberdene," Jack rebutted. "The media were already there, and he had already been introduced."

"He could have confessed," Aberdene countered.

"I thought he would. You thought he would. Who would have guessed that he would stay the course?"

"I would have," Archer interjected. "Study the man. You've got every fact there is about him except how many freckles he has on his back. He's a religious man. Personally, I think he's too smart for all that superstitious stuff; nonetheless, his religion plays a powerful role in his life."

"So?" Jack said roughly. "What's that got to do with anything?"

"Don't be dense, Jack," Archer snapped. "It has everything to do with it. He knows he's innocent and to say he is not would be a breach of his beliefs. Besides, he has friends and some resources. He's not going to crumble easily."

"What do you know about faith?" Jack asked harshly.

"Not much, except those that have it aren't quick to give up when the going gets tough."

"Ridiculous," Jack blurted out.

"You're missing the point," Archer said. "It doesn't matter if you believe in God; it only matters that David O'Neal does. Send him all the pictures you want, and all you'll be doing is providing more information for him to work with."

"What do you suggest?" Aberdene asked.

"Stop. You've got the ball rolling. The evidence has been planted. The more he states his innocence, the more guilty he will appear. Soon he'll be tied up in court, Barringston Relief will go broke from the asset freeze, contributions will dry up, and your problem will be solved."

Aberdene raised the clear cylinder to her eyes and studied its winged inhabitants. She spoke softly. "Did you know that the mosquito lives only sixty-five days? In that time it matures, feeds, and reproduces. Then it is gone. Not very long, is it? Just sixty-five days. Yet, there are two thousand species living from the equator to the Arctic Circle, from lowlands to mountaintops. They're everywhere. All they need is water to lay their eggs, and, for the female, warm-blooded animals on which to feed."

"Don't the males suck blood?" Archer asked.

Aberdene shook her head. "No. They're content with nectar and water. The females need blood."

"Typical," Archer quipped.

"My point is that they achieve what they're designed to do in a short time. I want the same thing. I want Dr. O'Neal to go away for good. I don't care how religious or moral or saintly O'Neal is. He must be dealt with. We'll stick to the plan. Understood?"

Both men nodded.

"We're right on track," Jack added quickly. "Everyone and everything is in place."

"Good," Aberdene said as she set the plastic tube on its end in front of her. The top of the cylinder had a friction-held cap. "What's the most deadly disease in the world?" she asked.

The two men looked at each other, puzzled at the abrupt change of subjects.

"What, no ideas from you, Archer?" Aberdene asked. "I would have thought you had an opinion."

Archer clenched his teeth. She was

playing with him. Baiting him.

"AIDS, I suppose," he answered bitterly.

Aberdene shook her head. "No, my dear Archer. Your disease is not the worst. I suppose you can feel grateful for that. And for the medicine I provide you to keep the virus in check. Expensive meds — twenty-five thousand dollars per year. Way out of reach for someone without the right insurance. But don't get me wrong. You've done a fine job, and I'm happy to give you what you need."

Archer said nothing. Just saying the acronym *AIDS* was painful. Being reminded of his dependence on the self-centered woman across from him only added to the pain.

"What about you, Jack?" Aberdene pressed. "Any ideas about the most deadly disease?"

Jack shrugged. "Cancer?"

"Malaria," Aberdene said, sounding like a teacher correcting a student. "Every fifteen seconds someone dies of malaria. Four a minute, 240 every hour. And how does one contract malaria? From mosquitoes similar to these." Without hesitancy, she pulled the top of the cylinder.

The two men stiffened as they watched several of the insects climb to the edge of the opening.

"*Anopheles* carry malaria," Aberdene said, her eyes fixed on the mosquitoes. "*Aedes albopictus* is also known as the Asian Tiger mosquito. It's a hardy little thing. Very resistant to insecticide. They came over from Asia on ships carrying used tire casings. *Aedes aegypti* mosquitoes, my personal favorite, are responsible for dengue fever, sometimes known as *breakbone fever* because of the pain it causes. Of course we can't forget those little guys who stowed away in water barrels on slave ships in the nineteenth century and brought yellow fever with them. Then there's the ever popular *Culex pipiens,* the common household mosquito. It carries the virus for encephalitis. That disease makes your brain swell. Quite a picture isn't it? A swelling brain in a rigid skull. Not a pleasant thing to witness, even worse to endure."

One of the mosquitoes took to the air and began to buzz around the room. Archer couldn't take his eyes off it. He began to perspire.

"Another fascinating thing about mosquitoes is their adaptability. Usually a little pesticide will do them in, but like all living creatures, they change."

Another mosquito took to the air.

"More and more species seem to tolerate the occasional spray of insecticide. Ironically, the viruses they carry tend to become more resistant to antivirals and other medications. Think of it: mosquitoes immune to insecticide and viruses untouched by current drugs. One could make quite the effective little weapon from these guys. Don't you think?"

Neither man responded.

"Now think of the flip side," Aberdene went on. "What if we could design mosquitoes to carry a weakened virus of some disease. It could bite someone and transmit the weakened virus, which in turn would inoculate the new host. That would make the lowly mosquito a harbinger of good — a living syringe. Boggles the mind, doesn't it?"

With a fluid motion, Aberdene brushed back her thick hair and then seized the plastic tube, lifted it three inches off the desk, and then slammed it down. The startled insects quickly escaped the container and flew around the room in random motions. One landed on Archer, who quickly brushed it off.

"Hey, what are you doing?" he shouted and stood to his feet. Jack joined him. Soon both men were swatting at the tiny swarm.

"Relax, gentlemen," Aberdene said with a laugh. "They're all males. They won't bite."

"You're crazy," Archer spat.

Slowly, Aberdene rose from her seat and crossed the room until she was standing face-to-face with the AIDS-ridden man. She raised a finger. "No," she corrected, "the last thing I am is crazy. Remember that."

She stepped to her office door and opened it. "Thanks for coming," she said.

The men hastily left the room. Aberdene stayed behind and admired her mosquitoes.

"Thanks for coming, Calvin," David said. "This is Greg Cheney. He says that he has something interesting for us."

Calvin shook the young man's hand and turned to David. "I'm glad you chose to meet here." David, Calvin, Kristen, and Greg were in a small office next to the communication department.

"It seemed wise considering all that you told me," David replied, remembering the revelation that the electronic sweep of David's office had indeed discovered several electronic listening devices. "But we can talk about that later. We don't want to

276

take up too much of young Mr. Cheney's time."

"No problem on time," Greg said. "I've got nothin' better to do today." Greg returned his attention to the electronic devices situated on a work station. "I didn't expect you to have video-editing equipment."

"We use it to edit video from our field workers," Kristen explained. "We use video for reports, promotions, education, and such."

"It's a pretty good system," Greg said. "It will speed things up." He placed the video he had been carrying into the cassette compartment and adroitly switched on the other equipment.

"Looks like you've done this before," David said.

"Like I said in the lobby, it's my major. I spend hours behind equipment like this." He turned a knob on a black control panel that sat on the desk. The tape began to fast-forward. "I made a copy of the report that aired on the news. That's what we're about to see." The image that had been burned into David's mind came alive on the monitor that sat on a platform above the editing equipment. The images scurried across the screen. Greg turned the knob again, and the image slowed to normal speed.

"OK," Greg said. "At first I just took the video at face value — a simple surveillance shot of a man caught in the act. No offense, Dr. O'Neal."

"None taken," David quickly replied. He felt his body tense as he saw the events play out before him. Glancing at Kristen, he saw that she too had tensed. Only Calvin and Greg seemed untouched by the display.

"Then I thought it might be interesting to see how much detail I could pull from the images. I assumed that the footage was shot with a secret camera. There are lots of them out there. Some have lenses smaller than the head of a nail. Anyway, I thought it would make a good school project. You know, analysis of secret tapes. That sort of thing. So I took my copy of the tape to the college and took a closer look. That's when things started to fall apart."

"Fall apart?" Calvin said. "How so?"

"Well, the first thing I noticed was that it was rather grainy. I assumed that it had been shot on film in low light. But that didn't make sense. Why use film when it is so much easier to use videotape? So I realized that I was seeing video noise, not grainy emulsion."

"Is that unusual?" David asked.

"Not particularly," Greg answered, his eyes fixed on the image. "When a dub is made from the original tape, a little quality is lost. If you make a dub of a dub, you lose a little more. What I was seeing looked like a tape several generations down from the original, like someone had made a copy and then gave the copy to someone else who then made a copy and passed it along. Do you see where I'm headed?"

"Not really," David answered. "I would expect that the news media received a copy and not the original. Those tapes are everywhere. Every television station got one as well as every department head in Barringston Relief."

"Let's not forget the FBI and the INS," Calvin said.

"I wish I could forget," David said somberly.

"Right," Greg said. "A copy. Not a copy of a copy of a copy. There's too much degradation of the signal for this to be a copy off a master."

"Which means that whoever sent these didn't have the original." Kristen leaned forward and studied the images. "Is that what you're getting at?"

"No," Greg answered quickly. "While that's possible, I don't think that's what happened at all."

"Then what?" Calvin said. David sensed his annoyance.

"I think the degradation in signal is intentional," Greg leaned back in the chair and watched the video. "I think the artist that did this is trying to muddy the water."

"Artist?" David raised an eyebrow.

"Computer artist," Greg answered. "A good one too. Really knows his stuff — or her stuff or their stuff, whatever."

"Can you prove this is the result of computer hocus-pocus?" Calvin inquired seriously.

"Ah, now there's the problem," Greg replied. "I'm no lawyer, so I don't know what constitutes proof. There's no doubt in my mind, but I don't know what a judge and jury would think."

"Why do I feel that you found something else?" David said. "What makes you so sure this is a fake?"

"I do have more. Let me show you." Greg reached out, took hold of the jogger knob that allowed him to change the direction and speed of the video, and cranked it to the right. The images raced by at high speed. The screen went blank for a moment before David's face appeared. It was large and filled the monitor. Greg twisted the control knob back to the stop position. The image of David's face was frozen on the screen.

"I used the college's computer editing equipment to make an extreme closeup of Dr. O'Neal's face. There it is," Greg said with the wave of a hand and a broad smile. "It's as plain as the nose on your face." He chortled.

"I don't get it," Calvin said. "It's just a closeup of David."

"And not a very good one at that," David added.

"Like I said," Greg replied. "It's as plain as the nose on your face." There was silence. "Look," Greg continued. "What's this look like?" He leaned forward and, with his index finger, pointed at a gray area under David's nose.

Unconsciously, David leaned forward. "What? Stubble? Five-o'clock shadow?"

"Shadow is right," Greg enthused. "Not five-o'clock shadow, but just your everyday shadow. Now you can see the border of the shadow caused by your nose and the light area next to it. Do you see that, Dr. O'Neal?"

"Yes. It looks like a faint diagonal line."

"Which way is it pointed?" Greg asked.

"To my right," David answered.

"Correct. Next question: Where was the light source in the room? I mean the room where the video was taken."

"I don't know," David admitted. "I wasn't looking at the furnishings."

"I can understand that," Greg said. "But I did look at the furnishings." He ran the tape back to the original scene and paused it. David could be seen at the end of the table with the two men on each side. "Where's the lamp, Dr. O'Neal?"

David studied the image, and for the first time looked at the room instead of himself. "To my right. In the corner. It's one of those contemporary lamps that shines the light up toward the ceiling."

"Correct again." Greg rubbed his hands together with excitement. "Now here's the big question: If the lamp is on your right, which way should your shadow cast?"

"To my left," David said softly. "But on the closeup it's going the opposite direction. They made a mistake. That proves it's a fake!" David clapped his hands.

"Maybe," Calvin said cautiously.

"It's a definite fake all right," Greg said. "But it's not a mistake. It's a tell."

"What do you mean?" Kristen asked. "What's a *tell?*"

Greg looked surprised. "None of you have ever played poker?"

"I have," Calvin said. "Used to play on a regular basis."

"So what's a tell?" David asked.

"A tell is something a player unconsciously does that reveals the nature of the cards in his hand. Some players when they get a good hand bounce their leg or raise an eyebrow or, if they were chatting a lot, suddenly become quiet. A good poker player will spend the first few hands studying his opponents to see if they display any tells."

David turned to Greg. "Are you saying this shadow is intentional?"

"Yup. He wants to give himself away. All the other shadows in the room are correct. I checked each one. They're all perfect except this one. He put that shadow there so someone would find it."

"Why?" Kristen asked.

"I have no idea," Greg said. "But there's more. I'm going to go back to the closeup and then advance the tape slowly. You tell me what you see." With quick movements, Greg adroitly did as he said. "Now watch and think simple."

The tape played. David's image was speaking.

"It looks . . . awkward," Kristen said.

"That's a good word for it," Greg said. "It's not Dr. O'Neal's face. It's a computer fabrication. Most likely a composite of actual video and computer modeling."

"Can they do that?" Calvin asked with surprise. "Can they put someone's face on someone else's body?"

"Oh, sure," Greg said. "It's done all the time. The technique was used in several music videos and in the movie *Jurassic Park*. You did see *Jurassic Park*, didn't you?"

"Sure," Kristen said. The men nodded.

"Do you remember the scene where the little girl falls through the ceiling and is hanging by one arm? There's a dinosaur below her that is getting ready to leap up and take a bite. Well, a stuntwoman actually did the drop, but there was a glitch in the shooting. When the stuntwoman dropped through the ceiling she acted out her part well, but she looked up into the camera. That meant the viewers would know it wasn't the child actress. Rather than reshoot the scene, they simply added the actress's face over the stuntwoman's. No one knew the difference."

"That's what they did here?" David asked.

"Probably," Greg answered. "The problem is speech. The human face is filled with muscles that work together. Everything from the twitching of an eye to a smile takes several, if not dozens, of muscles. It's hard to duplicate in a computer what the human face can do. Not impossible, but pretty hard. It also requires sophisticated and expensive equipment and someone who knows how to use it."

"Who would know such things?" Calvin asked. "I assume I can't just look in the yellow pages."

"The communities in and around Hollywood have companies that specialize in computer animation and computer-generated images. One of those companies could do it, or one of their employees. With the right equipment, that is."

"How hard is the equipment to obtain?" Calvin asked.

"Not hard at all," Greg answered. "All you need is money. With enough money and practice, I could do this." He nodded at the screen.

"You could create a tape like this one?" Kristen asked.

"No, not really. Not yet anyway. There is

as much art as there is technology involved here. Knowing what needs to be done is one thing; having the experience to do it is another. Whoever did this is a practiced artist. He's great."

"That's not the word I'd use for him," David interjected.

"You should thank him, Dr. O'Neal," Greg countered. "If he hadn't dropped these little clues in the tape you would never be able to prove this was a fabrication. Since videotape is purely an electronic media, it's impossible to trace physical changes. Unlike film, which has emulsions that can be analyzed, video comprises electronically recorded data. Since the image is really a recorded electronic signal, it can be easily manipulated. And there is no way to prove that such manipulation has occurred. You can't tell what the video camera really saw and what was added later. All you can do is look for mistakes in lighting, shadows, and detailed movements like that of a human face speaking. You're fortunate that the artist decided to give himself away."

"If he hadn't done it in the first place —"

"They would have got someone else to do the job," Calvin interrupted.

"They?" Kristen said. "How can we be

sure that it's more than one person?"

"It's a gut feeling at the moment," Calvin said. "Besides, I don't think a computer graphics artist would contrive such an intricate plan and then give himself away. No, someone has it in for David, and we're going to have to find out who that is."

David nodded. "Greg, could the same thing that was done on this video be done on still photos?"

"Oh, sure," Greg replied with hesitation. "That's easier yet, especially with digital cameras that record images electronically and can be directly downloaded into a computer. With a photo you're dealing with just one frame; with video hundreds of frames must be altered."

"So someone could take a photo and substantially change it?" Calvin asked.

"It's done all the time," Greg answered. "It's frequently done in fashion photography. You don't think those women really look that way, do you? The truth is that no photo or video can be fully trusted. More than half of all the commercials you see on television and nearly all of the movies have been electronically altered. It's the way it is now."

David sighed heavily. "Thank you, Greg,

you've been a big help. I knew the video was a fake, I just didn't know how. You've shown me that."

"You're not out of the woods yet, David," Calvin said. "A shadow under your nose is a far cry from having charges dropped."

"But it's a start," Kristen said. "At the very least we could call another board meeting and show them what Greg has found."

Calvin shook his head. "Let's hold off for a little bit. We need to think this through."

"I don't understand your reluctance," David said.

"David," Calvin responded firmly. "This is like a man walking through a minefield. He finds one mine and disarms it. Does he say, 'Whew, I'm glad that's over,' and then start off on a little jog? Of course not. He starts looking for the next mine."

"So you think there's more to all this?" Kristen said.

"I think there's a lot more to all this."

"In that case," David said, "I think it's time to start looking for the next mine."

Darkness hung in the room like an impenetrable shroud. The stark light of a computer monitor valiantly fought against the gloom. Dark as the room was, a greater darkness indwelled Archer Matthews. He sat motionless in his chair, body bent so that his head rested on his crossed arms. To his right was a bowl of empty pistachio shells, the sole remains of his dinner. Six inches from his head was the head of David O'Neal — a model of the man he had been paid to frame.

Slowly, he raised his head and stared into the unblinking eyes of the sculpture. "So how are you dealing with all of this, Dr. O'Neal?" Matthew's voice echoed in the near empty room. "It's not at all personal, you understand."

He picked up the bust and held it in his hands. He studied its shape, each line, each carefully crafted crease. Archer had used it to build a wire-frame representation of O'Neal in the computer. Using an electronic device, Archer had carefully traced all of the head's features and replicated them in the computer.

The sculpture had been a tool, but now it was a constant reminder that he was participating in the demise of a man whom he did not know. A man who nobly worked at easing the world's pain and suffering. That man — David O'Neal — stood on a crumbling precipice of public opinion. Soon he and his organization would be gone: O'Neal to prison, Barringston Relief to oblivion. All because of the work that he, Archer Matthews, had done. Without him, the frame-up would have been impossible.

Archer set the bust on the desk, leaned back in his chair, exhaled noisily, and rubbed his weary eyes. He had not wanted to frame an innocent man, but what could he have done? Elaine Aberdene had him in the palm of her hand. Archer needed her, not for work, not for income, but for life.

She and she alone had that which would keep him out of the grave. In fact, if it had not been for her, he would now be lying in some AIDS hospice waiting to exhale his last breath.

It was unfair to David O'Neal, he knew, but his life had been filled with the unfair, the inequitable. Archer was a true victim. He had not contracted AIDS through any act of his own. He had not used intravenous drugs, and he had never had a homosexual encounter. No, the HIV invaded his body because eight years ago a drunk had run a red light and crashed headlong into Archer's car.

He had been a senior in an East Coast college then and was on spring break with some friends. Like several thousands of other students, he had traveled to Fort Lauderdale for the weeklong intermission in classes. And like thousands of college students who filled the city streets, he spent his days sleeping and his nights hopping from one party to the next. It was while he and two friends were on the road to yet another party that a man, fresh from a tavern two blocks away, ran a red light and forever changed Archer's life.

When he had awakened, he was lying in a hospital bed with a concussion, two broken ribs, and a compound fracture of his left arm. There had also been internal bleeding. The lost blood had been replaced by a routine transfusion — an HIV-tainted transfusion. Somehow the blood they had given him had been overlooked in the routine screening for HIV. He could never prove it. He tried to sue for financial relief but had failed at every turn. The hospital had been able to "prove" that their blood was always tested and that such an event could never occur. When it was all over, Archer was left with a couple of scars and a terminal disease.

It took six years for the HIV to become AIDS. He took care of himself, having decided to surrender to death only after a fight. His doctors prescribed a course of medication that other AIDS sufferers called "the cocktail," but the course of treatment was expensive and he was underinsured. Since he made a good living working for one of Hollywood's premier special effects houses, he couldn't qualify for state aid to help pay the enormous cost of the medicine. Soon he was broke and desperate.

That's when Aberdene Pharmaceuticals had come along. Through an AIDS support group, he had heard that the drug company was looking for test subjects for a special set of trials. He applied immediately.

From the moment he was accepted, he was surrounded with secrecy. He could tell no one of the tests, not even family or friends. Since he had no family and very few friends, that had not mattered.

The people of Aberdene Pharmaceuticals were thorough and left no stone unturned about his life, his relationships, and his work. He was poked and examined and tested and then poked some more. Soon he was started on a one-time daily medication that replaced the cocktail, which had to be taken several times each day and at regular intervals.

It took less than a week for Archer to feel the difference. He had more energy, felt stronger, and enjoyed a natural euphoria that came with the drugs. There was no doubt in his mind that Aberdene Pharmaceuticals had come across the next big step in AIDS treatment. He wanted to tell everyone he met, but he had been sworn to secrecy.

"We must be very careful," they had told him. "Pharmacology is a very competitive business. Besides, we still have to obtain FDA approval, and we can't do that until the trials are finished."

So Archer kept the news to himself, ecstatic that he felt so well and consumed with guilt that he couldn't talk about it, especially to those who suffered from the same affliction. He watched as many fellow AIDS sufferers declined into abysmal weakness, ravished by one of the most tenacious diseases in the world, knowing that they wondered why he seemed so much more robust than they. Still, he kept the secret.

He had been in the program for a year when Jack LaBohm began visiting him. He asked Archer question after question about his occupation. How do computerized special effects work? What kind of equipment does it take? What programs have to be purchased? How long does it take to learn the craft? How can anyone tell if a video clip is real or fabricated? Jack had asked the last question a hundred times if he had asked it once.

Two weeks later, the bad news came. Each of the fifty volunteers in the research program were called in one by one and told that the trial run had been completed. Aberdene Pharmaceuticals was very pleased with the results, and Dr. Aberdene herself would push to have the medication made available as soon as possible. But that would take time. Independent testing had to be conducted. Massive amounts of paperwork needed to be filed, and the result had to be published in a reputable medical journal. In addition to all of that, patents, trademarks, and other legal matters had to be taken care of.

"How long will all that take?" Archer had asked when he sat in the office of Jack LaBohm. He was sure the other fifty had asked the same question and received the same answer: "Five years. Certainly no more than ten."

"But can't I continue on the medication?" he had begged. "I'll sign whatever release forms are needed. I'll sign a hold-harmless agreement."

Jack had shaken his head solemnly. "I wish I could say yes, but the laws of our country are very clear on these matters. We would be risking Aberdene Pharmaceuticals' reputation and exposing it to massive lawsuits. I'm afraid it's impossible."

Jack had been very patient with Archer, answering every question, countering every suggestion. At the end of the meeting, he had even offered Archer free use of the company's counselors. He then expressed his deep sorrow that he couldn't do more.

Archer had left that meeting more depressed than he had ever been. Thoughts, logical and illogical, erupted in his mind. He considered stealing several years' supplies, but he had no way to defeat the high-tech security that protected the nation's largest pharmaceutical firm. He thought of blackmail, extortion, and even retaliatory violence. But he knew it was all futile. He was just one small man against the laws of the nation and a major firm with more money behind it than some small countries possessed.

It was then that the next thought hit him. It was just a matter of choosing the right method. Gun to the head? Sleeping pills? Carbon-monoxide poisoning? A leap off a bridge over Interstate 15? It would have to be quick whatever it was. Suicide seemed the only choice for a reasonable man — a reasonable man who had no hope of surviving more than a couple of years.

As he drove home he masterminded several painless and quick ways to die. It was cowardly, he knew, but to his depressed mind, it was the only choice.

He entered his North Park home, a small house Aberdene Pharmaceuticals had rented for him while he was in the program, and noticed the phone answering machine showed one message. More out of habit than willful decision, Archer punched the play button. It was Jack.

"Archer," the message began, "this is Jack LaBohm. I've been thinking about your needs and . . . well, I think I may have found a solution. Dr. Aberdene needs you to consult on some matters and would be willing to pay you handsomely for it. Of course, we would provide whatever materials and, uh, supplies you need." Jack had stressed the word *supplies*. Archer immediately knew what he had meant. "Give me a call as soon as you get home. I'll be working late, so call at any time."

Archer had returned the call immediately.

Four months later, Archer knew he had been duped. True to their word, they provided him with everything he needed to do the work: computers, programs, models — everything, including the life-sustaining medication. All he had to do was sell his soul. That and destroy another man.

New concerns now worried him. After this "project" was over, what would happen? They wouldn't need him any more, and he knew too much. They could once again withdraw the medication or simply have him killed. Archer hoped, even prayed, that they would buy his silence with the medication, something to which he would readily agree.

Again he picked up the bust of David. "I'm sorry, Dr. O'Neal. You do great things, and I have no right to do to you what I have done, but I am desperate. You understand, don't you?" Archer felt that somehow, David O'Neal would understand, and that made Archer feel all the worse.

He set the sculpture down again and turned his attention to the computer monitor. He gazed at it blankly and then hit the enter key on the keyboard. The video began to play across the screen. He watched as Dr. David O'Neal did on tape what he had never done in life.

It was perfect. Everything was in place, including the little imperfection he had drawn in. It was a variation of something he used to do when he worked for the Hollywood effects business. On one frame in a scene he would put his initials. In film the frame would flash by too fast for anyone to notice, and only those with special equipment and knowledge of where to look would be able to find it. In those days it was his tag. Now it was . . . it was . . . he didn't know what it was, but he had to do it.

When the two-minute video reached its conclusion, Archer reached forward and turned off the monitor. The sole source of light in the room blinked out, and darkness covered him.

A breeze made heavy with moisture from the ocean blew across the small balcony of the twenty-seventh-floor hotel room. Aldo Goldoni, dressed only in plain white boxer shorts, sat on the thin, wrought-iron rail that separated the balcony from the 270-foot drop to the parking lot below. Indifferent to the danger, he rhythmically swung his legs back and forth and let the soft breeze caress his sweaty body. His chest heaved as he drew in a bushel of air with each inhalation. Perspiration trickled down his well-honed but thin body like rivulets of rain on a pane of glass. He faced the city lights, returning each sparkle with a glare of hatred.

Behind him his room lay in disarray. Mattresses were thrown against the wall; bedding was cast about in piles. The inexpensive chair and side table had been upended. Pages of the *San Diego Union Tribune* had been torn and cast about.

Aldo didn't care. He didn't care that the destruction was his fault. He didn't care that he sat exposed to the outside world. At the moment he didn't care who knew about him, who watched him. All he could see was the determined face of David O'Neal standing behind that fancy wood stand and boldly proclaiming his innocence.

He should have crumbled, Aldo thought. *What kind of man can see a picture like that and calmly ignore it?*

Aldo had crushed men stronger and more powerful than David O'Neal. That's what he did. He brought powerful men to their knees until they begged for mercy; then he would gleefully deny it. David O'Neal should be no different.

Anger began to rise in Aldo again. He could feel it inside, pushing, pressing to be released, to erupt one more time. He clenched his fists, digging his nails into hands already made tender by the repeated blows he had delivered to the motel mattress.

He should have crumbled right there, Aldo thought. *Right there, right then, he should have broken.* But he didn't, and that fact ate at Aldo.

Lowering his head, he forced himself to relax, working a mental exorcism on every infuriating thought. He forced himself to think of the one good thing that would come out of O'Neal's self-righteous behavior: Now Aberdene would be forced to up the stakes. That meant that Aldo could do that which he was best at — killing.

He looked forward to that call, and he knew with certainty that it would come. O'Neal was not going to roll over for anyone, at least not voluntarily. He possessed a rare courage, a courage exhibited only by those of great moral fiber or those with no morals at all. O'Neal was in the first group; Aldo in the latter.

Swinging his legs over the railing, he placed his bare feet on the balcony and strode purposefully into his room. His mind was made up. The time had come. First he would return the room to its original condition. It wouldn't do for the maid to come in tomorrow morning and see this. That would draw attention to himself. He hated attention. Next he would shower. Then he would call Jack. It was time to meet Aberdene herself. She would see things his way. He would see to that.

12

The early morning sun, unhindered by the usual drapery of morning clouds, poured into David's office. It was 6:30. After a night of unsatisfying sleep, David had come to his office early. On his desk were a large cup of coffee that gave off diaphanous wisps of steam that gently danced above the cup, an untouched cheese Danish he had picked up at the cafeteria, an open Bible that had been turned to the fifth chapter of Matthew, and the three terrifying photos.

Already David felt tension permeating his muscles, contracting them like a musician overtightening the strings of a guitar. He had begun his morning with a reading of the beatitudes, the nine blessings from the Sermon on the Mount. When David had been a pastor he had loved to preach from these verses. For him they summed up the entire mission of Christ: the reconciliation of God and man. In this passage he saw the heart's desire of the Savior to

302

bless His own, to comfort them in a way that could not be achieved in any other fashion.

David needed to be blessed. He needed the intervention of the divine, and he needed it quickly. Over the last twenty-four hours he had felt his resolve eaten away by the events that surrounded him. He knew he was being framed. That frightened and angered him. But it was the magnitude of effort to frame him that bothered him most. Who could hate him that much?

Blessed are the poor in spirit, for theirs is the kingdom of heaven.

He picked up the third photo, the one he had received right before the press conference, and studied it. He had not shown the terror-filled image to anyone. He ran a cautious hand across the photo, feeling its smooth surface. It wasn't a typical photo. Its size, like the others, was larger: 8½-by-11 inches instead of the typical 8-by-10 of processed photos. Before Greg had left yesterday, David had asked him about that. Greg had said that the pictures were not true photos taken with a standard camera and processed, but that they were color prints from a high-end color laser printer.

It wounded David to look at the photo. Each time he viewed it he was filled with the scorching pain of terror. He forced himself to study it, to take in its details, to find some clue, but it was a wasted effort. All he could see was the crushed shell of a red Mazda Miata engulfed in flames. The photo was taken — created, David corrected himself — from the rear of the car. It was clear enough to see the lifeless body of a red-haired woman slumped forward on the steering wheel. He could also see the vanity license plate above the rear bumper: RED HOT. It was the personalized plate that David had obtained as a gift for Kristen, a reference to her red hair and red car.

The fire was consuming the car. Even though the image was static on paper, it was alive in David's mind. He could see the flames licking up the gas from the ruptured tank and, filled with its power, consuming the combustibles in the car — the seats, the carpet, the rubber . . . the body.

In the upper left corner of the picture were the words *But the peasants — how do the peasants die?* David had already looked up the reference. They were the dying words of Leo Tolstoy. Calvin was right. The tormentor had a penchant for death. Such knowledge failed to comfort David. The idea of an educated assassin was all the more frightening.

He knew the person in the car was not his beloved Kristen. He knew that someone had fabricated the whole thing, but he could not expurgate the fear, shock, and terror the picture brought. He shut his eyes, squeezing them tight as if he could press the image from his mind, force it to drip away with the rising tears.

Blessed are those who mourn, for they will be comforted.

Another emotion flooded David's mind and heart — anger. Rage, like water that had spewed out of an old, eroded dam, inundated him, flooding his thoughts, his reason, his composure and carrying away the now shattered remains of his happiness. He wanted to lash out at those who had undertaken to destroy him and his work. Violent thoughts flooded his mind, but each thought was laced with guilt. His Christian faith did not teach him to hate, but to forgive. Could he forgive those who had done such vile things and had threatened Timmy and Kristen?

When he had been in church ministry, David had traveled to a retreat for ministers. It had been set at a campground filled with pine trees. A lake, large and captivatingly beautiful, was at the center of the camp. Pastors from all over the state had come to the camp for a time of fellowship, relaxation, and spiritual cleansing. The organizers of the camp had arranged for a couple of speakers to bring messages each night. One such message had left an indelible mark in David's memory. He had long since forgotten the speaker's name, but he did remember one line in the sermon: "The hardest people to forgive are not those who have done something to harm you, but are those who have done something to harm those you love." David understood that truth more now than ever.

Blessed are the meek, for they will inherit the earth.

There was a knock on the doorjamb. David looked up and saw Oz standing at the open door to his office. "You're in early, Oz."

"Actually, I've been pulling an all-nighter. I grabbed a few hours' sleep in one of the apartments."

David nodded. "Come in. Sit down. Where's Claudia now?"

Osborn crossed the office and took a seat opposite David's desk. David stacked the photos and turned them facedown.

"Just north of New Orleans and moving inland. She was downgraded to a four after crossing Cuba. The city took a beating, but because of the advance notice there has been little loss of life. The Red Cross and National Guard are pouring into the area."

"Property damage?"

"Extensive, but manageable. Cuba is a different matter. She took the worst of it. Tidal inundation, wind damage, flooding." Oz shook his head. "We don't have definitive reports yet, but the Cuban news footage out of the area is frightening. They're going to need medications to battle cholera and other diseases and, as you know, Cuba has always been chronically short of good medicine."

"And with our funds frozen we can't lift a finger to help," David said with disgust. "The best we can do is transfer medical materials and food from stockpiles in other countries. I have a report here that says we have some goods in Mexico that can be shipped to Cuba, but it's not enough. We're doing the same thing with supplies in India, but those won't last very long either. As it is, Mr. Barringston is paying the shipping costs."

"How are you doing?" Oz asked. "You've had a catastrophe of your own to deal with."

"I'm hanging in there," David admitted.

"Is that helping?" Oz nodded toward the open Bible.

"Yes, a great deal," David answered. "My faith is everything to me. Especially in difficult times. The Bible reminds me that other people have gone through worse things."

Osborn shifted his gaze out the window.

"What's on your mind, Oz?" David asked softly. "I think you have more on your heart than the tsunami and Hurricane Claudia."

"I'm not a very open man, David. I'm about as private as they come."

"I understand."

"Let me ask you a question," Osborn said, leaning forward in his chair. "What you said in the board meeting, is it true? You are innocent of all the charges?"

"You have my word on that," David answered quickly. "I can't give you all the details now, but we know for a fact that I'm being set up."

"Do you know by whom?"

David thought about the listening devices that were still in his office. "No, not yet. Some threats have been made, so I must be cautious."

"How are the others treating you?"

Osborn asked. "I mean, our fellow workers."

"Politely for the most part," David replied. "I have noticed a few whispering when I walk by. I suspect that if we can't get the money freed up soon, there'll be more tension to deal with."

"I know what that's like."

"Oh?"

Osborn dropped his head. David could see that he was weary and that the last few days had taken their toll. Over the years, David had become an excellent judge of character. When he hired Osborn, he felt that the man was genuinely brilliant, trustworthy, and a little haunted. Whatever haunted him was rising to the surface like an ancient shipwreck that had somehow regained its buoyancy.

"I don't talk about it much. But maybe it will help you. It's rather painful and embarrassing." Osborn shifted in his seat.

"I understand those two emotions," David said.

"Not long after I received my Ph.D., I landed a job teaching meteorology to undergraduates at the university. That was in 1989. I was only twenty-five at the time. I had been able to secure research funds for a team to study storm surges related to hurricanes. That was the year Hugo came ashore in South Carolina. It did seven billion dollars worth of damage and killed over five hundred people along its course. At the time I thought storms like that were magnificent, full of power and fury."

Osborn turned his gaze to unseen sights outside the window. David knew he was looking back through time.

"When the reports of Hugo's approach were made known, I assembled my team. Most were graduate students, but we had two undergrads with us. Exceptional students with a keen love for the study. Bob Hazelwood was one, Donna Gifford the other. They were engaged.

"Once we had an idea of where Hugo would make landfall, we flew in. Despite the evacuation notices, we worked our way to the ocean's edge. After all, we were there to study the storm surge. Part of our goal was to measure the force with which the surge came ashore and to gain an accurate measurement of its depth. We were also to videotape as much as we could. It's all tricky business, David. Very tricky."

"I can imagine."

"When the storm arrived," Osborn continued, "it came in with winds of 150 miles an hour. Debris was flying everywhere. I had seen scores of videos taken in hurricanes, but I had never actually been in one. It was incomprehensible." Osborn raised his hands to his ears and closed his eyes. "The sound . . . the sound was deafening. We had situated ourselves on the third floor of a six-story parking structure. The sides were open, so the wind whistled around the concrete corners. Rain propelled by the wind pelted us. It felt like we were being hit with grains from a sandblaster. And it wasn't just the wind, but the debris — plywood sheets, corrugated tin roofs, tree branches, twigs, everything — flying, spinning, tumbling."

David watched in silence as Osborn took a deep breath and let it out slowly. His face had paled. "It was . . . magnificent, majestic, so very powerful. I have never been so excited in my life. It was everything I hoped it would be. It was the reason for which I had been born." He shook his head woefully. "I got too caught up in it, David. I was too much in love with the storm. I didn't watch over my crew."

Osborn fell silent.

"What happened?" David prompted.

It took several seconds for Osborn to respond, and when he did his voice was just above a whisper. David had to lean forward over the desk to hear.

"For safety reasons, we had positioned ourselves to the east side of the building facing the ocean. The wind was more intense than expected, but it was the best way to monitor the incoming surge. It came in all right. Bob and Donna were videotaping the ocean as the surge arrived. We watched as the water along the beach began to rise. An eighteen-foot swell rushed over the beach and onto the streets. It carried with it small boats and pieces of beach structures. Bob and Donna were supposed to stay back in the parking structure and shoot through the open areas of the walls, but Donna got too excited. When the water came in she cried, 'I can't see enough.' Before anyone could do anything, she stepped right to the wall. A piece of corrugated metal from a nearby auto shop flew through the opening. It struck her on the forehead. Crushed her skull. She was dead before she hit the floor."

Osborn's eyes moistened, and his voice became raspy. "Bob was heartbroken. We all were. He sat on the wet concrete and held her in his arms, rocking back and forth, back and forth."

"And you were trapped in the parking structure," David said gently.

"Yes. The storm surge had flooded the streets, and the winds were too high to move her even if she had survived the accident."

"What happened then?"

"Bob dropped out of school, and I began to withdraw. My peers never said anything outright, but their glances and forced smiles said enough. It was my team and my responsibility to make it all work."

"But your team knew the risks when they went into it," David said.

"Did they? Donna was nineteen years old. What did she know of danger? I was the one with a Ph.D., and I didn't have any idea how bad it would be." He rubbed his eyes hard. "Because of me, one of my students became a statistic in the study of hurricanes."

"I had no idea, Osborn. None at all. I'm not sure what to say."

"Actually, I didn't come here to listen to you. I came so that you could listen to me."

"What do you mean?"

"David, I almost cashed it all in. I was willing to cast off my research, resign my teaching position, and go drive a truck. I couldn't look at my peers, knowing what they thought of me. But I didn't. I know how much this must weigh on you, but you must understand that not everyone is against you. I thought I was the butt of every joke told by my colleagues, until one came to see me. Dr. Julius Houston. He was the head of geophysics at the school. He stopped by my office, sat down, and said, 'Osborn, listen. We are people of science. We study, we research, we write what we learn. We're very good at those things, but like most people we are very poor at human relations. Nobody hates you. No one resents you. It could have happened to any one of us. Volcanologists lose people almost every year. That happens when you hang around volcanoes. Some sciences require risk. Yours is one of them. Now leave yourself alone and get back to work.'

"He was right," Osborn continued. "And I did just that. I sought out counseling to help me deal with the emotions, and I dedicated my life to the study of catastrophe. But this time I understood the human element."

"I'm glad Dr. Houston was there for you," David said.

"I'm trying to do the same for you. I'm

not good at these things. Physics, math, I'm good at. This kind of thing is beyond my understanding. But I do know this. I almost ruined my life by letting things happen *to* me rather than making things happen *for* me."

Osborn's last statement splashed on David like cold water. It was simple, but keenly insightful. *Is that what I'm doing?* David asked himself. *Am I just letting things happen?* He had not been completely passive, but he had not been as proactive as he could be.

"Thanks, Osborn," David said sincerely. "That means a lot to me, and it also makes great sense."

"Well," Osborn said standing to his feet. "I have a storm to monitor. I hope I wasn't butting in."

"Not at all," David replied as he too stood.

Osborn walked to the door, then turned back to David. "Those people in Bangladesh and India and Cuba need our help. I hope you can find a way to do that. They may speak different languages, but they are all Donnas who are dying much, much too soon."

"We'll find a way, Osborn. I promise you that we'll find a way."

Osborn flashed a small smile and left.

David sat down again and looked at his Bible. His eyes fell on another Beatitude.

Blessed are the merciful, for they will be shown mercy.

Then he read on: *Blessed are you when people insult you, persecute you and say falsely all kinds of evil against you because of me. Rejoice and be glad, because great is your reward in heaven, for in the same way they persecuted the prophets who were before you.*

Something happened deep inside David, at the place where the soul touches the heart, where the spirit touches the mind. He was no longer angry, no longer bitter. A change was happening, an alchemy of the spirit. What mattered was not revenge or even absolution, but the work to which God had called him.

Pictures of people he had never seen flashed in his mind — images of Bangladeshi, Indian, and Cuban families, each struggling for survival, wishing for the simplest basics of water, aspirin, and penicillin.

David turned the pictures over and took in their garish images. He was tired of waiting, weary of being passive. It was time to act. He had not chosen this battle, but he would not walk away from it. His commitment to fight back grew in intensity. There was more at stake here than his reputation, more than jail time. Lives hung in the balance, and his tormentors had tipped the scales. *Well,* David thought, *it's time to to them back.*

Rajiv watched as the red-tinted sun dropped behind the western horizon streaking a cloudless sky with pink. It was the first time in two days that he had bothered to notice the sun or sky, or even to think that his sunset was someone else's sunrise. He wondered about the "someone elses." Did they know of the rubble among which he now walked? Did they care about the decomposing corpses still buried in debris and mud? Would they send aid to battle the disease and starvation that was certain to come?

A male child, no more than five years old, sat on a mud-caked piece of lumber, sucking on dirty fingers. He stared emotionlessly across the devastated, alien-looking landscape. Rajiv realized that the boy sat in silence because the same wave that had destroyed his town with its incalculable weight of water had also destroyed the child's spirit. What the wave had done instantly to the buildings and homes of

Puri, it had done more slowly to the boy's mind. He was now numb, hungry, and patiently waiting for his parents to find him — parents who would never arrive.

A pair of Red Crescent workers struggled past him, carrying a stretcher on which lay the grotesque form of a dead woman. They too were weary, having worked nonstop for endless hours. *No one could be trained for this,* Rajiv thought. *Not this kind of pain, this kind of suffering.* He watched as the two workers, burdened by the load they carried in their hands and the one they carried in their hearts, walked by the boy with the dirty fingers in his mouth. He looked up at them expectantly, but they took no notice of him. Rajiv was sure that they had seen another child like him just a hundred meters away and would see yet another like him a hundred meters farther down.

Rajiv understood. For two days he had lain immobile in the yard of what had been his home, keeping close to him the only possessions that mattered: the tricycle of his missing daughter and the water-stained picture of his family. He had wept. He had cursed Allah. He had been smothered in depression. He had refused help. He had wished for death.

Slowly, however, reason and resolve melted their way back into his life. Now he could see the damage beyond his own home. Now he understood that many stood in an identical place to his. Rajiv began to walk.

At first he walked mindlessly, shutting out all that he saw, lost in his own grief and bitterness. But slowly he became aware of all the devastation that was around him. The destruction was incomprehensible. He fought the urge to seal himself off from reality, from pain. He forced himself to look, to see, to understand the wreckage of life and property.

He saw enough to scar the most insensitive of souls. But he continued to look, forcing himself to see what his mind did not want to see.

Rajiv continued his walk, his eyes down, his soul weighted by pain and sorrow. The boy who had looked up at the two Red Crescent workers looked up at him as he came close. Rajiv gazed down into the boy's deep brown eyes. He saw a hollowness there, an unfathomable emptiness.

There were too many boys like that one; too many little girls to help. He was just one man, a man whose life had been stripped from him in a violent act he had been forced to witness.

Too many lost little boys.

Too many helpless orphans.

Too many to help. Too much pain to ease. Too little resources to offer.

Rajiv walked on and thought of his family, of little Jaya, his lost little girl with the infectious giggle and the eyes that danced so beautifully when she laughed. He saw her, felt her, asleep on his lap as she did each night he was home. He could hear the simple, gentle serenade of her breathing, could see the rising and falling of her little chest.

The burning returned to Rajiv's soul, the conflagration of grief. He stopped walking. Tears, which he thought had been spent, once again poured from his eyes. He wished for death. He wanted to lie down on the ground and pray that it would swallow him whole.

But Rajiv did not collapse. Instead he turned and walked back to the silent little boy and took him in his arms.

Perhaps, he hoped to himself, *someone is holding my Jaya right now.*

The little boy wrapped his arms around Rajiv's neck, squeezed weakly, and then lay his head on his shoulder. He was instantly asleep.

Rajiv started walking again.

"Not to put too fine a point on it," Calvin said. "I think you're out of your mind."

"I knew you would feel that way," David said as he turned the wheel of the white BMW and directed the car north onto Interstate 5. "But I still think it needs to be done." He brought the car up to freeway speeds and then settled into the far right lane.

"I don't agree," Calvin said with agitation. "We should stay the course. Take each legal step as it comes our way. And," he added emphatically, "we need to get those electronic bugs out of your office and the conference room. If we had taken them out when the electronic sweep first discovered them, we wouldn't be having this conversation in a moving car. I don't know why you wanted them left there."

"Because it's our only contact with my tormentors," David said firmly. "Granted, the contact is only one way, but at least we could get a message to them if needed."

"And what would you say to them, David? 'Hey, guys, fun is fun, but it's time you stopped trying to destroy me and my

firm'? I'm sure they would respond immediately."

"You know what your problem is,
Calvin?"

"Yes, I attract crazy clients," he answered
harshly. "Mr. Barringston said you were a
bright man, quick on the uptake. At first I
agreed with him, but what you're sug-
gesting makes me rethink that."

"All right, maybe I am crazy. Maybe this
is insane, but your problem is that you
think too much like a lawyer."

"I *am* a lawyer."

"You were also a successful FBI agent.
What happened to that man? The one who
wanted to see the bad guys behind bars
and the good guys living their lives without
terrorism."

"He's dead."

"No, he's not," David countered quickly.
"He's sitting next to me. Calvin, this goes
beyond the normal criminal case. Many,
many lives are tethered to what happens to
Barringston Relief, and I can't allow this to
go on month after month. You know better
than I that this could take a year in trial or
more. I can't allow Barringston Relief's
assets to remain frozen much longer. It
would spell doom to a great many people."

"You're overreacting," Calvin said.

"Am I? Calvin, upward of thirty-five thousand people die each day of malnutrition, add to that those who are killed by controllable, treatable diseases, and the number skyrockets. Right now, as we sit in this car, the east coast of India is digging out from a tsunami. Worst hit was Bangladesh. Cuba has been devastated by a category-five hurricane. Havana has, by all early reports, been shredded. Who is going to their aid? Cuba, aside from a few alliances with Central American countries, stands alone in this. U.S. citizens are prohibited from conducting trade with Cuba. That includes medicines. As it is, we will have to send all our supplies through Mexico."

"I understand your feelings," Calvin said forcefully, "but as your attorney I must advise against this course of action. You can only hurt your case."

"Not if we can flush out my tormentors," David countered. "That video is too convincing. It's going to be introduced as undeniable evidence. Even I know that. What are we going to do? Plead no contest? Entrapment? If we don't prove — categorically prove — my innocence, Barringston Relief will cease to exist."

"I just want to keep you out of jail."

"Don't you see, Calvin? That is not enough. This isn't about me. It is about saving Barringston Relief and the people who depend on it for survival. Barringston Relief saves lives by being proactive, not merely reactive. It's time to take charge."

"I don't see this working, David. We don't know *who* is doing this. We don't *why* they're doing this. All we know is that they are resourceful and powerful. They've covered their tracks too well."

"What about the pictures?"

"That's another thing, Dr. O'Neal," Calvin said angrily. "You should have shown me that picture the moment you received it. Not the next day."

"OK, I agree that I shouldn't have kept that from you, but the whole thing caught me off guard — the boy, the picture, the news conference. I know now it was designed to shake me up, which it did." David paused to let the intensity of the conversation settle. "Will you send it off to the FBI labs?"

"Probably, but it won't do any good. You've been handling it, and whoever sent it is too clever to leave fingerprints or other evidence. The only fingerprints they found on the other photos were yours. That doesn't help our case."

"Will they be sending the originals back?" David asked. "All I have are the color copies we made."

"We shouldn't have done that either," Calvin admitted. "I hate releasing such things without a reference copy of my own."

"So we're not going to get much support from the FBI on this?"

Calvin laughed. "Let me explain something to you, David. Law enforcement agencies are not in the business of finding evidence of innocence. They're in the business of proving guilt. No agency, including the FBI, looks for evidence that will exonerate a person. They look only for evidence that will convict him. It took me a long time to realize that, and when I did, I discovered that I had sent an innocent woman to jail for ten years."

"So we're on our own."

"Largely, yes."

"That's why we have to take the initiative."

Calvin groaned. "This is crazy," he said more to himself than to David.

"Calvin," David began, his tone softer. "When you discovered that your investigation sent an innocent woman to prison, what did you do?"

"I made it my goal to prove her innocence."

"That's all I'm trying to do," David said. "Except I can't prove my innocence without first finding the true culprits. And the only way I can do that is to force their hand; make them break from their plan. You can understand that, can't you?"

Calvin said nothing. He looked out the side window at the passing scenery, but David doubted that he saw any of it. He was too deep in thought.

David and Calvin drove on in silence. They drove past San Diego Bay and on toward La Jolla. Minutes passed with agonizing slowness. Finally Calvin spoke. "All right, David, you win."

"You'll help?"

"As long as it stays within the confines of the law. If this goes bad, I don't want to be sharing a jail cell with you."

"I wouldn't have it any other way," David said with a small smile. It was a minor victory, but at least he was taking charge of his life. No longer would he be a passive victim; he would be an active participant.

13

Father Donovan removed his vestment and carefully hung it on the hanger in his spartan office. He was glad to be free of it. Although a light breeze had circulated through the cemetery, he now felt over-heated. It was not unusual for him to feel warm after a funeral mass and especially if there was also a graveside interment, but today he felt feverish.

The turnout at the mass for Beu Ribe had been generous. She had been a faithful member of the church all of her life and was beloved by the congregation. Her sudden death from dengue fever had sur-prised and wounded the church.

After leaving the hospital two days ago, the priest had returned to the church and said prayers for the saintly woman. He went back to visit her the next day. He arrived prepared to offer last rites. He found Beu incoherent, sweating pro-fusely, and in great pain. The doctors at the Barringston clinic offered her no hope.

Father Donovan performed last rites, took her hand, and watched her die.

Now the funeral was over, but the sadness and shock remained. The doctors had confirmed that Beu died of dengue hemorrhagic fever — a new, puzzling, and virulent strain. She had not been the first, and the doctors assured Father Donovan that she would not be the last.

He wondered about the disease and how it would affect his congregation. Surely there was something he could do. Already he planned to make an announcement to the congregation about the things they could do to control mosquitoes, but they had heard such things all of their lives. It was just a problem that tropical-living people faced.

Still, he wondered. Just how far will this go? Will the government become involved? There would also be a financial impact on his congregation if too many of the men became ill. How would he deal with those situations?

He felt tired and depressed.

He rubbed the small bite behind his right ear, and wondered what the future held for his congregation.

★ ★ ★

The drive from Cueva del Toro to Havana had been slow and tedious. Angelina's Papa had to watch very carefully as he drove the old automobile through washed-out, debris-laden streets. Once he had run over a board with a nail that flattened their tire. Angelina had watched in silence as her father changed it. He swore many times.

The car was crowded, and the humidity left behind by the storm was almost unbearable. Since Maria Marquez's house was destroyed, Papa had decided to bring Angelina's aunt's family with them. In the backseat were most of the Marquez clan. Two children shared the front seat with Angelina and her father. In the backseat children sat on the laps of their parents to make room. The car was crowded and hot, but no one complained. It was a small thing compared to what they had just been through.

Now Papa was very quiet. He said he was concentrating on the road, but Angelina knew that he was worried about her sister and their house. He wanted to get home as soon as possible, and that meant driving very slow. He had no spare tire to replace another flat. She could tell that the ordeal was eating at her papa.

"I see the city," Angelina said with excitement. "We are almost there."

"Almost, Puppet, almost," her father replied, his eyes fixed on the road ahead.

"I wish we could go faster."

"So do I, little one."

As they passed the outskirts of Havana's city limits, her father brought the car to a stop. His eyes were fixed out the driver's side window.

"Oh, no," he said morosely.

"What? What is it, Papa?" Angelina moved forward on the seat so that she could see. "Isn't that where you work?"

He answered with a nod. The building, a five-story glass-and-concrete structure, stood in skeletal silence. The windows on one entire side were missing, ripped from their places by a devilish wind. Papa swore some more. Angelina did not understand exactly what her father did at the Center for Agricultural Engineering, she did not even understand the name, but she knew that the water and wind could not have been good.

"Let's go," Papa said harshly. He sounded angry, but she knew that he was really afraid.

It took over an hour for the car to weave

through the destruction. Emergency workers scrambled about, some removing rubble, others aiding injured people. Buildings that had once stood tall and strong in the tropical sun now looked broken and beaten. Some houses had their roofs ripped away, just like the Marquez house. Commercial buildings were missing windows, and black tarpaper hung over their parapets. Pieces of wood, metal, and brick lay cast about. With no way to avoid the road hazards, the car lurched and bounced as it drove over them. Several times Papa had to stop to let firemen and policemen cross the cluttered street.

People, some with hastily bandaged injuries, wandered or stood in motionless disbelief at what the storm had done. They were as damaged emotionally as were the buildings physically. The corporate psyche of the people was as shattered as the glass that covered the ground, glinting in the cloud-shrouded sunlight. Nothing looked the same. The streets, houses, shops, and apartments were only vaguely familiar, landmarks of what once was.

Havana was wounded by the winds and rain that came only every few generations. Angelina took in the sight in silence. Each bit of debris represented the flotsam of a once-great city, now stripped and laid bare for all the world to see. She felt a profound sadness. The city's ruin was a violation of the security and comfort she had felt all her life. Angelina had survived the storm, but her innocence was a victim of the fierce power of nature.

Papa pushed on, his knuckles white as he held the steering wheel in a death grip.

"Two million people," he said aloud. Angelina turned to face him.

"What Papa?" she asked, confused.

"Over two million people live in this city." He shook his head. "In just two decades the city will be five hundred years old. Now look at it. I can only guess what the harbor looks like."

"It will heal," Maria said from the backseat. "We all will."

"Perhaps," Papa said, "perhaps."

They drove on with agonizing slowness. Angelina and her family lived in the newer area of the city, where structures had been built by subsidies of the former Soviet Union. The streets were wider and the buildings more impressive, though still damaged and marred.

Angelina held her breath as they rounded the corner that led to the street of their apartment. As they did, they passed the little church where her mother and she used to walk. All of its windows were in place; all of its tile still rested on its peaked roof.

"Look, Papa," Angelina cried with excitement. "The church is whole. It is strong. The storm could not hurt it."

Her father turned and looked at the small chapel. "It was sheltered by the taller buildings," he said without emotion. Angelina was not so sure.

"There it is," he said, nodding forward. "We're home." It took only moments for them to exit the car. Power lines, now dead, lay across the street. Branches and trees cluttered the sidewalk and road. "Careful," he said, stepping over broken tile. "Watch the children."

Water bled from the rooftops in trickles that cascaded from the opening that led to the courtyard. Angelina, holding fast to her father's hand, crossed under the archway and into the courtyard. Their apartment was the first one on the right. The window was broken, and the door was ajar.

"Wait here," Papa commanded.

"But, Papa —"

"Wait here, I said." Slowly he pushed open the door and went in. Angelina strained to look in the dark apartment.

Water from the floor above was pouring from the ceiling in a torrent.

"Papa, are they there?" Angelina cried.

Her father exited the apartment and shook his head. "The apartment is empty." His face was drawn with concern.

"Where are they?" Angelina asked near tears. "They should be here. Where are they?"

"I don't know, Puppet. I don't know."

Angelina lowered her head. "They should be here," she pined softly. "They should."

An ache, strange and familiar, filled her tiny heart. It was a new worry. Never had she imagined that the storm would take her sister. It was an old wound. She vividly recalled the day her mother died. She never wanted to feel that way again, never wanted to be singed by those hot pains and fears. Her bravery eroded like a saturated hillside ready to give way, and tears began to pool in her dark eyes. Juanita was gone. Her sister who teased her and laughed with her and scolded her for getting into her make-up and braided her hair and did her best to fill Mama's job after she died and —

"Father?"

It was a familiar voice. Angelina snapped her head in the direction of the sound.

"Father!" The words were excited, filled with joy.

Then Angelina saw her — Juanita. She was walking rapidly from the other end of the courtyard. Her obsidian hair, weighed down by water, lay flat against her head. She wore a light, flowered cotton dress that was soiled with mud. Behind her was Roberto, her fiancé.

"Juanita!" Angelina screamed as she ran for her sister, her father close behind. They met in the middle of the courtyard and embraced, arms intertwined. Angelina held her sister around the waist, and her father hugged them tightly, as if he feared that letting go would allow them to slip forever from his sight. He repeatedly kissed Juanita on the forehead.

A light rain began to fall from the remaining clouds. No one noticed. No one cared.

When the embrace ended, Angelina looked at her father. Rain dripped from his soggy hair; even more water poured from his eyes.

"We were at Mary Puntu's," Juanita said. "Part of her ceiling caved in and hit her on the head. It was just the plaster, but it cut her. I heard Angelina's voice and came out. I could not believe my eyes. I was afraid . . . afraid that . . ."

"We're all well," Papa said.

"I said we would be fine," Angelina said excitedly, tears of joy streaming down her face. "Didn't I say we would be fine, Papa?"

Her father laughed. "Yes you did, Puppet. Yes you did."

David watched dolefully as Calvin walked from the office and into the hall. He remained seated behind his desk, feeling weary, weak, and afraid. His stomach churned, and the muscles in his neck constricted into tight knots.

The die had been cast. They had acted out their part, their play. Calvin had sat in his chair and argued vehemently against David's proposal. It was a convincing portrayal, and David knew that Calvin had not been acting. He still opposed the idea. But that didn't matter now.

The conversation between the two men had lasted only twenty minutes. There had been plenty of give and take and emotion, and all of it had been transmitted by several listening devices they knew were in David's office.

Now there was nothing to do but wait. This was the hardest part.

David could script only his words and those of Calvin; he could not direct the actions of those who tormented him. He had no idea what form their response would take, but he was certain that they would react. He had to be ready.

His biggest fear was for the safety of Kristen and Timmy, but since they were confined to the upper floors of Barringston Tower, and since additional trained guards were patrolling the building, he felt that little danger could come their way.

He wondered again if he was wrong and Calvin right. Maybe this was reckless and inappropriate. Perhaps he should have waited for the investigation to be finished and then slugged it out in court. David shook his head. No, too many lives were at stake, and there was too little time.

When he had returned from his drive with Calvin where he had spelled out his plan, he found an update from Oz on his desk. Hurricane Claudia had devastated western Cuba. Havana, the country's capital, had been brought to its knees. Early estimates placed the dead at over five hundred and the property damage in the tens of billions. More would die from illness, contaminated water, and lack of food.

The word from the Bay of Bengal was no

better. Early on-scene estimates by the International Red Cross and its companion, the Red Crescent, the Indian and Bangladeshi governments, and Barringston Relief's own workers listed close to eighty thousand dead along the coast, an additional one hundred thousand missing, and innumerable injuries. Oz had tacked on a personal note: *David — double these figures.*

And Barringston Relief could do nothing about it. They were able only to send reserve supplies held in Central America and Mexico to Cuba, and from the inland areas of India to Bangladesh. Those supplies would be exhausted in less than two days. Barringston's funds had to be released, and the sooner the better. Each day that passed could be counted in lives lost.

David had done the right thing. There was nothing to do now but wait. And David hated waiting.

Jack swore to himself as he hung up the phone. He had not expected this. The question now facing him was how to tell his boss what his operative had just told him. The operative had been monitoring and recording the listening devices in O'Neal's office and conference room. They had been unable to bug his apartment, but had successfully set up a phone tap. O'Neal was the most monitored man in San Diego.

Perhaps, he thought, *I should wait until the tape gets here. That way she can hear the recorded conversation herself.* It took only a moment for him to change his mind. If he did that, she would question his delay. No, it was best to tell her immediately and just deal with whatever emotions she decided to throw his way.

Jack rose from his desk chair and stepped into the hall. His office was on the same floor as his boss. Although smaller, it offered the same view of the Pacific Ocean. The plaque on the door read, JACK LABOHM, VICE PRESIDENT, but he was more than an administrator. Dr. Elaine Aberdene may be the most famous drug researcher in the Western world, but she got that way by skirting, bending, and at times breaking the law. It was his job to take care of those matters that might prove embarrassing to Aberdene Pharmaceuticals or its founder. It was a job he had held for eleven years and one at which he demonstrated great skill. He always had the right connection and knew people who owed him suitable favors. Aberdene never had reason to complain about his service, and he was going to make sure that she had no reason now.

He looked at his watch as he started down the wide, carpeted hall — 3:15. She would be in the lab. Aberdene had a personal laboratory in which she ran her own experiments. In addition to being the most beautiful woman he had ever known, she was also a brilliant scientist. She was also the most quick-tempered.

The laboratory separated his office from hers, so it took only a few steps for him to arrive at his destination. He paused at the door. Her image filled his mind as it did a hundred times a day and a thousand times each night. Her thick mahogany hair shining in the light, her brown eyes, and her supple lips. Well, he assumed they were supple. He had never touched them. Jack would marry her in a minute even if it meant a life of total servitude to her volcanic emotions and self-serving plans. She, however, had shown no interest in him or, to the best of his knowledge, anyone else.

Jack knocked on the door and entered. He found her just as he had expected — hunched over a microscope.

"What is it, Jack? I'm busy."

"My apologies, but I thought you would like to know as soon as possible. O'Neal is changing the game."

"Oh?" she said without looking up.

"He just had a heart-to-heart with his attorney. He's going to call our bluff."

"Call our bluff? Don't be obtuse, Jack. Get to the point. How is he going to call our bluff?"

"He says that he can prove that the video is a fake. He plans to use the photos we sent him as further evidence that he's being framed."

"Not likely," she replied calmly. Her placidity made Jack nervous.

"He also said he knows who it is that's framing him and that he plans to make it public soon."

Aberdene raised her head, then turned toward Jack. Her eyes narrowed. "How can that be? Everything is perfect. The video and pictures are free of any evidence that could incriminate us."

"Maybe he made the Belize connection," Jack offered.

"Don't be stupid. There's no way that he could have connected our work in Belize to his firm."

"I'm sure you're right, but how can we know that for sure?"

"What we did there was done nine years ago."

"But the whole reason we're doing this is Barringston Relief's research on the dengue hemorrhagic fever that is being conducted there."

"I know why we started this, Jack," she snapped. Picking up a thin pair of tweezers from the worktable, she turned back to the microscope and picked up a small insect from the slide. It was immobile. Jack had seen Aberdene anesthetize the insects with a small amount of ether before. "This is why we're framing O'Neal," she said. "This mosquito and millions like it are making us rich, Jack. O'Neal can ruin that if he can connect the new DHF to us. It's not likely, but if our clients get wind that that's even a remote possibility, we could lose them. I've worked too long on this to let it slip away." She walked over to an aquarium-shaped container, opened a small port, and dropped the insect in.

"I'm aware of that," Jack said.

"Arbovirology, Jack. That's the future of medicine and warfare. Do you remember what I taught you about arboviruses?"

Jack nodded nervously. "Uh, yes. Arbovirus is short for arthropod-borne virus. A mosquito is an arthropod."

"Very good, Jack," Aberdene said. She leaned over and put her face close to the glass container. "There are five hundred mosquitoes in here, Jack, give or take a bug or two. Each one carries a virus — a virus I engineered. That makes them special. There are no others like them in all the world."

"Except Belize."

Aberdene stiffened, stood erect, and turned her attention to Jack. "Except Belize," she agreed. "Accidents happen. That virus was designed to respond to a special antiviral. It mutated. That happens a lot in the world of microbiology. It's not all that unusual to get one to two thousand mutations per million viruses per site per year. That's not a lot, but when you're dealing with millions of viruses that become billions of viruses . . . well, let's just say it adds up. Belize got away from me. That's all."

"But you do have a cure," Jack said. "Couldn't we just provide that? Aberdene Pharmaceuticals would be heralded as the lifesaving corporation, and you would win more awards. You'd become even more famous."

"No," she replied quickly. "Scientists are a curious bunch. That's why they're scientists. Sooner or later some nosy researcher or clever graduate student would start asking how it is that we came up with a cure so soon after a specialized, never-before-seen strain of DHF virus appeared. Too risky. Besides, I don't care about the awards or the fame. I care about the work and the money."

"Someone may find out all that anyway," Jack said.

"Not likely. Right now the only people close to doing that are Barringston Relief doctors in Belize. That's why David O'Neal and Barringston Relief must be discredited."

"If what he says is true, then he might be ready to blow the cover off all of this."

"So we step things up."

"Step things up?" Jack thought for a moment. "I suppose we could release the new video earlier than planned, but we won't get the full publicity value out of it if it comes in on the coattails of the first video."

"Forget the new video."

"Forget the video?"

"That's what I said." Aberdene went back to her stool and sat down.

"I'm afraid I don't understand," Jack replied. "We've worked so hard to fabricate that footage that it seems a waste —"

"Come on, think, Jack. We can't be concerned about cost and time. I don't think they can prove it's a fake, but suppose they can. Suppose that whiny little Archer Matthews made a mistake or even planted a clue, then we could be in real trouble. We lose everything. The people who want these mosquitoes would be more than a little upset. In fact, we could find ourselves floating facedown somewhere."

"I thought you said the U.S. military wanted the virus."

"They do, and so do a few other countries. Military is military. Just think of the advantage an army would have if it had only to fight soldiers who were stricken with DHF: Mosquitoes are the perfect weapon. Release them from a plane or plant them in some country near military institutions. They reproduce very quickly, and my little guys live far longer than the normal sixty-five days of the typical mosquito. My little friends are insecticide resistant. Nature provided that for me; I just encouraged it."

"If we're not going to use the video, what are we going to do?"

"Release the hounds, Jack. Release the hounds."

Jack rubbed his chin. This was the backup plan. It was the reason Aldo

Goldoni had been hired. "I understand. I'll get in contact with Aldo as soon as possible."

"Sooner," Aberdene said firmly. She stood and crossed the floor to where Jack was standing. She was the same height as he. She looked deeply into his eyes. A smile slowly crossed her face. "I've always liked you, Jack. You know that."

He could smell the sweetness of her hair and skin. Her lips parted seductively. Jack felt electrified. His skin tingled with excitement.

"You've been the best possible employee," she said softly. "I never would have made it this far without you. And I know that I can be difficult to work for. I'm just a little strong willed and opinionated, that's all." Her smile widened, revealing brilliant white teeth. She raised a hand and stroked his cheek. He felt flushed, dizzy over the attention he had desired for so long.

He was about to speak words of his love and admiration when she touched his lips with one beautifully manicured finger. "Shh," she mewed. Leaning forward she kissed him on the forehead.

She does know, Jack thought. *She does know of my feelings for her.*

"And Jack," she said, her voice silky with whisper.

"Yes."

"If this goes bad, you're mosquito bait. Understand?"

Impulsively Jack took a step back. Aberdene raised an eyebrow. She had been playing with him.

"I understand completely," he said tersely. "I'll make sure it's taken care of immediately."

"See that you do," she commanded. "Now leave me alone. I have work to do."

Without another word, Jack turned and stormed from the laboratory. As he closed the door, he was sure he heard her laugh.

"Thanks," David said, distracted by the file folder he held in his hand. He took the cup of Earl Grey tea from Kristen and set it on the coffee table in front of the sofa. She sat next to him.

"It's that bad, huh?" Kristen sipped her flavored herb tea.

"Huh?" David looked up from the folder and eyed her with confusion.

"Something's bothering you. Not that you don't have enough to think about."

David chortled. "Kristen the Amazing, mind reader to the stars."

She smiled. "More like absent-minded reader. The truth is, you narrow your eyes when you read bad news. Personally, I think it's endearing."

"You know me that well?" he asked playfully.

"I know all about you, Dr. David O'Neal. It's a power women in love possess. We women know the thoughts of our men, no matter where in the world they are."

"That explains why so many men are in trouble."

"Exactly."

David smiled, leaned back on the couch, and put his arm around her. He drew her close to him. The casual embrace felt good. Kristen fit David. Each time they would hug, he was amazed at just how right she felt. It was as if they had been designed to match, like pieces in a jigsaw puzzle. Each time he was forced to spend a day without seeing her was a day he felt incomplete. "I'm glad you could join me for dinner. Sorry you had to cook it."

"I thought that was a clever ploy on your part," Kristen said. "Invite me up to your place for dinner and have me slave over a hot stove." She laid her head on his shoulder.

"It could have been worse. I could have

played chef, but you would have been duty bound to eat it."

"So my cooking was really self-defense?"

"Any court of law would see it as such." David leaned over and gently kissed her on the lips. It was not a sensual kiss filled with passion, but an expression of profound love. "I've missed you these last few days."

"I've seen you every day of the last week."

"Only in passing or when others were present. What I miss is just being with you. The two of us alone, basking in each other's presence."

"We're alone together now," she said softly. "Timmy is in your room watching television or, should I say, sleeping through television. He's fast asleep on your bed."

"This hasn't been easy on him," David said wearily. "He's sensitive. My arrest frightened him a great deal."

"He's afraid that he is going to lose you. I have the same fear."

David held her tighter. "That's not going to happen. Not if I can do anything about it." David felt his resolve tighten within him like a well-wound watch spring. He had spent the afternoon and much of the evening wondering whether to tell Kristen of the latest photo and his plan to flush out his tormentors. The mental picture of him handing the fabricated photo to her and watching as she took in the image of her car in flames with her still behind the wheel had made his decision for him. He saw no reason to inflict such pain on her. He felt enough fear for them both.

There was a silence of words between them, but not an absence of communication. With Kristen nestled under his arm, her warmth pressed against him, they shared thoughts and emotions that were beyond the powers of language. The bond between them grew with each gentle breath taken, with each blink of a moist eye. Second after second ticked by with neither noticing their passing. Enveloped in a cocoon of love, time held no meaning.

"Do you remember the first time we did anything together?" David asked.

"Our first date?" Kristen said.

"No, before we were dating. It was soon after A.J. hired me."

Kristen nodded. "Coffee. Horton Plaza. We had cappuccinos."

"I had a turkey on rye with an iced cappuccino and you — oh, forgetful one — had a blueberry muffin and a mocha. I thought it was the woman's job to chronicle all those details."

"That's what we want you to think. What about that day?"

"I wish we could go there right now," David answered. "I wish we could sit in the summer evening drinking tall lattes and watching the window shoppers stroll the outdoor mall."

"Why don't we?" Kristen asked. "I've been cooped up in this building for too long. I could use some outside time."

"You know we can't do that," David said sourly. "It's not safe. Every time someone walked by, I would wonder if he was one of them."

"Or she," Kristen corrected.

"Or she," David agreed. "I would be constantly wondering if that person over there was taking pictures of me, or if the woman over there had a gun. I'm becoming paranoid."

"Paranoia is an irrational fear. You have a real reason to be afraid."

"That's just it, Kristen, I'm not afraid for myself. I haven't given that a moment's thought. All my fears are for you, Timmy, and Barringston Relief. My mind is constantly filled with pictures of something going wrong. Of Barringston being forced to go out of existence or of . . . of something happening to you."

"Nothing is going to happen to me," Kristen said, sitting up straight so that she could turn to face David. "Everything is going to be fine."

"How do you know that?" David said. "There are so many variables and so little time before the asset freeze begins to affect our work overseas."

"Faith, David. We are a people of faith. You know better than I do that it is our faith in our Lord that keeps us going in bad times."

"I don't want to be the spiritual wet blanket here, but bad things do happen to good people."

"True," Kristen agreed, "but not to us. Not this time."

"You don't know that."

"Actually I do, I just don't know how I know it."

"Gut feeling?"

"Spirit feeling," she corrected. "That's more tangible than some innocuous gut feeling. I'm not saying that I'm not concerned. Just the opposite. But I have an overall peace that we'll be able to do whatever we need to do."

"You're a remarkable woman."

"Not really. This peace is recent, just

today. When I first saw that video —" she broke off. "I don't think I've ever been so angry or so hurt. I wanted to lash out at anything that moved."

"Kristen —"

"I know it's not you in the video, but I didn't at first. In some ways I'm thankful that I saw it."

"Thankful?" David was puzzled.

"I know it sounds odd, even ridiculous, but the emotions that surfaced showed me how much I've come to love you. The sight of you — the video you — with that other woman infuriated me. It also wounded me deeply. That wouldn't have happened if I weren't in love with you. Now I know just how hard I've fallen."

David took her in his arms and kissed her. He held her tight. "There is no doubt in my mind that you love me, and there should be no doubt in yours that I love you. That's why we must be careful. We must keep you safe."

"That's one of the things that puzzles me," Kristen said, leaning back in the sofa again. "Why threaten Timmy and me?"

"To influence me, of course." David took his cup of tea and stood. He paced in front of the couch. "They want me to confess to something I didn't do. Clearly I pose some kind of a threat."

"Do you?"

"What else could it be?"

"Maybe it's not you that poses the threat. Maybe it's Barringston Relief, and as the chief executive officer of the organization you are the obvious target."

David thought for a moment. "What kind of threat would prompt such an elaborate ruse? Who could be harmed by our activities? We've had our share of run-ins with rebel groups in Africa and Central America, but I doubt that any of them would attempt this."

"I agree, but we can't rule them out."

"We can't rule anyone out," David agreed.

"Still, none of it makes sense, does it? I keep coming back to one question: What do they want? They haven't attempted to extort money, have they?"

"No," David answered.

"Barringston Relief deals with a great deal of money. Why haven't they asked for any? Because they don't need it. This isn't about extortion. So what is it about?"

David thought for a moment. "It's about controlling my actions. It's about painting me and Barringston Relief in the worst possible light. But I'm not sure what that tells us."

"Stay with me on this," Kristen said. "If we can figure out what they don't want, we might get closer to what they do want."

"Reverse logic?"

"Exactly." Kristen picked up her cup of herb tea and took a tentative sip. "We know that they don't want money. We know that they don't want any of our stored goods or research. If they did, they would have demanded it by now. Nor have they asked for any political changes. You know, get out of Rwanda or North Korea or something like that."

"They haven't asked for anything at all," David said.

"So what does it mean when you have nothing they want? My guess is that you have something that they don't want you to have."

"I don't know what that would be," David said, confused. "I'm not aware of anything that I've taken from anyone."

"What if they're afraid that you will take something? Or find something?"

"Like what?"

"I don't know," Kristen answered quickly. "That's the rub, isn't it? It must have been something in the last sixteen months, since you took over Barringston Relief. Probably more recent than that. What have you been working on?"

"You're the PR head; you know all that."

"We're brainstorming here, David. It doesn't matter what I know. What matters is talking about it. Maybe we'll stumble over something."

"OK," David acquiesced. He set his cup down and took his seat next to Kristen. "I haven't done anything spectacular. Mostly I've been learning the ropes of the organization and traveling."

"Have you made any changes in the day-to-day operations of Barringston Relief?"

David shook his head. "You mean like the banks we use, that sort of thing?"

"Anything like that."

"No. We use the same banks, same shipping companies, same airlines. Nothing has changed except the addition of the RRT. But I don't see how the rapid response team would be a threat to anyone."

"I don't either. What about your travels?"

"I've been to many places over the last year," David said. "Rwanda, Republic of Congo, Burundi, Sudan, North Korea, Madagascar, Belize, and a half-dozen inner cities. All of those trips were to meet with our workers."

"OK," Kristen said. "Is there anything unique about those countries? Anything that makes them stand out?"

"They're all unique," David complained. "Rwanda is on the verge of another bloodbath, as is Burundi. Sudan is abysmally poor. Same goes for Madagascar. North Korea is besieged by flood-caused famine. Do you suppose that's it? That someone is after Barringston Relief because of the work we do in North Korea?"

"Possibly," Kristen answered. "There are some pretty narrow-thinking people out there who can't see the pain for the politics. They may see our aid to North Korea as support for the Communist regime. Let's keep that one on our list."

"I don't know, Kristen. The Cold War has been over for years. I don't think anyone in this country sees North Korea as a threat."

"South Koreans might."

"That's true."

"What about Belize?"

"That one is a puzzle," David said sadly. "The report I was reading a few minutes ago is about Belize. There's a new strain of dengue hemorrhagic fever. It's growing into an epidemic. It's affecting all age groups but especially children. Even a priest in the area contracted the disease. The report said he died. As if that wasn't enough, one of our doctors has it. Her prognosis is not very good."

"Should we fly him home?"

"She, not he. No, the report said that she's being treated there. There's also a danger in spreading the disease to the United States."

"That's sad," Kristen said. "Does she have family?"

"Yes, and they're there with her. She was . . . is our lead researcher. She was making progress too. She had isolated the virus. She also discovered that the carrier was a special mosquito."

"Special?"

"I'm not sure what to call it," David said. "It seems to be a mutated form. It's resistant to pesticides and lives longer than the typical mosquito. This is going to require that we act fast. If we could act fast, that is."

David's face clouded over with anger. "I don't know who is doing this, but they're not just hurting me and Barringston Relief, they're killing innocent people abroad — in Belize and North Korea and Africa."

"Maybe that's what they're after," Kristen said. "Maybe it's hatred for the work we do that motivates them."

"How could they rationalize that?"

"How did Hitler rationalize the pogrom he led against the Jews? How is it millions of people can tolerate the cessation of unborn life and consider it a constitutional right? Every time the U.N. or the U.S. steps into another country to help a defenseless population like the Kurds, or the children of Bosnia, critics crawl out of every corner. How is it that U.S. citizens can arm themselves against their own government? People will believe anything and become anything to follow a cause."

"You're saying that someone is doing this to us because they hate some racial or political group?"

"It's possible," Kristen said.

"Possible, but not likely," David answered. "Groups like that are just as interested in making a name for themselves as they are in inflicting harm on someone else. And as you said, there are no demands. Whoever is doing this is not trying to get us to back away from some area like North Korea. They're attempting to put us out of business for good."

"That seems true enough," Kristen

admitted. "But we still need a *why*. If we had a why, we might be able to come up with a *who*.

"Let's go back to Belize for a moment," Kristen said. "You said that there's a new mosquito that is carrying this virus. Is that right?"

"*Mutated* is the word in the report," David answered. "It's basically the same mosquito that lives in the area, but it lives longer and is resistant to pesticides."

"But you also said the dengue virus is different too."

"That's right. It's more aggressive and more lethal than normal DHF. Apparently it mutated too."

"A mutated mosquito *and* a mutated virus in the same area?" Kristen's voice was laced with suspicion. "That seems odd, doesn't it?"

"I'm no biologist, Kristen. That's far from my specialty." David thought for a moment. "It does seem unusual though."

"Is there someone we can ask?"

"Most of the research teams have gone home. I suppose I could place a few calls."

"What about Oz? I know he's been staying in the building monitoring the storm. Do you think he might know?"

"His training is in the physical sciences, but he might."

David walked over to the phone and placed a call. He found Osborn at his desk. David invited him up for leftovers and a serious conversation. Ten minutes later, Osborn Scott was seated in a recliner next to the couch, a plate of leftover pork chops and mashed potatoes on his lap.

"Well," Osborn said between bites. "Entomology is not my specialty, but I do know something about mosquitoes. One doesn't study catastrophes for long without realizing that the disaster isn't over simply because the wind stops blowing or the earth stops shaking. Many more deaths occur after the event. In the case of earthquakes, deaths occur from aftershocks, fires, and damaged buildings. With hurricanes and flooding, there is also a problem with disease, especially in tropical areas. Large amounts of standing water are left and often overlooked by beleaguered officials. It's hard to worry about insects when there is so much death and destruction around."

He took another bite of his dinner and then continued. "I made a study of post-catastrophic complications in urban and rural settings. It was an interesting study, but frightening."

"How so?" Kristen asked.

"Living in the United States as we do, with all of our technology and easy access to medical help, we forget that many countries are still struggling to help their citizens. They are not equipped to spray insecticide over large areas to prevent the rise of mosquitoes or to treat cholera or to purify sufficient amounts of water. Such provisions are out of their reach.

"Take Cuba, for example," Osborn continued. "The same hurricane that is blasting New Orleans as we sit here now has devastated Havana. Which city do you think will recover more quickly?"

"New Orleans," David answered.

"Right," Osborn said, setting his plate down on the coffee table. "Why? It isn't because Cuba is backward. They have some excellent scientists and doctors. But because of trade restrictions against them, they are undersupplied medically. New Orleans has the entire U.S. government to support it."

"I want you to read something." David handed the report folder to Osborn, who took it and glanced through the pages.

"Interesting," Osborn said distractedly. "Insecticide-resistant mosquitoes and a variation of the dengue virus. Raises questions, doesn't it?"

"It did with us," Kristen answered. "Do mosquitoes and viruses mutate?"

"Oh, yes," Osborn said. "Mutations are normal in nature and in the laboratory. Of course, less than 1 percent are useful to the species. Most are harmful, even deadly."

"I don't follow," Kristen said.

"When I was in college," Osborn explained, "I took a class in genetics. I was required to take some life science classes even though I was a physical science major. As part of the class work, we were required to raise *Drosophila melanogaster.*

"What's that?" Kristen said with a grimace.

"Fruit flies," Osborn answered with a grin. "Sometimes called a vinegar fly. They're used in genetic research because they have a ten-day life cycle, which makes it easy to see results. It's easy to purchase mutated flies from several sources. By breeding nonmutated flies with those that have been altered by radiation, the student can actually see genetics at work.

"Anyway," he continued, "we were given white-eyed flies. Normal fruit flies have ruby red eyes. The white-eyed fly is a mutation. It's also blind. That's the way it is with mutations; they almost always harm the creature."

"So it is impossible for a mosquito to mutate and become stronger?" David asked.

"Not at all," Osborn replied quickly. "I said that mutations were almost always harmful. Insects are adaptive. It seems the more insecticides we use, the stronger the insects become."

"What about viruses?" Kristen asked seriously. "Do they mutate?"

"Absolutely," Osborn replied. "Viruses are, by comparison to other biological things, very simple. They're little more than DNA wrapped in protein. They mutate all the time, as do bacteria. That's why every few years there's a new flu bug out."

"So it's not unusual to see a new virus and a new mosquito in Belize?" David was feeling frustrated. He had hoped that they had found a connection. Something to go on, something to peruse.

"Now there's the catch," Osborn said. "If we were only talking about a heartier mosquito or a new virus, I wouldn't give it a second thought, but both appearing at the same time, well, it's not impossible, but it is unlikely."

"How unlikely?" Kristen asked.

"I couldn't say. That's a question for an entomologist and a microbiologist."

David thought for a moment. There was something here, but he couldn't put his finger on it. He felt as if he were attempting to catch a shadow.

"Let me ask this," David began. "You said that the fruit flies you used in college were artificially mutated. Is it possible to do that with mosquitoes?"

"I don't see why not," Osborn answered. "But I don't know why anyone would want to. The mosquito lives six times longer than the fruit fly. It would make genetic research too time-consuming."

"But what if there was another reason?" David asked.

"Like what?"

"I don't know," David answered. "But assume that someone wanted mosquitoes to live longer and be resistant to pesticide. Could that be done?"

"Again," Osborn said, "that's not my field, but I imagine that it could be done."

"And the virus?" Kristen asked.

"Possible," Osborn said. "Does this have to do with the trouble you're in, David?"

"It may, but I don't know. Right now I'm grasping at straws. Is there any way we can find out if someone is doing research on mosquitoes?"

"I could make some calls," Osborn said. "Surely there are scientists working with mosquitoes. There may be scores of them."

"Find out what you can," David said. "Maybe there is a tie to Belize."

"It's the least I can do for the man who shared his pork chops with me."

"Kristen cooked them," David said. "She's a woman of great talent."

"No doubt," Osborn said.

David's tone turned serious again. "Keep this under wraps, Oz. Go ahead and ask around, but be careful how you phrase your questions."

"I understand," Osborn said. "I just hope it will help."

"Me too, Oz. Me too."

14

Aldo Goldoni was a man of custom and routine. He rose from bed at 5:45 every morning, regardless of the time he went to sleep. He jogged three miles every day but Sunday. He read a minimum of one newspaper each day and three newsmagazines each week. He seldom watched television. Instead, he chose to read. Three books a week was his average. He preferred the classics.

He was also a man of idiosyncrasy. He exercised one hour and fifteen minutes each morning, not a minute more and not a minute less. He maintained a weight of 152 pounds of trim but not bulging muscle. He washed his hands and face every two hours. His food consisted mostly of vegetables, rice, and beans with only the occasional chicken breast for protein.

Goldoni was a man who was in love with himself, and that love was so deep, so compelling, so powerful that he could love no one else. Not his mother who watched over him for the fifteen years after his cocaine-captive father deserted the two of them. He was only five years old at the time. It wasn't that she was a bad mother, just incompetent. She knew nothing of boys and less of men. Over the years Aldo had come to understand that all men appeared stable and loving to his mother, when in fact none of them were capable of such legitimate behavior. The beatings that he and his mother took at the hands of the men she brought home from the dance bar where she worked had repeatedly proved that point to him.

He was a skinny, timid sixteen-year-old when the most formative event of his life occurred. He had walked home from school as he did every day, his textbooks and at least two books from the library under his arm. His mind was elsewhere as it usually was, lost in the stories of fiction or the past lives of others forever recorded in biographies. He took only mild notice of the strange car parked at the curb. There was always a strange car.

As he approached the front door he heard loud voices. But then he always heard loud voices. Boisterousness was the natural product of booze and drugs. It didn't matter to Aldo. He would walk through the door as he always did, go straight to his room as he always did, and lose himself in his books as he always did. He would avoid eye contact with his mother, maybe offering an unfeeling "Hi," but nothing more. No hugs, no kisses, no "How was your day?" He would also avoid the man, whoever it might be this time.

That day, however, had been different.

No sooner had Aldo closed the door behind him than he noticed piercing voices. The cacophonous tumult he heard was not alcohol-saturated revelry. He heard hatred and fear locked in battle. There was no laughter, just cries of pain that were nearly drowned out by vicious, obnoxious, poisonous words.

Aldo had never come to fully understand why he did what he did that day. Perhaps it was because he had just grown tired of his life or because that week he had received at school two beatings by boys twice his size. Perhaps it was just time to make a change, to seize control of his life.

That day had been his epiphany, his birth, his awakening. That was the day his universe found order and his life found meaning. That day he learned that being a victim was a choice he no longer wished to make.

Dropping his books to the floor, Aldo walked from the small entryway down the hall to his mother's bedroom. That is where he found her; that is where he found him. She was on the bed, her dress torn and her nose bleeding. A look of abject fear was draped across her face, the terror that death was just a blow away.

Standing above her was a monstrously large, ugly man with a pockmarked face. A sneer, the hybrid child of a grin and a snarl, was etched in his face. His shirt was unbuttoned, his trousers unsnapped.

The room was a shambles, the broken remains from a tornado of physical conflict. His mother's makeup, perfume bottles, and pictures that she kept on the dresser were scattered about. The floor was riddled with sharp shards of glass from the shattered mirror that hung over the dresser.

Aldo looked at his mother. Her arms were bruised and bloody. It was clear that her attacker had thrown her into the dresser and then onto the bed.

"What do you want, boy?" the man shouted demonically, gutturally. "Are you a hero or something?"

A peace settled on Aldo. A pleasant, unexpected peace. He felt no fear. He was untouched by apprehension. He smiled.

"Are you crazy or somethin'?" the hippo of a man spat.

It all had become clear to Aldo. At that moment he knew who he was, what he would be. Slowly he squatted to the floor and picked up an unbroken bottle of the cheap perfume his mother always wore.

The man turned toward Aldo.

Without a word, with a casual economy of motion, Aldo opened the bottle and raised it to his nose. It was sickeningly sweet with a hint of pungency, the latter a result of the alcohol base.

"Ahh," the ugly man sneered, "did I knock your precious little perfume bottle on the floor?"

Aldo looked at the man and cocked his head to the side. "You know, mister," Aldo had said, "the problem with stupid people is that they're always the last to know just how stupid they are."

"You little —"

"It's also true for ugly people. It's about time you knew that."

The man's eyes widened and his jaw clamped shut as if to dam up the fury inside. Grabbing the loose end of his belt, the man pulled it free of his pants, grasped the metal buckle, and slowly began to wrap the leather band around his hand. "I'm gonna make you wish you never saw me."

Aldo laughed. "Just seeing you was enough to do that."

The man raised his leather-clad fist and charged Aldo, screaming each step of the way. Aldo didn't budge. Instead, with a quick motion, he threw perfume in his assailant's eyes. There was another scream, this one of unbridled agony as the alcohol-based perfume permeated the tender tissue. The man crumpled to his knees.

Casually, Aldo removed a drawer from the dresser, emptied its contents of sweaters on the floor, and then swung it as hard as he could. It struck the cursing man in the side of the head. The screaming stopped as the obese assailant fell first to his side, then limply rolled to his back. A trickle of blood oozed from his right ear.

"Aldo!" his mother cried in shock.

Aldo crossed to the man, straddled his limp form, and then dropped his full weight on his chest. A rush of air raced from the man's lungs, accompanied by the cracking of bone. Aldo raised a fist and brought it down on the fleshy face of the man. He hit him again. And again. It felt good, liberating, invigorating.

He hit the man for his mother. He hit him for himself. He hit him for each time he had been teased and tormented at school, for each time he had taken a beating for being smaller than the other kids. He hit the man because Aldo's father had deserted them. He struck him for each man his mother had brought home over the years. He pummeled him for every night he had cried himself to sleep.

When it was over, the man who dared attack his mother and insult him lay motionless on the floor. Dead.

The courts were gracious, taking into account his legal standing as a minor and the fact that he had never been in trouble before. The court-appointed defense attorney had reminded the jury on several occasions that Aldo had done a brave thing in coming to the defense of his mother. He may have carried that defense too far, but in the heat and confusion of the moment, who can tell when the threat had passed?

Aldo was found guilty of manslaughter. The court sentenced him to five years in the juvenile detention system in the hopes of rehabilitating him. Aldo showed no emotion, no regret, no remorse, no sense of loss. Somehow, in a fashion yet unknown to him, Aldo had killed not only his mother's attacker, but he had murdered his own soul.

The state provided for his education while he was incarcerated. He proved an excellent student, able to grasp difficult concepts without effort. He excelled in chemistry and literature, but he learned more than the basics during his days behind the tall, chain-link fence. He learned how to pick a lock, turn off an alarm, build a small bomb, steal a car, and fence stolen goods. When he was released from his captivity, he left with far more knowledge than he had learned in the classroom.

He had also established a persona as a loner. The leader of a gang of inmates had attempted to show his dominance by making Aldo cower before the others. Aldo played the part for the moment. Two weeks later, the gang leader was found dead in the exercise yard, a strand of barbed wire encircling his neck. Aldo was never bothered again.

Aldo did not alienate everyone. Those inmates who had fathers entrenched in crime circles were courted. After all, Aldo would need work when he was released.

And his line of work was in demand.

One didn't need a business degree to know that the first rule of marketing was image. Aldo made a name for himself by identifying the most infamous hit man in the business and killing him. Aldo was never out of work after that.

Now Aldo had been freed to do the work for which he had so assiduously trained himself. It was time to review his plans, but unlike others who made notes or even used a computer to keep track of details, Aldo used only his mind. With a near perfect photographic memory, he began to recall the plans of the Barringston Tower. They had been easy to obtain. All it took was a small bribe to a small-minded government employee with a big drug problem.

Stripped of all his clothing, Aldo sat in the middle of his hotel bed, legs crossed in the lotus position, his hands resting on his knees. His eyes were closed. Had there been an observer present, he would have seen a man motionless, barely breathing. But inside Aldo's head, every page of the architectural plans were present.

He reviewed them. In his mind he ran up the floors in the stairwell, traveled the elevator system, walked the subterranean parking garages, and strolled the rooftops.

There were still unknowns. He didn't know what furnishings were in the offices except those he saw while disguised as a deliveryman. But those were the things that made his work interesting — that and the people. They were always unpredictable, but none had ever been a problem.

If he had a problem it was that he was too punctilious, too exacting. He never prepared just one plan; he prepared a set of them. For this job, he had formulated five approaches. They were all workable, all flawless, all creative, and all designed to do one thing: Kill Dr. David O'Neal.

"So why do you put up with it?" Archer asked. He was leaning back in his desk chair chewing on a red coffee stirrer. Behind him several television monitors cast a light tinted by the image they held — an image of David O'Neal.

"Put up with what?" Jack snapped back. He was seated in a nearby folding chair.

"With her and her games," Archer answered harshly. "She yanks your leash and you bark. It's pathetic really."

"Is it? What about you. I don't see you telling her off."

"I have a valid reason," Archer said. "She keeps me alive. She provides me with the only thing that may cure me. That's a pretty good reason, don't you think?"

Jack was quiet, morose.

"Let's see," Archer said, raising a finger to his chin and striking a scholarly pose. "If life doesn't motivate you, then love must. Is that it, Jack? Are you in love with the Mosquito Queen?"

"Mosquitoes don't have queens, you idiot," Jack snapped.

"It's a metaphor, Jack-man. A simple literary device. Still, I disagree. She *is* the queen bug. At least for those critters in her lab."

"Don't be disrespectful."

"Don't be disrespectful?" Archer laughed loudly. "Yup, it's love all right, and you got it bad."

"Shut up!"

"Why? You going to sick your mad-dog assassin on me? Have him kill me? I'm a dead man already, Jack. All that's left is the dying."

"Not if you don't do something stupid and mouth off to Aberdene."

"Oh, right. Do you think this is the end of it? What happens after your dog kills O'Neal? We're accessories, Jack. Heavy jail time. And do you really think that her majesty Aberdene is going to keep giving me the medication? Once this is done, my usefulness is over and she will cut me off."

"You don't know that."

"Don't be stupid, Jack. Of course I know it. And if you ever get in her way, she'll replace you and have dead flowers sent to your grave."

"She's not like that. She's a passionate researcher, a scientist who is willing to stretch the limits in order to find new cures to benefit mankind."

Archer guffawed. "Jack, you are in love, and love has turned your brain to mush. Benefit mankind?" Archer laughed uncontrollably.

"Shut up, you stupid computer jockey." He cursed and stood to his feet. "Don't make me —"

Archer sprang to his feet and stood face-to-face with Jack. "What?" he shouted. "Don't make you do what? Hit me? Beat me? Kill me? Look at me, Jack. I'm a sick man. I'm over the edge. I have had only a little sleep in the last week, and I've crossed the line. I no longer care, Jack. I no longer care. You wanna hit me? Then hit me. Go ahead. But don't expect me to just take it. I may be a skinny computer geek, but I'm a highly manic and motivated geek. Do you understand me? Am I getting through to your hazy, love-saturated brain?"

Jack took a step back, stunned by Archer's atypical outburst. "I didn't come here for all this. I came here to tell you the other video is out. Destroy it. And get rid of any other material you may have that could prove compromising. That includes whatever may be on your hard disk."

"That's a lot of work to be flushing, Jack. And once I do, there's no getting it back."

"That doesn't matter," Jack replied. Archer could hear the tension in Jack's voice. But there was more than mere tension. There was also apprehension and weariness.

"What's going on, Jack?" Archer asked firmly.

"Nothing you need or want to know about."

"She's sending him in, isn't she?"

"Who?"

"You know who — that killer."

"Just destroy the master tape and any copies you may have. I want the deck clean. Do you understand?"

"This is going too far, Jack. Way too far. It's out of control."

"Nothing is out of control. Just do as I say, and everything will be fine."

"Something must have happened to shake you up like this. A lot of time and money were put into that second tape. Aberdene wouldn't trash it unless she had to or no longer needed it. My guess is that it's the latter. What did O'Neal do?"

"Nothing."

"You're a liar," Archer spat.

Jack sighed heavily and rubbed his eyes. "This doesn't concern you. Just do as I say."

"It all concerns me, Jack." Archer was screaming, stabbing at the air with his thin index finger. "Haven't you been listening? We are accessories. Whatever happens now will just add to our guilt. I don't plan to die in jail, Jack. Maybe you're willing to pine away behind bars dreaming of your beautiful Aberdene, but I'm not."

Jack narrowed his eyes. "You will do exactly as I say, Archer. Exactly. You will not deviate from my instructions by as much as a millimeter, or you may find yourself the next in line after O'Neal. She can have you killed as easily as anyone else."

"There's got to be a way out of this, Jack. There must be some way we can be free."

"There's not. This is the hand life dealt

us. We will stay with it."

"Jack —"

"No! No more talk. No more discussion. No more speculation. Just destroy the tapes and electronic evidence. Burn this place down if you have to, but get rid of it."

"We've gone too far —"

Jack swore loudly, harshly. His face filled with red. Archer watched as he glanced around the room. His eyes fell on a glass paperweight. Seizing the heavy semi-spherical object, Jack swore again and hurled it like a baseball at the computer monitor that bore the image of David. Glass shattered, sparks erupted, and the monitor fell over onto the desk with an ear-pounding thud.

Archer cowered from the implosion and took two steps away from Jack. "Have you lost your mind?"

"Do what I say!" Jack began searching for something else to throw.

"OK, OK. You win." Archer continued to back away. "Just get a grip on yourself."

Jack stormed toward the door, then turned to face Archer. "I'll be back in two hours. I want everything taken care of by then. Got it?"

"Yeah, yeah, I got it."

"Make sure that you do, Archer. I have lost my last shred of patience with you."

"I'll take care of it."

Jack yanked open the door and charged through, slamming it hard behind him.

Archer stood in stunned silence and stared at the door. He wondered what he should do now. He knew whatever he did would come with a high price for someone, most likely himself.

With slow and gentle motions, David eased himself off the couch, taking care not to awaken Kristen, who had fallen asleep with her head on his lap. He slowly lowered her head onto a throw pillow, and she mumbled softly in her sleep.

Switching off the television, David turned and took in the lovely form of the woman who lay asleep on his sofa. Several strands of her red hair rested on her smooth cheek. David knew that beneath her closed eyelids were vibrant blue eyes that never failed to capture his attention. He watched as her thin frame moved rhythmically with each breath.

This was the woman he loved, and he was grateful to see her sleeping peacefully. He had been unable to bring himself to wake her. *Let her sleep*, he thought. *The couch is comfortable and, more important, close.*

David wished that he could keep her close always, but even more so now. Not a minute went by without the image of her in the pictures — one with the crosshairs of a rifle centered on her head, the other of her in a smashed and fiercely burning car. Those images were demons. They possessed his mind and stirred up fear and pain. That is what they had been designed to do. David wondered what kind of person could create such pictures. Clearly, a very unbalanced individual and a deadly one.

Despite the enhanced security he had ordered for Barringston Tower, he still feared for the safety of Kristen and Timmy. If something happened to them . . . He couldn't think about it.

It was all so unfair. He had done nothing to deserve this. All he had ever done was devote his life to God and to helping others. Why him? Why should he be singled out by some sadistic tormentor?

Those words brought a new image to his mind. Less than a week ago, Timmy had stood in David's office watching the video of the tsunami that had obliterated the coastal regions of Bangladesh and India. In his innocent, simple way, Timmy had asked the most profound of questions. A question that had plagued theologians and philosophers for millennia: Why do the innocent suffer?

Of course Timmy had asked it differently, more naively, but the question was the same. "Were they bad people?" Timmy had asked. David had assured him that they were not, but that had not appeased the young thinker. The next question had shaken David. "Why?" Timmy had asked. "Why did God let that happen?"

David had no answer then, and he didn't have one now. He knew the arguments for the existence of pain; he had read the books, but he still was without an answer that would satisfy either Timmy or himself. He could not explain the fairness of an undersea earthquake that created a record-breaking tsunami that inundated and killed tens of thousands of people.

They were not bad people. They were just people. People who loved and married and gave birth to a new generation. They felt pain, experienced joy, laughed aloud, wept in silence, had dreams, experienced fear. Their crime, their only crime, was living in the wrong place.

It wasn't fair, but it was life. It wasn't

fair that David was being terrorized and that the people whom he loved so dearly might be in danger. It wasn't fair that people he had never met, but whose life might be saved by Barringston Relief, would suffer and die because someone had a vendetta against him. It wasn't fair, but it too was life. And just like those poor souls in Cuba who had been bombarded by Hurricane Claudia and those around the Bay of Bengal, he would have to make the best of it.

Sitting and waiting for something to happen wasn't making the best of it.

David walked from the living area to the corner of the suite that overlooked the bay. The moon was high in the night sky. Lights from the downtown skyline flickered and winked like fireflies in a forest. A glass-topped work station complete with computer was next to the glass wall. David sat behind the computer and turned it on.

As he waited for it to finish its self-check and to automatically sign onto the network, he thought of Kristen asleep on the couch and Timmy, still sound asleep on David's bed. Somebody was using them as pawns in a horrible game. Someone had threatened their lives. David knew the threat was real.

They needed protection, and the only protection that David could think of involved his getting to the bottom of the matter. The police and FBI would be of no help; they were sure that he was the problem, not some mysterious person or persons. He was the target of their investigations, and they were dedicated to proving his guilt, not absolving him of a crime. He was alone in the matter. He could count on the support of a few people, but the weight fell on his shoulders.

There had to be a connection. Somehow and someway, David had become a threat. To whom, he did not know. His mind ran back to the discussion about the DHF virus and the new and improved mosquitoes. It was the only association he could imagine. He had been in Belize, and Barringston Relief was conducting research there. Could someone be threatened by that research? If so, who? Perhaps someone was responsible for the DHF outbreak and feared discovery. But again, who?

Raising his hands to the keyboard, David paused and wondered what his next step might be. Barringston Relief had one of the most complete databases in the country. From his terminal, David could access information on any country, see maps, search current events, watch special video reports, and more. It was almost too much information.

He typed in the word *Belize*. A moment later a color map of Central America appeared on the screen. He had seen all this before he had left on his trip. What made Belize special? It was a small country with just over two hundred thousand people. San Diego county was populated by ten times that many. It was a democracy with a decent life expectancy: sixty-six years for men, seventy years for women. The country was becoming a tourist attraction as more and more people discovered its cays, islands, and the world's second-largest barrier reef. In short, it was a pretty country but not an important one.

David's frustration expanded. "This is the wrong approach," he said softly. "I need more to go on." His eyes felt weary, gritty, but he had no desire to sleep. He felt like the solution was just out of reach. If he tried a little harder, worked a little longer, then he might make some headway. "Perhaps a shower and some fresh coffee would help," he said to himself.

Rising from his desk chair, he started for the kitchen and then stopped. He had caught sight of Kristen asleep on the couch. Turning back to the desk, he reached over to the phone and turned the ringer off. He didn't want anything to awaken her.

Greg listened impatiently as the phone at the other end of the connection rang. "Come on, Dr. O'Neal," he mumbled with frustration. "Pick up." He was excited about his new find and couldn't wait to share the news with David. It had taken some doing to get connected. First, he called Barringston Relief, but since the hour was late, he had been electronically transferred to the communications department. Only after insisting that it was vital that he speak to Dr. O'Neal did communications connect him directly to David O'Neal's suite number.

On the fourth ring there was an answer. "Hi, this is Dr. David O'Neal. I can't come to the phone right now . . ." Greg swore. He would have to leave a message.

The message machine beeped, indicating it was ready to record. "Dr. O'Neal," Greg said excitedly. "This is Greg Cheney. I'm at the video lab at San Diego State. I've found something important. I was going over the video and the copies of the photos you gave me. Remember how I told you about the tell in the video, the shadow that was cast the wrong way? Well, there's more of them, but you have to look real close."

The telephone lines could not diminish the excitement in Greg's voice. "I started with the assumption that if there was one tell, there might be others. So I chose a scene — the one with you, the blond lady, and the two bad guys — and broke it into several plots. I wanted all the players on the screen. Then I began a close examination of each area. If I were going to paint in a few clues, that's where I would do it."

Greg wished he were talking to a person instead of a machine, but this information was too important to hold on to. "I don't understand it, Dr. O'Neal, but maybe it will mean something to you. I started with the woman, magnifying the image as much as I could and still have some resolution. I found nothing special at first. By analyzing her facial movements during the kiss, I determined that she is a real person on a set, and not a later addition. Anyway, I started at the top of her head and worked down. When she leans over to kiss you . . . well not you, but whomever . . . you know what I mean. When she leans over, an earring becomes visible from behind her blond hair. It's a gold mosquito. Weird, huh? At first I didn't give it any thought. There are all sorts of weird earrings today, but I got suspicious when I was taking a close look at the briefcase with the money in it. There's a CGI — computer generated image — of a mosquito on several of the bills. And there's another one. The men at the table have small mosquito tattoos on their hands. Well, not really tattoos. These are computer generated. I doubt they actually exist on their hands. I don't know what mosquitoes have to do with anything, but I think they were put there intentionally. I bet the artist who did this either had second thoughts or was being forced into making the video and pictures."

Greg bounced on the balls of his feet. "Anyway, I'm going to keep working on this. The lab at the college doesn't have a phone, and I won't be able to hear the pay phone from there, so you can't reach me, but I'll call you in the morning."

Greg hung up and walked away from the phone.

David had taken his time in the shower, allowing the hot water to do its therapeutic work. He tried to push every thought from his mind, but there were too many of them. Too many fears, concerns, questions, anxieties, and no answers. Thirty minutes later he was back at his desk with a fresh cup of coffee in his hand. He leaned back in his chair and took a sip of the warm, dark liquid.

A small red numeral one on his answering machine caught his attention. He punched the play button and listened as the eager voice of Greg Cheney played through the tiny speaker.

David's subconscious started screaming.

He looked at the phone. Realization poured over him like a flood from a broken dam. His phone was still tapped. When Calvin had ordered the electronic search of the building, they had found listening devices in David's office and the conference room. They also had found that an external connection had been made to his private line. David had insisted that they be left in place. It was the only way of reaching his tormentors, the only way to flush them out. Now he regretted that decision with every fiber of his being. If they were listening in, then Greg could be in danger.

David had to warn him. How? The college was closed. He would never be able to make contact over the phone lines.

Bolting from his chair, David exited his suite and took the elevator down to the cafeteria. There he found a pay phone and placed a call to Calvin.

Aldo Goldoni dropped the handset of the phone back into its cradle. His operative had just informed him of a conversation between David O'Neal and someone named Greg Cheney. It was a loose end, and loose ends were not permitted. They had a habit of growing into problems if not dealt with properly.

A combination of anger and excitement wrestled within him. Anger because his plan was showing frayed edges that wouldn't be there if he had been allowed to act sooner instead of playing games of intrigue with his mark. But he was a hired hand, and he did what his client wanted. Usually.

There was, however, the excitement of having something to do. He would have spent the night waiting for dawn to signal his day of preparation. Now he would have something to pass the time instead of mere sleep.

Glancing at his watch, Aldo saw that it was 11:30. He would have to move fast, think on the run. But that was part of the excitement, the thrill.

Tonight would be a good one for Aldo. Greg Cheney would have a different opinion.

15

Calvin was more than angry. He was furious. The muscles were tense; his heart pounded with intensity; his hands were clenched on the steering wheel.

I told him that leaving the bugs in was a bad idea, he thought, *but no, he had to leave them in.* He slammed his hand on the wheel.

Taking a deep breath he calmed himself. He knew he was overreacting. David had been trying to help himself and others. He was a driven man, and if so much had not been at stake, if it was only his life that was in danger, then he would have been more willing to listen to Calvin. But the lives of scores of others depended on a quick reconciliation of the problem.

Calvin directed his car onto Interstate 8 and headed east toward San Diego State University. Despite the anger of the moment, Calvin knew that David was a man of determination and action. Doing nothing was and never would be an option for him. In many ways, the two men were cut from the same cloth.

The traffic was light as the night moved ever closer to being a new day. He wondered if Greg would still be at the school. His plan was simple: Find the campus police, inform them of the potential danger to one of their students, and accompany them to the video lab. SDSU was one of the largest colleges in the state, and Calvin had no idea where the lab was. He needed help, and the campus police could provide that. Besides, there was strength in numbers. Calvin hoped that whoever had gone through the trouble to tap David's phone lines would not arrive before him.

Calvin pulled his car onto the grounds of the college. San Diego State University was a compilation of white buildings clustered on a hillside that overlooked the long black ribbon of Interstate 8. Interspersed around the campus were large macadam seas of parking lots, now nearly empty of the thousands of cars that came here each day. Even in August, weeks before regular term started, the parking lots would be dotted with vehicles of students. Tonight, however, the lots were uncluttered expanses of blacktop.

He had never been on the campus before. He slowed his car and craned his neck as he looked for a sign that would direct him to the security office. He got his wish, but not as he expected. As he drove along the lot, he glimpsed red and blue lights. A security car was racing along the lot in front of him.

Calvin's heart sank; he feared the worse. His tires squealed, protesting the sudden acceleration as he stepped on the gas pedal. It took him a few moments to close on the patrol car. The police vehicle careened along the narrow roads that linked one lot to another. He watched as it screeched to a stop at an alley formed by a pair of two-story buildings. Parking, he grabbed his cell phone and quickly exited his own car.

The officer jogged down the open space, his keys and handcuffs jingling with each stride, resonating off the hard surfaces of the buildings. Ten strides later, he emerged into a large concrete plaza framed by classrooms.

He could feel his heart rate begin to rise as much from fear of what he may find as from the exertion of the run. He slowed as his fears became reality before his eyes. As an FBI agent he had seen many things, including violent death, but this was different. This was someone he had met. Someone who had taken it upon himself to help those he did not know. Now his enthusiasm may have brought him harm — maybe worse.

The officer slowed to a walk as he approached a first-floor door. Light poured from the doorway and the windows of the room and splashed onto the concrete plaza. Another officer stood at the room's entrance. Calvin drew close enough to hear.

". . . not good, man. Not good at all."

"Excuse me," Calvin said.

The two officers turned to face him. The one that had been standing in the doorway wore a name tag engraved with the name HILTON. Both men eyed Calvin suspiciously.

"Who are you?" Hilton asked harshly, stepping toward him.

"Calvin Overstreet. I'm looking for Greg Cheney."

"What's your business with him?" Hilton asked firmly. His expression was dour, his eyes cast a hard gaze.

"I'm an attorney. Mr. Cheney was helping a client of mine with . . . a project."

"May I see some identification, Mr.

Overstreet?" Officer Hilton moved closer to Calvin.

"Of course." Calvin reached for his wallet. "Is Mr. Cheney in there?" He nodded toward the lit classroom. In the distance sirens wailed.

"Yes." The officer looked at the driver's license that Calvin offered. "What brings you here now?"

"As I said, I'm an attorney, and I'm here to see —"

"Now," Hilton interrupted. "Why are you here now? Why this time of night?"

"He called my client and said he had some information to show him —"

"Who's your client?"

"That's none of your business."

"Isn't it?" Hilton snapped. "Cheney is dead. He's been murdered. You wouldn't happen to know any reason why someone would want to murder a college student, do you?"

Calvin's heart seized, and his stomach filled with bitter acid. His fearful suspicion had been right. "Any idea when it happened?"

"Not long ago. Maybe just minutes ago. Perhaps you know the exact time."

Calvin frowned. Hilton suspected him. "I only know that my client received a call about an hour ago."

"And you came right down? Odd, don't you think?"

"Look, Officer Hilton." Calvin was growing weary of the campus cop. "I'm a former FBI agent. I've seen more in a month than you've seen in your career. I had nothing to do with Cheney's murder."

"But you know more than you're telling."

"I've told you what I can."

"Well," Hilton said, nodding at a blue-uniformed San Diego police officer who was approaching. "I'll bet these guys will have a few questions for you too."

Calvin sighed. This was going to be a long night. Opening the cell phone in his hand, he began to dial a number.

"Who do you think you're calling?" Hilton asked.

"My client."

"That can wait. I'm not finished with you."

Calvin lowered the phone and glowered at the security officer. "Have I been placed under arrest?"

"No, but —"

"Since I'm not under arrest, I'll call whomever I wish." Calvin finished placing the call. The phone rang twice on the other end before being picked up. Calvin wasted no time. "David, we have a problem."

"It's my fault." David crossed the suite and sat heavily on the love seat that was positioned perpendicular to the couch where, until the phone awakened her, Kristen had slept.

"There's no way that's possible." Kristen rubbed her eyes. "You told me that he called you."

"But if I hadn't turned the ringer down, he wouldn't have left a message. I would have answered and could have stopped him."

"David, it's not your fault. It's a tragedy of the worst kind, but you did not kill him. A maniac did."

"But if I had been more careful, more alert, this wouldn't have happened."

"You don't know that. From what you told me, you did everything possible. You called Calvin. He's the expert. You even tried to get through to the campus police. It's not your fault that the switchboard was closed or that they don't answer their phones or whatever happened."

"I should have called the police."

"And said what? 'Hi, I'm Dr. David O'Neal, the man under investigation by the Justice Department, and I believe that a college student who is helping me prove my innocence may be in danger by the guys who are framing me.' I don't think that they would have believed that, David."

David buried his face in his hands. He was awash with guilt, deluged by sadness. He felt that he would soon drown from grief. The face of Greg hovered in his mind, the excitement in his voice as he shared his discovery with David echoed in his soul. An ache, deep, penetrating, and consuming, filled him, clung to him, dragged him down below the swirling waves of regret.

"David?"

Another innocent had suffered and died. Just like those in Bangladesh and India and Cuba. David didn't even know if Greg had family. Were there parents somewhere weeping over the brutal death of child? Were there brothers and sisters who would no longer hug one of their own?

"David?"

It was too much to think about, too much to experience. The people who did this had to be stopped and stopped soon. They wanted David. Why didn't they just come and get him?

That had been one of the concerns Calvin had voiced over the phone. "Take no chances," he had said. "Don't leave the building. Keep Kristen and Timmy nearby." David had no trouble hearing the fear in Calvin's voice. Bad had just gone to worse.

"David? Can you hear me?"

David looked up. Kristen's eyes were wide with concern. "I hear you." He rose from the love seat and walked back to the window wall. "They're out there, Kristen. Somewhere out there watching us. Hating us. Hating me. And whoever gets close to me is in danger."

"We'll make it, David. We'll survive. We'll come through all this."

"Greg didn't. All he did was try to help, and now he's dead." David shook his head. "I can't let it go on any longer. They must be stopped."

"You're not thinking of surrendering to their demands." Kristen was on her feet and, a few strides later, by his side. "You're not going to confess to something you didn't do."

"I don't know what I'm going to do, Kristen. I need to think."

David felt Kristen's hand on his arm. He turned to face her. He gazed into her eyes, eyes that radiated love and determination. She wrapped her arms around him. A second later, he returned the embrace.

The hug felt good to David, therapeutic. There was a strength that grew from the embrace. She rested her cheek on his chest.

Moments ticked by slowly. David wished that the rest of the world would dissolve, leaving just the two of them, new Adam and new Eve in a new world.

"David, I want you to listen to me." Her words were soft, heavy with concern, and enlivened by honesty. "When I first met you — when you first came to Barringston Relief — I was attracted to you. I found your humor and intelligence alluring. But a big part of you was missing. At first I thought it was remorse over the loss of your wife, but then I realized that it was more."

"More?"

"It was your faith. It wasn't gone, David, but it had been put on hold, tucked away in some dark spot of your life. Then we went to Ethiopia with A.J. It all changed there. That faith was back. In the face of the worst that life could show you, you reacquainted yourself with God. Your

Christianity began to bloom."

"I remember that day clearly." David held Kristen a little tighter. "It was one of the most important days of my life."

"I've been a Christian for most of my life, but like many people, my faith had been little more than something I did instead of something I was. When your faith bloomed again, so did mine. Your life reminded me of the difference belief can make. It has changed Timmy's life too."

"But?" David prompted.

"I think you're trying to do it all on your own again. I think you're cutting out the one who can help you most. God is still a part of all this."

David drank in her words. He had made no conscious decision to exclude his Savior from the events of the week. Indeed, he had found solace in the reading of the Beatitudes just a day ago. Still, his arrest, the tsunami, the hurricane, the threats against him, Kristen, and Timmy, and now the death of Greg occupied every corner of his mind, pushing out all that had been there before. His mind was full of questions and fears and concerns and problems and doubts, leaving no room for hope and peace and faith. Kristen had hit the nail on the head.

"I'm not trying to be preachy," Kristen said, her head still resting on David's chest.

"You should. You're good at it." David's voice was kind and tinged with humor. He felt her tighten her hug. "It's easy to get sidetracked and let the spiritual get pushed to the back. I'm prone to do that. You would think that a former preacher wouldn't be, but I am. It's a struggle for me to keep my faith in front where it belongs."

"I don't know why all this is happening, David, but I do know that we will come through it fine. I'm sorry about Greg. I feel bad. There's no way to explain what happened to him. I don't know why he had to die."

A sigh weighted with deep emotions escaped from David. "I don't know either. The other day, Timmy asked me why innocent people suffer. I didn't have an answer. Now I'm one of those who suffer, and as yet I still don't have an answer."

"Maybe there's not one."

David pulled back from Kristen and stared into her intelligent, moist eyes. "What do you mean?"

"I'm not much for philosophy, and I'm certainly no theologian, but maybe there is no answer to that question. At least not one we can understand. Maybe it's human chauvinism to think that we can have answers to all the questions we pose."

David thought about her words. "I have always been taught that all questions have answers."

Kristen shrugged. "Maybe they do, but that doesn't mean that we will know them. It doesn't matter anyway, does it? We're stuck in this problem no matter what. We didn't ask for it. It came our way. Unfairly perhaps, but fairness has nothing to do with reality."

Again David absorbed her words. She was right. He had ignored the power of his faith and allowed external circumstances to dictate his internal response. Evil was evil no matter how it manifested itself. Fairness was immaterial. What did matter, what could make a difference, was faith and love. Even though wickedness may have power over the body, it has no power over the soul. Perhaps that was one reason God had made man a spiritual being.

David took Kristen in his arms and held her tight. "Thank you," he said in whispered tones. "You're right. Maybe it's time I took the next step. Maybe it's time to pray."

★ ★ ★

The only thing good about the sudden change of events was that Aldo got to kill one more person than planned. It had been quick and lacked the flair he preferred, but a murder was a murder, and at times one couldn't be choosy.

The college kid had offered no resistance. He was young and naive. Aldo simply walked into the classroom — actually a video lab where students practiced what their professors had taught them — and asked for directions to the library. He didn't even need a disguise. The boy rose to his feet, said, "Sure, but it's closed," and walked to Aldo, who stood just inside the door. Ten seconds later, the college kid was dead. Aldo had struck him in the throat and crushed his windpipe. The young man was so stunned that he offered no resistance as Aldo stepped behind him, grabbed the kid's chin with one hand and the back of his head with the other, and wrung his neck, breaking it in one smooth motion. Aldo then walked away.

The bad part, the really frustrating part, was that Aldo had to accelerate his schedule. Now he had to do tonight what he had planned to do tomorrow. He hated changing plans. Changes meant possible mistakes, and he loathed mistakes. Still, it wasn't his fault, and it did mean that he would get to kill again. That was the upside.

Without wasted motion, Aldo closed the curtains of his hotel room and gathered all his materials. He had done his homework and had formulated five different plans. Now he had made his choice. It was plan three that he would use, and it was good — unique, different from anything he had done before. It required at least an hour's preparation, maybe a little more. He had no time to lose.

It would all start with a shower and a shave.

"What did he say?" Kristen asked.

David hung up the phone. "He would have to make some calls, but new security officers should arrive within a couple of hours."

"Will that be soon enough?"

"He knows his men." David walked over and joined Kristen on the couch. "He doubts that we even need additional people, but since Calvin and I insisted, he has agreed to it."

"Calvin called the security firm too?"

David smiled weakly. "Apparently he

didn't think I would or that I might be too distracted by Greg's murder."

"Calvin is looking out for us. He's a good man."

"He's certainly a cautious one."

"Is he still at the police station?" Kristen's face was drawn. The night was wearing long, and frustration was becoming heavier with each moment.

"He was when he called a few moments ago. The police are still questioning him. He thinks he'll be able to leave soon. Still, it doesn't look like he'll get much sleep tonight."

"After what you said about how Greg died, I don't know when I'll be able to sleep again."

"I shouldn't have told you." Kristen had seen David's reaction when he had been on the phone with Calvin. She had pressed him for everything Calvin had said. When he said that Greg's neck had been broken, Kristen had gasped and covered her mouth. David knew the revelation had made the danger all the more real. They were no longer dealing with threats but with a real assassin.

"Don't be silly. I insisted, I'm all right. Just having a shaky moment or two."

"Here," David said, patting his leg. "Lay

your head down. Maybe you can sleep a little."

Kristen complied, stretching out on the couch and laying her head on his leg. He began to stroke her soft hair. "I'm tired, but I don't think I can fall asleep."

"Think about something else," David advised.

"I wish I could, but I just keep seeing Greg's face."

David made no reply, he just continued to stroke her hair, allowing his fingers to caress her scalp and face. Slowly, lovingly, he continued the process. The suite was quiet. The moon shone in through the windows, bathing everything with a soft ivory light. A few moments later David listened to Kristen's rhythmic breathing, evidence that slumber had overtaken her. David offered a word of praise to God for the small miracle, then laid his head against the back of the sofa and closed his eyes.

An evil possessed Aldo, an evil that arrived before every job with freight-train punctuality, a black amoral mucus that oozed through his mind suppressing useless emotions like fear, regret, sorrow, and sympathy. The evil whispered in his ears, painted pictures on his mind, altered his memories.

On many occasions he had thought he had seen it out of the corner of his eye, just beyond reach. It was thick and black-green, formless and void, yet alive. It hovered. It reeked of all the death that Aldo had caused.

In weak moments, in those seconds between sleep and wakefulness, Aldo would be consumed by fear of the thing that consumed him. During those timeless, eternal seconds, he could see the faces of each person he had killed, each one he had tortured and maimed, their voices rising in a chorus that at first sounded pitiful, then mournful, then angry, then demonic. The cacophony of cries and threats from beyond the grave was the only thing that had ever frightened him.

But he wasn't frightened now. The Possession made it possible for him to do his job. The Possession was his empowerment, his motivation, his North Star. Without it, he would be just like the rest of the world: powerless, insipid, uninspired creatures who had little more value than cattle in a slaughterhouse. But the Possession made him different, invulnerable. Nothing could hurt him. No one could outthink him. No eyes could see his plans. No mind could match his. He was a god.

And he would prove it again tonight. What did it matter if plans had been accelerated by a day? This time tomorrow he would be elsewhere — Mexico perhaps, maybe Australia. Someplace with sun and water. That would be good. Sun and water.

But first things first. Taking a white washcloth he dragged it across the mirror, wiping away the condensation left by his hot shower. He started at the top and methodically worked his way down, not missing any part of the mirror. Then he wiped it down again. Then one more time.

His motions were slow and dreamlike, as if he were moving through a viscous fluid.

The Possession filled him all the more.

Looking in the mirror he saw his reflection looking back. But it was different from the reflection of yesterday or even of this morning. The face was the same. The bare body no different. The eyes — something behind the eyes. Something dark, something of wicked intelligence. It was the real him, the one who had been born that day as a teenager when he killed his mother's attacker. The him that had supplanted the teenage boy.

He taped a picture to the mirror. It was

an enlargement of a photo taken by one of the hired operatives. He studied the image, absorbing every detail.

With a twist of the knob, hot water began to run in the sink. Small billows of steam rose threatening to once again fog the mirror. He plunged cupped hands into the hot flow and brought the water to his face. It burned. It hurt. It made him feel alive. Water trickled down his stubbled chin and dripped to the bare skin of his chest, thighs, and feet.

Mindlessly he reached for the can of shaving cream that rested near the bowl of the sink. He pressed its button and watched as white foam erupted from its spout and into his hand. It felt smooth, silky, weightless. Raising the mound of lather to his nose, he inhaled deeply. Aloe.

Starting at his left ear, he spread the foam across his face, under his nose, over his chin, along his neck. Unlike the usual male routine that was done quickly and without thought, Aldo moved deliberately, like a dancer, like an actor, like a surgeon.

Preparation is everything.

He took the razor into his hand, twisted its base so the razor opened like a budding flower to reveal the new, unused double-edged blade inside. Aldo studied it for a moment before twisting the handle again, closing the tiny silver doors that held the blade in place.

Holding the razor in his right hand, he placed its sharp edge to his face, near the middle of his left ear. The razor felt cool to his hot skin. With slow, easy motions he dragged the blade down. He could hear it as it cut the hair on his face. Moving the razor he shaved some more. Then some more, leaving nothing but smooth skin behind.

The preparation had begun.

The twilight of sleep had come to David as he sat on the sofa, Kristen's head in his lap, his head resting on the sofa's back. He was not asleep. He was not awake. He was somewhere in between, in the mystical place where reality and dreams become one, where the rational held no more sway than the irrational.

David had struggled with sleep. He knew he was safe. The doors were locked, and a guard was nearby. The only people left in the upper ten floors were the employees in communications and a few die-hard workers. Still he was uneasy, and as he approached sleep, that uneasiness grew.

He worried. He worried about Timmy and about Kristen and about Barringston

Relief. He worried about those who needed his help right now. But he didn't worry about himself.

A prayer bubbled to his lips.

More hot water. Aldo washed his face again, then, after patting his face dry with a towel, he took a cotton ball, doused it with an astringent cleanser and rubbed it on his face. The sharp liquid burned as it touched his freshly shaven skin. He ignored it. He was lost in the labyrinth of his mind, of his plans, of the death he would soon cause.

Taking a woman's thigh-high nylon, he twisted it until it formed a band. He studied the picture again, taking special note of the eyes. He then placed the soft nylon cord to his forehead and wrapped it around his head, stretching the material as he did. The tension had to be right. Too tight and he would cut off the circulation. A quick knot at the front of his head finished the job.

He studied his eyes which had taken an almond, cat-eye shape. He examined the picture again, then his reflection. He was satisfied.

Sleep remained an inch from David's reach. It beckoned his weary and stressed

415

mind. Still he could not let go of the un-easiness, guilt, apprehension, and confusion. Those emotions and scores like them swirled within David like tumbleweeds in a dust devil. Despite his prayers with Kristen and despite his private petitions, he still had no peace.

Something he had memorized many years ago rose to the front of his mind, like a cork emerging from the ocean depths. A psalm written by a man who had known the fear of attack, who understood betrayal, who had fathomed the depths of faithfulness — King David.

The words of the ancient song floated between his conscious mind and the nether world of his subconscious:

> *The LORD is my light and my salvation*
> *— whom shall I fear?*
> *The LORD is the stronghold of my life —*
> *of whom shall I be afraid?*
> *When evil men advance against me*
> *to devour my flesh,*
> *when my enemies and my foes attack me,*
> *they will stumble and fall.*
> *Though an army besiege me,*
> *my heart will not fear;*
> *though war break out against me,*
> *even then will I be confident.*

It was Psalm 27. David had memorized it as part of his classwork in seminary. Then it was drudgery; now it was life and hope.

Aldo moved faster now. Moisturizer was followed by flesh-tone concealer that he applied under his eyes to mask the darkened skin of age. Satin-beige foundation came next. He took special care to apply the thick fluid along his dark beard line to mask any remaining shadow. Next came the eyeliner pencil. During his practice sessions this had always been the most difficult step. He was unaccustomed to putting pointed objects near his eyes.

The transformation was working as planned. He applied powdery eye shadow to his eyelids and the area just below his eyebrows. The eyebrows were the only things that caused him concern. His dark hair might provide a noticeable contrast. He had planned to bleach them tomorrow, but now his schedule had been unexpectedly pushed up by that interfering college kid. The eyebrows were a risk he would just have to take.

After applying blush to his cheeks, Aldo took a red lip liner and carefully traced the edges of his lips. He then applied pink passion lipstick and gently blotted his lips on a tissue.

With the makeup skillfully applied, Aldo stepped to the closet, swung open the mirrored doors, and removed a Styrofoam head from the shelf above the clothes rack. A red wig rested on the head. Aldo removed the wig and placed it over his scalp. The hair felt soft as it brushed against his bare shoulders. There was still more to put on before the transformation was complete: press-on nails, the silk shell top, blue woman's blazer, and black pleated pants, but even now the look was convincing.

Aldo's lipsticked lips parted in a grin as he stared at his altered image. "Well, Kristen. It looks like you have a twin."

16

"I'm so glad you could make it." Aberdene rose from the stool on which she had been sitting and stepped away from the lab bench. "I know it's late, and you've been working so hard."

Archer felt uneasy. Something wasn't right. Being summoned from the editing suite in the basement of the building to Aberdene's private laboratory was ominous. "What's up?" Archer asked with more bravado than he felt. Aberdene was being nice, which meant that she had something frightening up her sleeve.

"Did Jack tell you why I needed to see you?"

Archer shook his head and looked at the man standing by his side. His expression was grim. "No, just that you wanted me up here right away."

"That's good. I wanted to discuss this with you myself." Aberdene's eyes narrowed. "It seems that we have a problem."

"Problem?" Archer's heart began to pound fiercely.

"Oh, yes. Quite a problem. It seems that someone in our circle has decided to betray our operation. Any idea who that might be?"

He had been found out. But how? Archer swallowed hard. "No. No idea at all."

"I'm told that Dr. O'Neal received a phone call tonight by a young man named . . . ," she trailed off and looked questioningly at Jack.

"Greg Cheney," Jack said filling in the blank.

"Yes, that's it. Mr. Greg Cheney. It seems that young Mr. Cheney is . . . was the industrious type."

"Was?" Archer felt ill.

Aberdene ignored him. "Somehow he got hold of a copy of the videotape you made."

Archer shrugged with a confidence that he did not feel. "The tape was broadcast on all the television stations. He could have made a copy. Nothing unusual about that."

"That's how I see it. But that's not the real problem. You see, he was examining the tape. Running it through all sorts of tests. He found something."

"Not possible," Archer said defensively. "There's nothing to find."

"Oh, but there was. And not just one thing, but many things. We listened in on a phone conversation he had with O'Neal tonight. In fact, I have a copy of that conversation. Let me play part of it for you." She walked over to a small cassette player and pushed the play button. The words were tinny but easily understood.

Archer listened as Greg told David of the hidden mosquitoes in the video and how it was his belief that someone was delivering a message. Nausea swept over Archer. He had been discovered.

"This causes us some concern," Aberdene said easily, but there was a fire in her eyes and a hardness around her lips. "Why, Archer? After all I've done for you, why would you betray me?"

"Because what you're doing is wrong," Archer shouted. "I can't live with myself. I can't go on knowing that innocent people are dying because of your experiments."

"Those experiments will ultimately save lives," Aberdene snapped back. "A few may die, but it will be worth it."

"Worth it for you, maybe, but not to those people who die because of your supermosquito and virus."

"Don't you dare pretend to understand what I do!" Aberdene was shouting. "My research is important, significant, and beyond the understanding of a cretin like you! Do you know how long it takes to get a new drug on the market today? Do you? The red tape is enormous, the time lag cruel. People die every day for lack of medicines that have been demonstrated effective and safe but have yet to receive FDA approval. The drugs you take to keep your AIDS in check is unapproved. You're alive today because I chose to give it to you anyway."

"But your work in Belize is not curing anyone. It's killing them with your special brand of dengue hemorrhagic fever. I don't see how that helps anyone."

"How dare you presume to second-guess me!" Aberdene's face reddened. "DHF isn't the point, you tiny little man. I genetically altered the virus and then genetically altered the mosquito that carries the virus. In doing so I have proved that insects can be used to vector human-altered viruses."

"That way you can afflict entire populations with diseases that can only be cured by medications provided by Aberdene Pharmaceuticals. That's one way to make a buck in this business."

Aberdene laughed. "You're not so dumb after all, Archer. But that's just a side benefit. There are two other compelling reasons. One of which even you will approve."

"I doubt it," Archer snapped. The fear he felt was now being supplanted by resignation. He knew he would not see the sun rise again.

"Think of the military applications, dear boy." Aberdene began to pace. "Instead of dropping bombs and firing missiles, we can unleash a few million mosquitoes. Since they're pesticide resistant and live longer, they can have quite an effect on a region."

"You thought I would approve of that?"

"No, not that your approval is necessary. Come on, Archer, broaden your thinking. If I can genetically alter a virus to make it more virulent, why not alter a virus to make it weaker. That's what a vaccine is. A weakened form of the disease. That's how polio was defeated, except with polio and other diseases, the patient must come to the doctor. I plan to inoculate people against diseases by sending out mosquitoes that carry the altered virus. That begins the cycle. Mosquitoes then feed off their human hosts, obtain the new virus and then pass it on to other humans."

"Won't that put you out of business?"

"Not at all. There are plenty of diseases still left. And what nature doesn't provide, I can. No, I'm not worried about going out of business. In fact, countries will beat a path to my door to pay me large sums of money. You could have been part of all that."

"No thanks," Archer said. "I doubt you planned to let me live anyway."

Jack spoke up. "So you did plant clues in the video?"

"Of course I did, Jack. Don't be so thick-headed."

"I just wanted to hear it from your own mouth."

With explosive speed, Jack brought a crashing blow to the side of Archer's head. There was an explosion of pain and a moment of darkness. When his senses returned, Archer was seated on the floor. The side of his head pulsed with pain, and his ears rang.

"That's enough, Jack," Aberdene said. "You know how I hate violence."

"I'm sorry. I have a problem with betrayal."

"Your loyalty is commendable."

"What should we do with him?"

"Make sure he doesn't hurt us again," Aberdene said.

Her words made Archer laugh. The laughter made his head hurt all the more. He closed his eyes.

Archer felt himself being lifted to his feet. He opened his eyes and found himself staring at a crimson-faced Jack.

"What's so funny, little man?"

"You," Archer said with a chortle. "It's all over for you and the Mosquito Queen."

"What do you mean?"

Archer laughed again. He passed the fear stage of dying and moved into insolence. "Go ahead and kill me, Jack. I'm a dead man anyway. I've been dying for years. Inch by inch, I've been leaving this life. At least I'll die proud of one thing. I brought you down. Both of you."

"He's delirious," Aberdene said. "You hit him too hard."

"He had better shut up if he doesn't want me to hit him again."

"You're not so smart after all," Archer said. "My plan was perfect. They found exactly what I wanted them to find."

"It won't do any good," Aberdene said. "Aldo will have our problem taken care of soon. There will be so much confusion around the death of Dr. O'Neal that no one will be able to trace our work in Belize back to us.

The mention of Aldo sobered Archer. "You're killing an innocent man. A man who has done nothing but help other people."

"It is regrettable," Aberdene agreed. "But I can't help it if his organization has people doing research in Belize. I'm too close to making all this work. I can't have him and his organization mucking it all up. He's a pedestrian in the wrong place at the wrong time. It's not personal, it's business."

"Lady, you are one sick —" Archer doubled over when Jack's fist plowed into his stomach. He struggled for breath, but his paralyzed solar plexus refused to respond. He dropped to his knees.

"Jack!" Aberdene shouted. "That is enough!"

"He was being disrespectful," Jack said, still holding the front of the gasping Archer's shirt.

"I don't want to see any more of this," she said. "Get him out of here."

"What do you want me to do with him?" Jack asked.

"I'll leave that up to you. I just don't want it done here or on company property."

"Come on, Archer," Jack spat. "It's time for us to go."

Archer had no strength to fight back. He allowed himself to be dragged to his feet. Opening his eyes he looked at Aberdene, then, despite the pain, he smiled. He had won. He might not live, but he had won. It was the first time he had ever done anything for someone else, and it would cost him his life. So be it. Better late than never.

Jack dragged Archer from the room.

Slamming shut the door of the red Miata he had purchased two days before, Aldo gazed at himself in the rearview mirror.

He was a master of disguises, but this was one of his best. Had he been taller he might have chosen to disguise himself as Calvin Overstreet or even David O'Neal himself, but both men were much taller than he. Kristen was the best and only choice.

He started the car, inserted a tape in the cassette player, and turned up the volume. Music, hard-driving rock, pounded in the car, vibrating everything. He turned the bass up. Now he could not only hear the music, he could feel it. And it was as real as the evil that possessed him. Nodding his head in time to the music, Aldo pressed the gas pedal to the floor, and the car raced from the hotel parking lot. The clock in the car read 1:30.

"The hour has come," he said to himself. "Time to rock and roll."

The time had come. His hour had arrived. This was why he had been born. He was the one to make it happen. People needed him to rid themselves of human annoyances. It paid well, but that didn't matter. Aldo would have killed for free.

The drive from his downtown hotel room to Barringston Tower was less than ten minutes, but Aldo took a full half-hour. He drove the dark streets of metropolitan San Diego, his car rhythmically awash with the glow of streetlights. At first he noticed the other cars, the people walking the streets, the homeless, the hookers, the drug dealers, the police cars, but with each minute that passed he noticed them less. Instead he thought of David O'Neal and wondered how he was spending the last night of his life.

Calvin wanted only to go home, to climb into bed next to his wife, cuddle up to her, feel her warmth, and drift off to mindless sleep. He wanted to put the night's unsavory events behind him, to forget the countless questions he'd had to answer at the police station. Questions about how he had met Greg Cheney, how long he had known him, and how he knew he was in danger. The questions seemed unending, but he endured them, answering as honestly as possible. He doubted that they believed him, but they were left with no other choice. The police were intelligent people who followed the news. It didn't take long for them to associate Calvin with David.

There was one more matter he had to deal with before going home. In his phone conversation with David, he had made it clear that more guards were needed and had asked him to make the call to the guard service. He had made a follow-up call himself. Calvin wouldn't rest tonight unless he knew that the guards were in place. He would swing by and verify the matter personally.

Then he could go home.

Aldo steered the red Miata down the street that ran in front of Barringston Tower. He drove slowly. A guard, dressed in a white uniform shirt and black pants, stood at the front of the building. He carried a walkie-talkie.

This was no surprise to Aldo, who had kept close tabs on the number of guards that had been added and where they were stationed. By placing a call to the guard company and posing as a corporate client, he was able to determine the level of their training. He was neither impressed nor intimidated. He had made a second call to the firm's night dispatch office shortly before he left his hotel room. As anticipated, extra guards had been requested. It was an easy matter to cancel that request.

As he passed the guard, Aldo waved and smiled. The man waved back. Aldo pulled the car into the parking garage under the building and found an empty spot near the elevators. There was another guard posted there. Aldo exited the car.

Straightening himself, he took his first few steps toward the elevator. The low heel pumps he wore felt less stable than he wished, especially since he had shortened the heel of his right shoe to make his limp more realistic. Everyone who knew Kristen was aware of her congenital defect. Aldo could not overlook such a detail. Details, even details about shoes, had not been wasted on him. He had practiced walking in them for two days, pacing back and forth across his hotel room until they felt comfortable.

"May I help you, ma'am?" the security guard asked. He was a thin, tall man, no older than twenty-five.

"Hi." Aldo smiled. He spoke in a practiced falsetto. It would be difficult to maintain the image very long, but it would be good enough now. He doubted that any of these men had actually spoken with Kristen. "I'm Kristen LaCroix, the head of public relations here. I was just heading to my office."

"It's a little late to be coming to work, isn't it, ma'am?"

"Not if you're in public relations and your firm has been accused of laundering money. I haven't had a full night's sleep in three days."

"Well, the building is locked down for the night. You'll have to take the stairs up to the lobby and check in there. Oh, and the door from the stairwell into the first-floor lobby will open for you, but not the doors on the other floors. It's a security precaution. In case of a fire, people can exit into the stairwell, but you can't go the other way."

"That's fine with me." Aldo had anticipated this. Initially he had planned to walk up the fifty plus flights of stairs to gain entrance. He would have to go through the lobby. Before opening the door he turned and faced the man. He smiled broadly and winked. "Thanks for all your help," he said playfully.

The guard offered a casual, swaggering, two-finger salute. "Glad to be of service, ma'am."

Although he had had no doubts, Aldo was glad that he passed the first test. The guard didn't question his gender. He had passed as a woman. Now he needed to do it again. Climbing the one flight of stairs, he exited into the large lobby. The last time he had been here, he had been disguised as a reporter and had paid a street kid money to deliver the photo to David right before the news conference. Not that that had done any good. O'Neal had still asserted his innocence. Aldo swore under his breath.

Two uniformed guards were standing in the lobby behind a semicircular reception counter: one a thick, middle-aged man, the other an older, white-haired fellow. Aldo knew the latter was one of the Barringston night watchmen, not a trained security professional, but a "doorknob shaker." The first man had the look of a professional about him. There were three stripes on his uniform shirt — a supervisor. He looked fit. His hair was short, cut almost to the scalp. Aldo guessed he was retired military police. If things went bad, he would have to take him out first.

"Good evening," Aldo said in his falsetto voice and strolled confidently into the room.

The younger man turned and tensed. He eyed Aldo suspiciously, then smiled. Aldo returned the smile and turned his gaze on the older guard. The one thing that Aldo couldn't control was who would be on duty. He wondered how well the Barringston night watchman might know Kristen.

"May I help you, ma'am?" the hired guard asked. "I'm afraid the building is closed —"

"Oh," Aldo interrupted. "I'm Kristen LaCroix. I'm with the public relations department."

"Industries or Relief?"

"Barringston Relief. I'm preparing a press release for tomorrow. That's why I'm here so early."

Aldo walked closer to the reception desk and watched as the man typed Kristen's name into a computer. There was a short pause before a picture of Kristen appeared on the screen. The man looked at the image and then at the made-over Aldo. He nodded.

"All right, Ms. LaCroix, you can go up. Sorry for the delay, but we are paid to be careful. Since you're an employee, you won't need to be escorted."

"I understand. I'm glad you're here." Aldo started toward the elevators but stopped abruptly ten feet from their doors. He patted the pockets of the blue blazer he was wearing, then the pockets of his slacks.

"Is there a problem, Miss?" The older man asked.

"I don't believe it," Aldo exclaimed. "I left my security card at home. That's a good half-hour away."

"The elevators are locked down to general traffic," the younger man said. "You can't use them without a security card."

"Could one of you loan me yours? I really have to do this work, and I don't want to lose an hour driving home and back. As it is, I almost fell asleep driving down here."

"We can't do that, ma'am," the old man began. "It's against the rules —"

"I'll have to escort you," the other man broke in. He offered a grin that was just shy of a leer. It was all Aldo could do not to laugh.

"That will be fine with me," Aldo said. "You can sit in my office and watch me work if that makes you more comfortable."

"Hmm," the man said as he walked to the elevators and inserted his security card into the slot near the door. "What floor are we going to?"

"Fifty-second," Aldo said as he stepped into the cab of the elevator. He turned and winked. A second later, the guard was in the small compartment. He inserted his magnetic card, and the elevator doors closed.

The two watched the floor-indicator lights above the door as the elevator began to rise. "Public relations, huh? You must be one smart cookie."

Aldo smiled demurely and looked down at the floor. "Smart enough, I suppose, and . . . what . . . what is that on the carpet?"

The guard looked down. "I don't see anything —"

Aldo took one side step away from the man, rocked on his left foot and threw a fast, brutal kick to the side of the guard's left knee. There was an audible snap, followed by a cry of pain. As the man crumpled, Aldo struck again, this time with an elbow to the temple. The guard was unconscious before he hit the floor.

Quickly Aldo reached into the pocket of his blazer and extracted a small roll of fiber-enhanced packing tape, pulled a six-inch piece loose, and placed it across his victim's mouth. He pulled a longer piece free and taped the man's ankles together. Another long piece secured the man's feet to the metal handrail that circled the inside of the cab. Removing the guard's handcuffs from their holder, Aldo cuffed the man's right hand, pushed the free end through the handrail, and cuffed his other hand. The guard was immobilized and hung like a hammock in the elevator.

Aldo took the security card and dropped it into the pocket of his coat. "That's step one," he said to himself.

The elevator continued its climb. Aldo had only moments to complete the next step. With a body trussed up in the cab, he could not allow the elevator to descend to the lobby again. He could not push the emergency stop because it would set off alarms. No, he had to gain control of the elevator from within the cab, and there was only one way to do that.

He wasted no time kneeling in front of

the control panel, his attention focused on a small keyhole under the rows of plastic buttons that selected the floors accessed by the elevator. Reaching in his other pocket, Aldo removed a locksmith's tool kit and began working on the keyhole, which was the override that firefighters used to control elevators in emergencies. By using the override, Aldo could gain complete command of the elevator cab, but he had only seconds to pick the lock.

After years of practice the long, picklike tools felt familiar in his hands. He probed for tumblers and found them, just as the elevator passed the fifty-first floor. Working patiently, as if he had hours instead of moments, Aldo worked the lock. It turned, and the doors opened. He was on the fifty-second floor, just where he wanted to be.

Taking another strip of tape, he placed it across the face of the door to block the light beam that crossed the threshold of the elevator cab. The beam was an electronic safety measure to prevent the doors' closing on a passenger entering or exiting the cab. With the beam broken, the doors would not close, and the elevator would remain stationary. It would be there when Aldo needed it, and he would need it.

He stood, straightened his clothes, and

exited into the lobby of the fifty-second floor. He had been here before dressed as a deliveryman. At each end of the lobby was a long corridor that led to various offices. Choosing the hall on the right, Aldo walked casually toward the rest rooms. He saw no one. No workers. No guards.

The rest rooms were just a few steps away from the junction of the lobby and corridor. He paused in front of the two doors. Glancing down the hall in both directions, Aldo made certain he was not being observed. A woman entering the men's rest room might draw unwanted attention. Seeing no one, he stepped through the door. As with all commercial rest rooms the door led to a small niche that in turn led to the spacious room itself. The light was on, which caused him to hesitate. He had assumed that at a little after two in the morning the lights would be off. Could some late-working employee be inside? He peeked around the corner and saw a wall lined with six urinals. No one there. He stepped into the room, crouched down, and looked under the stall doors. No feet. He was alone.

Stepping to the middle stall, Aldo opened the door and closed it again. Standing on the seat of the toilet, he pushed up one of the suspended ceiling tiles and reached into the dark void. He searched with his hand for a moment and then extracted the briefcase-size package he had concealed there after delivering the videotape to Kristen.

He stepped down from his perch, exited the stall, and stepped over to the sink counter. He set the package down and stripped off its brown-paper wrapping, revealing a small aluminum case. The shiny case reflected the soft fluorescent lights overhead.

Like a briefcase, the container had two latches, a lock combination for each, and a hinged top. Aldo dialed in the combination and released the latches. Without hesitancy, he opened the lid. Everything was there.

Aldo smiled.

David awoke with a start. A sound. A soft ringing. He sat up on the couch and blinked hard. He had drifted off. Looking at his watch he saw that it was just before two.

The phone rang again. David rose and trotted across the room. He was hoping the phone would not wake Kristen as she lay asleep on the couch.

"Yes," he said with a tone more sharp than he meant.

"Dr. O'Neal," the voice on the other end said, "this is Fred Weaver down in communications. I'm sorry about the lateness of the hour, but we have a standing order to notify you if we regain contact with our missing workers in Bangladesh."

"I'm glad you called," David said, his heart picking up a beat. Communications was the only department that operated twenty-four hours a day. With workers around the globe, Barringston Relief could not expect them to call during West Coast office hours. Every worker could be contacted or could make contact any time of day. "Have you heard something?"

"Good news, Dr. O'Neal. I have both workers on satellite link. Did you have a message for them?"

"Yes, but I want to give it to them myself. I'm on my way down." David hung up the phone. For the first time in a week he had some good news. Two workers thought dead were alive.

He walked back to the couch intending to tell Kristen, but he stopped. She was sound asleep, unperturbed by the phone. Since he was only going to be gone for a few minutes, he decided not to wake her.

She wouldn't even know he was gone.

David headed for the door.

Aldo enjoyed the thirty-five ounces of weight the Beretta 98FS, nine-millimeter semiautomatic pistol brought to his hand. The silencer attached to the muzzle would add a few ounces and slow the bullets down to just below the sound barrier, but that was plenty fast enough to do the job. Better silence with a slower bullet than maximum power with lots of noise. Stealth was still the order of the day.

Closing the aluminum case and snapping shut its latches, Aldo took it with his left hand and, holding the gun in his right, exited the rest room, pausing only long enough to be sure his movements were unseen by anyone who might have entered the corridor. The communication room was on this floor, and he knew that department never closed.

With quick steps, Aldo moved to the elevator. The door was still open. Once inside he glanced at the still unconscious and trussed guard. He frowned. It would be better if he could have disposed of the man, but that would take time and a chance discovery would complicate things. Killing him would be easy, but that, too, would be counterproductive. A single killing would make the news. A multiple killing would draw more attention and community outcry. That would place even greater pressure on the local police to find the killer. Not that they could. But wisdom called for as prudent a path as possible.

Reaching down, Aldo pulled the tape from the door, allowing the sensor to complete its circuit. The doors closed immediately. Taking the magnetic card he had removed from the guard, Aldo inserted it into the scanner and then pressed the plastic button marked 53.

The elevator began its one-floor journey up.

Among the debris-laden winds of emotion that had been swirling through David's mind, one of the most unrelenting had been the missing Barringston workers in Bangladesh and India. The Bangladesh workers had been the closest to the tsunami impact. It was an unspoken belief that they had been killed along with thousands of Bangladeshi.

Now the two missing workers were found and had made contact with communications. David bounced on his heels with excitement as he waited for one of the elevators to arrive. The building had six electric cable elevators, but only three opened on the fifty-third floor and only employees with special magnetic card keys could direct the elevator to the top level.

A small ding sounded as the central elevator opened. David stepped in and punched the button for the next floor down.

17

Partly from impatience, partly as a test, Calvin pulled his car to the curb in front of Barringston Tower. A young man in uniform sat on the front steps, smoking a cigarette. He gazed nonchalantly at Calvin as he exited the car and walked toward the entrance.

"Hi," Calvin said with a grin that belied his real emotions. This kid seemed barely awake. Granted the hour was late, but it was his duty to be alert.

"Hi," the young man said.

"Nice night, isn't it?" Calvin asked.

"Boring is more like it." The security guard took one last drag on the cigarette and then flicked it to the sidewalk.

"You don't like your job?"

"It's all right, I guess. It beats real work."

Calvin nodded at the walkie-talkie that rested on the concrete step next to where the man was sitting. "Does your radio work?"

"Sure. Why?"

"I was wondering what your supervisor said when you told him that I just pulled up."

"Oh, I didn't tell him." The guard reached into the front pocket of his uniform shirt and retrieved another cigarette.

"Interesting," Calvin said easily. "So I could kill you right now and no one would know the difference?"

The young man's eyes widened, and he started to rise.

"Do you know who I am?" Calvin's voice was terse, pointed.

"No."

"Then why are you sitting on your butt? Do you have any idea why you're here?"

"I'm guarding the front door."

"No you're not, you're killing time. My name is Calvin Overstreet. I'm the guy who hired your firm to protect my client. It's a good thing that you don't care for your job, because when I'm done talking to your boss you won't have one. Get on your feet."

The young man complied.

"Where are the additional guards?"

"I don't know what you're talking about."

"I'm not surprised. There were supposed to be additional guards added tonight."

"Are you expecting trouble?" The guard was off balance, nervous.

Calvin was becoming more infuriated each moment. "Yes, Einstein, I am. That's why I called for more people. Has anyone approached the building?"

"No — well, yes."

"Which is it?" Calvin demanded. "No or yes?"

"A car with a woman in it drove into the parking garage. But it's OK, we have a guard posted down there."

"Have you talked to him? Who was the woman? Did she drive out or is she still in the building?"

"No I haven't talked to the other guard —"

"So for all you know, he could be dead. Right?"

"I would have heard something."

"This is unbelievable," Calvin said loudly. "I want to talk to your supervisor."

The young man hesitated.

"Now!" Calvin shouted.

"He's in the lobby."

"Take me to him. Right now, son. Take me to him right now."

"But I'd have to leave my post."

"You left your post hours ago." Calvin grabbed the young man by the arm and steered him toward the front doors.

Once inside the lobby, Calvin released his viselike grip on the guard's arm and marched toward the older uniformed man behind the counter. The man wore a different uniform. Calvin recognized it as the one worn by the building's night watchmen. As soon as the man saw Calvin marching through the lobby, he raised his walkie-talkie to his mouth and keyed the microphone.

At least this guy has something on the ball, Calvin thought. "I'm Calvin Overstreet, Dr. David O'Neal's attorney. You'll find me in the database."

"One moment, Mr. Overstreet," the night watchman said. He sat down and keyed something into the computer.

Calvin heard the opening of a door. He turned to see another guard enter the lobby from the stairwell. *The guard from the parking structure,* Calvin reasoned. *Good. At least he's responsive.*

The night watchman studied Calvin closely, then did the same to the picture of Calvin that had popped up on the computer screen.

"You check out, Mr. Overstreet."

"Thank you." Calvin turned to the young guard who had followed him into the lobby. "Do you see how this is done?"

The older guard nodded at the one who had come through the door and who now promptly turned and went back downstairs to his post. "How can I help you, Mr. Overstreet?"

"There were supposed to be more guards added tonight. Do you know why that hasn't happened?"

"No, sir, that's the first I've heard of it."

"Where's the supervising guard?"

"He accompanied Ms. LaCroix up to her office."

Calvin was nonplussed. "What? Why would Kristen need to be —" He paused. "Are you saying that she had been outside the building?"

"Yes, of course."

"That must have been the woman I saw," the young man said.

"That doesn't make sense. She wasn't supposed to leave the building." Calvin thought for a moment. "Are you sure it was Kristen LaCroix?"

The older guard nodded. "I don't know her well, but who could forget that red hair? I may be a senior citizen, Mr. Overstreet, but I ain't dead. Besides, she was in the database."

"And you say the supervisor accompanied her up to her office?"

"Yes. She had forgotten her card key, and —"

"She didn't have a card key?"

"No, she said she forgot it at home."

This wasn't right. Calvin wondered why Kristen would leave the building, then come back at such a late hour. "How long ago did all this happen?"

"Maybe twenty minutes. Perhaps as much as a half-hour."

"And he's not back?"

"Well now, that is odd."

"Can you phone her office from here?" Calvin asked urgently.

"Yes, but I'd hate to disturb her."

"Disturb her," demanded Calvin. "I'll take responsibility."

"OK." The night watchman picked up the phone. "Let's see," he said as he scanned a list of extensions that had been taped to the telephone. He punched in a number.

"Let me have the phone," Calvin said. The guard relinquished the receiver to him. Calvin listened as the phone rang and rang. "No answer."

"Maybe she's in the head or something," the young guard said.

Calvin glowered at him. "Are you willing

to take that chance?" He returned his attention to the man behind the counter. "Punch up her apartment. She's staying in employee apartment twelve."

The guard did as he was told. Calvin sighed. He had a bad feeling about this. A very haunting, fearful feeling.

When the elevator doors parted on the fifty-third floor, Aldo was in a crouched, three-point stance, the Beretta pointing out the opening, ready to fire. He knew that at least one guard would be on this floor. He could not allow him to radio an alert.

No one was there.

Aldo straddled the threshold between the elevator cab and the lobby, his gun pointing forward. The elevator doors started to close but immediately opened again when the sensors detected his presence. Aldo listened quietly, wondering if the ding of the arriving elevator had alerted the guard.

Nothing.

He stepped back into the elevator, seized the packing tape he had used earlier to block the light sensor, and quickly placed it across the door. The elevator was his escape route, and he wanted it ready when he returned.

Where was the other guard? Aldo could think of only three places: in the rest room down the hall, in the stairwell sleeping or smoking a cigarette, or in O'Neal's apartment. The stairwell would be the easiest to determine. If the guard went in there, he would have to block the door open. The only doors that opened from the stairwell were the doors that led out to the basement, into the first-floor lobby, into the mechanical room just above this floor and the roof. All other doors were locked as a security precaution. Aldo was sure they would do this, and the guard on the parking level had said as much.

Unlike the floor below, this level had only one corridor that ran the width of the building. From the hours Aldo had spent poring over the plans of the building, he knew every necessary detail.

The stairwell first, Aldo thought.

With military precision, he moved quickly down the corridor to the stairwell farthest from O'Neal's apartment. After he had traveled half the distance he stopped. There was no need to go any farther; he could see that the door was closed.

He turned and headed toward the other stairwell. There it was. The door was slightly ajar, propped open by a roll of toilet paper that the guard must have taken from the rest room. The rest room was a redundancy of design. Aldo knew that every floor had the same setup. Even though O'Neal's suite was the only part of the floor occupied, the rest rooms remained from the days before Barringston Relief took charge of the upper ten floors. The guard had to be just behind the metal fireproof door. With a catlike stealth, Aldo approached. He paused near the door, his ear inches away from the opening. He could hear the man's shoes scuff against the concrete landing. The man cleared his throat. The malodor of burning tobacco wafted its way out of the stairwell and into the hall. Aldo smiled to himself. This was going to be easy.

This would have to be quick. A scuffle might be noisy enough for O'Neal to notice. He checked the safety on his gun. It was off. Grabbing the edge of the door, Aldo opened it with a jerk and stepped onto the landing. The guard spun in surprise but had no time to react. The butt of the pistol struck the man on the forehead.

Stunned, he stepped back. His feet came to rest on the edge of the landing, which provided no purchase. He waved his arms wildly trying to regain his balance, but

Aldo had no intention of letting that happen. Raising his foot just a few inches off the floor, Aldo kicked an easy fluid motion that struck the guard on the inside of his right ankle and knocked his foot from beneath him.

The man fell backward, landing hard on the concrete treads. Aldo heard the sound of bone breaking. The momentum of the fall forced the guard into a backward somersault. He came to rest on the next landing down of the U-shaped stairs. He didn't move. From even a half-floor up, Aldo could tell that the guard had breathed his last.

Aldo had not intended to kill the man, but he had made no effort to prevent his death. If the guard died, he died. It made no difference.

Now he had to deal with the other guard, the one trussed up in the elevator. There was a small chance he would come to and make enough noise to attract attention. That would not do at all.

Stepping from the stairwell, Aldo cautiously worked his way back to the elevator, every sense honed and heightened. The guard was still unconscious. Opening the aluminum case, he first removed a narrow knife and quickly cut through the tape that bound the unconscious man's feet. Bits of tape remained stuck to his pants legs. Aldo released one hand so that the cuffs could be removed from the rail. Aldo wasted no time cuffing the guard again.

Next he pulled an inch-long glass container wrapped in a tight cotton mesh from the aluminum case. It was a vial of ammonium carbonate — smelling salts. The vial broke easily in his hand. He waved the pungent container under the guard's nose. He groaned, jerked, and then groaned again. A few seconds later, the man's eyes blinked open.

Aldo watched as the stunned and beaten guard's expression went from confusion to astonishment to fear.

"Hi," Aldo said in a sweet, endearing voice. "Remember me? I'm your date for the evening."

The man started to speak, but the duct tape across his mouth made it impossible. He looked down at his handcuffed wrists. Anger clouded his face.

Grinning, Aldo raised the pistol and pressed it to the guard's forehead. "Now, now. Let's not get in a huff. You know how sensitive we girls can be. Stand up!"

With painful slowness, the man struggled to his feet. Aldo kept the Beretta pointed at the guard's head. He hobbled, his right leg refusing to support its share of his weight.

"Out of the elevator," Aldo commanded. His words were quiet in volume but loud and unmistakable in tone. As the man limped across the threshold, Aldo gave him a shove. The man staggered but kept his balance. "One peep out of you and I'll send a nine-millimeter round through your head. Do you understand?"

The man nodded and walked toward the corridor.

"Turn left," Aldo ordered. "Move to the stairwell. There's someone I want you to see."

Limping as he moved, the guard struggled forward.

When they reached the stairwell Aldo commanded: "Open it. Get inside." The man hesitated, but Aldo drove his point home by pressing the gun into the back of the guard's neck. "Now."

They stepped onto the landing. Aldo made sure the toilet-paper roll remained in its position, propping the door.

The sight of his coworker crumbled in a heap on the intermediate landing below terrified the guard. It also angered him.

Despite his taped mouth, he bellowed, turned, and swung his cuffed arms at Aldo's head. But Aldo was too quick. Ducking just enough so that the guard's futile swing would miss him, he brought a knee up into the man's stomach. The guard doubled over.

"Bad mistake," Aldo said as the guard struggled to catch his breath. "Don't they teach you guys anything?" Aldo brought another knee up in a vicious kick to the face. The force of the blow righted the man. He stood dazed, swaying like a sapling in a stiff breeze. "You shouldn't have done that. You really shouldn't have tried to hit me."

Aldo raised the gun and squeezed the trigger once.

"I don't like this." On the outside, Calvin seemed frustrated and annoyed; on the inside he was terrified. "I've tried her office, no answer. I've tried the apartment she's staying in, still no answer." He paused in thought. "Ring David."

"David O'Neal?" The older guard asked.

"Yes, David O'Neal. Hurry up. And while I'm on the phone, see if you can't get hold of the guard up there. Let him know that something may be going down."

"Got it."

Calvin's stomach tightened into a knot as he heard the phone ring. "Come on, David," he said under his breath. "Pick up."

Aldo raced back to the elevator, retrieved his case, and quickly walked to the door of the suite. He paused, straightened his pants and blouse, and smoothed out the blue blazer. He also checked the wig he wore.

"Showtime," he whispered to himself.

He set the case down, knocked on the door, and picked up the case again. He waited.

Nothing.

He knocked again and listened carefully. This time he heard a muted, "Just a minute." But it was a woman's voice, not a man's. Why hadn't O'Neal answered?

He also heard the phone ring.

Kristen was seated on the edge of the couch wearily rubbing her eyes. She had been deep asleep when the knocking came at the door. It had taken her a moment to realize that it was not part of a dream. She stood and took a few steps toward the door. *Where is David?* she wondered. *He was just here. Maybe he's in the bathroom or he went to bed. I bet he forgot his card key.*

When she was three steps from the door, the phone rang.

"Unbelievable," Kristen said to herself. She started to turn away from the door and toward the phone, when there was another knock. She felt torn between the two. Since the phone had an answering device — she had left several messages on it herself — she opted for the door.

The phone rang again.

Kristen turned the lock and put her hand on the doorknob. A disquiet, nebulous and undefined, percolated within her. Attributing the feeling to the lateness of the hour, Kristen turned the round knob. The door opened easily.

"Forget some— ?" she asked as the door swung open. Her words choked in her throat. Before her stood a woman with red hair cut in the same fashion as hers and wearing clothes similar to those in her own closet.

"Like looking in a mirror, isn't it, darling?"

The voice was wrong, but Kristen couldn't put her finger on it. Her heart seized as the woman in the doorway brought a gun up and pointed it in her face. She backed up as the mystery woman

458

stepped forward.

The phone rang again. It seemed to annoy the woman. Kristen watched as her eyes darted around the room then returned her gaze to Kristen. Without taking her eyes from her, the woman set an aluminum briefcase on the floor. "Where is he?"

"Who?"

The intruder's face hardened; her eyes seem to spark like struck flint. "Get real, woman! Whose suite are we in?"

The truth of the situation flooded Kristen's mind. This must be one of the people responsible for all of David's trouble. She felt foolish for opening the door.

"I asked you a question." The woman's voice dropped a full octave.

"He was called out of state."

The unwanted visitor charged forward with eye-blurring speed. Instinctively Kristen flinched, attempting to dodge the rapidly approaching fist. The blow staggered Kristen, who tottered backward, her jaw aflame with pain. The impact was so stunning that she didn't remember falling or landing on the carpeted floor.

She blinked hard. Her vision was blurry, and there was a profound ringing in her ears. The skin tightened along her jaw as the tissue beneath began to swell. As her eyes cleared she noticed that the woman with red hair was gone.

Was it over?

Kristen willed herself to rise. She stumbled on uncertain feet. Grabbing the back of the couch, she steadied herself. Faintness descended on her. Nausea welled up like a pot boiling over on a stove.

As she waited for her equilibrium to return, Kristen looked around the room. The door was still closed. The metal briefcase was still there. The sight of it made her heart sink. Why would she leave the briefcase?

A sound to her right hooked her attention. She snapped her head around and immediately regretted the motion. Pain raced down her neck and back. She saw the woman exiting David's bedroom.

"I didn't find O'Neal, but I did find this." She was pulling Timmy by the arm.

"Ouch," Timmy protested. He rubbed his eyes. "Leave me alone."

"Shut up, kid." The woman pushed Timmy forcefully. He stumbled forward and fell to his knees. A cry of pain erupted from his lips.

"Leave him alone." Kristen wondered

how this woman could be so mean. Kristen stepped forward, her hands clenched into tight fists.

The woman raised the gun and pointed it at Timmy. "Careful lady," she croaked. "I'm trained to do things that would give the Mafia nightmares."

"Who are you?" Kristen demanded.

"A professional with a job to do. Now where is O'Neal?"

"I told you."

"That he left the state? O'Neal is out on bail. He's required to stay in California. Now tell me where he is or I start hurting people."

"I don't know," Kristen said forcefully. Anger and indignation were replacing fear.

"Another lie?" The woman raised an eyebrow.

"It's the truth. I fell asleep on the couch. When I woke up, he was gone. I thought you were him."

The woman glared at Kristen, who felt as if she were being examined with eyes that could see right through her. "Do you think he left the building?"

"I told you that I don't know. He said nothing to me, and even if he did, I wouldn't tell you."

"You're a bad man," Timmy said. "Go

461

away. Leave us alone. We don't like you. Go away."

Bad man? That was it! Timmy had seen what Kristen couldn't. This wasn't a woman, it was a man dressed to look like her.

"I told you to shut up, kid."

"No. I don't have to. You're not my boss."

The man took a step toward Timmy.

"No," Kristen cried. "Timmy, be quiet."

"But —" Timmy began.

"No, Timmy," she commanded forcibly. "No more talking. I don't want to have to tell you again. Do you understand?" Kristen felt remorse for yelling at Timmy, but he didn't understand the danger, couldn't conceive of the madness of the man with the gun.

"OK," Timmy said. He got up off the floor slowly and sat on the couch. "I'm sorry."

Kristen's heart sank. Timmy was trying to be brave. A man, dressed as a woman, broke into the suite, rousted him out of bed, held him at gunpoint, pushed him to the floor, and she yelled at him. Tears welled up in her eyes. She would explain it all to him over an ice cream sundae when this was all over —

assuming they survived.

"You're quick, lady. I'll give you that." The man no longer made an attempt to alter his voice.

"David's not here, so why don't you just leave?"

"Yeah, right. I went through weeks of planning so that I could get up here and say, 'Gee whiz, this didn't work out the way I wanted. I guess I'll go home now.' " He waved the gun at the sofa. "Sit down."

Kristen complied. "Now what?"

"Now we wait."

David exited the communications office with a manila folder in his hand. It was the written report about the Bangladesh workers. He was ecstatic. He had just finished speaking with two Barringston workers previously thought lost. The night before the tsunami struck, they had taken the children of the orphanage to Ramu. Everyone was safe — at least in Bangladesh. There were still two missing workers in India.

Despite the time, David had called the families of the workers to let them know that their loved ones were safe. They were two of the best calls he had ever made. Now he looked forward to telling Kristen.

At the bank of elevators, David inserted his card key. The middle elevator opened immediately. David stepped in, reinserted his key, and depressed the button marked 53. The elevator began its short ride up.

A soft ding sounded his arrival, and David stepped from the elevator car. As he did, something caught his attention. He paused and turned. The doors to the elevator next to the one he had just been in were open.

Odd, he thought. Stepping to the elevator, David looked in. The doors remained opened. Bits of brown tape hung from the handrail. David walked in. Something dark and moist on the floor caught his attention. Squatting down, he took a closer look. He touched it with his middle finger. Red. Sticky.

Turning, David noticed another piece of tape across the door. He crossed the threshold into the lobby, took hold of the tape, and pulled. The doors immediately closed.

A deep piercing flash of fear stabbed him. It was falling into place. He studied the deep rust-red smudge on his finger. Blood. But whose blood?

A sudden storm of anxiety swept in. Kristen! Timmy! He had to be sure they were safe. The guard. Where was the guard? David had not seen him when he left the suite. His mind was so fixed on the discovery of the workers that he had not even thought to wonder at the watchman's absence.

Cautiously, David first worked his way to the corridor, which he surveyed closely looking for any clues that an intruder might be present. He saw none.

He came to the door of his suite and placed his hand on the doorknob. The door should have been locked. He remembered locking it as he left. As slowly as he could, he began to turn the knob. It turned easily. It was unlocked. Had Kristen awakened and stepped into the hall to look for him? Could he take that chance?

The answer was no. He faced a dilemma. On the other side of the door were the two people he loved most. They could be in danger. They might even be dead.

His first impulse was to charge through the door and attack. But he hesitated. Not out of fear for his own life, but out of fear that he might fail and become the cause of Kristen and Timmy's death.

Think, he told himself. *Think.*

Gently, David returned the doorknob to its previous position. He leaned forward, pressing his ear to the door and holding his breath. He listened.

"He doesn't answer his radio."

Calvin looked at the older guard and saw the concern in his eyes. "There's no answer at David's either. Something is wrong, very wrong." He began to pace. "We have two missing guards, an unknown woman who looks like Kristen, and no one is answering at David's."

"I think we should call the police," the young guard said.

Calvin ignored him. "Let's assume for a moment that your guards have been taken out of commission. That means the perpetrator may have one of their radios. She will be able to listen in on all transmissions. That makes the radios useless."

"So what do we do?" the Barringston guard asked.

"You call the police," Calvin said to the older guard, then to the young rent-a-cop he ordered, "You talk to the other guards. Don't use the radio. Understand? Walk over to them and tell them to take a position out of sight but near any possible exits. If this person is associated with the ones who have been setting David up, I doubt she would have any compunction about putting a bullet in someone's head. Including yours. Have you got that? We don't need any John Waynes here tonight."

"But she's just a woman," the younger guard protested.

Calvin clenched his jaw. "She's surely armed, and you're not." Calvin regretted not insisting on armed guards. David had nixed the idea, fearing that it would cause undo concern among the employees who had enough on their minds. "A fast-moving bullet doesn't care who fired it. A gun is a great equalizer. She might be half your size, but with a gun she's a giant. Besides, she may not be working alone. The best we can do is observe. The police can take it from there."

"What are you going to do?" the older guard asked.

"I'm going up," Calvin replied flatly. "You have a master card key, don't you?"

"Yes."

"Give it to me."

"I'm not sure that's wise. Especially if she may have taken out two guards already."

"Give me the key. I'm going up."

Reluctantly the guard passed the card key to Calvin. Calvin started toward the elevators.

★ ★ ★

Click. Clack.
Click. Clack.
Kristen tensed. With each new metallic sound she became more apprehensive. She and Timmy were seated side by side on the sofa. The man in the red wig sat behind them. Although she could not see him, she guessed that he was playing with the hammer on the pistol. Cocking it, releasing it.

Click. Clack.
"Is that really necessary?" Kristen asked.
"I like it."
"Figures."
The man sighed. "It's been my experience — and I'm very experienced — that when faced with danger such as this, people fall into one of two groups: those who whine and plead, and those who become mouthy. You, Kristen, fall in the latter."

"Why are you doing this?" The question sounded like a line from the countless action pictures she had seen. She had always thought it was a lame question; now it was the only one she could think of.

"It's my job. You're the head of public relations for Barringston Relief. That's your job. I assume you're good at it, that you have a talent for it. True?"

"I guess so."

"Don't guess. You're a smart woman. Be assertive. Of course you're good at what you do. Well, I'm good at what I do. I have certain skills and am unencumbered by needless emotions."

"Needless emotions?"

"Sure. Guilt, remorse, regret, sorrow, fear."

"You have no fear?" Kristen asked. "I find that hard to believe."

"I find it hard to believe that you'd think I care about your opinions," the man snapped. "I have no fear. I haven't had any since I was a teenager."

"You're not afraid to die?" Kristen shifted in her seat. In the wake of terrorist activities, she had once read an article about hostages. Experts said that conversation often led to a bonding between terrorist and hostage, making it more difficult for the abductor to kill the abducted.

"Not a bit. A man dies and that's it. It's the living that mourn." He laughed. "I have yet to hear a dead man complain about being dead."

"What if death isn't the end?"

"What? You mean like heaven and hell?" He laughed again. "Save it for gullible

Sunday school kids, lady. There's no heaven. There's no hell. There's just this old, tired world and me."

"And you?"

"Well, there are others, but they don't matter. Evolution has bred all this. This situation isn't all that different from what you find in nature. More sophisticated, perhaps, but basically the same thing. Your boyfriend, David, has stepped into someone else's territory, and that person wants protection. I'm the one who specializes in providing that protection. It's nothing special, really."

"That's a pretty pathetic view of life, don't you think?"

Click. Clack.

"If I did, I wouldn't be here now, would I?"

Click. Clack.

Kristen shuddered. Had she gone too far? Had she irritated the man?

"I think there's more to death than just nonexistence. What if you're wrong? What if there is a hell?"

"Then, my dear Kristen, I shall conquer it. Better to rule in hell than serve in heaven."

Kristen guffawed.

"What's so funny?" the man snapped.

"Where did you get that little bit of philosophy? A bumper sticker?"

Click. This time there was no clack. No easing of the pistol's hammer into its resting place.

In for a penny, in for a pound, Kristen reasoned. "Despite your actions, you seem like a fairly intelligent man. Surely you can see the fault in that statement. No one rules in hell. The cartoon picture of Satan standing with pitchfork in hand tormenting poor lost souls is just that, a cartoon. Satan is going to be the most tormented of all. What do you think hell is, mister? A stroll through the bad part of town?"

There was silence, then the soft sound of feet on carpet. Something cold and hard touched Kristen on her swollen jaw. She cut her eyes to the side and saw her captor. He had removed the blazer, but the silk shell top and red wig were still in place. He gently dragged the barrel of the gun along her cheek and ear as if caressing her with it. The metal felt cold and foreign. She trembled. A chill of terror trickled down her spine.

"I am my own god and my own devil. There is none beside me. There is none like me. I can bring pain or pleasure. The choice is mine."

He pressed the side of the gun next to her ear. Every muscle in her body tightened.

"Don't insult my intelligence." He spoke threateningly. "I have an IQ of 145; I've taught myself four languages; I have a photographic memory." His voice deepened in anger. "Don't lecture me. Don't imply that I'm stupid."

Clack.

He had returned the hammer to its forward position.

"You leave her alone," Timmy shouted.

"Shut up, kid," the man bellowed. "You're starting to get on my nerves. Do you understand that? Are you smart enough to grasp that?"

"I'm smarter than you think," Timmy boasted.

"That's enough, Timmy," Kristen said firmly. "It would be better if you sat still and were quiet."

"But —"

"Still and quiet, Timmy. Please." Kristen made strong eye contact. Timmy relented.

"OK. But I gotta go to the bathroom."

"Too bad, kid. You're not going anywhere."

"But I really, *really* gotta go," Timmy insisted.

"Let him go to the bathroom," Kristen

said. "We're fifty-three floors up. What's he going to do, jump out a window?"

"All right, kid, but make it quick. Do you hear? Quick, or I'm coming in after you."

"I'll be quick," Timmy said as he leaped from the couch and sprinted toward the bathroom.

David pulled back from the door. He could not make out all the words, but he heard three voices. Kristen's, Timmy's, and one he didn't recognize. He was simultaneously relieved and terrified.

Relieved because Kristen and Timmy were alive and sounded unharmed. Terrified because a stranger was in his suite holding his loved ones. David had to assume the man was armed.

The real question was what to do next. He played with the idea of storming into the apartment. He would have the advantage of surprise. Perhaps he could tackle the man before he could harm Kristen and Timmy. If so, they might be able to make an escape. But logic kicked in hard. It was more likely that David would be shot and killed in the act. With him dead, the abductor would have no reason to keep the other two alive. As horribly ironic as it seemed, Kristen and Timmy might be safer with David at some distance.

But he had to do something. It was just as likely that the kidnapper would get frustrated and kill them anyway.

David walked away from the door to the elevator lobby. He began to pace. The thought of the danger that was just a few steps down the hall tormented him. He had to do something, but it had to be right, smart, and logical. He struggled to suppress his emotions while freeing his mind.

David paced some more. He prayed. He fumed. He prayed again. The elevator indicator chimed. Instinctively, David ducked around the corner into the hall. The elevator could be bringing anyone up. Maybe the man in the apartment had an accomplice or even a dozen accomplices. For all David knew, all the guards were dead and the building had been taken over by a mob of hit men. He could take no chances.

Desperately, David looked for a weapon. His eyes traced the hall but at first found nothing. A big, heavy fire extinguisher was mounted on the wall. It might serve as a decent weapon against one, maybe even two men — provided they didn't have guns. It was his only choice.

Dropping the folder, he took the metal

canister from its rack. David set it down, seized the neck just below the handle and nozzle, and quietly stepped to the corner formed by the hall and lobby. He prepared to swing and swing hard.

David strained his ears to listen, hoping to hear voices or to get some clue as to who was stepping from the elevator. He heard only the slow padding of shoes on the lobby carpet. Taking a deep breath, David raised the fire extinguisher, stepped forward, and prepared to strike.

Calvin's eyes widened, and he brought up his arms. David was barely able to redirect his swing so the metal cylinder missed his attorney's head.

"David! You're all right."

"Quiet," David commanded. He pushed Calvin to the back wall of the lobby. In a voice barely above a whisper he said, "I just got back from communications. Someone is in my apartment. I could hear them talking. Some man is holding Kristen and Timmy."

"Man? You're sure you heard a man's voice?"

"Yes."

"You didn't hear a strange woman's voice?"

"No. Should I have?"

Calvin explained about the "Kristen" being escorted to her office.

"Kristen has been in my apartment all night. She hasn't been out of my sight except for the twenty minutes or so that I was down in communications."

"It must have been a disguise."

"I can believe it. This whole thing has been nothing but smoke and mirrors since the beginning."

"What about weapons? Are there any weapons in the building?" Calvin asked.

"There are none on the Barringston floors, that much I know. Do you think I'd be swinging a fire extinguisher if there were?"

"Swell," Calvin said. "So we have a professional hit man holding two hostages on the top floor of a fifty-three-story building, the extra guards didn't show, and the ones that are here aren't carrying guns, and we're armed with a fire extinguisher." He shook his head. "This is not good, not good at all. At least the police are on their way."

"That's a plus."

"I'm not so sure. If our bad guy gets nervous, things could go from bad to worse."

"How so?"

"Look, David, the police are trained for

476

many things, including situations similar to this one. They have hostage negotiators and sharpshooters. But this is not a typical situation. Those things are fine if you're dealing with a trapped bank robber or some depressed husband who has taken his family hostage. Our bad guy is a professional. Some negotiator isn't going to talk him into giving up."

"I agree with the professional part. Whoever it is that has set me up with those videos and sent those pictures has put a lot of thought and money into this. They certainly aren't going to hire some two-bit hood." David paused. "What will the police do when they get here?"

Calvin looked across the lobby at the hall. "They'll send a patrol car, maybe another as backup. First officer on the scene will talk to the guards and attempt to assess the situation. A couple of officers may come up here, so go easy with that fire extinguisher. Once they know that it is a hostage situation, they'll call for supervisors, SWAT, hostage negotiation. Most likely they'll evacuate the building."

David studied Calvin. "You don't think that'll work, do you?"

Calvin shook his head. "Most times yes, but not here. If she . . . he is the professional I think he is, then we've got real trouble. There's a good chance that he might kill Kristen or Timmy."

"Why?" David was shocked. "They're his safety net."

Again Calvin shook his head. "Two hostages are more difficult to handle than one. He knows that. By killing one, he sets the tone for negotiations. I'm sorry, David."

"I'm not going to let that happen. Not while I breathe. We must do something."

"There's another problem too. If I've pieced this together right, we have a man dressed like Kristen. If the police give up on negotiations and charge the room, they could mistakenly shoot the wrong person."

David sighed heavily.

"Animals become more ferocious when trapped," Calvin said coolly. The transition from attorney back to FBI agent was easily seen. "It's going to be the same for him. What we need to do is give him a way out. At least a way he thinks is out."

"Or give him me. I'm the one he wants. This whole thing orbits around me. I don't know why, but it does."

"He would still need a way out."

"I can become his hostage and . . ." David trailed off.

Calvin finished the thought for him.

"And he can kill you as he makes his get-away. I don't think so, David. We don't release control. We maintain it. Use it to our advantage."

"I wasn't aware that we had control."

"We may have more than we think."

There was a deep, palpable silence as dark as the night outside.

"OK, here's what we do," Calvin said.

18

"What's in the case?" Kristen asked. The previous ten minutes had passed in utter and oppressive silence.

"Did you watch cartoons when you were a kid?" the man said. *Click. Clack.* He was still playing with the hammer of the pistol.

"Sometimes."

"Ever hear of Felix the Cat? Well, that's my magic bag of tricks."

"What's in it?" Kristen persisted.

"If I told you, the magic would be gone. Wouldn't it?"

The man's flippancy was wearing on her. "What happens if David doesn't come back? Maybe he's on to you."

"No one is on to me," he replied flatly. "No one knows I'm here."

"The guards must have seen you enter the building."

"Correction. They saw *you* enter the building."

"The red wig is a close match, but you

don't look that much like me. At least I hope I don't look like you."

"The resemblance has to be only good enough to create the illusion. That's the problem with hiring rent-a-cops. They don't know the people well enough. I passed right under their noses."

"Maybe."

"No maybe about it. Not even the guard who escorted me saw through my disguise. Another ten minutes and he would have made a pass at me."

"What happened to the guard?"

"He took the stairs down." The man laughed.

"What's that mean?"

Before he could answer, there was a knock on the door. The abductor was on his feet and pressing the gun to the back of Kristen's neck. "Who could that be at this hour?" His voice was a whisper.

Kristen grimaced in pain as the man ground the gun into her skin. "How should I know? I don't live here. I just fell asleep on the couch."

He leaned over and put his lips next to her ear. Strands of hair from the wig brushed her face, and his breath rolled along her cheek. She felt ill.

"This is how it is going to go," he said.

"You're going to answer the door. Open it only partway. If it's David —"

"It's not — oww!" The end of the silencer dug into her flesh.

"Shut up and listen. If it's David, step back and let him in. If it's someone else, get rid of them."

"And if it's the police?"

"You're all dead."

Kristen rose and crossed to the door. Just before she turned the handle, she heard a whispered, "Hold it." Turning, she saw the man grab Timmy by the back of the shirt and lead him to the side of the door. The barrel of the gun was pressed under Timmy's chin. He said something to Timmy that Kristen could not hear. Timmy, eyes wide in fright, just nodded.

Once in place next to the door, the man motioned with his head that Kristen should continue. She turned the knob and opened the door about six inches. Peeking out, she saw Calvin.

Calvin's heart was pounding, and his mouth was dry. He forced a smile. "Oh, hi, Kristen. I didn't expect to see you here." A glance was all it took for him to realize the fear she felt.

"I . . . I fell asleep on the couch."

482

"I'm sorry to wake you, but I have some good news for David. Is he still awake?"

She shook her head. Calvin shot his eyes to the door and back asking an unspoken question. Kristen caught it. She nodded slightly as she said, "He's asleep. He's not feeling well."

"I can imagine. Anyway, I've found a way to get the Justice Department to unfreeze Barringston Relief's assets, but I need a couple of signatures first. If David could sign them first thing in the morning, I'll send a messenger around to pick it up. Then you guys can get back to the business of helping people." Once again he cut his eyes to the door and then back at Kristen asking again the unspoken question. This time he scratched his chin with his thumb, his index finger extended straight. He was making a sign for a gun.

Kristen nodded twice. "I'll make sure he gets it. I know he'll be pleased."

"Thanks," Calvin said lightly. His stomach seized into a tight fist of a knot. "Again, I'm sorry I woke you. If you'll just take this folder," he held out the manila office folder David had brought up from communications, "and have him sign where I've indicated, we can get this monkey off our back."

483

Calvin held the folder back making Kristen reach for it. "I'll be sure to do that, and —"

He grabbed her arm and pulled hard while simultaneously ramming his shoulder into the door. Calvin watched as Kristen was turned sideways by the forceful opening. He pulled again, spinning her into the hall. David was there. He snatched her by the blouse and pulled her down the corridor toward the stairs. Calvin heard him yell, "Run!"

The door unexpectedly pulled open. Calvin, who had been pressing against the door with all his strength to make an opening wide enough to pull Kristen through, fell headlong into the apartment.

It was something Calvin had not anticipated.

David pushed Kristen along the hall, interposing himself between the door to his suite and her. He turned briefly, looking over his shoulder. Two holes exploded through the door at head height, casting splinters into the air. Gunshots.

"Timmy!" Kristen was screaming. "Timmy is still in there."

"I know," David answered forcefully. "Keep moving. To the stairs. Don't stop.

Run. Keep running." It wasn't supposed to have worked this way. The man was supposed to bolt into the hall where Calvin would distract him and possibly subdue him. That would give Timmy a chance to run. But Calvin disappeared into the apartment. David's fear tripled.

The stairway nearest David's apartment was only a dozen steps away, but it seemed a thousand. In his mind, he could hear the door open and the man with the gun laugh maniacally. He could feel the impact of hot bullets in his back. So far it was only his imagination, but David knew that the nightmare could become reality in less than a second.

Kristen reached the stairwell door with David close on her heels. She paused. David did not. Reaching around her, he clutched the horizontal panic bar, sandwiching Kristen between him and the door. David pushed the bar with his hand and Kristen with his body. They careened through the opening.

Kristen gasped. David, still holding the door open, turned in the direction of her gaze, fearing that some coconspirator had been lying in wait for them. Instead, he saw the broken and shot bodies of the two guards lying unmoving on the intermediate landing five feet below them.

"Oh, David."

"Later. Upstairs. Run."

"Where?"

"There's a machine room above this floor. Calvin and I checked it. The door is open. Now go."

"What about you?"

"I'm going back for Timmy and Calvin." David didn't wait for a reply. He bolted back through the door and into the hall.

His heart was pounding, his mind praying, his anger growing. It wasn't supposed to work this way. It was falling apart. Sprinting down the hall, he came to the door of his suite. He paused for a second, took a deep breath, then charged through.

When Calvin fell through the opening into David's suite, he wasn't sure what to expect. He was pretty sure that he would be shot. Instead, he stumbled across the threshold, falling forward. He did a shoulder roll, springing to his feet.

Looking to the door he saw the woman/man with the gun. He also saw something that sent chills of terror through his soul. Timmy was wrestling with the man in the wig.

"Stop it! Stop it! You're a bad man."

Timmy was young in mind, but he possessed the body of a twenty-four-year-old man. Adrenaline fueled by fear and concern had given him explosive strength. Timmy had kept Calvin from being shot.

"Get off me, you stupid — oww!" The scream of pain came when Timmy bit the gunman's hand. It was a brave act that was rewarded with a knee to the stomach and a left-handed punch to the side of the head. Timmy dropped in a heap. Calvin knew by the way the boy fell that he was unconscious before he landed on the floor.

But Calvin had no intention of letting the brave young man be treated so brutally. Before the attacker could fully turn, Calvin was on him, full weight flung forward with the determination of an NFL tackle. The two men crashed into the wall. Several pictures fell from their perches and crashed to the floor.

Immediately, Calvin spun the smaller man around so that his gun hand was pointed away from Timmy. A shot was fired. It pierced the carpet and ricocheted off the concrete floor and into the ceiling. He wanted the man on the floor flat on his back. There Calvin could use his greater size and weight to pin him and limit his mobility. Wrapping both arms around the assailant, he lifted, preparing to send him crashing to the deck.

He wasn't fast enough.

The gunman, arms confined by Calvin, pulled his head back and then brought it crashing down into Calvin's face. The blow was stunning. Red and yellow splashes filled his sight. Calvin's knees buckled; his stomach turned at the pain. Darkness plunged in from the edges of his eyes. He fought the encroaching blackness, willing himself to hold on to consciousness and to remain on his feet.

Blinking hard, he involuntarily dropped his arms and staggered backward. His vision blurred, then cleared in time to see a foot sailing at his head. Instinct told him to move, but his body was unresponsive. The roundhouse kick landed on the right of Calvin's jaw. There was a snap and searing pain. Again he staggered but remained standing.

Another kick. This one landed just below his ribs. The air in his lungs was forced from his lips, his solar plexus, convulsed by spasms, became paralyzed. He could not draw a breath. Calvin dropped to one knee and looked up into the bore of the pistol aimed at his head.

The gunman smiled.

★ ★ ★

When David exploded into the room, his eyes fell directly on a woman with red hair. She was aiming a pistol at a crimson-faced, heaving Calvin. He knew this was no woman but a man in disguise. A man hired to kill him. A man who had threatened and harmed those whom he loved. A man who participated in bringing Barringston Relief to its knees when it needed to be its strongest. Out of the corner of his eye, he saw Timmy curled up on the floor, unmoving.

In the fraction of a second it took to take in the scene, parts of David's personality dissolved. Fear evaporated, caution melted away, personal protection became meaningless. All that mattered was stopping this man.

David charged. By nature he was not a physical man, although he kept in shape by playing racquetball twice each week, a habit he had learned from A. J. Barringston, his mentor. But when properly motivated, the least physical of men could become juggernauts of force, driven by passion, propelled by love.

Without missing a beat, David continued toward the gunman, pushing himself forward with as much thrust as his rage-empowered legs could muster. He could see the assailant's eyes widen at the sudden sounds of David's entry and of the piercing scream he uttered as he propelled himself forward.

David — head down, arms out — left the ground. He hit the attacker with such force that electric bolts of pain struck every nerve. The force carried both men across the living room and into the desk with the computer near the picture window. The desk's glass top came down in large shards of shark-toothed glass.

David and the gunman lay dazed and bleeding on the floor.

The gun! David thought, fighting to hold onto consciousness. *Where's the gun?* He rolled on his side and tried to raise himself to his knees. Glass dug into the flesh of his hands and legs. He wiped his face with the back of his hand. Blood. *Must find the gun.*

Next to him the man screamed in fury. Swearing. Streams of curses, maledictions, and fulmination filled the air.

David stood to his feet. *Gun. Gun. Does he still have it? Where is it?* Blood trickled into his eyes.

"I've been waiting for you." The attacker stood, less affected by the crashing blow than David. The gun was in his hand and aimed at David's sternum. *This man is*

490

tough, David thought.

The wig the man wore was twisted, uneven, and hanging in his eyes. He grabbed it and threw it to the floor. His face was cut in several places, and rivulets of blood dripped from his chin, splattering the silk top he wore. A piece of glass protruded from his cheek. He took it between two fingers and slowly extracted it. If it caused him pain, he didn't show it. "I've gone through a lot of trouble to find and kill you."

"Aww," David said sarcastically, too angry to care about his own safety any longer. "You shouldn't have got all dressed up for me. I already have a girl."

"Why is it that people just this side of death turn into smart alecks?"

"Nothing to lose, I guess."

"You're about to lose everything," the man said. "It would have been a lot easier if you had just confessed to the crimes."

"I didn't commit any crimes." *Keep talking, David,* he said to himself. *Buy some time.* He hoped and prayed for a miracle. "Why should I confess to any?"

"Because it would have saved your life. But you missed that opportunity. Now you get to die."

"I've been ready to die for years. Today

is as good as any."

"No one is ready to die. It's not natural. We all claw at life. Trust me, I've seen many people beg for just one more day."

David smiled. "You won't see it here. What about you? Are you afraid to die?"

The gunman laughed. "To quote Woody Allen, 'It's not that I'm afraid to die, I just don't want to be there when it happens.' Death happens. That's all there is to it. You die tonight, I another night. But we will both die. See if you recognize this one: 'As the waters fail from the sea, and the flood decayeth and drieth up: so man lieth down, and riseth not: till the heavens be no more, they shall not awake, nor be raised out of their sleep.' Can you place it?"

"It sounds familiar," David conceded.

"Job 14. It's from your own Bible. Pretty depressing, isn't it?"

"You need to look deeper. Try this on for size: 'See in what peace a Christian can die.' Do you know who said that? Joseph Addison, English essayist of the eighteenth century. Those were his dying words. I think they were good ones. But best yet are the words of Paul the apostle: 'For to me, to live is Christ and to die is gain.' Can you understand those words?"

"Very good, Dr. O'Neal. I'm impressed.

Not enough to spare your life, but I am impressed." The gunman brought the pistol up and aimed it at David's head. "The night wears on, and I have new jobs waiting."

Slowly David stepped back and to the side until he backed into the glass wall that overlooked the city. Glass crunched under his shoes with each step.

"Not afraid to die, huh?" A grin grew on the man's face. David watched as the grin dissolved into a sneer. His lips parted to reveal blood-stained teeth. David steeled himself for the inevitable. He wondered if he would die instantly or if he would linger in pain before breathing his last. He thought of Kristen and of his deep love for her. Her face filled his mind as did the face of Timmy.

Emotions began to swirl in him like marbles in a blender. *So this is what it is like to face death.* Instead of fearing pain, he was more concerned about dying with dignity. He didn't want to embarrass himself or Barringston Relief, but mostly he didn't want to embarrass his Lord.

A soft pop exploded from the muzzle of the gun. David stood his ground. Glass exploded behind him as the floor-to-ceiling picture window exploded into cubes of tempered glass and rained down on the floor, the planter, and the street fifty-three stories below. Night air rushed in where the window had been. David turned to his attacker.

"You missed." Through the jagged opening came the ululation of distant sirens. They would have been a welcome, hopeful sound if they were not so far away.

The man's face was drawn with anger. Wrath radiated from his eyes.

"What's the matter?" David asked. "Didn't I flinch enough for you?"

"You're too stupid to plead for your life."

"I told you, I've been ready to die for years. It's the great adventure. The famous evangelist Dwight Moody called it his coronation day. Why should I fear my coronation?"

"You're crazy. You know that, don't you? You're nothing but a superstitious freak."

"I'm not the one who's afraid to die. One of us has to be, right?" Behind the gunman, David saw Calvin slowly stand and waver. It was clear that he was in great pain. David had to buy more time.

"Ever heard of Pascal's wager?" David asked.

"Pascal? The mathematician?"

"The very same. He was a strong Christian. He once said to an atheist, 'If I'm wrong and there is no God, I lose nothing; but if you're wrong and there is a God, you lose everything.' That's a paraphrase, but I'm not at my best right now."

"It's a fool's bet," the man said. "You're asking me to change my life for a myth."

"You stand to lose more than I do."

"Nice try, Dr. O'Neal, but no dice. It's time for you to die."

Calvin started forward, but the gunman heard his heavy, unsteady footsteps and spun on his heels. He fired two shots. Calvin stumbled backward and fell to his side with a scream of pain. He moaned and thrashed on the floor.

David was moving before the gunman fired the second shot. He was not experienced in any form of fighting, but he was motivated by fear for his friend's life. As the gunman turned back to David, he was greeted with a fist to the face. David had put his full weight into the punch, which rocked the man, split his lip, but didn't cause him to fall.

David reached for the gun but was only able to grab the man's wrist with both hands. David felt the air leave his lungs as a fist caught him in the ribs. He held on.

Another blow to the ribs, but this time it was from his attacker's knee. Bones broke. Fire raged through David's torso, but still he hung on. Another shot was discharged, striking the second floor-to-ceiling window. Glass again rained down.

"No one" — another kick to the ribs — "hits me!"

Another kick. More bone-breaking noises. David dropped to a knee, but still he held on. It was all he could do. It was his only hope of survival. If this man was going to kill him, he was going to have to work for the privilege. David refused to lie down and die. He had Timmy to live for — if he was still alive. He had Kristen. He had a work that changed the lives of millions. He would not surrender his life; it would have to be dragged from him.

From his crouched position, David gathered all his strength and pulled down on the man's gun arm while springing to his feet with all his might. David's aim was on target. The top of his head hit the gunman square on the chin. He knew he had hurt him by the pain that filled his own skull and neck.

David pulled backward, hoping to free the gun, but his strength was waning. Blackness began to engulf him, drown him.

He stumbled back, still holding tenaciously to the assailant's arm. The man followed him, careening forward out of control. David sensed his legs were weak, and he prayed that the man would fall unconscious.

The two men fell to the floor, rolling over each other trying to gain the upper position for control. But each time David found himself on top, he immediately found himself falling toward the floor again.

Glass from the shattered window dug at his back and arms. The gunman began to swear. His face was twisted into a monstrous, demonic mask of pure rage. They rolled one more time, but not to David's advantage. He was pinned to the floor; the man sat astride him. David fought to keep the gun pointed away from himself and toward the broken window, but his opponent was stronger and better trained. No matter how much David resisted the gunman, the pistol moved inexorably closer to his head.

Then, in a move that surprised David, the assailant pulled the gun in the opposite direction. David's grasp slipped. One second later the barrel was pressing between David's eyes.

"You surprise me, Dr. O'Neal." The gunman was sweating and breathing heavily. "I had you figured for a quitter, but you've proven an almost worthy opponent. Not that I care. Not that it matters. You're a dead man anyway."

A dark object emerged from just outside David's vision. It was large and moving fast. There was a crash as the object careened into the man. The force was sufficient to knock the man off David. The gun went flying.

"You leave David alone!" Timmy was screaming. The gunman moaned. Timmy had picked up the heavy desk chair and flung it as hard as he could. When the chair made contact with the assailant, David heard a crack. He had no idea if it was a bone or the chair breaking.

"You leave him alone! Do you hear?"

David looked at Timmy, who seemed to tower above the floor. His face was marred by blood and bruises. His nose was bleeding. But he seemed to take no notice of it.

The gun! David scrambled to his feet. Everything hurt — the glass in his back and arms, the broken ribs, the strained muscles — but he rose to his feet. He saw the gun on the floor near the gaping hole where the window used to be. The same force that had knocked the gun from his attacker's hand had also knocked the attacker in the same direction. The gun and he were only two feet apart.

David started for the weapon, but he wasn't fast enough. The gunman grabbed it, rolled on his back and aimed up at David, then Timmy, then back to David.

"Back up. Back up now," he commanded. His voice had changed. It was now charged with animalistic rage, with evil. He rose to his feet, swayed, and grimaced in pain. "Who dies first, O'Neal? Huh? You or the kid? One of you gets to watch the other die. Who wants to be the lucky one?"

He raised the gun to shoulder height. The attacker stood only a foot away from the open window frame. The glass under his feet crunched as he set his stance. "You've been a challenge, Dr. O'Neal. A real challenge."

David was stuck. If he charged, he would certainly be shot and Timmy soon after that. There was nothing he could do. He was going to die.

"I think it should be Timmy," the man said with a bloody smile. "That should cause you a little more pain."

Instinctively, David stepped in front of Timmy, interposing his body between the boy and the barrel of the gun.

"Such bravery, Dr. O'Neal," the man said mockingly. "How do you know the bullet won't go right through you?"

"I'm willing to take the chance." Then to Timmy he said, "I love you, buddy. You know that, don't you? I love you more than I can say."

"I know," Timmy said softly. "I love you too."

"Timmy, I want you to leave now. I want you to run."

"I don't want to leave you." Timmy's voice choked with tears.

"Don't argue. The police should be in the building by now. Find them. They'll take care of you."

"But —"

"Don't argue with me, Timmy. Do as I say." David's voice was loud and firm, but laced with sad kindness.

The gunman sneered. "I'll kill him before he's halfway to the door."

"No you won't," David said confidently. "I won't let you."

"How are you going to stop me?"

"Now, Timmy! Run!"

Timmy turned and sprinted for the door.

David watched as the attacker quickly brought the pistol around toward Timmy, but David was already on the move. The gun came back to bear on David. There was a muffled sound as a shot traveled through the silencer. A second later he heard the door to the apartment fly open as Timmy ran for his life.

The bullet smashed into David's right shoulder, but David didn't care. It didn't matter. Nothing mattered but stopping this man. The shot slowed David's forward momentum but not enough to stop him completely. He fell forward in a lumbering crash to the floor. He slid along the broken glass, his torso smashing into the shins of his tormentor and knocking his feet from under him. The man crashed face first on top of David. Both slid along the floor.

David opened his eyes and found himself looking down fifty-three floors to the street below. He could see police cars, tiny from this distance, with their red lights flashing. He had hoped to hit his attacker straight on, propelling them both into the empty air. It would have meant his death too, but he had resigned himself to that fact. *Greater love has no one than this, that he lay down his life for his friends.*

The man exploded in fury as he sprang

to his feet. He kicked David in the ribs, then in the head, then in the ribs again. Darkness swirled in David's head.

"I have had enough of you!" His voice was venomous. Distant. "I'll kill you with my bare hands if I have to."

"Here, here, here." David heard another voice, excited and panicked. It was Timmy's voice.

"Run, Timmy," David croaked, his words barely above a whisper. "Run." Another kick caught David in the face. He was staring down the dark tunnel of unconsciousness. He fought to stay alert. He wanted to meet death with eyes open.

"In here, in here." It was Timmy's distant, frightened voice.

The kicking stopped.

Click. A metallic sound.

David rolled over on his back and stared into the muzzle of the cocked gun. "I'm still not afraid to die," he croaked.

A demonic sneer spread across the man's face. He quoted slowly with poetic evil: "And I looked, and behold a pale horse: and his name that sat on him was Death. Revelation 6:8."

The sound of shuffling feet filled the room. "Police! Don't move!"

The man spun around, aiming the pistol

at the uniformed men who had barged through the open door.

"That's him! That's him!" Timmy yelled.

"Put the gun down," a police officer commanded. "Do it now."

The gunman threw his head back and screamed a deep, guttural cry. He returned his attention to David. "I never, never lose." He snapped the gun back toward David. The room was filled with the report of police handguns. The sound was deafening in the apartment.

The man recoiled as several bullets struck him in the chest. He staggered backward toward the open window.

He stepped into nothing and plunged headlong to the street below.

David slipped into unconsciousness.

Epilogue

Angelina, her father, her sister, and soon-to-be brother-in-law walked outside their water-soaked apartment and into the street. Hand in hand they patiently strolled through the rubble-lined walkway. Overhead the Caribbean sun shone brightly in a cobalt blue sky. A gentle, humid breeze meandered through the streets of Havana. Other families walked in the same direction.

"You'll like it, Papa. The people are very nice."

"It's been a long time, Puppet. I haven't been in church since I was a little boy."

"That's all right, Papa. God still remembers who you are."

He picked her up and held her tightly in his arms. A single tear escaped his eye. "I'm glad to hear that, little one. I am truly glad to hear that."

Angelina hugged her father's neck.

Rajiv banked the aircraft and looked

down at the heavily populated land below him. From this altitude it looked serene, untroubled. Behind him lay Bangalore, ahead of him Vijayawada where the medical supplies he carried from the Red Crescent and Barringston Relief would be offloaded and distributed to the many emergency clinics along the coast. His Cessna was a far cry from a cargo plane, but every little bit helped. Besides, he could land at the smaller airfields that could not accommodate the larger planes.

Leveling the plane, he checked his compass, air speed, and altitude. All were normal. Next he checked the passenger seat. The orphaned boy he had found two days before was sound asleep. He was a good traveler and seemed to enjoy the time spent in the airplane. The boy had already made several trips with Rajiv. The two were becoming inseparable.

The boy was not a replacement for his family. No one would ever occupy the place they held in his heart. But Rajiv's heart had grown enough to allow one more person in, one tiny, helpless little boy.

Who knows? Rajiv thought. *Maybe he will become a pilot.*

David stood weakly before the assembled board of directors of Barringston Relief. Every part of him hurt. The doctors had taped his broken ribs, patched the gunshot wound in his shoulder, and stitched the numerous cuts on his back, arms, and legs from the broken glass. They dosed him heavily with antibiotics and ordered strict bed rest. They could do nothing for his blackened eyes and swollen jaw. If there was any consolation, it was that Calvin looked worse than he did and had proved to be no better a patient. Both men had left the hospital early. Both men had work to do.

David looked down at Calvin, who sat in a wheelchair next to him. Calvin's wife stood nearby, unhappy about her husband's determination to leave the hospital for this meeting but clearly happy that he was alive. He would recover from the gunshot wound to his arm and leg.

The board of directors sat in stunned silence at the video they had just seen. A frail-looking man named Archer Matthews had confessed to being the technician behind the framing of David. He had listed each step in the process, told how the videos could be proven as fakes, stated his reasons for his actions, confessed to the crime, and implicated Dr. Elaine Aberdene as the mastermind behind the plot to destroy David O'Neal and Barringston Relief.

"Let me make sure I have this right," Bob Connick, the company's CFO said. "This Aberdene woman is responsible for the epidemic of dengue hemorrhagic fever in Belize, and she was afraid that our researchers would find out what she had done nine or ten years ago?"

"Right," David said. "As you heard on the tape, she had developed and cultured a mutated virus and mosquito, ideally to understand how the disease was spread and to find a cure. She infected unsuspecting patients and then used their blood to pass the virus to the mosquitoes that would then pass it on to others."

"She was creating a market," Calvin added. "But she was also developing a weapon for the military. She believed that she could also spread a vaccine through a mosquito bite."

"Unbelievable," Connick said. "And by framing David, she could bring our research to a halt."

"Exactly," David agreed. "Killing our researchers would only draw attention to the area she was hoping to keep in the shadows. By attacking me, she could bring down all of Barringston Relief."

"But what about the alien smuggling?" Kristen asked. "How did they manage that?"

"Allow me," Calvin said. "The INS interviewed the captain of the ship again. He denied everything at first but soon caved in. He was paid to carry the undocumented aliens and say that David had hired him. He even posed in the video. He was never going to have to work again. The Central Americans themselves thought that they were being smuggled into Florida and found out too late that they were being taken south and through the Panama Canal. It was a horrible trip for them. Most had families remaining in their native countries. The captain had threatened their loved ones. They were terrified. If they didn't stick to the story about paying for passage through Barringston Relief workers in their countries, then great harm could come to their families."

"That's horrible," Kristen said. "And they're all being deported?"

"Yes," Calvin answered.

David spoke up. "I've already asked our workers in the field to see what they can do for the families. It will take some time, but we hope we can do something."

"What about the extra guards?" Kristen said to Calvin. "I know David called the security firm, and he said you did too. What happened to them?"

"I was furious about that," Calvin answered. "I called the owner as soon as I was able. I was going to read him the riot act. Turns out that someone called not long after we did and asked if extra guards had been requested. He then said that there had been a change of plans and canceled the request. Want to guess who did that?"

"I don't have to," Kristen said. "It was the attacker, wasn't it?"

Calvin nodded. "The police have identified him as Aldo Goldoni. They were able to run his fingerprints. I don't want to be too indelicate, but after a fifty-three-story drop, there wasn't much else they could use. Very little is known about him, except that he had been sent to a reform camp when he was a teenager."

Bob Connick rose to his feet. "I need to say something." He looked at David, then at Archibald Barringston. "David, I believed the tapes and made every effort to have you relieved of your position. I . . . I owe you, Mr. Barringston, the board of directors, and every Barringston Relief worker an apology. I should have believed in you more. I will tender my resignation after this meeting."

"No, you won't," David said with a grin that made the bruises on his face hurt. "I almost believed the tapes myself. You were looking after the welfare of our firm. We have too much work to do. I don't need to be looking for a new CFO."

Stunned by the kindness, Connick sat down. "Thank you."

"What happened to Archer Matthews?" Barringston asked.

Calvin spoke up. "I'm sorry to say that they found his body early this morning at the bottom of Torrey Pines Cliffs. He had been shot in the back. That's near Aberdene's firm. Apparently they discovered he had doctored the videos so they could be identified as fakes. He made the tapes so that he could continue to live, but he sabotaged his own work and made this video. He knew he'd be discovered sooner or later. He mailed the tape we've just seen to David's office and another one to mine. It was quite a sacrifice."

"And Aberdene and LaBohm?"

"Missing," Calvin said. "The FBI thinks they may have skipped the country. Her company has a corporate jet. It left Montgomery Field two nights ago. Apparently they had planned to be out of town when the murder took place and thereby have a ready alibi should they need one. The flight plan said they were headed for Phoenix, but they never arrived. Most likely they kept going south out of the country. She's a very wealthy woman. She could live anywhere in the world."

"It's frightening to think that she is still out there," Kristen said.

David nodded slowly. "We have work to do. Even as we meet here, the rapid response team is meeting in another conference room. Bob Connick, Kristen, and I need to join them. Osborn Scott is pulling everything together. Calvin tells me that the Justice Department should unfreeze our assets in a few days. In the meantime, we are diverting whatever resources we can from our storage areas in different countries.

"Tonight's news will play portions of the video we've just seen. Kristen is already working out the public relations nightmare that will come with that revelation. I plan to hold a news conference tomorrow morning."

"Are you going to be strong enough for that?" Barringston asked with concern.

"Oh, yeah," David said with a smile. "I wouldn't miss it for anything. Once the word gets out about this, I expect that things will get back to normal. In short, ladies and gentlemen, we are back in business."

Applause filled the room.